MULTIPLE EXPOSURE

MULTIPLE EXPOSURE

Ellen Crosby

SEVERN
HOUSE

First published in the USA in 2013
by Scribner, a division of Simon & Schuster, Inc.,
1230 Avenue of the Americas
New York, NY 10020.

This trade paperback edition first published in Great Britain and the USA in 2022
by Severn House, an imprint of Canongate Books Ltd.

severnhouse.com

British Library Cataloguing-in-Publication Data
A CIP catalogue record for this title is available from the British Library.

ISBN-13: 978-1-4483-0859-0 (trade paper)
ISBN-13: 978-1-4483-0860-6 (e-book)

Typeset by Palimpsest Book Production Ltd.,
Falkirk, Stirlingshire, Scotland.

For André,
with love, and for the next thirty years

How often have I said to you that when you have eliminated the impossible, whatever remains, *however improbable*, must be the truth?

—SHERLOCK HOLMES, IN *THE SIGN OF THE FOUR* BY ARTHUR CONAN DOYLE

Multiple exposure: the superimposition of two or more individual exposures to create a single photograph. The technique can be used to create ghostly images or to add people and objects that were not originally there to a scene. It is frequently used in photographic hoaxes.

PROLOGUE

I've been in too many war zones not to recognize blood when I see it, but I did not expect to find it smeared on the whitewashed walls and puddled on the black-and-white harlequin tile floor when I opened my front door.

It's just past midnight as my taxi driver pulls up to the curb on the quiet, dark cul-de-sac where we live in north London. I'm back after two grueling weeks of work in Iraq, a photo shoot on the new postwar architecture of Baghdad, pastels and sleek modern structures blooming incongruously alongside exquisite medieval buildings and the rubble of destruction.

I open the arched wooden door to the half-timbered Tudor cottage Nick and I rent in Hampstead and call out that I'm home. Outside, the cab pulls away now that the driver, an elderly gentleman with an old-fashioned sense of chivalry, believes I'm safely inside. When Nick doesn't answer, I figure he's already upstairs, either in his study—he's been working so hard lately—or in bed reading. A bottle of Veuve Cliquot will be chilling in the silver bucket he bought at a flea market after the seller swore it was used at the Château de Condé for the wedding of Edward VIII and Wallis Simpson. There will be red roses, for passion, on my pillow.

You don't have to tell me. I know I'm lucky.

Then I see blood, illuminated by a swath of golden light from the lantern at the front door. Frantically, I begin turning on lights throughout the silent house. The blood is dark and rust colored, but I can tell it's recent, not more than four or five hours old. The last time Nick and I spoke was in Istanbul as I boarded my connecting flight. Just before I hung up he told me he loved me, as he always does, and I started to say, "Love you more," because that's our routine. But my phone, down to a sliver of a battery, died before I got the words *out. I never got to tell him that one last time, and it still haunts me.*

I set down my equipment bag and suitcase and unstrap my tripod, which I wield like a saber as I follow the path of blood spatter. Signs of a struggle and someone being dragged. A partial handprint on the wall of our sitting room, like a child's art project. I call Nick's name, hoping he's still here, and pray he hasn't bled out. The house has a tomblike stillness about it and somehow I know his attacker or attackers are gone.

And so is Nick. In the sitting room, a bottle of Scotch is overturned, the clear liquid leaving a dark wet stain on the Bukhara carpet I brought back from an assignment in Afghanistan. His glass has rolled under the settee, and his book, John Julius Norwich's Byzantium: The Early Centuries, *lies splayed open on the floor.*

Upstairs, the blue-and-white Amish wedding ring quilt on our bed is gone. The blankets are askew, so it was probably dragged off in haste and I know that is how he left the house, bundled in the quilt under which we'd made love so many times.

Otherwise, our bedroom looks as it always does, and his clothes are still hanging in the armoire or folded in his dresser—suits arranged by season, shoes and work boots lined up in two rows, ties draped over the antique rack I found in a shop on Portobello Road. Sweaters, underwear, socks organized neatly in the drawers.

The computer is switched off in his study. His desk is immaculate, as usual. Nick doesn't leave work around, not in his business.

I stand there for what seems like ages, wondering whom to call: 999, which will bring officers from the Hampstead police station? Scotland Yard?

But I know what I'm supposed to do and reach for my phone.

I call Nick's people and they come. The regional security officer from the American embassy and a bland man with a forgettable face who says his name is John Brown.

That's it. That's all I, Sophie Medina, can tell you with

absolute certainty about the night my husband, Nicholas Canning, was abducted from our home. Everything else, the rest of that night—sirens wailing, bright lights strobing the quiet darkness, doors slamming, voices raised in alarm— is a blur.

ONE

Timing is everything. Sometimes setting is everything, too. Lord Allingham, or Baz, as he was known to me, waited until we were standing in Innocents' Corner in Westminster Abbey before he told me he had it on good authority Nick might still be alive. I knew his sources went all the way to the top since Baz is a senior minister at the Foreign Office, responsible for all foreign and common-wealth business conducted by the House of Lords. He also has contacts at MI6, the Secret Intelligence Service, since he served on the Joint Intelligence Committee, although that's something he'll never, ever talk about.

Baz wasn't smiling, so I knew his news about Nick would be one more wrenching development in what had become a sensational and well-publicized manhunt: *American Oil Executive Vanishes in Bloody Abduction*. It had taken a royal wedding to knock the story, complete with lurid speculation that involved aliens and a distant planet, off the front pages of the British tabloids.

Tomorrow would make exactly three months since Nick disappeared. There had been no note, no ransom demand, no one contacting me or Crowne Energy, Nick's British employer, to claim responsibility or announce that he had become a pawn in a political agenda half a world away. If Nick's cover had been blown—he was an operations officer with the CIA's clandestine service—it never surfaced that he had been outed. To my surprise, not even the tabloids hinted that Nick might be a spy.

A week after the abduction, a group of German hikers found a dark green Citroën with more of Nick's blood staining the backseat and inside the trunk, along with his wallet. They hadn't even taken his ID or credit cards. The car had been abandoned next to a grove of pines off a small slip road on the Col de Tende, the mountain pass between France and Italy. I flew to Nice and joined the multinational search: five intense days combing pine forests and climbing scree-covered slopes while bearded vultures circled overhead, until the odds of finding him were almost nil.

By the time the search was called off, everyone—my family, Nick's sister in California, our friends, his colleagues—had begun gently urging me to stop hoping and make peace with the fact that we might never find his body. To come to terms with the likelihood that he was probably dead, especially after the body of Colin Crowne, his boss, had been discovered a few days later in Vienna, floating in the Danube River not far from OPEC headquarters.

Which made Baz's news all the more incredible.

I gripped my damp umbrella with both hands and said, "Where is he? Is he all right? When can I see him?"

Baz clamped his arm around my shoulder and pulled me close, brushing a strand of hair off my face like a protective older brother. The rain was falling, fine and sharp as needles, on this unseasonably cool early August day as we entered the Abbey, bypassing the queue of visitors—one of the perks of nobility. Steel gray clouds hung so low in the sky that London had the closed-in feeling of being inside a bell jar. The scent of damp wool mingled with Baz's cologne—Santal by Floris, very sensual—as he hugged me close.

Kings and queens are crowned and buried in the Abbey. Poets, statesmen, philosophers, and a few of the less-than-great who bought their tombs in the days when a burial spot was for sale are immortalized here. I stared at the effigies of the two infant daughters of King James I; above them, a casket contained the bones of the boy king Edward V and his brother, supposedly murdered in the Tower by their uncle Richard III in the 1400s. It would be just like Baz to deliberately choose this tragic corner of Henry VII's chapel, screened behind the altar where Edward the Confessor's coronation chair and the mythical Stone of Scone sat, as an appropriate stage because of the irony of the setting and his news.

"I don't know a good way to tell you this, Sophie, so I'll just give you the unvarnished version." Baz began walking, pulling me along with him. He and I are the same height, five ten, but he's fair-haired and solidly built, the latter serving him well since he still plays weekend rugby to keep in shape. I have the lean, willowy figure of my American mother and the dark hair and olive skin of my Spanish father, a man I know mostly from old photos in European football magazines. Age-wise, Baz is ten years my senior, which makes him forty-eight.

"Come," he said. "Let's carry on, shall we?"

I nodded, suddenly glad for the strength of Baz's arm around my shoulder, though I knew what he was going to do: deliver bad news sideways while we were walking and in motion. That way he didn't have to look me in the eye. Nick used to do that. Eventually I realized it was a defensive tactic so he wouldn't have to deal with the possibility of watching me dissolve into floods of tears. Men come so unglued when a woman starts to cry.

Except I don't fall apart easily and Baz knew that. I'd been tough and strong throughout this entire nightmare.

"What is it?" I asked him. "Just tell me."

Around us, tourists and visitors had begun filing out of the chapel. Evensong would begin shortly in the Quire and visiting hours would be over. Whatever he had to say, it wasn't going to take long.

Baz squeezed my shoulder. "Nick's been spotted in Russia."

I could feel the blood leave my face.

"Oh, God, Baz. If he's there, the mafia got him, the Shaika," I said. "Right before he was taken Nick told me their threats had been escalating. It wasn't enough just to pay protection money anymore. He and Colin were worried the Shaika planned to intimidate their workers and eventually force them out so they could step in and take over their operations. The Shaika got him, didn't they?"

Baz shook his head. "Not exactly."

"What do you mean, 'not exactly'?"

"We don't think they kidnapped him."

He was watching me as though he expected me to understand. And he had said "we."

When you live with a man who has chosen the shadowy, truth-altering world of espionage, you commit to his secrets and duplicity. As far as I knew, no one besides me—not even Nick's sister or Colin Crowne, his boss—was aware that Nick led a double life. His degrees in geology and physics led him to work for Crowne Energy, a small oil exploration company that had been searching for oil near the Caspian Sea. But it was his native fluency in Russian that caught the interest of the CIA, which believed his job was the perfect cover to report on a dangerous and politically unstable Russian republic that was a hub of arms and drug trafficking.

To be honest, even I didn't know what my husband really did.

"If I don't tell you anything, Sophie," he used to say to me, "then you don't have to lie."

Now Baz was talking as if he _knew_. I played my role anyway.

"Sorry, I'm not following you. If the Shaika didn't kidnap Nick, then what is he doing in Russia?"

We stopped in front of the starkly modern blue stained-glass window dedicated to the airmen who flew in the Battle of Britain: heroes of a grateful nation, men who made the ultimate sacrifice for king and country.

Baz's answer, dropped into the respectful silence, caught me off guard. "We wondered if you might know why he's there?"

"Good God, what makes you think that?"

"Do you, Sophie?"

"No. Of course not. Until five minutes ago, I thought he was . . ."

"What?"

I moved out of Baz's embrace. "I don't know. Dead, I guess."

"I thought you never gave up hope?"

"I didn't. But with every day that passes, it gets harder."

Especially because one of Nick's people at the embassy had been keeping me informed of their search. They'd pinged the GPS on his phone and got nothing. No credit card movement, no e-mail use, no phone calls.

He was gone, completely gone.

Considering Nick's line of work, I had to ask. "He's not in prison, is he?"

"No."

"Then where . . .?"

"He was seen in Moscow by one of our operatives. It was Nick, all right, though he's rather changed. A beard and different hair color. Thinner." Baz paused. "He was getting on the metro. At Kuznetsky Most . . . Kuznetsky Bridge."

Baz watched me absorb that information. Nick knew Moscow well since he often stopped there on business trips to Abadistan, the Russian republic where Crowne Energy had set up operations to drill a test well, searching for oil. And thanks to a grandmother who taught him the language as a child, as I said, Nick spoke Russian fluently and with a native accent.

"What's he doing there?" I repeated Baz's question.

His voice hardened. "Sophie, it's become clear that Nick probably staged his kidnapping. It would explain a lot. He may even have had help because he did a bloody good job, no pun intended. Very thorough, very convincing. I mean, we know Colin required everyone to get basic medical training before departing for Abadistan since you can't even get an aspirin there, much less a syringe, so Nick's perfectly capable of drawing his own blood. Over a period of time he could have collected enough to create a realistic-looking crime scene."

I started to protest, but Baz wasn't done.

"The lads surmise that he must have had a boat ready to take him across the Channel once he got to the coast after leaving London. Though knowing Nick and his capacity for sheer gall, maybe he strolled onto the ferry, nice as you please, and no one noticed him."

"No." I didn't want to believe any of this, but the "lads" he was talking about probably worked at Vauxhall Cross. The headquarters of MI6, also known as Legoland.

"I'm sorry, love. I hated to tell you, but I wanted you to hear it from someone who cares about you. No doubt Nick's people at the embassy will be contacting you soon. I'm sure they'll have questions as well." He paused and said so softly that I had to lean closer to catch his words, "Under the circumstances, you must wonder who Nick's working for these days. It rather looks as though he might be peddling information to the highest bidder."

For a long moment, I couldn't think of a thing to say. In all the time since Nick disappeared, those early harrowing nights trying not to imagine whether he'd been tortured or just mercilessly executed, followed by the unendurable loneliness as weeks dragged by after that car was found in the mountains, I had never—not a single time—considered this.

"You mean Nick betrayed Colin, sold out Crowne Energy?"

"For openers."

"You are out of your mind." My voice rose in a little bubble of hysteria. A woman walking by stopped and gave me a curious look. "He would never do something like that."

Baz noticed the woman and touched a finger to his lips, gesturing silence. "I think the possibility has to be considered."

"No, it does not." I would not let him go there, not allow this horrible accusation to take root and flower.

"What about Colin?" he asked.

"You know as well as I do, Baz." I took a shaky breath and continued. "Colin's body was found in Vienna, in the Danube. The same people who kidnapped Nick went after Colin next."

"And when we all believed Nick was dead, that theory made sense," Baz said. "Sophie, love, I trust you understand why I can't go into detail, but we believe Crowne Energy discovered oil reserves in the Caspian Sea off the Abadi coast when they drilled that test well. To say that discovery would radically alter the political situation in an unstable part of the world is an understatement. However, the only way to confirm what Colin and Nick found would be to review their well logs." He paused and added, "Unfortunately, they're missing."

I wondered if Baz knew that piece of information through his contacts in MI6, or because his Foreign Office portfolio also included international energy policy. With London as the world's second largest oil trading market and Britain as a declining but significant exporter of North Sea oil, Baz knew all the players.

"What are you saying?" I asked.

"I'm saying that perhaps Nick has those logs and he's selling information about what Crowne Energy discovered in Abadistan," he said. "With Colin out of the picture, he's the only person who knows what's in them. As a geophysicist—or, to use your delightful old-fashioned American term, a doodle-bugger—he also has the skills to interpret the seismic data."

"Nick wouldn't sell out anyone, Baz. Forget it."

"I wouldn't have thought so either, but how do you explain his turning up suddenly in Russia?"

"Maybe someone made a mistake," I said. "Nick is Russian, or half Russian, from his mother's family. It could have been someone else at that metro station who looks just like him."

Baz shook his head. "No."

I wrapped my arms around my waist, suddenly bone chilled and weary. "It can't be Nick."

"Why are you so sure?"

I took a deep breath and fought to keep my voice rock steady. "Because he wouldn't do this to me."

"Oh, my poor darling—" Baz started to pull me into his arms again, but I backed away.

"Don't pity me," I said. "I can't bear it."

"There's something else," he said. "You may as well hear it all."

I swallowed hard and nodded.

"Our people have gone back to Vienna," he said. "In case we missed something in the first go round regarding the suspicious death of one of our citizens."

"Like what?"

"Maybe Nick met up with Colin in Vienna," he said. "Maybe Colin had the well logs and now Nick has them."

"You mean, Colin gave Nick the logs before he was killed?" But I knew that wasn't where Baz was going.

"That's one possibility. The other possibility they're looking into is that Nick took them." He gave me a worried look. "After he killed Colin."

TWO

My husband is not a murderer. There are things you know in your heart, believe with all your soul, in spite of what anyone tells you or however convincing the "proof" to the contrary appears to be. I didn't know the secrets Nick kept for the CIA because I couldn't know them, but I will swear to you that these things are true: He is an honorable, trustworthy, and loyal friend; a patriot who would die for his country; and a loving husband who would hang the moon someplace different if that's what I wanted.

How Nick metamorphosed from kidnapping victim to murder suspect who had killed his boss and good friend because of a set of technical documents, even if they were as priceless as an original copy of the Magna Carta, was something I didn't understand that day in Westminster Abbey. Nor did I understand it in the three remaining weeks before I left London and moved home to Washington, D.C.

Baz had been right. Within twenty-four hours after he dropped that bombshell news, I got a call from one of Nick's contacts at the embassy who said they had a few questions for me in light of "new developments." When I showed up at their office on Grosvenor Square, the atmosphere was, to put the best face on it, tense. What became clear right away was that no one except me believed the man getting on the Moscow metro was a case of mistaken identity.

At any time during the past three months, Ms. Medina, did your husband contact you?

No, he did not.

Can the CIA count on your cooperation to let us know if he does reach out to you?

Of course.

My own questions received similar terse replies except they were mostly *no comment* or *we can't say.*

Wasn't it possible Nick was on the run from the local Russian mafia, known as the Shaika, who had been pressuring Crowne Energy to turn their operations over to them?

No comment.

Did they honestly believe Nick would murder Colin Crowne, a man he liked and respected, in cold blood, and then dump his body in the Danube River?

We can't say.

As they requested, I'd gotten Nick's black diplomatic passport out of the safe at home and turned it in that afternoon. He never flashed it around since he always traveled on his blue passport; the dip passport was a last resort, a get-out-of-jail-free card that guaranteed a swift evacuation from anywhere in the world and no questions asked. I hadn't been sorry to surrender it. In my line of work as a photographer for IPS, International Press Service, being a diplomatic spouse is a liability if you travel as I often do to war zones and places where it's smarter to keep your nationality to yourself. Get hijacked or captured by the wrong people, and diplomats, U.S. government employees, and their dependents are the first to be singled out of the group and shot. If they're lucky.

A few days after that first meeting, I was invited back to Grosvenor Square for another session—you don't say no to the CIA, even if it sounds like a request rather than a demand—this time to go over the months leading up to Nick's disappearance. Eventually the relentless probing, like picking a scab that will never heal, took its toll as I told my story. And then told it again.

Surely Nick's behavior had changed in the weeks and months before he disappeared; some minor, telling details that, though they seemed insignificant at the time, could now be recognized as big, glaring clues? How could I not have noticed something? Anything? They say that the wife is the last to know, and you think, *Sure, what a lie: Of course she knew. She just turned a blind eye.*

Was that what I did?

That evening after they were finished with me at the embassy, I went home and headed straight for the bottle of Scotch on the sideboard. I poured a drink, and another, and another as I sat for hours in the velvet darkness of our sitting room among the shadows and negative space, curled up in the nubby blue-and-green tweed settee by the hearth where Nick and I had spent so many nights together reading and talking. The CIA had painted a picture of a stranger, not the man I knew and loved.

Occasionally a car would drive by as I nursed my Scotch, the hum of the engine slowing as it turned off the main road into our cul-de-sac. Like clockwork, just after the *News at Ten* ended, my neighbor's front door opened and closed and I heard his footfalls as he went out for a last smoke. Then the metallic click of his lighter followed by the jaunty firefly glow of a cigarette as he sauntered over to the green across the road with his pair of Westies. After a while he finished his fag and went back inside, leaving me alone with my thoughts, which kept coiling back to the night Nick vanished.

What if I'd caught an earlier flight? Paid for a cab all the way from Heathrow instead of first taking the train to Paddington? But mostly what I wondered was this: Was my husband of twelve years, the man I loved with all my heart and whom I believed—no, I *knew*—loved me so much he would die for me, capable of staging a scene of such blood and violence, knowing I would be the one to discover it? And so I racked my brain, going over and over it again, searching for the tiniest clue, the least little hint, to prove that Baz and the CIA and MI6 were all comprehensively wrong: that Nick was a victim, not a villain.

The official explanation for why I was leaving London was that I'd finally decided it was time to return home to the States to be near my family after a difficult and tumultuous period in my life, to grieve in private. The unofficial reason was that the media assault and attention had been overwhelming. From the beginning, the British tabloids had latched on to me as the story unfolded, inflating my life into a sympathetic sob-story drama of the brave, beautiful wife who courageously "soldiered on alone." A press photo taken in Egypt when I was shooting an excavation site at the Valley of the Kings popped up everywhere. My head scarf had slipped onto my shoulders and I was completely sweat drenched, but the picture somehow made me look as sultry and exotic as an extra on the set of *Lawrence of Arabia.*

So far the press hadn't gotten hold of the ugly new rumor concerning Nicholas Canning, the missing-and-presumed-dead American businessman: that he was alive, well, and, apparently, hiding out in Russia. But sooner or later, word would leak out and public sympathy would turn to shock, and that would be followed by scorn. Then derision.

But until that happened, I was given strict instructions that any information pertaining to Nick's whereabouts had to remain our little secret, or maybe our Faustian pact: mine, the CIA's, and MI6's. I was not to breathe a word to anyone, not even Nick's sister or my own family.

I gave notice at IPS, quitting my dream job as a senior photographer, and persuading Perry DiNardo, my boss, that a big good-bye bash wouldn't be appropriate under the circumstances. Instead I took everyone in the bureau to drinks at Ye Olde Cheshire Cheese on my last day.

If I had wanted to turn the screw any tighter and make my departure more wrenching than it already was, I picked the perfect venue to do it. The sign outside the pub on Wine Office Court listed the monarchs who had ruled Britain since the place had been rebuilt in 1667 after the Great Fire destroyed it. We were given tables in the Chop Room next to the fireplace, something I figured Perry had arranged, since these were the sought-after seats once occupied by Charles Dickens and Samuel Johnson.

The mingled scents of woodsmoke, sawdust, and beer and the centuries of history and tradition that sifted through the air like dust motes assaulted me with a rush of nostalgia as I walked through the door. In a few days I would lose all of this, lose *London,* trading it for the land of strip malls and fast-food chains, where "old" might mean built before 1970.

Perry seemed to sense my melancholy mood because he gave my hand a squeeze and touched his beer glass against mine.

"I'm going to miss you," he said.

"I'll miss you, too." I couldn't look at him.

He'd been a good boss, who always backed his people, no matter what we did or where in the world we were. His over-zealous devotion to the job, to always be where the story was, had come at a price: three marriages that saddled him with enough alimony and child support to keep him paying someone until they lowered his casket into the ground.

"Instead of getting married again," he told me during yet another acrimonious court battle with an ex-wife, "I'm going to do what Rod Stewart said he was going to do. Find a woman I don't like and just give her a damn house."

But the bosses in New York loved him, just as women continued to love him and he couldn't help loving them back, so the London job was his for as long as he wanted it. He'd been especially kind to me during these last few months, making sure my assignments were relatively close to home in case there was any news of Nick, deflecting questions and criticisms from the big suits, as he called them, about whether I was still up to the job. I heard about the remarks anyway; every newsroom in the world leaks worse than a bad sieve when it comes to office gossip.

There was one night about a month ago when things nearly unraveled between Perry and me, and I suspected he was remembering it now, just as I was. We'd both ended up traveling through Venice for separate reasons, and if there had ever been a moment when vulnerability, loneliness, booze, and recklessness might have intersected in a bad way, it was our unwise decision to adjourn to my room for a nightcap. Perry was between girlfriends; the day before had been my wedding anniversary. It happened so fast, Perry getting up to pour me another glass of wine and then suddenly he reached for me and I was in his arms, just so damn dog tired of keeping up a good front for the world. Missing Nick like crazy and needing someone, anyone, to hold me and make the hurt go away.

Thank God we stopped when we did, because it would have changed everything. I felt him go tense, just as I did, and for a long moment we stood locked in that embrace, his cheek against my hair, his thumb stroking my back, breath warm in my ear. He sighed softly as I struggled to regain my composure and I was grateful he pretended not to notice when I wiped my eyes on his shirt. Then he kissed my forehead, chucked me under the chin like I was a kid, and told me to lock my door after he left. We never spoke about that night again.

Like everyone else sitting around the table tonight, I'm sure he assumed Nick was dead and I was still coming to terms with it.

"It's not too late to change your mind," he said to me later, after the others had left, more hugs and good-byes, and it was just the two of us. "I didn't hire anyone to replace you yet, Medina. Not that you're easily replaceable, you know? Who else am I gonna find who turns in travel vouchers with mileage expenses for riding a camel?"

I grinned. "Which you unfairly denied."

"I'm serious," he said. "You don't have to go. You're damn good. It *is* going to be tough finding someone to take your place."

"Probably because whoever you hire will expect to be paid a living wage," I said and he laughed. "Thanks for the offer, Perry. I know you've taken some heat for me, that I wasn't pulling my weight lately, and I appreciate it. But I made my decision. It's time to go home. Besides, the estate agent rented our house the day I gave notice. I've got to go through with it now."

"That must have broken your heart," he said. "You and Nick loved that cottage. I remember you talking about maybe buying it one day."

I nodded and concentrated on my beer, trying not to remember the trilling delight of the young woman who came through the house with her husband and baby daughter, listening to her fall in love with its charms, just as we'd done twelve years ago. Our only home as a married couple.

"What are you going to do when you get back to Washington?" Perry asked.

I shrugged. "Look for a job."

"I wish there was an opening in our D.C. bureau, but they're going to be making more cuts soon." He gave me a sideways glance and grimaced. "Don't repeat that, okay?"

"Leaving the cleaning staff to do our jobs, once they get rid of a few more bodies? Come on, Perry. There's no more meat left on the bone. There's not even any bone left on the bone. How can they keep cutting?"

"There's always the marrow. We can suck that out." He sounded like he wasn't joking. "But listen, I know a guy. Old friend from the hood growing up, another *paesano*. Luke Santangelo. He's a one-man band, owns his own agency, and he's swamped with work. It might be a good fit for you right now."

He fished in his back pocket for his wallet, thumbing through a thick wad of bent and tattered business cards and old receipts until he came to a blue-gray card with the words FOCUS PHOTOGRAPHY printed in white. The *O* in *Focus* looked like a camera lens.

"Here." He handed me the card. "I'll call him, tell him about you, if you want."

I looked at the address. Cady's Alley, Georgetown. An upscale address, next to the C&O Canal.

"Thanks. I appreciate this. Let me think about it and get back to you."

"Look, Medina, are you blowing me off?"

"I would never do that."

"Oh, yeah? How about, 'My e-mail wasn't working so I didn't see your memo about not being authorized to fly home business class'?"

"I didn't see it. Give me a break. I was in Ulan Bator. They were using a camping stove in the aisle back in economy and people brought their livestock on that flight." I drank my beer. "Please don't take this the wrong way, but that job doesn't sound like me."

"How do you know it doesn't? You think I'd send you to a guy who makes his living taking Christmas card snaps of happy families all wearing the same color clothes?"

"Well, no—"

"Damn right I wouldn't. Look, Luke called me this morning. You know what he's got coming up in a couple of weeks? That big exhibit at the National Gallery. The one in D.C., not London. And guess who's behind it? Arkady Vasiliev." He eyed me. "Aha. Knew I'd get your attention. Remember those Easter eggs he bought, the Fabergé eggs that nobody knew belonged to the Romanovs? He loaned them and a bunch of paintings some czar used to own to the National Gallery, and he's throwing a party the night before the opening. Luke's the photographer."

Perry had my attention, all right. Arkady Vasiliev owned Arkneft, the biggest oil production company in Russia, and had amassed enough wealth in the past few years to land on the *Forbes* list of the world's billionaires. The discovery of two previously unknown imperial eggs in an attic trunk in a village near Kent, England, had sent the art world into a frenzy of curiosity about their provenance. Vasiliev had doubled the bid of the Kremlin Armoury, which claimed the eggs belonged in their museum because they were part of Russia's patrimony, and now he was thumbing his nose by putting them on display in Washington.

Nick had met Vasiliev at an international energy forum in Oslo, plus Vasiliev lived mostly in London these days since he felt safer there than in Moscow, so they'd seen each other at a couple of industry conferences. Last year we'd been surprised to get an invitation to a party at Vasiliev's tricked-out luxury home in Belgravia soon after he'd acquired the Fabergé eggs. I drew the short straw at work and spent the weekend in Berlin, much to my disappointment. Nick got to see the gaudy mansion and the eggs during a private viewing with Mrs. Vasiliev. The imperial eggs, he said, were spectacular but the house looked like someone's idea of a Borgia palace with a bit of Disney and Vegas thrown in.

"So," Perry said, "have you changed your mind about my calling Luke?"

A chance to see the Fabergé eggs and to meet Arkady Vasiliev, who had become something of a recluse ever since a waitress tried to poison him a few months ago at a Moscow discotheque appropriately named Club Decadence, intrigued me. And then there was this: My wedding gift from Nick had been an exquisite Fabergé pink-and-gold guilloché basket-weave snuffbox that had belonged to his grandmother, a gift from Nicholas II himself to Nick's great-grandmother. The tantalizing history of my own precious link to the vanished world of Fabergé had always seemed like something out of a fairy tale. I had listened for hours to Nick's babushka's stories of growing up in Old Russia, tales of sleigh rides and skating parties with red-cheeked men and dark-eyed women, lavish masked balls, all-night feasts where everyone danced and sang while someone played the balalaika—a magical, unreachable land of gaiety and exuberance at the back of the North Wind.

"All right," I said to Perry. "I've changed my mind."

Perry's grin said he knew I'd be hooked when he brought up Fabergé. "No problemo. I'll call Luke first thing tomorrow," he said. "You owe me."

"I have no doubt you'll collect."

It was the wrong thing to say and I knew it as soon as the words were out of my mouth.

"Bet on it." He searched my eyes while I struggled to keep a poker face and not look like I understood what he meant. "I know it's too soon, but I can't get that night in Venice out of my head."

"I'm sorry," I said, "but it just wouldn't work for us."

"I'm not rushing you. Just promise me you'll at least keep my number on speed dial. Maybe someday you'll change your mind."

"I won't change my mind," I said. "But I will keep your number on speed dial. I promise."

He leaned close and ran a finger along the back of my hand. "You're a beautiful woman, Medina. Very sexy and desirable. When you're ready, at least give me a chance."

I kissed his cheek. "You're a good man and a dear friend."

His eyes locked on mine and that's when I realized how tough it was going to be to keep the bombshell development that Nick might be alive a secret, especially from people who loved me and loved him. Secrecy, stoicism, and silence, Nick used to tell me. And there was one other term he used that always struck me as odd: face maintenance. Perry believed I was a grieving widow. I couldn't let the look on my face give me away, couldn't let Perry see anyone but the woman he expected to see.

"There is something," I said, to break the awkward silence.

"What? Just tell me. Anything . . ."

I smiled. "You could be like Rod Stewart and just give me a damn house."

He said nothing for a long moment before he roared with laughter. "In your dreams, Medina. How about a beer, instead?"

*   *   *

The next day, as a courtesy, John Brown, one of the men who showed up after I called Nick's people the night he disappeared, came by with a driver from the embassy to take me to Heathrow for my flight to Washington. When we pulled up to the British Airways entrance at Terminal 5, the driver got my bags out of the trunk of the car as John Brown handed me an envelope.

"What's this?" I asked.

"Your contact in D.C.," he said. "His name is Napoleon Duval. If you need anything, call him. If we find out anything, he'll be in touch."

"No one's seen Nick since that one time in Moscow," I said. "If it was Nick."

"It was. And, believe me, we're looking for him and we'll find him."

I shivered. "What happens then?"

"I'm sorry, Ms. Medina," he said. "We can't say."

THREE

A few days after I arrived in D.C., Luke Santangelo interviewed me in the light-filled industrial warehouse he'd transformed into the studio of Focus Photography and told me I wasn't the right person for the job. To be honest, not five minutes into our meeting, that had been my gut feeling as well.

Though Luke was drowning in work as Perry had said, he was looking for a fresh-faced kid, someone young, hopeful, and right out of school who would be willing to work like a slave in gratitude for landing a job as a real photographer instead of waiting tables or doing something in retail at the mall. It also explained the modest salary he was offering, a minor detail Perry had neglected to mention.

That Luke was meeting me strictly as a favor to Perry became obvious the moment I realized Perry had given me a recommendation that made me sound like the next Annie Leibovitz. That was strike one why I was overqualified for the position. Strike two was an offhand remark I made about the framed Robert Capa quote hanging above a beat-up black credenza in a corner of the room. *If your pictures aren't good enough, you're not close enough.*

I told Luke that before I worked for Perry I had a boss who liked to say that if you were sent to photograph a fire, you didn't get the right shots if you came back and your eyebrows hadn't been singed off.

Luke leaned back in his chair and picked up his water bottle, tossing it back and forth like a ball. He was good-looking in a dark, Mediterranean way—Perry hadn't told me that, either— thick, curly hair flecked with gray, dark brown eyes, a prominent nose that looked like he might have broken it once, and the kind of intense stare that made me want to look down and check for undone buttons in strategic places or run my tongue over my teeth in case I'd smeared lipstick on them.

I hoped Luke might at least smile or make some lighthearted quip, but all he said was, "So did you singe them off?"

"Not me. A friend. They don't grow back, either."

He gave me that double-barrel stare and said, "What happened to you, if it wasn't your eyebrows?"

"A bullet grazed me in a firefight."

He unscrewed the cap to his water bottle. "Where'd you get that?"

I presumed he was asking where in the world I had been, not to see the scar under my left breast.

"A highway outside Khartoum. I was traveling with a group from the U.N. High Commission for Refugees and the Red Cross to the camps in Darfur. We got held up by bandits," I said. "Our guards were twenty feet away getting water at a well."

"This job isn't going to be that exciting. Not even close."

"I know that. That's why I'm applying for it."

He shook his head. "Sorry, but I don't get it. You could work for *National Geographic,* the *Post,* the *Times,* the AP. Write your ticket with stuff like this." He tapped his finger on a photograph I'd taken of a group of women in brilliant jewel-colored saris, part of a wedding procession in Rajasthan, India. Then he added, and I knew this was strike three and the kiss of death. "Plus you're Charles Lord's granddaughter. You're photographic royalty."

He was right. My grandfather, one of the legendary post–World War II photojournalists, was an early member of Magnum, the iconic photo cooperative that began in 1947. His friends were its founders, and even bigger legends; people like Henri Cartier-Bresson, Robert Capa, George Rodger, and David Seymour, whom Granddaddy called "Chim." Edward Steichen, who put together the world-renowned *Family of Man* exhibition when he was photography director at the New York Museum of Modern Art, had been a neighbor until he passed away in the 1970s.

Growing up, I spent summers at my grandfather's house in Connecticut because my mother, then a single parent on the verge of living on welfare, couldn't afford to pay anyone to look after me or send me to camp when school was out. What she didn't know was that Granddaddy turned me loose in his darkroom, giving a twelve-year-old free rein around toxic chemicals as he taught me about developing film and making prints. All the while he'd recount outrageous, uncensored tales of his exploits and adventures on assignment for *Life* or *National Geographic* and the models he'd worked with for *Vogue*. I knew then that was the life I wanted, but I also learned my craft from a master, and I knew what a gift he was giving me.

"Surely my grandfather's reputation isn't a liability, is it?" I asked Luke.

"Of course not. But it does make it harder to understand what you're doing here."

It was a fair question and I'd already prepared my answer. "I moved back to Washington because it's home and I have family and friends here. For the past twelve years I've been on the road practically nonstop. I'm looking for a job where I'm not always living out of a suitcase or a backpack," I said. "I'm done with war zones and wearing flak jackets and sleeping in tents."

His eyes narrowed. "Doesn't fit your profile."

"It does now."

What I wanted—actually, what I needed—was to do something that gave my life structure and order, work that would keep my mind occupied so I wouldn't drive myself mad with worry and anxiety about Nick.

"Perry told me about your husband," Luke said. "It sounds like you've been through hell. I'm sorry. I'm sure it's tough coming back here and starting over."

I nodded and looked away, staring at the art and photography on the walls. The photos of people caught in the business of everyday living, little vignettes of life, were Luke's—I knew that instinctively—and he had a knack for making something ordinary seem extraordinary and worth noticing, a keen eye for detail. The original paintings and prints were also his, an extension of his photographic style. I liked the fact that, unlike some photographers I'd worked with, Luke seemed to understand the symbiotic relationship between photography and art. Perry was a journalist: The reason we took photos was to report a story, tell what happened. Luke seemed to subscribe to Ansel Adams's school of thought, that photography is a creative art, much more than a medium for factually communicating ideas.

"I'd like to work with you," I told him. "We're different as photographers, but we'd complement each other as a team. Perry pulled out his whole bag of tricks to get me to talk to you and I bet he did the same to you. He knew you were looking for an assistant to set up your lights, and he didn't tell me the salary was what you'd pay a grad student from the Corcoran."

One of Luke's eyebrows went up as he said in a bland voice, "That's Perry for you. He always was an operator, even back in high school."

For a long moment the only sound in the room was the quiet whooshing of the air-conditioning. This guy was hard to read.

Finally I said, "So was he wrong and we're wasting each other's time here, or do you want to talk about this?"

Luke took a swig from his water bottle. "Are you always this pushy?"

I sat back in my chair and folded my arms. "Let's put it this way. I always get the shots I need for my assignments. I'm diplomatic when I need to be, but there are times when it's just best to be direct and say what you mean. I'm also currently unemployed, which is a heck of a motivator."

I caught the tiny flash of respect in his eyes. "All right, let's say we could work something out. You have a salary in mind?"

My IPS wages, plus Nick's income from Crowne Energy and the CIA, had allowed us to take advantage of London's cosmopolitan cultural life, to enjoy its restaurants, theaters, and art galleries. We knew we were lucky, but we never took those luxuries for granted. After Colin died, the substantial paychecks from Crowne Energy stopped coming, but Perry had given me a small bonus when I left and the CIA was still paying Nick, so I had some income, plus our savings.

I named a figure that I thought was reasonable given my

experience and credentials, and Luke's eyebrow went up again, but this time he looked intrigued.

"Let's go into my office," he said. "I need to do some math."

I followed him across the large, sunny room with its gleaming hardwood floors and whitewashed walls. His office was the only permanent space in the studio; he'd configured the rest of the boxy two-story brick-and-stone warehouse so that a series of interior modular partitions could be moved on rollers to accommodate whatever size room he needed for a photo shoot.

A desk with a supersize Mac and a half dozen external drives probably used to back up photos sat on his desk. He indicated the chair opposite his desk and I took it.

Luke sat down, hit something on a keyboard that made his computer screen flicker to life, and began clicking as he studied various screens. A bloodred folder with *Empire of the Firebird: The Rediscovered Treasures of the Imperial Romanov Dynasty* stamped in gold sat on a corner of his desk next to a framed photo of Luke with his arms around an attractive blonde and a pretty teenager who was the mirror image of the woman. They were standing on what looked like the deck of a cruise ship, all of them relaxed and laughing at something the photographer must have said or done.

"My wife, Leslie, and our daughter, Tara," he said.

I hadn't realized he'd stopped working and was watching me. Perry had told me Luke lost his wife to cancer two years ago.

"They're lovely," I said. "And I'm sorry for your loss. Perry told me about you, too."

"Thank you." For an uncomfortable moment he looked like he wished he could turn that photograph around so I couldn't see it and I wished I could do it for him.

"How long were you married?"

"Eighteen years. She was eighteen and I was nineteen. We were a couple of kids." He cleared his throat and went back to his computer screen, but a muscle twitched in his jaw and my heart ached for him.

"Would it be okay if I take a look at that folder on the Fabergé exhibit?" I asked.

"Help yourself," he said without looking up. "I got the gig to shoot a private party the night before the opening at the National Gallery. The director of public relations is a friend of a friend."

"Have you seen it yet? The exhibit, I mean?"

"No." He stopped working again, ran both hands through his curly hair, and leaned back in his chair. "Arkady Vasiliev, the Russian billionaire who's loaning the two Fabergé eggs and the paintings and icons to the gallery, won't allow anyone to see it until the night of the party. Nobody from the press got in for a preview, no advance interviews, no photographs, nothing. Moses Rattigan, the PR guy at the National Gallery, said those are Vasiliev's terms and they have to go along with them."

"That's odd. You'd think he'd want the publicity, wouldn't you?"

He shrugged. "Actually, all the secrecy worked in his favor. The tickets were gone the first week you could get 'em. I heard people are selling them—free tickets—on eBay for a hundred bucks or more. It's crazier than 'Bloom Watch' during cherry blossom week. The press are calling it 'Egg-Mania.'"

"Egg-Mania?" I said. "Seriously?"

"Don't look at me. I didn't invent it. Haven't you been following it in the news?" He made a face. "'D.C. Goes Nuts Over Eggs.' 'We're So Egg-cited and That's No Yolk.'"

I laughed. "I guess I missed those stories."

"Don't worry. I'm sure there'll be more."

"Well, the Fabergé eggs are a big deal," I said. "In Russia they symbolize the end of the Romanov empire. After that, the Communists took over and life changed forever."

"To be honest," he said, "I'm more interested in the paintings and icons than I am in two eggs with rubies and diamonds plastered all over them."

"You might change your mind after you get a chance to look at them," I said. "Nick—my husband—saw them. He told me they were fabulous."

Luke shook his head. "Vasiliev's people said no one had seen them. That's why this world premiere is such a big deal, the first time they're on display anywhere. The Firebird egg was never even mentioned in Fabergé's records, so nobody

knew it existed. The other one was lost after the Bolsheviks
assassinated the czar and his family before Fabergé got a
chance to give it to them."

Fabergé's last known imperial egg, the Blue Tsarevich
Constellation Egg. A miniature blue crystal clock with the star
constellation from the night Nicholas and Alexandra's son,
Alexis, the heir to the throne, was born. The stars were all
rose-cut diamonds.

"You mean it's the first time they're displayed in public," I
corrected him. "We were invited to a party at Arkady Vasiliev's
home in London. I was away that weekend but Nick went."

"You're personal friends with Arkady Vasiliev?"

"Not me, I've never met him," I said. "Nick knew him
professionally; they'd met once or twice. The only time he
saw Vasiliev that night was in a receiving line in a room made
entirely of crystal. Their house was so huge you could drop
Buckingham Palace inside and lose it."

"A room made entirely of crystal? Jesus." Luke rubbed his
chin. "How'd your husband end up seeing the eggs?"

"He asked Tatiana, as simple as that. She took him upstairs
in one of the elevators to the wing with their private art gallery."

"Jesus," he said again. "Who's Tatiana?"

"His wife."

"Must be his ex-wife," he said. "His girlfriend's running
this show. Lara Gordon. A real knockout, young enough to be
Arkady's daughter. Her mother is Katya Gordon, the Russian
art scholar from Columbia. The Gordons are the reason the
exhibit is opening in Washington instead of Moscow or
London. Lara wanted her mother to be the curator and get the
credit for scoring a world art coup and Vasiliev wanted to
please his hot new honey."

A new girlfriend, an American girl. I'd been so preoccupied
with my own life and avoiding reading the tabloids that I'd
missed the news that Vasiliev and Tatiana had split up.

I said to Luke, "I'd love to photograph that exhibit and I'd
really like this job."

He gave me another assessing look and picked up a black
marker, scribbling something on a legal pad. He spun it around
and pushed it over to me.

"Here's my final offer of a salary," he said. "I'm still getting out of hock for the equipment and the rent on this place is pretty stiff. It's all I can afford right now."

I looked down at what he'd written. He'd sweetened the deal, but I'd be making less money than I did in London, significantly less than the household income that had included Nick's CIA pay and his salary at Crowne Energy.

"I'll take it," I said.

FOUR

L uke set things up so I was cleared to work as a second photographer at Arkady Vasiliev's private party at the National Gallery of Art the following week. The two of us had already stopped by the museum to take test shots and check lighting, so we had done our homework, but Seth MacDonald, the gallery's director, still wanted us to come by for a final after-hours meeting the night before the event. I have photographed heads of state whose staff didn't require this amount of hoop jumping and security, but Luke told MacDonald that he, Alicia Jones, and I would be there at six sharp on Tuesday.

The first day I worked at Focus, no one showed up to sit at the receptionist's desk and I wondered if it was there for show. Then Luke told me he had hired Alicia—Ali—a few weeks before he took me on, agreeing to let her keep odd hours because she occasionally worked nights as a vocalist with a local jazz band. If the salary I made was anything to go by, Luke wasn't paying Ali much either, so accommodating her schedule must have been part of the quid pro quo for the paltry pay.

Ali said she met Luke when he saw her by the side of the George Washington Parkway one night, leaning against her car with the hood up. A cool, pretty twentysomething with glossy jet-black hair wearing a strapless jade-colored cocktail dress and stiletto heels, waiting for a chivalrous knight to come along and help a damsel in distress. He jump-started her car, found out she was unemployed during the day, and offered her a job.

Ali and I were in the office after hours one evening, drinking white wine and waiting for Luke to get back from a photo shoot for a client's annual report, when she told me that story.

I had retreated to one of the black leather Barcelona chairs in the reception area, where I sat cross-legged in my usual work uniform of jeans, T-shirt, and Keds. Ali was perched on her desk, dressed in a vintage black-and-white hound's-tooth suit, peep-toe heels, one leg crossed over the other, her lustrous black hair marceled like some retro movie star.

She looked at me from under heavily mascaraed eyelashes and said in a husky voice, "So what about you? Where are you from? You know, we could be sisters we look so much alike. Or, at least, cousins."

She was right. The first time I saw her had been like looking in a mirror at my twenty-year-old self, except that Ali was curvaceous and girly, whereas I was reed slim, a grown-up tomboy.

"My father—my biological father—was from Spain. My mom met him and fell madly in love when she was an exchange student in college. She dropped out when they got married, but it didn't last. He played football for Real Madrid, so he was always traveling. After the divorce we went back to the States," I said, "and when I was fourteen we moved to Virginia when she married my stepfather."

"¿Hablas español?" Ali asked.

I nodded. "But I learned it in school. What about you?"

"Anglo dad, mom's from Peru," she said. "Luke told me you used to live in London. He said you just moved back here."

"I did."

"And?"

I didn't know how much Luke had said, but she would find out sooner or later. So I gave her a sanitized version of Nick's disappearance and my decision to move home and put my life in order.

Ali drank some wine and swept a wave of hair off her face, as though she were vamping for some invisible admirer. "You still think he's alive, don't you? Your husband."

For one crazy moment, I thought about giving her the whole complicated answer. Instead I said, "The odds are that he's not."

"That's not what I asked." She made a fist and pumped it against her chest. "You can feel it here. You're a woman. You *know*."

She slid off the desk and walked into Luke's office for the wine bottle in his refrigerator. A moment later I heard her singing, "My Baby Just Cares for Me."

My God, her *voice*. It was a voice to give you shivers, make you think about smoke-filled nightclubs at closing time and sad saxophones and a table for one. I shut my eyes and listened as the words about Lana Turner's smile and races and high-tone places soared into the perfect acoustics of the room and echoed off the rafters.

I thought about Nick, who only just cared for me . . . didn't he? Where was he now and what was he doing? Ali came back into the room and I avoided her eyes as she filled my glass to the rim. We sat together in the brooding silence and drank as it slowly grew dark outside.

Later I wondered if she had deliberately chosen that song.

On Tuesday evening, Luke and Ali pulled up in his Jeep in front of the Mall entrance to the National Gallery of Art for the meeting with Seth MacDonald, the museum's director, just as I arrived on a mint green Vespa, my new purchase from a GW student who was ready to move up to a motor-cycle. Ali grinned and gave me a thumbs-up. Luke looked astonished.

"Doesn't that thing run on a hamster wheel?" he asked.

"Two." I chained the front tire through an empty bike stand across from the gallery entrance. "Okay, I'm parked. What about you?"

He made a face and drove off to find a spot while I waited for them at the top of the steps. By early September, summer is a distant memory in London, but in D.C. the temperatures still languished in the high eighties and the air felt as humid and sultry as if it were the dog days of August. The one differ-ence is the light: In the few weeks since I'd been home, it had shifted from a hard, pure glare to the softer, golden slant that signaled autumn.

A security guard let us in the gallery and said the director was finishing up some paperwork in the Founders' Room, which was just off the main lobby. Dark paneling, an enormous chandelier, oil paintings of the museum's benefactors lining the walls, the Founders' Room was furnished like an upscale gentlemen's club. An overstuffed sofa and club chairs were grouped around a large marble fireplace flanked by multitiered candelabra, and an antique clock that had stopped working sat on the mantel. All that was missing was the sherry and a butler to serve it.

Seth MacDonald looked up from signing papers at a Queen Anne desk in front of the room's only window. I'd seen photos of him and read enough not to expect a white-haired soft-spoken art historian. Ten years ago he'd been a controversial choice as the youngest director in the gallery's history at age twenty-nine. Within a few months he'd quashed his critics by persuading the Vatican to loan the museum never-before-seen-in-public paintings from the pope's private chapel and charming two high-tech billionaires with significant collections into making a permanent bequest in their wills. Since then, he had become best known for his populist talent for staging crowd-pleasing events that brought in hundreds of thousands of visitors who'd never set foot in the National Gallery because they'd believed art was too highbrow or mystical.

The international premiere of the lost Romanov treasures with its two previously undiscovered imperial eggs and the drama, romance, and intrigue surrounding their provenance was right up MacDonald's alley: a blockbuster exhibition that had already distributed free advance tickets in the tens of thousands. The backstory only added to the fairy tale: a Russian oligarch's desire to please his beautiful young American girl-friend who was devoted to her mother, an art history professor who was the exhibit's designer.

MacDonald came around from behind the desk to shake our hands. Though he wore a conservative charcoal suit, his tie was either something that Picasso painted during his Cubist period or the creation of a child gone wild with crayons, and I thought I saw rainbow peace signs on his dark socks.

"Thanks for coming," he said. "I won't keep you long. I just wanted to go over a few details for tomorrow. Mr. Vasiliev has some rather precise and unusual requirements. This needs to go like clockwork."

"You won't even know we're here, Dr. MacDonald,"

Luke said with smooth assurance. "We know how to stay out of the way."

MacDonald seemed relieved. "Excellent. Please call me Seth. And, if you're interested, when we're done I can give you a quick tour of the exhibit. You'll be the first visitors. It's quite a feather in our cap that Mr. Vasiliev chose the National Gallery to host the world premiere of the lost imperial eggs."

His face grew animated when he mentioned the Fabergé eggs, but feather or no feather, the exhibit had clearly come with strings attached, maybe even a whole ball of string. I'd read about Arkady Vasiliev's path to oligarch superstardom in the British newspapers. And Nick had filled me in on details that didn't make it into the press. Twenty-some years ago, Vasiliev had lived in a tiny two-room apartment in Moscow and stood in daily queues for such basic items as toilet paper and butter, which had been hard to come by in the old Communist-run Soviet Union. Now, after picking off Russia's state-owned oil production company for a pittance during the gangster capitalism Yeltsin years, Vasiliev had privatized it and watched the value soar into the billions. Then he acquired the lifestyle, which included owning a fleet of boats, a pride of houses, and a gaggle of jets.

Luke glanced at Ali and me and we nodded. "We'd love to see it," he said.

We followed Seth into the marble-columned rotunda with its statue of a winged Mercury poised on top of a tiered fountain. The fragrance of hundreds of red rosebushes surrounding the fountain scented the air, and the place was eerily silent except for the rushing sound of cascading water. Fading daylight flickered from the high-domed Rotunda skylight and the skylights that ran the length of the museum's two mirror-image wings. This wasn't the first time I'd been in a museum or cathedral or temple after hours and had it virtually to myself. It always gave me goose bumps and the breathless feeling of molecules swirling differently, the place coming to life as though paintings had eyes that followed you and statues flexed stiff muscles like they did in kids' movies. Once the noisy, boisterous tourists with their guidebooks and cameras and bored children had departed, the space filled up with the weighty stillness of centuries of greatness that I found intoxicating.

"Come." Seth cut into my thoughts. "Let's walk and we can go over everything one more time."

He ticked off items on his fingers. Two hundred guests. More roses specially flown in from California and alabaster urns lining both sculpture halls filled with long-plumed feathers dyed scarlet and gold to evoke the mythical Firebird. Twenty-four-karat gold-flecked Cristal champagne in Waterford flutes. Vasiliev's personal French chef arriving by private jet from London.

"There'll be lighted ice sculptures of the two lost Fabergé imperial eggs," Seth said. "Red for the Firebird, blue for the Constellation egg."

"How come no fireworks on the Mall or changing the color of the lights on the Capitol dome?" Luke asked when he had finished.

Seth's laugh was rueful. "You jest. The Park Service nixed the fireworks. I don't think changing the Capitol lighting occurred to anyone, thank God. And the National Symphony is on tour. Mr. Vasiliev is making a significant financial donation to the gallery, so anything he wanted he got as long as we could accommodate it."

Based on what I knew about Vasiliev, so far this sounded pretty tame.

"What else did he ask for?" I said.

"I have a small suite—an office and a conference room—that I use occasionally when I need a place to work where I won't be disturbed," Seth said. "You won't find it on any gallery map because it's located in a corridor that's accessible only through a somewhat hidden door in the cloakroom. Mr. Vasiliev wants the suite available for his private use, just in case."

Ali looked puzzled. "Just in case what?"

Luke and I exchanged glances and Seth gave her a heavy-lidded look.

"Just in case he wants it for whatever he wants. And he requires absolute privacy," Seth said. "He also requested a fully stocked bar, all top-drawer liquors and wines, and silver bowls filled with Beluga caviar to be placed there."

Ali seemed like she might be trying to imagine whatever-he-wants, but Luke said, "Seth, your PR guy, Moses Rattigan, told us we could use your office to store our equipment. We might need to get back there for fresh batteries or whatever. Is that going to be a problem?"

Seth looked concerned. "I hope not. The room Mr. Vasiliev really wants is the conference room. We can close the connecting door between that room and my office, if necessary. There's also a lock on the door to an office supply closet where you can keep your things. I'll arrange for you to borrow the key for the evening."

"We'd like to see that closet and the setup," Luke said. "We need to make absolutely sure our gear is safe."

"You can have a look at it as soon as we're done here," he said. "Come, next I want you to see the stage for Dr. Gordon's talk. We had to make some changes after she did her walk-through."

Seth led us through the West Sculpture Hall, its elegant bronzes burnished by the diffused light of spotlights suspended from the skylight fretwork. This was the wing of old master paintings: Dutch, Flemish, Spanish, French, Italian—and the only painting by Leonardo da Vinci in the western hemisphere, a fifteenth-century Florentine bride named Ginevra de' Benci. I trailed behind the others, stopping to glance into each gallery.

Seth doubled back and found me, the patient, polite expression of someone used to herding wayward visitors written on his face.

"Sorry," I said. "I couldn't resist. It's been years since I've been here. It's such a fabulous museum."

"Enjoy having it to yourself now because you won't be able to look into these galleries tomorrow," he said, smiling. "There'll be screens up everywhere. We can't have someone accidentally splashing a glass of wine on Jacques-Louis David's *Napoleon,* you understand. The only spaces that will be open during the reception will be the Rotunda, the East and West Sculpture Galleries, and the two garden courts. The *Empire of the Firebird* exhibit is in a gallery by itself off the East Garden Court, where we often showcase temporary exhibits."

Luke joined us and caught the end of Seth's comments. "What about the lower level?"

"It will be closed. All guests will enter the gallery through the Mall entrance as you did this evening," Seth said. We walked into the West Garden Court, where rows of folding chairs were set up in front of a small stage.

"I wanted you to see where we relocated the podium," he went on. "Katya Gordon's request. I'll begin by making a few remarks, thanking Mr. Vasiliev for his generosity, and then introduce Katya. She'll give a brief talk about the collection, the history of Fabergé and the Romanovs, and anything else she wants to talk about. All guests will receive a ticket when they arrive specifying the time when they can view the exhibit. If all goes according to plan, the reception ought to end around nine thirty."

He led us back through the Rotunda into the East Sculpture Hall. Here the galleries were filled with eighteenth- and nineteenth-century paintings, American, British, Spanish, and a magnificent gallery of the Impressionists; the sculptures were white marble.

"Last but not least of our host's requirements concerns you three," Seth said. "No photographs of the exhibit. Mr. Vasiliev controls all official photos and he owns all rights. I presume that's been made clear to you?"

"Don't worry. Moses told me that violators would be boiled in oil. So we get it," Luke said. "Not to mention he plans to stick to me like glue to make sure I get pictures of everyone you want photographed. Sophie's going to take candids, as well as the detail photos of the party, like those ice sculptures and the roses and urns with the red and gold feathers."

Seth nodded. "Excellent. In that case, how about a tour?"

The shadows in the museum had lengthened as the light from the skylights faded and became opaque. Now only spotlights illuminated the sculptures and paintings, and the gallery lighting took on a lambent, dreamlike quality. We followed MacDonald into the East Garden Court. In the center of the room golden light poured onto a fountain in which two cherubs played on a lyre and backlit the arcade behind a row of Ionic columns. Rosebushes of every color surrounded the fountain, and in each corner of the room a small garden area was heavily planted with ferns, palms, and other greenery whose branches arced over the walkways. Benches, wrought-iron chairs, and small tables had been placed around the perimeter of the room. In a far corner, a grand piano was cordoned off behind red velvet ropes.

"It's beautiful," Ali said.

"The lighting reminds me of an Impressionist painting," I said.

"I thought you would appreciate it." Seth smiled. "I come here when I get a free moment, just to sit and enjoy the tranquillity. That fountain used to be on the grounds of Versailles, along with the one in the West Garden Court."

Ali pointed to the piano. "Do you hold concerts here?"

He nodded. "We also have a terrific summer jazz series in the outdoor sculpture garden across the street. It's just wrapping up for the season, but I'll make sure you get a schedule before you leave. I think you'd enjoy it . . . I believe you're a professional singer?"

Ali was wearing another vintage outfit—fitted chartreuse skirt and matching bolero jacket, her thick, dark hair pulled up in a chignon, smoky eyes, and kiss-me red lips. I'd watched Seth noticing her as we'd toured the museum, her surprised reactions and comments giving away that this was her first visit ever to the National Gallery. A potential convert for Seth, someone he could perhaps win over and persuade that this beautiful building wasn't just a series of rooms filled with old paintings by dead men.

Ali looked surprised that he had taken the time to find out about her. "I am," she said, blushing. "And I'd like a copy of your concert schedule."

"I'll see that you get one," he said. "Come. Please follow me."

We walked past a scarlet banner suspended between two columns with EMPIRE OF THE FIREBIRD: THE REDISCOVERED TREASURES OF THE IMPERIAL ROMANOV DYNASTY written on it in gold calligraphy. The exhibit was laid out in a series of interlinked rooms connected to a central octagonal room. Though the imperial eggs had received the lion's share of media attention and hype because of the dramatic way they'd been discovered and the fact that one of them had never been heard of until now, the exhibit also comprised an eclectic collection of art and icons whose common thread was that everything had once belonged to the Romanovs and had vanished for nearly a century, lost in the chaos and turmoil of a revolution that disdained—and even tried to destroy—anything the royal family had owned. The exception, as homage to the Firebird egg, was a series of paintings from the Firebird fairy tale by Viktor Vasnetsov, a Russian artist known for his mythological and historical subjects and a contemporary of Nicholas and Alexandra. According to Seth, the curator of the Vasnetsov Museum in Moscow was a close friend of Katya Gordon's and this was the first time the paintings had ever been exhibited outside Russia. In the smallest room hung half a dozen never-before-seen oil paintings by Alexander III's wife, Maria Feodorovna.

"Not many people knew the empress was an amateur artist," Seth said as we stood in front of a still life of a table set for a meal. "These paintings are valued, of course, because Maria did them."

He saved the octagonal room, with its specially built cabinets displaying Fabergé's ruby-red Firebird and sapphire Blue Tsarevich Constellation imperial eggs, for last. In the pure white light of dozens of tiny spotlights they glittered, dazzling baubles created to please two empresses but ultimately symbolizing the brutal and merciless end of the Romanov's decadent empire.

I heard Ali's sharp intake of breath as Luke muttered, "Jesus."

"Exquisite, aren't they?" Seth said. "Fabergé created fifty-two imperial eggs that we knew of, until the discovery of the Firebird egg. So now there are fifty-three."

"Why fifty-three?" Ali asked. "And why eggs?"

"Because in the Russian Orthodox faith, it's common practice to exchange eggs at Easter," he said. "These were Easter gifts. Alexander III began the tradition in 1885 when he went to Carl Fabergé, who was a well-known jeweler in St. Petersburg, and asked him to design an Easter egg for his Danish wife, Maria Feodorovna.

"Fabergé's design appeared to be quite simple, a plain white enamel egg. But inside the egg was a pure gold yolk and inside the yolk was a tiny hen. And inside the hen was a diamond miniature of the imperial crown and a ruby pendant. Maria was enchanted, as you can imagine. And so began a tradition that would continue for three decades. When Alexander died, his son, Nicholas II, continued the gifts. Though by then Fabergé was designing two eggs, one for Maria and another for Nicholas's wife, Alexandra. It ended, of course, in 1918."

"What happened in 1918?" Ali asked.

Seth said in a bland voice, "As you probably remember from your history classes, the Bolsheviks assassinated the entire royal family—Nicholas, Alexandra, and their five children—by firing squad in the basement of a home in Ekaterinburg. The czar's mother, Maria Feodorovna, had escaped earlier to the Crimea, and later to Britain. But the others were mowed down in cold blood, believing they were going to have their photographs taken."

Ali absorbed that information in shocked silence, but I knew this story only too well. Nick's grandmother's family had also fled Russia as Maria had done, a terrifying trip on an over-crowded boat with no food and almost no water for four thousand people. The ship barely made it out of Sebastopol, those on board watching weeping friends and family members abandoned on shore as gunfire from the approaching Red Army grew louder. My heart still pounded every time I thought about that harrowing trip, heard Babushka's raspy voice as we sat in the tiny kitchen of her Paris apartment drinking tea that she'd insisted on making in a samovar. Nick would translate for me as a curl of acrid smoke from her favorite Gitanes Maïs—she used a Bakelite cigarette holder, which seemed so glamorous—enveloped us.

"Are you okay, Sophie?" Luke asked me.

I looked around, momentarily convinced I'd caught the wisp of a scent of black tobacco and yellow corn paper. "I'm fine," I said. "Just thinking about what Seth said."

"The display card says that neither Maria nor Alexandra ever saw these eggs," Ali said. "Was it because Alexandra had been killed and Maria was gone?"

"Yes and no. In the case of the Constellation egg, you're correct," Seth said. "But the egg was to be Alexandra's had she lived, not Maria's. The Firebird egg was also supposed to be for Alexandra, until Fabergé decided not to give it to her."

"How do you know they were meant for Alexandra?" Luke asked.

"Come. I want to show you something," Seth said as we walked over to the Constellation egg. "You see the beautiful detailed etching on the blue stone? It depicts the night sky on the date Alexis, Nicholas and Alexandra's son, was born. It was the last imperial egg Fabergé ever designed. Until it turned up in that trunk in England, we believed he never finished it because it was supposed to be Alexandra's gift in 1918. It probably explains why there's no surprise inside, as there was with all the other eggs."

"What about the Firebird egg?" Ali asked. "If nobody even knew about it, how do you know Alexandra was supposed to get it?"

"We don't know for sure," he said as we moved to the other case. "But the egg is red, the color of blood. Alexis, who was the heir to the throne, had hemophilia, meaning a fall or a bruise could cause him to bleed to death. The odds of him living to adulthood were poor and his death would change the Romanov line of succession. So his parents tried to keep his illness a secret for as long as possible. By now, though, Fabergé had become the imperial jeweler. He was known and trusted by the royal family, so we presume he knew about Alexis. And from 1906 on, Fabergé never designed an imperial egg in any shade of red, so as not to remind Alexandra of her son's bleeding."

We stared at the exquisite ruby- and diamond-studded Firebird egg, perched on a gold stand on top of a white velvet pedestal. The tiny surprises, a jeweled gray wolf and a golden-maned horse from the Russian fairy tale, sat at the base of the pedestal.

"When do you think it was made?" I asked.

"It's hard to know for sure since there were no records, but our best guess is 1904 or 1905, when Nicholas didn't commission eggs for the empresses. If you recall, those were the years of the Russo-Japanese War, and Nicholas thought it was in poor taste to show such blatant ostentation during a time of hardship for his people," Seth said. "Now, Alexis was born in 1904 and quite possibly Fabergé didn't know about the hemophilia that early, so maybe he went ahead and designed the egg then. Once he found out about the little boy, though, he decided not to give it to Alexandra. But it was too beautiful to be destroyed and, for yet more unknown reasons, Fabergé didn't sell it to one of his other wealthy clients."

No one spoke for a moment. Finally Ali said, "That's so sad."

Seth gave her a kindly look. "Think of it this way: These eggs are the legacy of a gift of love from a husband to a wife and a son to a mother. They've outlived an empire. There was a time the Bolsheviks were so desperate for Western hard currency that Joseph Stalin sold ten Fabergé eggs to Armand Hammer, the American businessman, based on the weight of their jewels. Then, in order to drum up public interest—the United States was in the middle of the Depression and people didn't care about a few Russian trinkets—Hammer took the eggs all around the country like a road show, displaying them in upscale department stores."

Luke whistled softly as Ali made a final slow tour of the eggs.

"More than ten thousand people have tickets to this exhibit," Seth said. "There's an almost obsessive interest in the imperial eggs now. Not only because they once belonged to royalty but also because there's so much tragedy and mystery surrounding their history after they came into the possession of the Bolsheviks. Each one has its own story, starting with the lives of the women for whom they were created to an eccentric cast of characters and wheeler-dealers who bought, sold, smuggled, and even stole the eggs."

Luke met my eyes through the glass case of the Firebird egg, and I knew now that he understood what I had said to him about what the eggs symbolized the day he interviewed me.

"This was fascinating," he said to Seth. "Thank you."

"Especially for letting us see them like this," I said. "It was sort of magical having them to ourselves."

"I've felt that way, too, when I've been here by myself. Though it's going to be a different story when the exhibit is open to the public." He smiled. "And now, shall we have a look at my office and the storage closet?"

As he'd told us, the office and conference room were accessible through an unobtrusive door in the cloakroom, which adjoined the Founders' Room. Seth pushed a recessed panel in the wall and the door sprang open.

"Open sesame," Ali said, awed. "Is it a secret passageway?"

"Yes." Seth nodded as we followed him down a corridor whose only lights were a few bare electric bulbs. We stopped in front of a door marked PRIVATE.

"There's a metal security door just around the corner," he said. "It leads to a subterranean corridor running the width of the museum, from the Mall to Constitution Avenue."

Ali disappeared to check it out. "It looks like the door to a dungeon."

"You're almost right," Seth said as we crowded into his small office. The walls and surfaces were covered with posters, photographs, sculptures, scale models, and architectural adornments that had been part of previous museum exhibits. The desk was a door set on top of a pair of Ionic columns, and a colorful foam topiary of fruit and flowers sat on top of a file cabinet. I instantly fell in love with the room, with its colorful random juxtapositions.

"I don't know if you were aware that the gallery was built on the site of the old Sixth Street railway station," Seth was saying. "It's probably most famous for being the place where President Garfield was assassinated in 1881. There's a plaque in the underground passageway commemorating the spot."

"Why is there a passageway under the museum?" Ali asked.

"I can't go into a lot of detail, but it leads to a climate-controlled vault. Something we might need in case we ever have to temporarily store some of our most valuable paintings in an emergency and there isn't sufficient time to get them out of Washington," he said.

"You mean like a terrorist attack?" Luke asked.

"Well, that's the first thing you think of today, but don't forget, John Russell Pope designed the building in the 1930s," Seth said. "At that time the precedent was something less apocalyptic, but equally devastating: the War of 1812, when the British burned Washington—the White House and the Capitol being the two most prominent buildings damaged in the fire. And during World War II, the director of the Corcoran Gallery was so worried about the capital being bombed he secretly moved many of their finest masterpieces to the basement of a high school in Winchester, Virginia."

"Can anyone use that tunnel?" Ali asked.

"It's closed to the public," Seth said. "But since the passageway has a door that leads to the kitchen of the Garden Café, which is our lower level restaurant, we've decided to leave the access door up here unlocked the night of the reception. That way Mr. Vasiliev's chef and some of the waitstaff can get back and forth between the upstairs and downstairs without going through the Rotunda."

Luke glanced at me. "We'd better make sure our stuff is locked up if there's going to be that much traffic through here."

"You said you had a key?" I said to Seth.

"Moses will have it for you tomorrow night."

"The public relations director," Luke reminded me. "Moses Rattigan."

Seth nodded. "I'll see you all here at six sharp."

We went back to the main lobby, where Seth waved off the security guard who leapt to his feet to unlock the double doors of the Mall exit.

"I'd like a word with Sophie in private, if you don't mind," Seth said as everyone shook hands.

Luke looked surprised, but all he said was, "Sure. Ali and I will wait outside. Good night, Seth."

The leather-clad door closed with a quiet thump and I said, "Is something wrong?"

"It's about your background check," Seth said. "Everyone who will be here tomorrow had to be vetted by Mr. Vasiliev's people. I thought you should know Mr. Vasiliev himself phoned me to inquire about you, particularly your being a last-minute addition to the list of people who will be here tomorrow. Do you know him? Personally, I mean?"

"No," I said. "But my husband knew him for business reasons."

He nodded. "Luke mentioned that to Moses . . . and about what happened to your husband. I'm terribly sorry for your loss."

"Thank you," I said. "Look, Seth, is there going to be a problem with my working at this reception?"

"Not at all. But I was curious why Mr. Vasiliev was especially interested in you."

"I'm sure it's because of Nick," I said. "When he . . . disappeared . . . the story made the headlines of the British papers for quite a while."

"I see," he said. "I appreciate your clearing that up."

He said good night and held the door for me. Outside the air felt warm and muggy and the eastern sky over the Capitol glowed with the sapphire brilliance of the Constellation egg. Above the Washington Monument to the west, the orange-red setting sun made the treetops look as though they were on fire.

"What was that all about?" Luke asked. He and Ali were waiting next to one of the enormous columns under the portico.

"Apparently you told Moses Rattigan that Nick knew Arkady Vasiliev, and Moses told Seth," I said. "Seth wanted my version, specifically whether I knew Vasiliev . . . you heard what he said about everything needing to go perfectly. I guess he just wanted to double check."

Luke looked concerned. "So everything's okay?"

"Yup. 'Night, you two. See you tomorrow." I ran down the steps to the Vespa before Luke could probe any further.

I drove along Madison Drive wondering what had prompted Arkady Vasiliev to personally call the director of the National Gallery of Art to ask about me. Nick's CIA contacts had warned me to tell no one my husband was alive.

Had Vasiliev somehow found out? And if so, who had told him and what did he want with me?

FIVE

Experience has taught me two things when someone says, "I'm afraid there's a small problem." First, the problem is never small, and second, it's about to become my problem.

Luke, Ali, and I were standing in the main lobby of the National Gallery of Art with our equipment when Moses Rattigan made that statement just after we'd arrived. I liked Moses right away. He had a basketball player's height and rangy build, stylish long gray hair, dark dancing eyes that hinted at a good sense of humor behind scholarly horn-rimmed glasses, and a Caribbean lilt to his voice that seemed to soften the impact of what he'd just told us.

"What small problem?" Luke asked, shooting a glance at me. I gave him an imperceptible shrug. Whatever it was, we'd handle it.

Before Moses could reply, the main door to the museum opened behind us and the security guard said, "Good evening, Dr. Gordon. The director is waiting for you in the East Garden Court. He asked me to tell you that he'd like to have a word with you before the guests arrive. I'd be happy to let him know you're here."

I couldn't resist turning around. Katya Gordon was probably in her early fifties, a stunning ash blonde with pale skin and cool gray eyes. She reminded me of Queen Jadis, the White Witch in *The Chronicles of Narnia,* whose magic brought endless winter to her kingdom during her hundred-year reign.

"Very well. Tell him I've arrived." Katya's Russian accent was faint but distinct, and she sounded annoyed. I wondered how she got along with Seth and whether she had something to do with Moses's small problem.

"Yes, ma'am," the guard said.

"Katya, my dear." Moses strode toward her with his hand extended. "You look absolutely stunning tonight."

Moses bent over Katya Gordon's outstretched hand and kissed it, a courtly gesture that earned him a fleeting smile. He was right. She looked gorgeous in a deep blue couture suit: shawl collar, nipped waistline, and pencil skirt with a sexy kick pleat slit. An unusual amber necklace, matching earrings, black slingback heels.

"Thank you, Moses," she said. "Can you see to it that my notes are put at the podium in the West Garden Court?"

"Right away." He summoned the guard and slipped him Katya Gordon's folder in a neat sleight of hand. "Before you join Seth, I'd like you to meet Luke Santangelo and Sophie Medina from Focus Photography. And this is Alicia Jones, their assistant."

Katya looked us over and murmured, "Nice to meet you," with all the sincerity of an Election Day politician. Then she moved away, the staccato tapping of her heels on the marble floor echoing as she walked toward the Rotunda.

Moses waited until she was out of earshot and said, "Well, now you've met Katya Gordon, the exhibit curator. Working with her was . . . quite an experience. She oversaw every detail, everything had to be just perfect. Of course, Mr. Vasiliev backed her to the hilt."

"It looks wonderful," Luke said in a neutral voice, and Ali and I murmured polite agreement.

Moses winked and said, "As my mother used to say, every hallelujah's got an amen—all good things must come to an end—and I can tell you I won't be too sorry to say that final 'amen' to this one. No one's ever tried to get us to change the architecture of the building before." We laughed and he added, "Why don't we finish our conversation in Seth's office, where we'll have privacy and you can get your equipment safely stowed?"

He touched the magic panel in the cloakroom wall and the door to the hidden corridor opened. A white-jacketed waiter pushing a cart filled with liquor followed us. Moses let us into Seth's office and disappeared into the conference room to have a word with the waiter. Ali peeked through the connecting door and let out a surprised whoop.

"The silver bowls with the caviar in them are big enough

to take a bath in," she said as Moses joined us, closing the
door behind him.

"Don't get any ideas." He grinned and wagged a finger at
her. "Those fish eggs cost nearly as much as one or two of
our paintings."

"What did you want to talk to us about?" Luke asked.

"Ah, yes. A little situation that caught everyone by surprise.
We're going to have another high-profile guest this evening.
Yuri Orlov, the Russian ambassador. Originally he didn't plan
on attending, but at the last minute he obviously changed his
mind." Moses leaned against Seth's desk and crossed one foot
over the other. "I'm sorry to get you involved in this, but we
need to keep as much distance between him and Senator
Hathaway as possible. Anything you can do to, uh, assist
would be greatly appreciated."

Scott Hathaway was the U.S. Senate majority leader and
the husband of Roxanne Lane Hathaway, a member of the
National Gallery's board of directors and one of the VIP guests
attending tonight. You couldn't swing a cat along the Mall
without hitting a museum that had received a significant
donation from Lane Communications. The Lane Educational
Center, which endowed promising young artists, was located
across the street in the museum's East Building.

"Why do those two need to be kept apart?" Luke slung his
camera strap over his shoulder and adjusted the camera so
the lens nestled protectively against the small of his back.

Moses sighed. "What I'm going to say can't go beyond this
room."

Luke eyed Ali and me. "We know how to be discreet," he
said. "In our business, you have to know how to keep your
mouth shut."

"I appreciate that," Moses said. "First of all, is anyone
familiar with the name Taras Attar, the Russian author and
politician?"

Luke and Ali shook their heads, but I said "I am" and hoped
I sounded blasé, instead of like huge puzzle pieces were
suddenly slamming together in my brain.

Taras Attar was Russian, as Moses said, but he was also
ethnically from Abadistan, where Crowne Energy had been

drilling their test well for the past few years. Though Nick never said anything to me, I always figured that part of his brief for the CIA was reporting on the escalating violence in the region because the Abadis were pushing for independence from Russia, as many of the other former Soviet republics had done.

Moses seemed surprised that I'd heard of Attar, but he continued. "Well, as I'm sure Sophie is aware, Taras Attar is from a region of Russia called Abadistan, which is a hotbed of political unrest at the moment. They want to be an independent country and the Russians want them to remain in the fold. If they do succeed in breaking away, Attar is probably the guy who'll be their new president. He's good-looking, talks in poetic and highly quotable sound bites, and was educated in the West—here and the U.K., in fact. He has less of an accent when he speaks English than I do."

Everyone smiled and I said, "Attar just wrote a book that was translated into English. I read a great review of it the other day. It's a memoir about growing up in the former Soviet Union woven between chapters on Abadistan's contribution to world culture all the way back to Alexander the Great."

Moses nodded. "Or, if you're Yuri Orlov, the Russian ambassador to the U.S., it's a manifesto that subliminally promotes independence. But Sophie's right; the book is getting a lot of buzz in certain circles. Attar's coming here to promote it as soon as he wraps up touring in Britain."

"What does this have to do with Senator Hathaway?" Luke asked.

"Ah," Moses said. "This is where it gets tricky, where you guys come in. Scott Hathaway and Taras Attar are old friends who went to Georgetown University together years ago. So when Attar's in D.C. next week, the senator is hosting a book signing for him at the Library of Congress and it's causing the Russians considerable heartburn. Hathaway says it's a literary event celebrating the publication of a friend's book, and the Russians are calling it a backhanded way of showing solidarity with the Abadi people. They also view it as meddling in what they claim are internal Russian affairs."

"What do you think?" Ali asked.

Moses gave her a tolerant smile. "I think I want peace in the wigwam for the duration of this evening, that's what I think."

"You don't really believe Yuri Orlov would get into something with Senator Hathaway tonight, do you?" I said.

Moses cleared his throat. "Well, I certainly hope nothing happens. But we're already dealing with a couple of touchy issues from the get-go. It's not exactly a love fest between the ambassador and Arkady Vasiliev, either." He started ticking items off on his fingers. "First, Mr. Vasiliev outbid the Kremlin Armoury for the Fabergé eggs. Second, he approached an American museum to stage the international premiere, something the Russians perceive as a slap in the face. In fact, it was the unspoken reason neither Orlov nor anyone from the Russian embassy planned on attending tonight. Third, and possibly adding insult to injury, many of the paintings in our original collection were purchased from the Hermitage by Andrew Mellon when he was in Russia in the 1930s. A number of them once belonged to Catherine the Great."

"Don't tell us you're worried Orlov might try to take the art off the walls and repatriate the paintings to Mother Russia?" Luke said with a grin.

Moses smiled and gave him another rueful look. "I don't believe that's going to be a problem, but I thought I'd mention it so you have the whole picture, so to speak. However, the alcohol is going to be flowing freely tonight, if you get my meaning. And Ambassador Orlov has a reputation for, ah, plain speaking when his, ah, tongue has been loosened."

"So we're not supposed to let him drink too much, either?" Ali asked.

"No. Figuring out a discreet way to handle that is just one of the many plates I need to keep spinning tonight," Moses said as the phone on his belt chirped that he had a text message. He looked at it. "And now, folks, I do believe it's showtime. That was Seth. Mr. Vasiliev and his entourage have arrived."

When I finally saw Arkady Vasiliev, he was standing in front of the fountain in the Rotunda with his arm around a dazzling dark-haired slip of a girl. She wore a short cream-colored dress that looked like it was spun out of gossamer and showed off a perfect golden tan. Around her neck hung a diamond necklace with a blood-colored ruby pendant the size of a small egg. As I watched, Vasiliev leaned down and whispered in her ear. She gazed up at him and smiled and nodded.

So this was Lara Gordon, Katya's daughter. She possessed her mother's exotic beauty, but without the forbidding and haughty demeanor. No wonder Vasiliev, who had to be at least twice her age, had fallen for her. A man could feel immortal with a girl like that on his arm. Or in his bed.

As for Vasiliev, he was as I remembered him from pictures in the London newspapers. Boyish looking, close-cropped salt-and-pepper hair, aquiline nose, high cheekbones, and the exotic slant of Tatar eyes behind rimless glasses. Nick described him as unfailingly polite on the few occasions when they'd met. But just now there was something in his eyes that gave me chills—once you got past the gee-whiz look of amused curiosity—a hint of a predatory show-no-mercy streak that no amount of Midas-like wealth or spectacular yachts and jets and mansions or his carefully cultivated image as a philanthropist and patron of the arts could erase. Even Lara Gordon, who looked as fragile and innocent as a Botticelli angel standing next to him, did nothing to dispel the aura of thuggishness he exuded.

His eyes fell on me, zeroing in on my cameras, and a little jolt of electricity zinged down my spine. I returned his stare and gave him a dutiful smile since he was, after all, paying my salary tonight. Someone called my name, or I thought so, and I looked away. When I turned back, Vasiliev and Lara were gone. Behind me guests began pouring in through the main entrance, filling the Rotunda and overflowing into the sculpture galleries. Before long the voices reverberating off the vaulted ceilings became an indistinct, echoing roar, like the sound of the ocean inside a seashell.

I forgot about Arkady Vasiliev and his stony stare and got to work.

Ali found me in the Rotunda after Katya Gordon had finished her talk and guests were slowly beginning to file through the exhibit. "Luke wants to know if you need anything, whether you're all right."

"I'm fine." We retreated to a spot between two enormous black marble columns where we could people-watch from the sidelines. "How's he doing?"

"Luke? Great. He could talk you into posing standing on your head or even naked, if he wanted to. He's real good with people."

"I noticed."

I'd watched him earlier, his knack for making his subjects relax, putting them at ease until they forgot he was holding a camera and began acting naturally. Changing angles as he laughed and joked, waiting patiently until he nailed the shots we were expected to get, and then diving in to try something different, more creative.

Ali leaned against one of the columns. Tonight we'd all worn black: Luke in a smart-looking Armani suit and open-neck shirt that made him look James Bondish, me in silk palazzo pants, a lace-and-silk sleeveless top, and a beaded cashmere shrug I'd bought in Paris, and Ali in a low-cut concoction straight off the cover of a 1950s pulp novel where some red-lipped sultry-eyed dame vamped below the caption "She Always Gets Her Man." We'd both pulled our hair back in ponytails—my reason was practical, to keep it off my face while I was working, but Ali had curled her hair and wore pretty tortoiseshell combs that only added to her sexy, flirty look.

"Do you know if Senator Hathaway has arrived yet?" I asked her. "I saw his wife but not him."

"Moses told Luke that Hathaway's going to be late because the Senate's still in session."

"That could be good news. Maybe he'll miss Ambassador Orlov. Whom I saw a few minutes ago, by the way. He looks like he ate something that gave him heartburn."

"I'll tell you what's giving him heartburn," Ali said. "Arkady Vasiliev. Not feeling the love when those two are standing next to each other. You can tell Orlov's in a real snit to be playing second fiddle to Vasiliev. The more he drinks the louder he gets."

"How much has he had to drink?"

"Enough to float an ocean liner, that's how much," she said. "Speaking of ocean liners, I met Lara Gordon. Can you imagine what it's like to be the girlfriend of a guy as rich as Vasiliev? He owns seven houses and three yachts. Not even yachts. They really are ocean liners. They flew over here in his Airbus. It's like a flying palace."

She sounded wistful.

"Hey, he owns the houses and boats and jet," I said. "She's just using them until he moves on to the next girlfriend. He left his wife, you know. And kids."

"How can you be so unromantic?"

"Easy. There's a difference between love and lust. And there's no guarantee her fairy tale will have a happy ending."

"You think he doesn't love her?"

"I don't know. He probably does today. But she's young enough to be his daughter. And I think someone like Arkady Vasiliev believes everything and everyone is expendable."

"He does seem sort of like a mafioso kind of guy, doesn't he?" She started humming the theme from *The Godfather* under her breath.

I shushed her and we both started to giggle.

"Well, I could see him committing murder if someone got on his bad side." Ali grabbed onto the column and peeked at Vasiliev. As she swung around, she knocked into a waiter carrying a tray of hors d'oeuvres. He lost his footing and the tray and dishes sounded like crashing cymbals as everything hit the marble floor. The noise caused a momentary lull in the conversation as heads swiveled to see what had happened and then the buzz started up again.

Ali's hand flew to her mouth. "What a klutz I am . . . I'm so sorry."

The waiter gave Ali a perfunctory smile and mumbled "It's okay" as a barrel-chested bartender who had been serving drinks at a bar in the Constitution Avenue lobby came over to help retrieve skewers of grilled scallops, dishes of wasabi, and sesame-encrusted crab cakes.

Ali and I started to help, but the bartender, who brought a rag to wipe the floor, waved us away as the waiter picked up the destroyed tray and disappeared.

"Don't worry," the bartender said. "At least it wasn't a tray full of drinks. We'll take care of it."

Ali threw me a guilty look and said, "Guess I'd better get back to Luke."

"Try not to run into anyone else on the way," I said.

She grinned. "What I'm really hoping is I run into a rich Russian sugar daddy who'll invite me to live on his ocean liner."

"Just don't spill his drink on him."

Ali winked and flashed me a radiant smile. Then she sashayed into the crowd and was gone.

Ali wasn't the one who found a rich Russian: I was. Rather, he found me. I walked into the Founders' Room, where a half dozen of the more elderly, fragile guests had taken refuge from the crowds and were sitting on the sofa and club chairs surrounding the fireplace. I was in the midst of photographing a group who were standing under the portrait of Andrew Mellon when a man in a dark suit who'd been shadowing Vasiliev tapped me on the shoulder.

"Mr. Vasiliev would like a word with you," he said in careful English. "Now, if you please."

He'd phrased it like an invitation, though I knew it wasn't.

"Why me?"

"That is for Mr. Vasiliev to say. Follow me."

I knew where we were going: to the caviar-and-serious-booze conference room. Vasiliev's bodyguard led me to the cloakroom and knew the secret panel to push that opened the door to the back corridor. As soon as I stepped inside the conference room he closed the door, leaving me alone with Arkady Vasiliev, who sat at the far end of the table speaking staccato Russian into his mobile phone. Vasiliev held up a finger to signal he'd be only a minute and pointed to the caviar and well-stocked bar. I gave him a polite smile and shook my head. No drinking on the job.

I stood, since he hadn't indicated I should sit, and waited until he finished his conversation. I can't read or write Russian, but I'd heard Nick speak the language often enough to pick up a few words. Unfortunately I had no idea what Vasiliev was talking about, though it sounded like he was trying to placate someone. He took off his glasses and rubbed his fingers across his forehead as he repeated, *"Nichevo, nichevo."* An all-purpose word that meant whatever you wanted it to mean: "Don't worry about it" or "It's nothing."

Vasiliev finally ended the conversation and set his phone next to him, folding his hands together and steepling his fingers. "Please take a seat."

I put my cameras on the table, pulled out the chair across from him, and sat.

"You are Sophie Medina?"

"Yes."

The boyish cockiness on display when he'd been standing with Lara Gordon in the Rotunda was gone, replaced by a grim-faced businessman. Vasiliev picked up his glasses and put them on. "Also the wife of Nicholas Canning?"

"Yes."

"What are you doing here?" Asked in a nonthreatening way.

I decided to take him literally. "Taking photographs of your reception. I'm a professional photographer."

The veneer of courtesy disappeared. "That is not what I meant. You are a professional photographer who only became employed by Mr. Santangelo and Focus Photography last week."

I wondered how long he planned to keep asking questions when he appeared to know the answers, but I wasn't going to tell him anything I didn't have to. "That's correct."

"You knew Mr. Santangelo had been hired to work here tonight."

This time I couldn't figure out if he actually knew the answer or if he was fishing for information.

"My former boss in London is an old friend of Luke's. He recommended me for a job at Focus when I decided to move home to Washington," I said.

Vasiliev sat back in his chair, folding his arms across his chest. His fingers were short and square, the nails manicured, but his hands looked like they had the brute strength to crush things and break them.

"You did not answer the question."

"I'm a photojournalist, Mr. Vasiliev. I used to work for a news agency that sent me all over the world covering wars, politicians, natural disasters, you name it. No disrespect, but this is pretty tame stuff for me. Perry, my former boss, told me about the Romanov exhibit at the National Gallery and your reception," I said. "He thought it might make the position at Focus seem more appealing since your . . . since my husband saw the Fabergé eggs at your house in Belgravia not long after you acquired them. You invited him . . . us . . . to a party."

That surprised him. "You have been to my home?"

"No, I was in Germany covering a G-8 summit that weekend. But Nick went, as I said."

Vasiliev picked up his phone, turning it over and over while he considered my answer. "Where is your husband, Ms. Medina?"

Nick used to say that it wasn't lying if you stopped talking when you got to the end of what you knew was true. "I have no idea. His body was never found after he was abducted from our home."

Vasiliev tossed the phone on the table. It landed with a clatter as he leaned back in his chair. "Of course it wasn't. How could it be, when he's still alive?"

Who told him that? Did he *know*—how could he? Or was he baiting me again? It felt as though the air had suddenly been sucked out of the room.

I chose my words carefully. "I haven't heard from him since the day he vanished."

Vasiliev looked incredulous. "I don't believe you."

"Believe whatever you like. It's true."

He made a clicking sound of disapproval with his tongue. "Come, come, Sophie, don't play games with me."

"I'm not."

"But you know he's alive, do you not?"

I forced myself to say, "He would have gotten in touch with me."

Vasiliev studied his manicure. "If it's true that you haven't heard from him, perhaps he has no wish to be in touch with you. Maybe he has met someone new, another woman. Or maybe he has simply grown tired of you."

A ghost of a smile crossed his face, a taunt.

I kept my face perfectly composed. "You're wrong. Not Nick. He would never do something like that. My husband loved me."

"If he loved you, he would find a way to let you know that he is alive, that he is okay."

Vasiliev was going to pursue this ruthlessly, wear me down and play mind games that made me doubt Nick's love and fidelity. As long as I didn't take his bait, I'd be okay.

"If he's not alive, he couldn't get in touch with me, could he? And if he is alive, there was a lot of blood in the car in the mountains, Mr. Vasiliev," I said. "Maybe he's sick or injured. There are a lot of reasons why I wouldn't have heard from him . . . maybe he just can't."

"You are a clever woman," he said. "But I believe you are lying."

I'd had enough and now I snapped at him. "Mr. Vasiliev, do *you* know that my husband is alive? Do you know where he is? Because if you do, I'd be interested in knowing myself."

He leaned forward and there was a razor edge of menace in his tone. "I am going to tell you something. If Crowne Energy discovered oil in Abadistan, that oil belongs to *Russia,* do you understand? It is *ours.* That means we need to have all data, all reports concerning what they found, whether it was a producer, what yield they expected. Now that Crowne Energy has abandoned their facility, I want that information."

The well logs.

Of course he wanted them. He owned Arkneft, the largest oil production company in Russia. As for his patriotic claim that any oil that had been discovered belonged to Russia, what he really meant was: *It's mine.*

"Crowne Energy didn't abandon their facility." I held my ground. "The Shaika moved in and disrupted their work, extorted money from my husband and his boss, and intimidated their workers."

Vasiliev glared at me. "You do not know what you are talking about. Listen to what I am telling you. I will pay for those documents. I will pay well."

"I don't know anything about any documents," I said.

"I doubt that is true." Vasiliev stood up and I felt the chill emanating from him, and his anger. "But I know your husband does."

As he walked by me, heading for the door, he leaned down and said, "Do not underestimate me, Sophie, and don't fool yourself that I believed your little charade just now, either. I will get those logs by whatever means it takes. Right now, I am willing to do it the easy way, so everyone wins. But I am not a patient man. Remember that."

I didn't look up or acknowledge him. But I did jump, as I suspect he intended me to do, when he slammed the door on his way out. The noise sounded like a gunshot.

Then silence.

SIX

I was still sitting at the conference table when the connecting door to Seth's office opened a crack. A second later it swung completely open and Ali stood there gripping the doorknob with both hands.

She'd heard. By the scared look on her face, she'd heard all of it. If Vasiliev found out she'd been eavesdropping, if he even suspected she'd been in the next room . . .

"Ali," I said, trying to keep the panic out of my voice, "how long have you been here?"

"Are you okay, Sophie?" she asked. "What was that all about?"

"I'm fine," I said. "Answer my question."

"Don't worry," she said. "He didn't know I was here."

"How much did you hear?"

She shrugged. "Everything. The walls between these rooms are pretty thin."

I stood up. "You need to forget it, do you understand? Don't repeat a word of this to anyone. The meeting, the conversation . . . it never happened."

"Arkady Vasiliev threatened you, Sophie. And he thinks your husband is alive," she said. "Is he? Is it true? I knew you thought he was, I just knew it."

"Ali, stop!" I clenched my fists. What I really wanted to do was clap them over her mouth. "Stop asking questions. You don't know what you're getting into."

"What are you going to do?" she asked. "This is like being in a spy movie."

"No," I said, my voice rising. "No, no, no. It is not. It's the real thing. And I'm not going to do anything except carry on like nothing happened. And you're going to do the same. But right now we need to get you out of here so Arkady Vasiliev doesn't put two and two together and realize you were next door when he thought he and I were having a private conversation."

Ali gave a little one-shoulder shrug. "That's easy. I'll just take the tunnel to the other side of the gallery. I can stop off in the kitchen . . . one of the waiters told me there's an awful lot of food."

"You'd better get back to Luke. He's going to be wondering what happened to you."

"Oh, come on," she said. "What's the harm? I'll just take a quick peek. Sue me for having a little fun at a glam party."

I opened the conference room door and listened. All we needed was for Vasiliev to have posted one of his bodyguards there, but the hall was silent. I turned back to Ali and said, "There's no one there. I'll see you back in the Rotunda in a few minutes, okay?"

She grinned, putting her arm over her mouth and nose like she was wearing a veil. "I always wanted to be Mata Hari."

I groaned. "Just go."

She left, and a moment later, the metal door at the end of the corridor scraped open and then closed. A text message from Luke chirped on my phone.

Where are you? Hathaway just arrived. Orlov still here.

This evening couldn't end soon enough.

I left through the passageway door to the cloakroom and walked into the Founders' Room in time to see Scott Hathaway standing in the lobby trailed by half a dozen dark-suited men and women who looked like members of his staff. A group of admirers surged around him—everyone seemed to want to touch him—and he waded into the crowd, laughing and chatting, backslapping the men and kissing the women. I'd run into Hathaway on a couple of occasions when he was overseas with some congressional delegation, and I'd always found him to be smart, personable, and well liked. Plenty of his peers lived up to the stereotype of foreign trips as party junkets or shopping sprees to fun or exotic places with taxpayers footing the bill, but Hathaway wasn't one of them. Nor did he have the parochial ugly American view that the world revolved around Washington because the United States was the center of the universe.

Tall and lean with an athlete's erect posture, dark blond hair turning white at the temples and just beginning to recede at the hairline, he was handsome in a craggy patrician way. Just now he was charming his fans with his crinkle-eyed grin and a sonorous voice that cut through the buzz of conversation, especially his thick-as-mustard Boston accent, all dropped *r*'s and elongated *a*'s.

"Scott!"

Hathaway looked up as his wife waved and called to him from the Rotunda. I had seen Roxanne Lane Hathaway from a distance for most of the evening. She was a pretty, petite redhead who moved with an easy charm and grace, a good foil for her husband.

I heard him say, "Theah's the boss. I'd better get over there and join her. Good seeing you, Danny-boy. Stu, keep an eye on your pretty bride befoah someone steals her."

Danny-boy or Stu leaned over and said something that made Hathaway roar with laughter. Hathaway patted the man on the back and moved toward his wife just as Yuri Orlov and his embassy entourage walked into the East Sculpture Hall. The two men saw each other instantly. I thought Moses had been exaggerating when he implied that a meeting between Orlov and Hathaway might be as combustible and drama laden as the gunfight at the O.K. Corral. But there was Orlov, a stocky, compact man with a bullet-shaped head and the florid face of a heavy drinker, barreling down the hallway toward the Rotunda, his body tilted forward as though battling a fierce headwind, and Hathaway standing there watching him, just like Wyatt Earp waiting for the Clantons and the McLaurys.

I raised my camera and a woman's voice said in my ear, "Put the goddamn camera down or else. No photos of this meeting, got that?"

I obeyed, adding, "You could have said 'please' put the goddamn camera down."

One of Hathaway's aides. Dressed in a severe black suit, white silk blouse, black kitten heels, very young and very pretty, except for the glower on her face. "Please," she said through gritted teeth and with not much sincerity and left to rejoin Hathaway who, by now, had extended his hand to Yuri Orlov.

Orlov's group closed ranks around him; Hathaway's people muscled in behind their boss. I lost sight of Roxanne, but a few guests had stopped to watch the meeting.

"Good to see you, Mr. Ambassador." Hathaway sounded friendly and upbeat. "Especially on an occasion that showcases your country's magnificent cultural heritage."

Orlov played along. "It's good to see you, too, Senator. I did not know you were so interested in Russian art."

Hathaway flashed his genial smile. "Ah, but you're mistaken, Yuri. I try to visit the Hermitage, the Pushkin, and the Tretyakov every time I'm in Moscow or St. Petersburg. And my wife is on the board of directors of the National Gallery. She's been telling me about this exhibit for months."

"Excellent," Orlov said. "But you would be wise, Scott, to confine your interest to Russian art and refrain from supporting the literature of terrorists who plot against my government."

There was a long moment of silence as Hathaway ducked his head and appeared to consider his response to Orlov's polite insult.

"Now, Yuri. First, he's no terrorist, and second, you're talking about something that's an entirely private matter. Third, this is the United States of America." Though he continued to smile, his tone had turned professorial and no-nonsense and the Hahvad-yahd accent more pronounced. "Freedom of speech is one of our fundamental rights, what-evah or whoevah the source. You know that."

Orlov snorted. "Don't pull that with me, Scott. Do you really believe that this book signing you're hosting for Taras Attar has no political significance? What message does it send to the Abadi rebels? I tell you what: that they have a friend in the United States of America. Come, come. I give you credit for more intelligence than to pretend otherwise."

A tiny muscle flexed in Hathaway's jaw and his eyes narrowed, but he held his tongue and his manners. "I've known Taras longer than I've known you. We were classmates at school thirty years ago. As far as I'm concerned this is a personal matter, a favor to an old friend, and it's my business. There's really nothing further to discuss."

Orlov, on the other hand, had been drinking all night, and his boiling point was lower than Hathaway's. His ruddy face became even more flushed and he shook his finger at Scott Hathaway. "This is *not* finished, Senator. We will not tolerate this situation, do you understand?"

The room became silent as Orlov's ultimatum hung in the air and then started spinning, a dangerous, shimmering taunt. I caught a blur of motion that was Seth MacDonald moving swiftly across the Rotunda on his way to defuse this ticking time bomb about to go *boom*. Roxanne Hathaway, flaming red hair, glittering one-shouldered electric green dress, also hurried toward her husband. Before either of them could reach the two men, or Hathaway could counter with *Or else, what?* Katya Gordon appeared, sliding her arm through Orlov's, and murmuring to him in Russian.

Whatever she said appeared to mollify him because he gave her a curt nod and said something that sounded like "*Udachi.*"
Good luck.

Katya turned to Scott Hathaway. "Senator, it would be my pleasure to give you a private tour of the *Lost Treasures* exhibit."

She extended her hand as Seth and Roxanne surrounded Orlov and began talking to him in soothing voices, distracting him as they ushered him toward the exit.

Hathaway shook Katya's hand. "Thank you. That's very kind. And you are—?"

Katya's smile froze as though she was stunned Hathaway needed to ask. "Dr. Katya Gordon. I am the curator of this exhibit." She paused and added in a stiff voice, "I beg your pardon, but I thought you would remember me. You and I have met before."

Hathaway gave her a tight smile. "Of course. Forgive me, it's been awhile. I'd be delighted if you'd show me the exhibit, but I don't want to impose with so many other guests here tonight. I'm sure you're much in demand."

"It's no imposition at all." Katya turned to Hathaway's aides, who were starting to fall in line behind the two of them.

"Ladies and gentlemen, I'm sure you wouldn't mind allowing me to give the senator a private tour? Please check your tickets, as they are printed with the time you yourselves can view the exhibit. In the meantime there is plenty to eat and drink, so please enjoy yourselves. I'll have Senator Hathaway back to you shortly."

The young woman who'd ordered me to put my goddamn camera down didn't look happy at being untethered from Scott Hathaway, who was already walking toward the East Garden Court with Katya Gordon. As she joined her colleagues who were drifting over to one of the bars, something flickered across her face, an emotion I couldn't quite read. Anger, maybe.

"What was that all about?" Luke said in my ear. "What did I miss?"

I hadn't heard him come up behind me and I jumped. "Yuri Orlov going at it with Scott Hathaway. Katya Gordon rescued Hathaway and took him off for a private tour. Seth and Roxanne Hathaway practically had to get Orlov in a headlock so they could escort him to the door."

"Damn, I would have paid to see that," he said. "Sorry, I didn't mean to scare you. Everything all right? You seem sort of keyed up."

"Me? No, I'm perfectly fine." I changed the subject. "I tried to take pictures of the Orlov-Hathaway meeting, but some twelve-year-old from Hathaway's staff threatened me with bodily harm when she saw my camera. I guess they're exempt from child labor laws on Capitol Hill."

Luke grinned but he shook his head. "We're getting paid to take pictures of people having a good time, not the Russian ambassador and the Senate majority leader about to duke it out in the middle of the National Gallery."

"They'd be newsworthy pictures."

"Newsworthy for International Press Service, not for Focus Photography. So don't go there. We wouldn't get invited back to the next soiree if we pulled that crap." He held up the key to Seth's closet. "I need to get a fresh battery for my flash. You okay? Need anything?"

"I'm fine," I said. "I'm going to wander down to the East

Garden Court and wait for Katya Gordon and Scott Hathaway.
Get them to pose for a few pictures."

"Great," he said. "Catch you later."

Not anger, but jealousy. I figured it out while I was lingering
by the fountain where the two cherubs that had once graced
the courtyard of Versailles played the lyre. Hathaway's aide
hadn't been angry that Katya Gordon spirited off her boss
and forbade everyone else from tagging along. She'd been
jealous.

An affair between her and her boss? Or was she just besotted
with Hathaway and he didn't know or wasn't interested?
Powerful older men and pretty young women—you almost
expect it these days. I filed that thought away as a heavyset
African-American man wearing a navy blazer with a badge
with a gold eagle insignia and the words PROTECTIVE STAFF
NGA came up to me.

"Sorry, miss. No photographs allowed here."

"I know," I said. "I'm one of the official photographers for
tonight. They're paying me to take pictures. I was hoping to
ask Dr. Gordon and Senator Hathaway to pose for a couple
of shots after they leave the exhibit."

"In that case, no problem," he said. "But it's gotta be out
here. They're being real strict about the no-photo rule. I
already had to ask a lady and her daughter to delete pictures
on their phones even though there are signs up all over the
place."

"I understand," I said. "Dr. MacDonald and Mr. Rattigan
made sure we were aware of that restriction."

"Good," he said. "Senator Hathaway and Dr. Gordon have
been in the gallery about fifteen minutes. Oughta be coming
out soon. She asked to have the place to herself, so I had to
shoo everyone else out. I don't think they're gonna take long.
You can hang around here and wait if you want."

"Thanks," I said. "I'll do that."

I had counted on Katya Gordon and Scott Hathaway leaving
the exhibit through the main door, figuring she'd end her tour
with the Fabergé eggs just as we'd done the day before with
Seth. If they did, it would bring them back into the East

Garden Court. What I'd forgotten was door number two, a side exit off the room where Maria Feodorovna's paintings were displayed. It led to a lobby, a set of staircases, and a small atrium with a glassed-in balcony overlooking the 4th Street courtyard between the East and West buildings of the National Gallery. By the time I remembered that other door, I'd moved to the opposite side of the East Garden Court near the entrance to the East Sculpture Hall.

I looked up as the museum guard raised his hand and pointed to the atrium: They'd used the side door. From where I stood, the fountain blocked my view, but I could still get my shots of Katya Gordon and Scott Hathaway because they had to come through the East Garden Court in order to get to the East Sculpture Hall and the Rotunda.

Unless the reason they'd chosen that exit was that it was next to those staircases to the lower level.

What if Hathaway had decided to leave the museum after Katya's private tour? The Senate majority leader probably had enough clout to persuade the guards downstairs to let him out the first-floor exit. I cursed and flew across the East Garden Court. If I had to take my photos in the atrium, I'd have to deal with the mirrored reflections from the glass, plus the glare of lights through that balcony window. Spotlights glinting off the East Building across the street and, in the plaza below, a lighted semiunderground fountain alongside pyramid-shaped skylights that would glitter like massive diamonds.

Instead what I saw as I walked around the little fountain were the profiles of two silhouetted figures in an emotional conversation, a man and woman who had clearly met long before that encounter a few minutes ago in the Rotunda. They were standing too close, their body language too intimate, and they were completely engrossed in each other, oblivious of me as I watched what looked like an argument, maybe even a lover's quarrel.

I moved near one of the pillars, raised my camera, and fired off a couple of shots. Without a flash and at this distance, I'd be lucky to get anything, but through the lens of my telephoto I watched Scott Hathaway vehemently shake his head as Katya Gordon grasped his arm, insisting on something he didn't want to hear.

Then Katya spoke, her words clear and distinct. "You have no choice, Scott. You know that."

I lowered my camera. Their discussion—or argument—was finished. Besides not wanting to be caught eavesdropping, I knew neither of them would be interested in smiling for a photo together after that exchange. I had taken about half a dozen steps when Katya Gordon said in a loud voice, "You! The photographer. What are you doing here?"

I stopped and turned around. "I was hoping to get a couple of pictures of you and Senator Hathaway after you finished touring the Fabergé exhibit, Dr. Gordon."

She looked stunned, but then her eyes narrowed as though she was trying to figure out how long I'd been here and whether I'd overheard her conversation with Hathaway.

Finally she said, with icy finality, "That will not be possible. Leave here at once. I thought it was made clear to you and your colleague that any photography of the exhibit is strictly forbidden. Did you not understand?"

"Of course," I said. "That's why I was waiting out here."

The museum guard, who'd conveniently disappeared behind another column on the far side of the courtyard, now stepped out from the shadows and joined us. Katya turned her ire on him.

"Where have you been? You're supposed to be watching that door." She pointed to the exhibit entrance like a furious parent confronting a teenager who just wrecked the family car. "Did you see her take any pictures?"

The guard folded his hands together and shook his head, placid and unruffled by her tirade. "No, ma'am. She must have just walked in a second ago. I been here the whole time, just wanting to give you and the senator a little privacy, so I scooted out of the way."

Katya's gaze shifted from the guard to me as though she was trying to decide if she'd just been fed a pack of lies. "I could confiscate your memory card, you know," she said to me.

I couldn't tell if she was bluffing.

"You could, but you don't need to," I said. "You're going to have all our pictures anyway once Luke and I download and process them."

Except the ones we didn't show her.

After a moment she pursed her lips and said, "Make sure I do."

She left the East Garden Court, head high, still bristling with anger. The guard and I exchanged glances.

"Thank you," I said. "I owe you."

"She been acting like that the whole time, bossing everybody around, talking to us like she owns this place." He snorted. "A couple of the old-timers who been here their whole life got so fed up, I swear, if she was on fire they wouldn't spit on her. It's not her museum and it don't belong to Mr. Vasiliev, neither. I don't care how much money he spent tonight. It belongs to the American people. That's you and me, sweetheart."

I blew him a kiss. "It is you and me, isn't it?"

He grinned and gave me a thumbs-up. "And don't you forget it."

By the time I got back to the Rotunda, I decided to swap my memory card for a new one on the off chance Katya Gordon reconsidered and got the bright idea that I should hand it over to her anyway. I found Luke by the Firebird ice sculpture and asked him for the key to Seth's closet.

"What for?" he said.

"My memory card's full. I need to get a new one."

He gave me a quizzical look. Fifteen minutes ago I'd told him I was all set when he asked if he could get me anything from the supply closet.

He handed me the key, but all he said was, "Did you get pictures of Hathaway and Katya Gordon?"

"No. I think he slipped out the back way while she held me off at the pass."

"Pardon?"

"There's a staircase off the East Garden Court," I said. "I think he took it, probably tried to leave the building through the lower level, after all that drama with Yuri Orlov."

"That's strange. You'd think Katya could have persuaded

him to stick around for a photo op," he said. "Good publicity for the exhibit."

"Maybe she tried." I palmed the key. "Anybody lurking in the conference room while you were back there getting your battery?"

"Nope. I took a look around, too. Doesn't look like the room has been used all evening. Nobody's eaten or drunk a thing. What a shame if it goes to waste. All that caviar and expensive hooch."

I put on my poker face. "Yeah, a real shame."

"Maybe they'll give out doggie bags."

"In your dreams."

He grinned and hooked a thumb at the Firebird ice sculpture. "You got pictures of this and the Constellation sculpture at the beginning of the evening, right?"

"Of course. Why?"

"Take a look," he said. "The Firebird's starting to look like a rooster on a bad day. The clock for the Constellation egg is a big blue lump. The electrician had to turn the lights down before they ended up with two giant ice cubes to dump in the big fountain. Wouldn't that have been something?"

He chuckled as I surveyed the sculpture. He was right. The Firebird's magical tail feathers drooped like he'd been caught in a downpour.

I smiled. "Well, at least they lasted for most of the evening. Plus it's nighttime now so it's darker in here. Maybe no one noticed."

In the past half hour the daylight streaming through the skylights had faded, becoming as flat and black as obsidian. In the soft, pale light and crisscrossing shadows, the gallery seemed enchanted, like something out of a dream. A stray beam from a spotlight burnished Luke's profile like one of the bronzes in the West Sculpture Hall.

He seemed to be in high spirits just now, an adrenaline rush of elation and relief that the evening had gone so well for us. I liked him this way; the last few days he'd been as serious and intense as if we were planning a military campaign. Once or twice I'd wanted to say or do something irreverent that would make him laugh and lighten up. But he wasn't Perry and I didn't know him that well, so I'd held my tongue.

"Find me after you get your memory card, okay?" he said. I nodded. Back to business. "I'm going to ask around, see if Hathaway really did manage to leave since everything's locked up downstairs. Maybe I can still get him to pose with Vasiliev or Katya Gordon," he added.

I wouldn't try to get Katya Gordon and Scott Hathaway together if I were you. I almost said it, but I didn't want to do anything to ruin his perfect evening, a success for Focus and for him.

"Sure," I said. "Good luck."

When I walked into the cloakroom a few minutes later, a different guard in a navy jacket with the gold eagle emblem tried to stop me from using the door to the private corridor.

"It's restricted, miss. The restrooms are on the other side of the Rotunda."

I held up Seth's key. "I'm one of the photographers. My equipment is in Dr. MacDonald's office."

"In that case," he said, "go right ahead."

The hallway was cool and silent. I let myself into Seth's office, unlocked the closet door, and got a new memory card out of a pouch in my backpack, swapping it with the full one. As I closed the compartment on my camera, the metal door at the end of the corridor opened and closed. I heard foot-steps—more than one person—stopping outside the conference room.

I flipped off the light switch as whoever it was—presumably Vasiliev and a companion—walked in next door. Maybe I could just wait until they were finished, as Ali had done, because I had no interest in meeting Arkady Vasiliev again, especially not here. Apparently neither Seth nor Moses had let him know he didn't have the total privacy and exclusive access to this suite that he'd demanded. If he found out now, there would be hell to pay.

But it wasn't Vasiliev in the next room after all. I heard two male voices and finally identified them as a Russian and an American. The Russian talked like he was running the show; the American sounded nervous and ill at ease.

"Stop walking around and sit down," the Russian said in a flat, toneless voice.

"I want a drink," the American said and blew his nose.

"No drink. This is business. Hey, don't touch that. I told you, leave everything alone."

"Why do we have to do this tonight?" A chair scraped like the American was sitting down.

"Here. Take this. You'll get a text message on the day to confirm it's still on. Afterward get rid of it. A Dumpster or the river. In the meantime, don't do anything stupid like using it for personal calls. Understand?" the Russian said.

"I don't want it, you keep it. I changed my mind. I'm not going through with this anymore." It sounded like the American slid the phone across the table. "It's too risky and it's a crazy idea, anyway. What if I get caught?"

The Russian slid the phone back like they were playing shuffleboard. "Too late, my friend. He'll be here in three days and we're only going to get one chance while he's in the country. You can't change your mind because you know too much. And you weren't sorry to take the money . . . why do you think we chose you? You needed it."

"I'll give it back—"

The Russian cut him off. "Do what you're told and every-thing will be fine. Changing your mind would be very bad for your health. Do you understand what I'm saying?"

I gripped my camera until my fingers cramped and bit down on my lip.

"You can't threaten me. This isn't Russia, where you can get away with stuff like this; we got laws here."

The Russian laughed. "For a smart guy you're being very stupid."

"I'm not stupid enough to be an accessory to murder." The American's voice rose and he sniffled again like a dripping faucet. Allergies? A cold? A user?

"Shut up," the Russian said. "You're not *doing* anything. All you have to do is keep your mouth shut. You see nothing, you know nothing. Turn your back, that's it. Everything will be okay, no problem."

My heart was hammering like war drums, and for a wild

moment I wanted to just get the hell out of here, run as far away as I could. Then I thought, *Calm down and breathe. They don't know you're here, just like you and Vasiliev didn't know Ali was here. Just be quiet and you'll be fine.*

I heard a noise like a cat being strangled; it was the American's high-pitched hysterical laugh. "You expect me to believe Hathaway is going to go along with this crackpot idea? He's going to turn his back, too, let you just pull this off? No way, man. Why don't you kill the guy in Russia? It'd be a lot easier if you did it there."

"Shut up," the Russian said again, "and listen to me. You talk to anybody—*anybody*—about this and they'll have to look through every Dumpster for a hundred miles to find what's left of you, if the body parts are even recognizable. Do you understand?"

In the pocket of my silk evening pants, my phone made the distinct sound of an incoming text message. I stopped breathing, closed my hand over the phone, and flipped the switch to silent mode.

"Christ, what was that?" the American asked. "You got someone on the other side of that door listening? Checking me out?"

The door to the storage closet was still open. I stepped inside, closed the door, and prayed. The connecting door creaked open.

An eternity passed before the Russian said, "It's empty. There's no one here. Someone left a phone on the desk. That's what you heard." He must have picked it up. "Yeah, there's a bunch of text messages on it."

The door closed and the next time the Russian spoke he was back in the other room, his voice now too muffled for me to understand what he was saying.

I hung on to the closet doorknob, weak-kneed with relief. Thank God for small blessings. I hadn't seen that phone— probably Seth's—among all the items on his desk, but I was grateful it had been there.

I waited in the suffocating blackness until I was sure they were gone. When I opened the door, a ghost current of air brushed my arm, nearly sending me back into the closet. My phone vibrated in my pocket again. I pulled it out. Two text messages from Luke.

Where are you?

Hathaway just left.

I shut off the phone and threw it in my equipment bag with shaking hands. If I heard what I thought I did, someone— probably working for Arkady Vasiliev—had just finalized plans for the assassination of another Russian, someone who was arriving in the country in three days. When did Moses say Taras Attar was coming to the States? A couple of days . . . three days?

More incredibly, whoever the target was—Attar or someone else—the assassin was going to have help pulling it off from two Americans. The scared guy I'd heard in the next room.

And Senate Majority Leader Scott Hathaway.

SEVEN

I ran down the corridor toward the buzz of voices audible through the door that led to the cloakroom. That conversation couldn't have happened, or I misheard what they said.

Except I didn't.

I felt a sharp little twitch of nerves between my shoulder blades. What now? Tell someone? Seth? Luke? Keep it to myself and say nothing?

I reached for the doorknob as the door sprang open from the other side.

"Sophie!" Seth grabbed my arm to catch me as I stumbled back, shielding my cameras to keep them from whacking the wall. "I'm sorry, I didn't expect you there. Are you all right?"

The cloakroom had been nearly empty a short while ago. Now it was filled with guests who crowded around us as they waited to retrieve briefcases, backpacks, evening jackets, and other items that hadn't been permitted in the museum. Seth stepped into the hallway with me and shut the door as I checked my cameras to make sure nothing had gotten banged up.

"I'm fine. I was just getting something from your office."

"You didn't happen to see a phone in there, did you? I've misplaced mine somewhere."

"It's on your desk." *And you have no idea how glad I am it was there.*

"What a relief. I am always losing that thing." He sounded tired and distracted. "I'd better go get it. I'll see you later."

He opened the door and I slipped into the crush of people still waiting in line for their things. Luke found me at the desk in the Founders' Room a few minutes later.

"Where've you been?" he said. "I texted you twice."

"Oh, gosh, sorry. I ran into Seth and we started talking. Everything all right?"

He sighed. "Katya Gordon wants to see our photos first thing tomorrow."

Somehow that wasn't a surprise. "Did you manage to get her together with Scott Hathaway?"

"No, just some pictures of him with his wife and a couple of the deep-pocket donors. Moses was happy about that."

"What about Hathaway and Arkady Vasiliev?"

Luke shrugged. "Vasiliev left his own party early. He and Lara Gordon took off with a bunch of his people twenty minutes ago."

Twenty minutes ago. That meant Vasiliev was gone before I overheard the conversation in the conference room. So who knew about that room besides him and probably whoever was part of his inner circle? Who else would have used it?

"Earth to Sophie?" Luke tapped me on the shoulder. "Are you listening to me?"

"Yes, of course. We've got to get the pictures edited right away."

"Yeah, that, too." He gave me a sideways look as Ali joined us, hopped up with excitement, bright red lipstick freshly applied, her party face on. I thought I smelled alcohol on her breath, but I couldn't be sure.

"Do you guys need me anymore?"

Luke glanced at me and I shook my head. "I think we're good," he said. "Don't you need a ride home?"

"I'm all set, thanks."

"A date?" Luke asked as her cheeks bloomed a pretty shade of pink. "You met someone? Here?"

"Your Russian sugar daddy." I teased her, smiling.

Ali put her hands behind her back like a little kid and flashed a don't-you-want-to-know smirk. "Maybe tomorrow morning I'll call you from a yacht somewhere in the Caribbean and tell you how delicious it is to have a life like Lara Gordon's. I'll be eating caviar from silver bowls big enough to take a bath in."

"What are you two talking about? Whose yacht? What about Lara Gordon?" Luke asked.

Before she could answer him, something dark and urgent

pushed itself into my mind. "Ali, where did you just come from? Were you downstairs in the kitchen again?"

Because if she had been in that corridor, maybe she'd seen one or both of the men who'd been in the conference room. Maybe she'd walked right by the Russian or the American in the underground passageway and maybe she could pick him out, just maybe, if she spent some time looking through our photos. If we'd managed to get a picture of him— or them.

"Whoa, wait a minute. Time out." Luke held up his hand. "We weren't supposed to be anywhere near the kitchen. That food and all the booze were strictly for the guests."

Ali cut me a look like I had violated sisterhood solidarity by ratting her out. "One of the waiters asked if I wouldn't mind taking a tray down to the kitchen because they needed it, and he was stuck upstairs. I wasn't going to tell him no."

"Just now?" I said.

"A couple of minutes ago."

"Did you see anybody—?" I began.

Ali shifted her weight from one foot to the other. "Can we talk about this tomorrow, please? I'm going to miss my ride . . . I need to go. I'll see you guys in the morning."

"Ali—" I said, but she was gone.

Luke waved a hand. "Let her go. Come on, we need to get our gear from Seth's office. They're about ready to turn out the lights on us."

Reluctantly, I followed him. It sounded as if Ali might have seen at least one of the men in that corridor. It was a missed opportunity letting her leave when she'd have a clearer memory of the encounter, though by tomorrow we'd have downloaded our photos, which might make it easier to identify him.

"Are you all right?" Luke asked.

"Yeah," I said. "I'm fine."

We found Moses tidying up the conference room, which had been completely cleared out, the bottles of alcohol and bowls of caviar whisked away. "Well, all that hoopla for nothing," he said. "No one even used this room."

"How do you know?" I looked around. "How can you tell?"

I had been here with Arkady Vasiliev; so had two men plotting murder. Surely there was some trace of our presence, some clue left behind that would give up our secrets? To me it still possessed an aura of what had happened here, like the foul odor of something rotting. I was almost surprised that neither Moses nor Luke wrinkled his nose and said, "What's that awful smell?"

Moses gave me an odd look. "I'm just guessing. No dirty glasses or dishes. No open bottles. Room neat as a pin. I can't imagine having a meeting with a fully stocked bar and bowls of Beluga caviar, and then not eating or drinking anything."

"So what happens to all of it?" Luke asked.

"Everything that was in here is being delivered to Mr. Vasiliev's hotel in Georgetown. All the other food, all the hors d'oeuvres, will go to local homeless shelters and soup kitchens. He was kind enough to agree to that."

"That was generous," I said.

Moses nodded, joining us in the office as Luke unlocked the storage closet.

Luke passed me my backpack. "Thanks for letting us use this place, Moses. It came in handy." He tossed him the key.

"No problem." Moses pocketed it and watched us disassemble our cameras and pack them into Velcroed compartments in our backpacks. "Everything go okay for you guys tonight? No problems or complications?"

"Nope. Nothing. It all went great," Luke said. "We'll start editing the pictures right away, hopefully have something for you before the weekend."

"Katya's pretty keen to see what you've got." Moses made a face. "Not that I'm rushing you, but she and Lara would like them tomorrow."

"We'll do our best. I promise you'll have them as soon as possible." Luke picked up his gear and said to me, "All set?"

I nodded. We followed Moses back out to the cloakroom and walked into the silent Founders' Room, which was now lit only by the golden light of the candelabra sconces on either side of the fireplace mantel and a few tiny ceiling lights that twinkled like night stars.

"Seth asked me to say good night and thanks," Moses said

as we stood next to the leather-clad exit doors. "I'm still hoping I can talk Mr. Vasiliev and Katya into letting us use a few of your pictures for the lifestyle sections of the *Post* and *Trib,* and maybe a spread in *Washingtonian.* Surely they don't need all of them for that coffee table book they're putting together."

He shook Luke's hand and, to my surprise, leaned over and gave me a one-armed hug and a quick buss on the cheek. "It's been a pleasure working with you both. I'll be in touch."

The door thudded behind us, and Luke and I were alone on the columned portico, overlooking the dark, quiet Mall. My Vespa, pale and washed out under a streetlamp, was the only vehicle still parked on the street. The glass facade of the Air and Space Museum glittered across from us, the lights reflecting off antique silver airplanes and rockets that had traveled to the moon, all now suspended in the air by tension wires.

The federal part of Washington grows quiet at night; no one lives here. At the end of the day, receding taillights stream toward the bridges and highways and to other parts of the city—Adams Morgan, Brookland, Tenleytown, Anacostia. Office lights still blaze here and there inside the massive government buildings along Constitution and Independence Avenues if the cleaning staff is in or someone is burning the midnight oil, but mostly the place is deserted.

The museum itself was dark except for the soft glow of the torchères on either side of the doorway and the lights shining through the wrought-iron grillwork that covered the two windows. On our left, the lighted Capitol dome looked serene and peaceful; to the right, a pair of red lights winked off and on at the top of the Washington Monument like reptilian eyes.

"You going to be okay driving this thing at night?" Luke asked as I stowed my bag in the Vespa.

"Fine. I owned a Vespa in London. Fastest way to get around a city," I said. "They're useless in bad weather, but tonight's lovely."

"Still feels like summer." He nodded and segued back to work. "We ought to start editing right away, you know."

"You mean you want to go back to the studio now?" I stopped in the middle of pulling on my helmet. He hadn't mentioned the two of us working all night until just this second.

He yawned. "No, I'm beat. I don't know about you, but I need a second wind. How about if you do what you can at home tonight and so will I? We'll pick up from there in the studio tomorrow."

"Fine," I said. "See you in the morning."

He nodded and yawned again.

"Where are you parked?" I asked.

"Next block. By the East Building." He pointed behind him. "G'night."

I started the Vespa and it grumbled to life. A moment later Luke was a small dark smudge in my mirrors as I sped down Madison Drive. At the 9th Street ramp just after the outdoor sculpture garden, a vehicle turned onto Madison behind me. The driver pulled up too close for comfort so I flicked the handlebar for more speed. He sped up and I veered to the right to let him pass. The headlights swerved right, too, flashing in my mirrors as he closed the gap between us.

Years ago Perry had sent everyone at IPS to a five-day boot camp in northern Scotland that taught survival skills to journalists who worked in hostile environments and war zones. The ex–Special Forces team who drilled us educated us about what to do if we were caught in a gunfight or would-be kidnappers stopped our car, scary stuff like that. Mostly we were taught to think fast, know our surroundings, and have a plan. When the other guys have guns and you have a camera, your options are limited, and the faster you react is the difference between living and dying.

Whoever was driving that car—a kid fooling around, a drunk, or someone who knew exactly who I was—was going to win this drag race in about thirty seconds. All he had to do was hit my rear fender and plow me off the road.

Madison is a one-way street that runs along the Mall and goes downtown. Across the way, Jefferson Drive goes uptown toward the Capitol. He was still on my tail as we raced down Madison, approaching the Natural History Museum on the right.

I shifted my weight as a counterbalance and drove up the ramp onto the sidewalk, looping behind the big car. It was black, a Ford Explorer or a Chevy Suburban, one of those cars that are built like tanks. Tinted windows. I didn't get a look at the license plate because I didn't have much time before I figured his reaction to what I'd done would be to shift into reverse. I zoomed across the road and up the crosswalk toward the Mall as his brakes screeched. A few seconds later, I heard a motor grinding and the whine of a car backing up. I hit the gravel pedestrian path and prayed for no potholes, since Vespas aren't great on uneven surfaces, especially in the dark.

I sped across the Mall to Jefferson Drive and turned left, heading toward the Capitol. For once I wouldn't have minded seeing the light bar of a park police cruiser come to life next to the Smithsonian Castle, an officer pulling me over for illegal joyriding on the National Mall. But Jefferson was as dark and deserted as Madison had been, except for the pale necklaces of streetlights lining the paths and the two parallel streets.

I made two quick rights and turned on Independence Avenue, heading downtown once again. By the time I zipped through the city and reached my hotel in Foggy Bottom, I knew I'd lost him for good. What I didn't know was whether he'd been waiting for me, or if it was just some driver out for kicks. It's been years since D.C. owned the title "Murder Capital of the U.S.," but the city still has its share of crime— drive-by shootings, random violence—where the victim is unknown to the assailant and did nothing except show up in the wrong place at the wrong time. Maybe that's what happened to me: a woman alone at night, an easy target on a putt-putt scooter.

Or maybe Arkady Vasiliev wasted no time turning up the heat, letting me know he was serious about getting the well logs from Nick—if he even had them. I pulled into the parking lot behind the Roosevelt Executive Hotel and chained the Vespa to a bike rack. If that car had been driven by one of Vasiliev's bodyguards—Nick said the Russian mafia word was *byki,* which literally means "bull"—I'd been lucky this time. But from now on, I'd have to watch my back.

I let myself in the rear door with an oversized key. The Roosevelt hadn't entered the twenty-first century; no key cards here. The lobby was dimly lit and empty. Unlike a regular hotel, no one manned the front desk after eight in the evening. There was a courtesy phone for emergencies and a laminated piece of paper with instructions on whom to call, but that was it. I had wondered if you phoned at, say, two in the morning, whether whoever showed up would be wearing a bathrobe and slippers.

Someone at the embassy in London had told me about this place, an out-of-the-way budget-friendly apartment-hotel on a quiet, leafy street at the edge of the George Washington University campus. The occupants were mostly returning ambassadors and diplomats, international business travelers, and Kennedy Center performers who kept to themselves. I rarely saw the same people in the elevator or the lobby.

It was a small building, only eight stories high, but all the apartments had good-sized balconies; from the top floor, which was mostly occupied by VIPs, you could see the Kennedy Center and the Potomac River. My little one-bedroom apartment was on the second-floor corner facing the back, with a view of the parking lot and the row houses on H Street.

I unlocked the door and went inside. The place was dark and silent, exactly as I'd left it. I flipped on all the lights, and in the cocooned familiarity of the two small, furnished rooms, I calmed down and wondered if, after everything that had happened tonight, I was overreacting about being followed, letting myself get spooked for no good reason.

There was a half-full bottle of Cabernet Sauvignon on the kitchen counter. I got it, poured a glass of wine, and found the floral-print zippered bag where I kept my passport in the top drawer of the bedroom dresser. Tucked between the cover and first page was the business card John Brown gave me that day at Heathrow: the phone number for Napoleon Duval, my CIA contact in the United States. Tomorrow I'd call Duval, tell him what happened at that meeting with Arkady Vasiliev, and see what he had to say.

I brought the business card out to the living room and set

it on the desk beside my laptop. What I was less sure of was what to do about meeting number two, the one between the Russian and the American. Tell Duval about that, too? I could just imagine how my end of the conversation would go.

No, sorry, I don't know who either of the men was. I didn't see them, so I couldn't identify anyone except, possibly, by his voice. I believe the victim might be Taras Attar, the Abadi politician and author, but I have no idea where or when they plan to murder him. Oh, by the way, Senator Scott Hathaway is one of the accomplices.

Duval would think I was a lunatic and he might even question whether I was telling the truth about my conversation with Vasiliev as well. Maybe he'd decide I had a few screws loose, the distraught wife of a missing operative using an attention-getting ploy to make sure her husband hadn't been forgotten about.

My backpack sat on the floor next to the desk. Inside were my cameras and the memory cards filled with photos I promised Luke I'd start editing. Tonight I needed to get to work, take my mind off everything. Tomorrow I'd meet Duval, figure out what kind of guy he was, and take it from there.

I refilled my wineglass, changed into jeans and a T-shirt, and downloaded eight hundred and sixteen photos from a card reader onto my laptop. Luke told me he'd taken about nine hundred pictures. Editing them—cropping, retouching, adjusting highlights and shadows—and then culling them and selecting the best ones to send to Katya and Lara Gordon would take time.

I scrolled through the pictures. Sometimes you can get lucky if, say, the lighting is exactly the same in a group of photos because you can make adjustments by doing what's called batch editing and that speeds up the process. But because of the skylights in the National Gallery and the shifting light and shadows as it grew dark outside, most of these pictures would have to be edited one by one.

The half dozen shots I'd taken of Katya and Scott Hathaway on the atrium balcony were, as expected, too dark to make out much detail. Maybe if I enhanced them, played around a little, I'd have some luck, but that project would have to wait.

I did spend some time taking an extra-close look at photos of both Scott Hathaway and Arkady Vasiliev, checking to see if anyone—one of Hathaway's aides or Vasiliev's bodyguards—showed up regularly in the background.

Thinking about it logically, it made sense that the American was probably on Hathaway's staff. And Vasiliev, who had exclusive access to the conference room, would have told the Russian he'd have complete privacy for a meeting there. Yuri Orlov had left the National Gallery by then, and when he'd swept out of the museum it looked like he'd taken his retinue with him, like a king with his court, so I didn't think the Russian worked for him. But Luke had said that Vasiliev had also left early. Hadn't he taken his entourage with him, too? Did someone stay behind? Or had a third party borrowed the conference room for that clandestine meeting and Vasiliev had no clue?

The pictures I'd taken of Hathaway before his aide shut me down showed the senator surrounded by women. And Vasiliev's security people all looked like identical Russian Rambos: built solid as tractors, with stares that would pin you to a wall and freeze you there, earpiece and wire running into the suit jacket, hands clasped at the waist.

I gave up trying to figure out who I was looking for and went outside to my balcony. It had cooled off, the night breeze rustling the gauzy privacy curtain and the air soft and sweet as cream. A nearly full moon had risen above the treetops and the late-night traffic was a distant buzz. I heard banging—at first I thought it was the apartment below or something on the street—until I realized someone was knocking on my door.

I didn't know a soul in the building and it wouldn't be a manager at eleven o'clock at night. But when they're coming for you, they don't knock first, do they? I went inside and picked up a poker from a set of fireplace tools next to the electric fireplace—the Roosevelt is like that, little touches of unreality to create the illusion of home—just in case.

I stood next to the door and said, "Who is it?"

"Pizza delivery. Sophie? Hey, open up. I brought dinner."

I quit holding my breath. It was Luke.

"Give me a minute." I went over and shoved the poker back where it belonged.

"I figured you'd still be up," he said when I opened the door. "Did I catch you at a bad time?"

He had changed, too, from the Armani suit into faded jeans and a bright yellow polo shirt. His equipment backpack was slung over his shoulder and he was holding a white delivery pizza box that smelled fragrantly of fresh tomato and basil.

"I had the water running in the bathroom," I said. "What are you doing here? And how did you get in?"

"Followed someone who was kind enough to hold the door."

How did he get so lucky? Every time I got here after the doors were locked for the night, I had to fish out my key because the place was always deserted and silent as a tomb.

"How'd you find out which apartment was mine?"

He gave me a quizzical look. "Do you think I could come in and we could talk about this? The pizza's getting cold and I don't want to wake your neighbors."

"Pardon? Oh, sure. Sorry."

He walked in and set the pizza box on the kitchen counter. "There was nobody at the front desk so I walked around until I found the mailboxes in that little room off the lobby. Your name is on 2F."

I nodded, feeling dumb. "You're right. I forgot."

He set his backpack down. "Are you a fugitive from the law or in a witness protection program so you don't want anyone finding you?"

"Of course not." I reached for the bottle of wine. "Drink?"

He nodded and I said, "I'm just curious why you didn't call before you came by?"

"I did and my equipment bag rang." He reached into his jeans pocket and pulled out my phone. "Didn't you miss it? I figured you needed it tonight, so I picked up the pizza and came over. There wasn't time to send smoke signals to warn you."

His equipment bag. I'd dumped the phone in it while I was in Seth's closet, thinking it was my bag. He handed me the phone and I gave him a glass of wine.

I smiled. "Fair enough. Sorry for sounding paranoid. And thanks."

"Are you all right?" he asked. "Or are you always this jumpy?"

It was the second time he'd asked me that tonight.

"I'm fine." I refilled my own wineglass. "I'm also starved. The pizza smells great. Thanks for bringing it."

"You're welcome. As long as I'm here, I figured we could eat and then get some work done together, if that's all right?"

I nodded and got plates and paper napkins. "I had no idea my phone was gone. And I got 'the lecture' when I moved in here. Don't let anyone follow you in. Everyone's supposed to have their own key, et cetera, et cetera."

"That explains no one at the front desk and no security guard," he said.

"We're supposed to be our own security. That's why the rent is so reasonable. They don't even have video cameras."

"I guess your neighbor figured not many people turn up to break into a place and bring pizza, so she made an exception." He looked around. "It's a nice apartment."

"It's perfect for what I need now. You can rent by the month, so I took it while I was waiting for my shipment from London."

"When does that get here?"

"It came a couple of days ago. Everything's in a warehouse in Baltimore until I figure out what I'm doing next."

"I thought you told me you have family living in D.C. Can't you move in with someone for a while?"

"My mother and stepfather live out in Middleburg," I said. "And I have a stepsister and stepbrother who are a lot younger than I am. Lexie just finished undergrad. She lives near Eastern Market with five other people and her bedroom is the size of my bathroom. Tommy's studying to be a doctor. He's working in Honduras for a year."

"I guess Middleburg would be a hell of a commute."

"It would." Not to mention I'd have to live with my mother. "I need to find a place in town. It's nice tonight. How about if we eat on the balcony?"

I'd left two red pillar candles and a fire starter on the small patio table. Luke lit the candles while I brushed twigs and dried leaves off the folding chairs.

"How'd your pictures turn out?" he asked.

"Pretty good. How about yours?"

"Same." He set down his pizza. "You know, if this is going to work out—you and me—I have to get something off my chest."

"What?"

He gave me a long look. "We need to be able to trust each other."

I said in an even voice, "I trust you."

"That's nice," he said, "but it's not mutual. You've been edgy and evasive all evening. When are you going to tell me what's going on? Whatever it is, I'm pretty sure it has to do with the reception tonight and I think I have the right to know what it is."

In my marriage, trust had so often depended on what was *not* said, a secret that needed to be kept, a confidence that could not be betrayed. Woven through it all like a bright thread was complete faith in the other person. That was the only way it worked.

Luke didn't have faith in me, but I couldn't tell him what he wanted to know. The meeting between Vasiliev and me was strictly for Napoleon Duval's ears. I couldn't get Luke mixed up in that. But what would he say if I told him about the American and the Russian?

"Well?" he said.

"How about if I open another bottle of wine?"

"As bad as that?" he said, getting up. "Sit tight. I'll do it. I saw another bottle of red on your counter."

When he came back, I said, "You're right. There is something. But I'm warning you, you're not going to like it."

He looked grim as he filled my glass. "I was afraid of that. What happened?"

"I heard something tonight," I said, "when I went back to Seth's office to get that memory card. Two men came into the conference room, a Russian and an American. They were there about five minutes, maybe a little less. They were discussing a plan to assassinate someone. Another Russian. I'm pretty sure it was Taras Attar."

Luke set the wine bottle on the table. "Are you serious?"

"That's not all. I think the American works for Scott Hathaway. It sounded like Hathaway's mixed up in this, too . . . or at least he knows about it."

Luke gave me a sideways glance, his eyes glittering like a cat's in the golden candlelight. "Scott Hathaway is involved in a plot to assassinate a Russian that you think is Taras Attar? You're sure about that?" His voice was flat with disbelief.

We'd been speaking quietly so as not to disturb my neighbors. Now our voices dropped to whispers like we were conspirators ourselves.

"The American said something to the Russian that made it sound like Hathaway knows what's going to happen. The Russian told him all he has to do is turn his back . . . maybe Hathaway is supposed to do the same thing."

Below us in the Roosevelt's parking lot, someone started a car, a late-night run for cigarettes or beer, or maybe a midnight rendezvous. The moon had disappeared from view, leaving a bronze-tinged night sky bright from the glow of city lights, too bright to be able to see any stars.

"And why would Scott Hathaway do something like that?" Luke leaned back in his chair and folded his arms across his chest. He sounded like an adult parsing each sentence of a child's tall tale, until finally we both would agree that someone had a vivid imagination, didn't she, making up a story like that?

I knew he wouldn't believe me. "How the hell should I know why he'd do it?"

"Calm down. Jeez, don't bite my head off."

"Then don't patronize me."

He blew out a long breath and laid both hands palms down on the table, fingers splayed like he was trying to compose himself. "All right, sorry. Let's start over. Do you know who these guys are, other than a Russian and an American? You're sure about their nationalities?"

"Yes, I'm sure. And no, I don't know who they are. I told you. I heard them, but I didn't see them. The Russian knew about the conference room, so I imagine he worked for Vasiliev. As for the American—" I shrugged. "It's a guess, but I figure he works for Scott Hathaway. He showed up with a bunch of aides, remember?"

"Okay. Why are you sure they were talking about Taras Attar?"

"I'm not one hundred percent sure. But they said something about a guy who was arriving in a couple of days . . . and that he was a Russian who lived in Russia."

"You're also positive these guys mentioned Hathaway's name?"

I nodded. "The American did."

"You're right. It is a hell of a story." Luke took a bite of cold pizza. "What are you going to do about it?"

I couldn't tell if it was a dare or a challenge, but I didn't think he knew himself how to handle this because of what it might unleash. The possible consequences not only for me but also for Focus, repercussions that could boomerang back to the National Gallery of Art.

"What do you think I should do?" I said.

He was silent for a moment. "I don't know. What's the post-nine/eleven Homeland Security slogan? 'If you see something, say something.'"

On my way over to the National Gallery this evening I'd followed a car with a bumper sticker that had the stars and stripes on it. An unblinking eye peeking out from among the stars, and fingers, like they were parting window blinds, parting the stripes. Underneath were the words ONE NATION, UNDER SURVEILLANCE.

That's who we were now. Our brothers' keepers.

"All right, say I call somebody. Who is going to believe me when I bring up Scott Hathaway? You didn't." I gave him a pointed look. "You still don't, do you?"

He took too long to figure out his answer.

"See?" I said.

"You have to admit, it's pretty far-fetched." He sounded defensive. "Especially when you can't prove anything. You heard what Moses said tonight. That conference room looked like nobody ever set foot in it."

"My stepfather always says, 'When in doubt, do nothing.' I'm not going to do anything, at least not right now."

Luke gave me another sideways look. "Okay," he said. "Your call."

A fresh gust of wind rattled the dry leaves in the corner of the balcony, stirring them into small cyclones and extinguishing our candles. We sat in the darkness in uncomfortable silence.

I'd just taken a giant leap of faith and unburdened myself to Luke because he said he didn't trust me. Not only did it seem like that hadn't changed, but I would bet good money he was wondering who the hell he'd gotten mixed up with.

And how soon he could gracefully get rid of me.

EIGHT

After that we went back inside to start editing photos. Somewhere through a neighbor's open window, a clock chimed midnight.

"Should I make a pot of coffee?" I said.

"Sure," Luke said, though by now neither of us needed it. We were both wound up, the tension in the room as thick as a stew.

He set up his laptop on my dining table so he could watch me as I worked at the desk. I tucked Napoleon Duval's business card into the top desk drawer since I didn't need Luke seeing that and moved the pictures of Katya and Scott Hathaway to a different folder on my computer.

"How much longer are you going to keep staring at me? I'm starting to feel like a lab specimen under a microscope," I finally said without looking up.

"I'm not staring at you. I'm staring at these pictures, at any male who looks remotely Russian, wondering if he's your guy." He was frowning at his computer screen.

"Too bad the pictures don't come with an audio track so I could listen to the voices." I pushed my chair back and stood up. "The only photos I have of Scott Hathaway with someone from his staff are pictures with women. I know a couple of men walked in with him."

"All my pictures are group portraits with his wife and the people Moses rounded up. Donors, Friends of the National Gallery," he said. "I already looked through them."

I went into the kitchen and got the coffeepot, filling our mugs.

"Did you bring your copy of the guest list?" I said. "We could at least check names."

He unzipped his backpack and pulled out the list, scanning it. "Only two men, unless Ashley is a guy. Eric Nettle, his chief of staff, and David Epps, deputy chief of staff."

"I wonder if either of them is deep in debt? The Russian said he knew the American needed cash, so he must have done some homework and figured out who was vulnerable."

Luke set the list on the table. "Hathaway certainly doesn't need money. What's his motive?"

"I don't know," I said.

"What makes you so sure the Russian works for Vasiliev?"

"I suppose it's possible he works for Yuri Orlov." I went back to my desk and sat down.

"Maybe, except a diplomat of Orlov's stature doesn't arrange to have a political opponent assassinated on foreign soil." Luke sipped his coffee, looking thoughtful. "Though, if he did, it wouldn't be the first time. Remember that crazy Iranian government plot to assassinate the Saudi ambassador to the U.S.? It was like something out of a bad movie. They found a used-car salesman and got a Mexican drug gang involved. At first nobody official believed it because it was so weird."

"I remember. I read about it in England."

"Though if it was Orlov, he wouldn't team up with Hathaway, not after that scene tonight," Luke said. "And you said you're positive Hathaway's involved."

I had to agree with him. "Okay, not Orlov and Hathaway, but I definitely think the target's Attar."

"Hathaway and Attar are good friends. He wouldn't be part of any plan to murder Attar, or turn his back and let someone else do it," Luke said. "This doesn't work on any level. In fact, no combination of players we've come up with works."

"So far. If we had more information, maybe we wouldn't be going around in circles."

"Fair enough, but not tonight. It's late, we're not thinking straight anymore, and I'm starting to screw up editing these pictures." Luke closed his laptop. "Why don't we call it quits? It's nearly two o'clock."

I put my laptop to sleep. "Fine with me."

He packed up and at the front door laid his hand on my shoulder.

Here it was. He was going to ask me to e-mail him my pictures after I was through editing them and tell me not to bother coming in tomorrow.

"What is it?" I said.

"I'm just going to bring this up once and then I'll shut up," he said. "I've been through what you're going through now. The first year's pure hell. Some days you don't think you can even get out of bed."

It took a moment for it to sink in that he wasn't talking about letting me go. He was talking about his wife's death.

"Do you think maybe you're just so stressed that you could have been mistaken about what you heard tonight?" he asked.

I hated doing this, letting him believe it was true that Nick was gone, but I had no choice. "No. I'm not mistaken. I'm sure about what I heard. And thank you for caring enough to ask."

"Then are you also sure these guys didn't know you were in the next room listening to them?"

"Positive."

"Lock up after I go, all right? Including that balcony door. You're only on the second floor."

"I'll be fine. Don't worry."

But he waited in the hall until he heard me slide the dead bolt into the jamb and latch the chain. I leaned against the door and listened to the whir of the elevator as it stopped on my floor. The door slid open and shut, then I heard the quiet hum as it descended.

I locked the sliding door and closed the drapes before turning off all the lights. After that, I stripped off my clothes, went to bed, and fell into a restless, anxious sleep. When the late-night alcohol-and-caffeine-induced crazy dreams came, they were of two faceless men who talked about murder as they slowly melted into puddles like the Wicked Witch of the West in *The Wizard of Oz*. Then Nick called my name as I ran through a fun house of mirrors that led to nothing but dead ends.

By six thirty I was up, dark smudges under my eyes, a pot of coffee on, back at my desk. The first thing I did before I resumed editing was check e-mail, my morning ritual. Nick's CIA bosses were still monitoring his accounts, which had all gone dormant, but I couldn't let go of the foolish hope that

I'd be sitting there one day as an e-mail came in, moments after he'd sent it from wherever in the world he was, a link as fragile and finespun as a cobweb, and the heading would be: I'M OKAY COMING HOME LOVE YOU.

But there was no joyful homecoming message, just the usual overnight barrage of mail, including a short, terse note from Perry, all lowercase, no punctuation—his usual chatty style— asking how I was doing. Baz had written a longer letter, asking the same thing with more finesse. I replied to each of them that I was fine, employed (thanks, Perry), and settling into life back home.

Then I typed in every e-mail address Nick had ever used and, on the subject line, wrote: *Mom's Birthday Present.* Years ago we had devised a coded way to communicate with each other in case something went wrong, an innocuous-sounding letter involving a family member and some fact the other person knew was patently wrong.

> *Darling, last night I checked the Internet again for Mom's birthday gift, looking for that book she wants, the one that's been so hard to find. I might have located a copy, but someone else wants it very badly and is apparently willing to pay well for it. Not sure what to do next and could use your advice. Love.*

If Nick saw this—*if*—I hoped he'd realize someone had approached me about the well logs. My mother's birthday was in January and the gifts she favored generally involved a pale blue Tiffany's box or something in a velvet bag. I hit Send and heard the whoosh of an outgoing letter. Then I poured more coffee and went back to editing last night's pictures.

After an hour, my neck had a crick in it and my joints felt stiff. In London I would have gone for a run on Hampstead Heath to unwind. I got up and went out on the balcony. The early-morning sky was threaded with clouds tinted the mother-of-pearl shades of an oyster shell. A trash truck banged Dumpsters in the Roosevelt parking lot above the escalating noise of rush-hour traffic. Last night's reception and those two meetings in the conference room had been replaying in a loop in my head, the undercurrents of threat and menace speeding up until they became a dangerous-sounding whine.

I went inside and took a long hot shower, sluicing away the voices and convincing myself it would be all right once I talked to Napoleon Duval.

But when I called the number on his card at precisely nine o'clock, his phone went straight to voice mail. "Leave a message."

No name, no *you've reached* and his number. He sounded tough and uncompromising. I lost my nerve, disconnected, and decided to try again later.

At nine thirty I parked the Vespa beside Luke's Jeep in the postage-stamp space he rented next to our building. A large black SUV with official government plates and shiny enough so I could see my reflection was illegally parked by the bright yellow-and-red Big Wheels Bike mural on the corner of 33rd Street and Cady's Alley.

Even before I walked through the front door I knew this was bad news. The office was empty—no Ali furtively reading fashion magazines at her desk—which meant whoever belonged to that car was in Luke's office behind closed doors. I heard the sound of a chair scraping, and a moment later, Luke's door opened.

A good-looking African-American man with the build and attitude of an ex-Marine stepped into the room. He was about three inches shorter than me and probably in his fifties. His gray-flecked hair was military short, he wore gold wire-rim glasses, and the fatigue lining his well-lived-in face and the deep crow's-feet around his eyes looked permanent. Navy blazer, khakis, white polo shirt with a logo partially obscured by the jacket, and wing tips as shiny as his car.

Luke was right behind him, looking rumpled and tired. His eyes went straight to me.

"Sophie," he said, "this is Special Agent Napoleon Duval with the National Counterterrorism Task Force. He stopped by to talk to us about that matter we were discussing last night."

I had been in midstep when Luke uttered the man's name,

and the shock of it nearly froze me right there. Duval's face gave away nothing—another disciple of face maintenance—so I kept my expression neutral as well, though I knew he'd caught that tiny flinch. Dammit, Luke had called someone—not Duval, I was sure of that—in spite of what we'd agreed last night: that it was my decision how to handle this. And, *poof*, Napoleon Duval, my CIA contact, appeared like he'd been conjured out of thin air, though he'd apparently been secunded to a special task force. No wonder he hadn't answered his phone when I called; he was probably in the middle of interviewing Luke.

We shook hands and I said, "How do you do, Agent Duval?"

"Very well thanks, Ms. Medina." He pulled out his wallet and handed me a business card. "As Mr. Santangelo said, I'd like to have a word with you, ask you a few questions. Perhaps we could take a little walk, get some fresh air?"

Duval had a light Texas drawl, more of a twang, actually. It sounded like he was asking me for a date.

"Of course," I said. "I just need a quick word with Mr. Santangelo about a project we're working on. Our client is very anxious. If you can give me a minute, I'll meet you outside."

So I can strangle him while you're not looking.

"Take your time," Duval said. "I'll be right outside."

I waited until the door shut behind Duval before I swung around to confront Luke. He held up his hand. "Before you say anything, it's not what you think."

"Is that so? And what exactly do I think?"

"That I ambushed you."

"Damn right."

"Look, I ran into a neighbor this morning when we were both walking to our cars," he said. "He works for Homeland Security, something in intelligence, but you know how it is with those guys. They can't tell you anything."

No fooling. "Go on," I said.

"So I described a hypothetical situation without going into detail, of course, and asked his advice on how to go through proper channels if I wanted to let someone know about it."

"And?"

"And apparently it's like calling the fire department and saying you think you smell smoke coming from under your attic door, but maybe you're wrong," he said. "They don't give advice or deal in what-if. They sound the alarm and send fire trucks and guys with axes and hoses to your front door ready to bust into your attic."

"Great," I said, "just great."

Luke ran both hands through his hair. "Look at it this way: At least you'll get it over with and then we can forget about it."

I shook my head. "I don't think it's going to be that simple. I'll be back after Duval finishes chewing me up and spitting out what's left."

"Relax. He and I had a perfectly civilized talk. It went much better than I expected. He told me I did the right thing, so don't worry. Nothing's going to happen. Tell him what you told me and you'll be fine."

I opened my mouth to tell Luke precisely how wrong this was going to go, and thought better of it. He really had no idea why I was upset.

"Sure," I said finally. "Wish me luck."

Duval was leaning against the Batmobile when I got outside, looking at something on his phone. "You got that client matter all straightened out?" he said.

I pulled his CIA business card out of my pocket. "They gave me this at the embassy in London and told me you're my contact in the U.S.," I said. "I tried to call you this morning, but I got your voice mail."

Duval glanced at the card and scrolled through his phone again. "What time was that?"

"Nine o'clock."

"What's your number?"

I told him, and he nodded, verifying my call. "Why didn't you leave a message?"

"I didn't want to, under the circumstances," I said. "I also assume it's no accident that you turned up after Luke called."

"You assume right." Duval clipped his phone to his belt. "Why don't we head down to the river? It's a nice day."

I'd half expected him to tell me he wanted to take me for

a little ride where we'd end up in a nondescript office building downtown or on the other side of the Potomac somewhere in Virginia where I'd sit across from him at a table answering questions he'd fire at me like a baseball pitching machine. I hadn't figured he'd want to take a walk in the park.

"We can take the canal towpath and cut through Grace Street," I said. "It's a lot more pleasant than dealing with the crowded sidewalks on Wisconsin and M."

"Lead the way," he said.

We turned right at the bike mural and took the little pedestrian bridge over the C&O Canal. Upstream you can see the Potomac River from the towpath, because the canal—all 184.5 miles of it—roughly follows the contours of the river. But by the time you get to Georgetown, the Potomac is a few blocks away, and instead, newish redbrick office buildings and old stone walls rise like a canyon on either side of it.

Duval and I clattered down the steep metal staircase, the sound of our footsteps reverberating off the buildings. On this bright, sunshiny September morning when the air was soft and warm, the kind of day when you felt good to be alive, I expected to see joggers along the towpath or even the backlit silhouettes of people traversing the other bridges farther downstream. Instead we were completely alone and the place was eerily silent. No one looked out an office window or seemed to notice us, and I briefly regretted suggesting that we not join the jostling throngs on Georgetown's main streets.

"So, how about if you tell me what happened last night at the National Gallery?" Duval said, as though we were getting back to a conversation that had been temporarily derailed.

I thought he might take notes, but maybe he'd written down what Luke had told him and now he just wanted my firsthand account. By the time I'd finished my story, we'd reached the cut-through to Grace Street.

"You have no idea who these men were?" he asked. "You notice anything, like an accent, maybe? Speech tic?"

"The Russian had a deep voice. The American had a cold and he sounded scared."

"What else?"

"I think they were talking about a plan to kill Taras Attar

when he's in the U.S.," I said. "They kept talking about a
Russian who would arrive in three days."

"They never mentioned his name?"

"No."

At the intersection of Grace Street and Wisconsin Avenue,
Duval and I turned right and continued down the steep sidewalk
toward the river and the waterfront promenade. The thundering
traffic noise and the roar of planes landing and taking off from
Reagan Airport were deafening.

Duval raised his voice as we turned downriver toward the
Kennedy Center. "Do you have any reason to believe these
men knew you were in the next room?"

"No," I said.

He took off his glasses and stared at me. "Meaning all we
have is your word you overheard a conversation that appears
to involve the Senate majority leader having prior knowledge
of an assassination plot of a Russian you presume is Taras
Attar."

It sounded worse coming from him. "Yes."

Duval and I kept walking until we reached the elaborate
fountains at Washington Harbour.

"There's something else I need to tell you," I said. "Luke
doesn't know about it."

Duval put his glasses back on. The lenses had darkened in
the sunlight so I could no longer see his eyes. "Speak freely."

I told him about being summoned to the meeting with
Vasiliev and that he'd informed me he wanted the well logs
and any information on the test well Crowne Energy had drilled
in Abadistan. I said he expected me to be his messenger because
he was convinced I had a way to contact Nick.

"What did you say?" he asked.

"I asked him how he knew Nick was alive," I said. "He
didn't feel like sharing that information."

"You had a busy evening, Ms. Medina," Duval said.

"Not by choice." I ignored the little dig. "This time I had
a witness. You can verify that conversation with her."

Duval stopped walking. "What witness?"

"Ali Jones . . . Alicia Jones, the office receptionist. She was
in the next room getting an extra set of flash batteries. After

Vasiliev left the conference room, she came in and told me she heard the entire conversation."

"I didn't see a receptionist when I came into your office."

"She might have had a late night last night."

"I see," Duval said. "You got a home address for her, a phone number?"

I pulled out my phone and looked through my address book. "Just her cell phone. Luke has her address."

"Never mind. I'll get everything from him," he said. "Back to you and this talk. Did Mr. Vasiliev threaten you in any way?"

"He told me his patience lasted only so long," I said. "And as I was leaving the National Gallery, a black SUV pulled up behind me on Madison Drive. I think the driver was trying to run me off the road, or at least scare me."

"You think?"

"Before anything happened I got away and lost him. Maybe it was random, but later I wondered if Arkady Vasiliev wanted to make sure I knew he meant business and that was his way of warning me."

"You want to tell me how you lost an SUV on a Vespa? Driving down a one-way street on the Mall?"

I said, surprised, "How do you know I drive a Vespa?"

He pointed his index fingers at his eyes. "Sometimes we're very low-tech. The only vehicle outside your building when I arrived was a Jeep. When I left, a Vespa was parked next to it and you had shown up."

"Oh."

"So how'd you lose that car?"

"I took a shortcut across the Mall on one of the footpaths. He didn't follow me."

Duval's mouth twitched. "I see."

We had nearly reached the end of the shops and restaurants and office buildings that made up the Washington Harbour complex. Duval veered over to the river and leaned against the safety rail with his back to the Potomac as though he was just there to people-watch and enjoy a lazy day. I joined him, since it seemed like the logical thing to do.

Duval seemed to be mulling what I'd said, and his silence

was making me nervous. "Are you in contact with your husband, Ms. Medina?" he asked finally.

"No."

"Have you tried to get in touch with him?"

"I've sent him e-mails. He doesn't reply."

"When was the last time you did that?"

If he didn't already know the answer, he could find out soon enough. "This morning."

"Why, particularly, this morning?"

"To tell him about that conversation with Arkady Vasiliev."

"Either of those stories you just told me—the meeting with Vasiliev and the discussion between the two men—is disturbing on its own," Duval said in his light drawl. "Taken together, I'm not sure what to make of them—or you—yet."

I had figured it might go down this way. The man who was supposed to be my lifeline to information about Nick was telling me he didn't know whether to take me seriously or consider me some kind of kook.

Duval folded his arms and tapped his fingers on his elbows like he was playing an arpeggio on a piano. "Did your husband ever discuss the political situation in Abadistan with you, talk about how he felt about what was going on? For example, do you know if he sympathized with the Abadis or was he pro-Russian?"

He did think I was a kook. Or at least naïve enough to tell him that Nick and I had pillow talk where he spilled secrets about the clandestine need-to-know world he operated in.

"Give both of us a little credit, Agent Duval. Nick never discussed his work with me and I knew enough not to ask."

"Your husband didn't confide in someone as intelligent, well traveled, and politically savvy as you, Ms. Medina? I find that hard to believe."

I shrugged. "Thanks for the flattery. But if I don't know anything, I don't have to lie. Keeps life simple. That's how we operated."

"Is that so?" Duval said, and I couldn't tell if he was being serious or sarcastic. "All right, let's just see where we are here. Right off the bat a couple of things jump out at me and that always gives me heartburn. One, where is Nicholas Canning and why doesn't he come in? Two is you, Ms. Medina, and your role in all this. It seems like an odd coincidence that you show up as one of two photographers at a gig at the National Gallery where Arkady Vasiliev will be present, practically materializing out of nowhere. Mr. Santangelo told me you just started working with him and, in fact, that was your first assignment. He also happened to mention that you were particularly interested in—and knowledgeable about—Mr. Vasiliev's exhibition. In fact, he said you discussed it at length during your interview."

"That's because—"

Duval kept going. "Don't you think it's more than a little convenient that you were right there last night to act as an intermediary between your husband and Arkady Vasiliev?"

"Give me a little credit," I said, snapping at him. "If I were making this up, don't you think I'd invent something less outrageous than overhearing an assassination plot that somehow involves the Senate majority leader? I had no idea Vasiliev was going to seek me out and say what he did."

"Is that so? Well, here's the thing. As I piece together this story, there are a lot of coincidences," he said. "Unfortunately I don't believe in coincidences, especially not that many. They bother me."

He seemed to believe Nick and I were somehow working together, that we had orchestrated events in order for me to meet Vasiliev at the National Gallery.

"What you're implying is wrong, Agent Duval. I didn't set up anything or plan anything."

"Then you either have impeccable timing or an unfortunate talent for being in the wrong place at the wrong time," he said.

"Probably the latter." I felt like he'd knocked the wind out of me. "Look, Vasiliev found out somehow that Nick's alive. I'd like to know how or who told him. In London I was told that my husband was spotted getting on the Moscow metro. Once. Has he been seen since then? Do you know where he is now?"

"No, we do not know where he is now." Duval gave me a severe look. "And we'd sure like to know. So if you hear from

him, I want you to call me night or day. Next time leave a
message, you got that?"

"Yes."

"And do not screw around with me."

I kept my voice level. "I wouldn't dream of it."

"About that other conversation, we'll be looking into that
as well. But when all is said and done, a lot of roads seem to
be leading back to you, Ms. Medina. So it goes without
saying"—he pointed to his eyes again with his two fingers—
"that I'll have these trained on you. I'll be watching you."

NINE

I passed on Duval's offer to walk back to Cady's Alley with him since he had to get back to his car. After telling me I was now under his microscope, it was a safe bet we weren't going to segue into a chatty conversation about the summery weather or the Nats' chances of making it to the playoffs. He gave me one last shrewd, assessing look before wheeling around and walking briskly back toward K Street. Ten seconds later, he was on his phone, which remained clamped to his ear until he disappeared from view.

I gave him a ten-minute head start before I walked back to the office. The big black car was gone and Luke was at his desk, working at the computer.

"Hey," he said. "How'd it go? You were gone awhile. Duval came back and asked for Ali's contact information. What was that all about?"

I leaned against his doorjamb and wondered if Luke had deliberately sabotaged me when he told Duval that I'd been interested in and knowledgeable about the Vasiliev exhibit during my job interview. How had the conversation started? Who brought it up, Duval or Luke? If it was Luke, then maybe he, like Duval, didn't buy the story that the only reason I applied for the job at Focus was because Perry pushed me into doing it.

Ever since Nick disappeared, my life had gone like this, my own personal Möbius strip. I'd start out thinking something was two-sided then, wham, it would turn into a smooth-edged single surface and I couldn't find the beginning or the end.

Last night Luke told me he didn't trust me. Now I wondered if I trusted him.

"I guess Duval's just dotting his *i*'s and crossing his *t*'s," I said. "Remember when you were at my place yesterday and you looked at me like I'd just grown another head after I told you what I heard?"

He nodded.

"Duval gave me the exact same look, except he thought I'd morphed into a Hydra."

Luke let out a long breath. "I'm sorry. I had no idea it was going to blow up into something like this. I still think we did the right thing. And anyway, it's done now. We can forget about it and move on. We need to get back to editing."

We did the right thing. I would have done it differently. He had no idea.

"Right," I said. "Back to editing."

I started to walk over to my desk—I had my own workspace now, a windowless alcove at the back of the studio—when he called out, "Have you heard from Ali, by the way?"

"No. You?"

"I just left a voice mail. Didn't tell her about Duval because I didn't want her freaking out, but I asked her to call me."

"It's just after ten thirty. She could still show up here."

"I wish she were more reliable," he said. "She seemed more interested in partying than working last night."

"Talk to her," I said. "She's a good kid. She's just young."

An hour later my mobile rang and the display read *Washington Tribune*. I almost let it go to voice mail, but if I did that, I'd get another call and then another, until I finally picked up.

Grace Lowe was the first person to befriend me when my mother married Harrison Wyatt, my stepfather, after we packed up our tiny walk-up apartment in Queens, New York, to move to Harry's sprawling two-hundred-acre horse farm in Middleburg shortly before my fourteenth birthday. Right now Grace was just about the last person I wanted to see.

She had flown to London the day after I got back from the mountain search on the French-Italian border and stayed with me for a week. She made sure I ate and slept and changed my clothes and stumbled through the days and nights, until she finally had to get back home to her family to be there for all the important end-of-the-school-year activities—proms, awards ceremonies, final concerts—for her son and daughter. After that we talked regularly on Skype, usually midnight my time, or even later—I had insomnia for a while—when she got home from work. But in the last few weeks, ever since I'd found out Nick had been seen in Moscow and was possibly linked to Colin Crowne's death, I'd been avoiding her. I went off-line so I didn't see her calls, explaining in an e-mail that I was too busy with the details of moving back to the States and promising we'd catch up when I got home.

I saw her once, a few days after I moved into the Roosevelt. She came by with roses from her garden, a chilled bottle of fizzy white, and Chinese takeout, ready for an evening of girl talk. The two of us curled up on opposite ends of the sofa with the remnants of kung pao chicken, shrimp with lobster sauce, and a half-eaten carton of fried rice littering the coffee table. The visit hadn't gone well; I pleaded a headache and told her I was jetlagged and overwhelmed. She left as soon as we finished eating, her mouth puckered in a line of bewildered hurt.

"I'll call you," I said, but I hadn't.

Now she was trying again.

"Hey," she said in a clipped tone when I finally answered. "I know it's last minute, but are you free for lunch? You can't duck me forever, you know. And don't you dare tell me you're not ducking me."

She was done being polite and solicitous.

"I'm not ducking you," I said. "I'm sorry, Gracie, I really want to, but I'm sort of backed up at work."

"Fine. If you don't tell me what's going on," she said in that same no-nonsense voice, "I'm going to call Harry and your mother and tell them I'm worried about you, tell them you're shutting out your oldest and dearest friend, and that you haven't been yourself since you moved home."

"You wouldn't."

"Oh, yes, I would. Your mother would haul you off to a resort spa before you could say seaweed wrap or diamond-and-ruby facial, and Harry's just dying to buy you a new wardrobe or a new car or build you a new house because he wants you to be happy again."

"All right." I rubbed the bridge of my nose with my thumb and forefinger. First Duval, now Grace. I could feel a tension headache building behind my eyes like gathering storm clouds. "Please don't call anyone. Can we have lunch tomorrow, maybe?"

"Sure," she said, like she was going to drop it. "I guess I can wait until then to find out what really happened last night between Scott Hathaway and Yuri Orlov at that National Gallery reception. That must have been a hell of a scene."

I sat up in my chair. "What are you talking about?"

"We ran a piece about it in *Lifestyle*. With a photo."

"You did?" Where the hell had they gotten the photo?

"You mean you didn't know? Oh, for cryin' out loud, no wonder our circulation numbers are in the toilet. Even my best friend doesn't read my newspaper."

"Of course I do. It's sitting right here on my desk. It's been a busy morning. I didn't get to it yet."

I tapped a key on my computer and searched for "*Washington Tribune.*" Seth and Moses had been adamant about privacy because Vasiliev had insisted on it. All we needed was for them to think Luke or I was the source of that picture.

The story popped up on my screen, complete with an unflattering picture of the beet-faced Russian ambassador and Hathaway, with a make-my-day swagger, as he leaned in toward Orlov. Some wag who wrote the headline called it "Empire of the Firestorm" and the reporter who wrote the gossipy piece equated it to a return of the cold war.

"I know you're typing," she said. "Paper on your desk, my ass."

Grace had the hearing of a bat and the eyesight of an eagle.

"That's someone at the desk next to mine," I said. "How'd you get a reporter into that party last night? It was closed to the press. Who took that photo?"

"Have lunch with me today and I'll tell you," she said. "In return, you tell me what's going on—because I know something is—and I won't call Caroline and Harry. I can pick up sandwiches at the Late Edition and take a cab to your office since you're so busy."

I wished I'd had the opportunity to introduce Grace to Nick's people because she'd make a first-class interrogator. She just wears you down until you say "uncle."

"Why don't we meet somewhere in between my office and yours?" I said. "A park, maybe? It's gorgeous out."

"How about Dupont Circle by the chess tables?"

"Can we do it in an hour? I've got some editing to wrap up."

"Twelve thirty. Be there," she said, "or else."

The first time I laid eyes on Grace Lowe in English class at St. Michael the Archangel High School I hated her. She had been named for Grace Kelly thanks to her mother's romantic obsession over an American actress's fairy tale marriage to the rich, handsome prince of Monaco; growing up, her family's nickname for her was "Princess." Grace looked and acted exactly like her namesake: blond, beautiful, patrician, perfect, and aloof. I thought she was a horrible snob.

But a few weeks after school started, a gang of girls confronted me one afternoon as I was walking home alone, teasing me in crude ninth-grade Spanish about my dark skin and hair, my heritage, and that I must be someone's rejected child, a bastard, probably, because I looked nothing like my Anglo mother and stepfather. Grace showed up out of nowhere, returned the girls' crudeness with some equally crass remarks about their own family relationships, and before we knew it, fists were flying and it turned into an all-out brawl. She ended up with a dislocated finger and I had a hell of a shiner and two bruised ribs, but we held our own against four slow-witted bullies and had marched home together arm in arm, bloodied but unbowed. Over time, the story of our amazing bravery and martial prowess grew into a whopping tale that bore no resemblance to reality, but no one ever teased me again, and Grace and I bonded during the next few weeks of detention and cleaning up litter on the school grounds.

She was already waiting at a park bench near the chess tables when I arrived, still as gorgeous and alluring as the other Grace flying along the Grande Corniche in that convertible with Cary Grant at her side in *To Catch a Thief.*

She saw me and stood up. Our hug was awkward.

"Hope you're hungry," she said. "I brought you tuna on sourdough . . . it used to be your favorite."

"It still is," I said. "Thanks, Gracie. What do I owe you?"

She gave me a look and said, "An explanation."

We sat and she doled out the deli bags, passing me a bottle of water. Across from us two African-American men played chess, whiling away a pleasant afternoon in retirement.

I hadn't been to this part of town since I'd returned home, but Dupont Circle hadn't changed in twelve years. Still bustling with the lunchtime crowd as it always did: men from nearby offices in rolled-up shirtsleeves and ties flung over their shoulders, women with skirts hiked up to take advantage of the last slanting rays of summer sunshine, students from Johns Hopkins just down Massachusetts Avenue reading or sitting and talking in groups. As always, the prime real estate was the steps of the two-tiered fountain—Washington, like London, is a city of fountains—which was as packed as the beach on Labor Day weekend with lovers and friends and sun worshipers listening to a trumpeter play "When I Fall in Love" like he meant it.

One of the lazy weekend pastimes Nick and I had enjoyed in London had been a long afternoon walk along one of the paths of the city's many parks. Our favorite was St. James's, bounded by the Mall, Birdcage Walk, and Horse Guards Road, with its beautiful lake and postcard-perfect view of Buckingham Palace. We'd bring stale bread from home to feed the rare breeds of swans, ducks, geese, and pelicans that lived on Duck Island. At the end of the day we'd walk over to the Blue Bridge, where we'd watch the setting sun gild the palace walls and turrets and towers or catch the graceful arc of the Eye as it slowly revolved.

"Sophie," Grace said, "you're a million miles away."

"Sorry. Just . . . thinking."

She set her sandwich on the deli wrapper. "Remember I told you Ben and I bought a summer place in North Carolina last winter? On Bald Head Island? It's lovely and tranquil and the beaches are deserted after the kids go back to school. No cars allowed, so the only way to get around is by bike or golf cart. It's heaven. The house is yours for as long as you need it. I can come with you or you can stay there by yourself. But I can't stand seeing you all wrecked up like this." She covered my hand with hers. "I know it's been hell with everything that happened to Nick. And you haven't even had any real closure since they never found him."

"Thanks." I squeezed her hand tight. "Your house sounds wonderful, but right now I need to keep busy. I'm not sure I could handle solitude. Maybe later."

She nodded and snapped her fingers, a quick syncopated beat like she'd just thought of something. "Hey, I know. Why don't you come over for dinner? Ben and the kids are dying to see you, and that includes your fifteen-going-on-twenty-one-year-old goddaughter. We'll throw some steaks on the grill and Ben will make his award-winning margaritas. How about tomorrow, Friday night?"

She still wanted to save me, make everything okay again. "Let me check and get back to you . . ."

"About *tomorrow*? You don't know what you're doing *tomorrow*?" Her voice went up in disbelief. "I still have your parents' number on speed dial. Just sayin'."

In the poignant silence that followed—broken by cheers as someone across the way triumphantly called out "checkmate"— I knew I couldn't keep doing this. I couldn't keep putting up barriers and shutting everyone out of my life because of secrets I was forced to keep and fears I couldn't share. Grace, who'd stuck by me ever since that after-school battle so many years ago, wouldn't turn her back on me if she knew the truth: that my husband was alive somewhere, on the run, and his name had been linked to the grisly murder of his boss in Vienna. Was that what I was scared of? I'd have to listen to a lifetime litany of I-told-you-that-boy-was-no-good-but-you-wouldn't-listen from my mother, but Grace would never utter a word against Nick because she knew I loved him.

"There are some things I can't talk about right now," I said. "Can you just trust me that I'll tell you when I can?"

"Are you in trouble?" she asked.

"I . . . no. I'm not. Just . . . trust me, Gracie. Please? And I'd love to come to dinner tomorrow. Thanks for inviting me."

She cocked her head and stared past me, her mouth tight with the realization that I wasn't going to take her into my confidence, no matter how dear our friendship.

"Hey, you were going to explain how you guys got someone into that reception last night." I needed to change the subject. "And please don't be angry with me, okay?"

She sighed and squared her shoulders. "We didn't have anyone from the paper there," she said in a quiet voice. "Apparently Hathaway went back to the Hill, some last-minute Senate business. He ended up drinking in his Capitol hideaway with a couple of members of his staff, and he was in a pretty foul mood. Our Senate correspondent ran into one of the staffers after she moved on to the Hawk 'n' Dove. Hathaway's person was pissed off and she'd had a few, so she started talking about some scene with Orlov at the National Gallery." She shrugged. "It didn't take our reporter long to find a couple of independent sources who confirmed it. And someone had a camera phone."

I wondered if the angry staffer had been the young woman I thought had a crush on Hathaway. "That was lucky." *For you, not us.*

"So what happened?" she asked. "Were you there?"

I nodded. "There's not much to say that you don't already know. Actually, you got everything right, except for the cheesy comment about it being the worst face-off between Russia and America since the Cuban missile crisis," I said.

"That's *Lifestyle,*" she said with the ghost of a grin. "Never let the truth get in the way of a good story. So how'd it end?"

"Katya Gordon, the Russian art history professor who organized the exhibit, showed up and charmed them into neutral corners. Then she disappeared with Hathaway and gave him a private tour while his wife and the director of the National Gallery helped Orlov find the exit," I said.

We ate our sandwiches in silence until I said, "Do you know much about Scott Hathaway, whether he's a skirt chaser?"

She eyed me over her water bottle. "Why do you ask?"

"One of his aides—I think she was about twelve—was acting sort of possessive around him. I just got a vibe . . . something like that."

"Ben says they're called 'Hathaway's Hotties,'" she said. "He's got an almost all-female staff. Every single one of them looks like a Victoria's Secret model but brainy as hell—Rhodes

Scholar or top of their class at some Ivy. Ben said he's thinking of instituting the same policy for his committee staff. I told him, 'Do that, buddy, and you're sleeping with the dog.'"

I laughed. Ben Glass was majority staff director for the Senate Foreign Relations Committee. He'd come to the Hill straight out of Johns Hopkins, where he'd gotten his master's in international relations. His boss, the senior senator from Virginia and chairman of the committee, had been in office longer than some marriages last.

"Hathaway has at least two men working for him," I said in an offhand way. "His chief of staff and his deputy chief of staff. They were on the guest list last night. Are they hotties, too?"

She flapped her hand. "Eric Nettle and David Epps. They've been to our Christmas parties once or twice. Eric could be Hathaway's kid brother, same Boston Brahmin way of walking, talking, and preppy dressing—*pahk the cah in Hahvahd yahd.* If you go for that type, I'd say he's good-looking."

Eric Nettle hadn't been the American I'd heard talking to the Russian. Not with an accent like that. "What about David Epps?"

She shot me a curious look. "David looks like a teddy bear or a hairy Pillsbury Doughboy. Round glasses like Harry Potter, round face. Spends a lot of time at the track at Charles Town betting on the horses. Supposedly he wins a lot. He's smart as a whip."

"Oh." In other words, someone with an expensive gambling habit—though it didn't sound like he had a money problem, or at least one that he admitted. "Also from Boston?"

"No," she said. "I forget where he's from. Why do you want to know about them? Are you thinking about . . . getting out again?"

"Oh, God, no. I mean, *no.*" I turned bright red.

Grace licked mayonnaise off her thumb. "Ben knows where all the bodies are buried, Soph. You can ask him about Eric and David tomorrow night. Eric's married, by the way. David is . . . between wives."

"I'm more interested in their boss," I said.

"He's married, too."

"I *know*. Give me a break, okay? What I mean is, after last night, I'm curious about Hathaway's friendship with Taras Attar. Hathaway really fought for him and told Orlov to take a hike. I wondered why."

"You can ask Ben about that, too," she said. "The committee has been holding hearings on ethnic conflicts and human rights abuses, focusing on places that aren't often in the spotlight. There was one on Abadistan last spring."

She crumpled her sandwich wrapper and held her hand out for mine. I gave it to her and she got up, dumping our trash in a nearby rubbish bin.

"By the way, I called Johnny B. Good yesterday to catch up. He happened to mention that he hasn't seen you since you got back."

She didn't say it, but she didn't need to: I was avoiding Jack O'Hara, too. Johnny B. Good was Grace's nickname for Jack, the first boy who ever kissed me, my first love. The romance was never destined to be—we were fifteen—but what came out of that relationship was a friendship that had become very dear to me. And later, it all made sense when Jack told me after he finished undergraduate school that he had decided to become a priest, to move to Rome and enter the Jesuit order. Now he was a professor of ethics at Georgetown Law School.

"I've called him," I said to Grace. "We've talked. I'm not a total recluse, you know. He's been busy with the start of classes, plus he was on a retreat."

Grace gave me a pointed look. "You ought to see him, Soph."

"I will."

But the first time I saw Jack, I knew his eyes would fasten on mine and he'd bore holes right through my carefully constructed facade until he got to the walled-off place I'd been able to keep hidden from Grace. He wouldn't settle for being pushed away, put off, or deflected by promises of honesty and truthfulness down the road.

". . . whether you'd be interested and I told her I'd ask," Grace was saying. "So what do you think?"

"About what?"

She flashed me a martyred look. "I *asked* if you were looking for a place to live because a good friend of my mother's owns two Victorian row houses on S Street." She waved a hand behind us. "Up that way, between Seventeenth and Eighteenth."

"I wasn't going to look until I found a job," I said. "But my lease is running out at the Roosevelt, so I ought to start trying to find something soon."

"This place is supposed to be gorgeous."

"I'm sure it is, but I can't afford a Victorian row house off Dupont Circle. I'm not that rich."

"I'll bet you can afford this one. It's not the whole house, just the top two floors. India lives in one of the houses. Years ago she and her husband converted the other one into duplex apartments. An antiques dealer rents the lower levels and India kept the upstairs place for out-of-town friends and family. My mom said she's finally decided the antiques dealer travels so much she'd like to find someone to move into the upstairs apartment. She's looking for a person who'll be around on a more regular basis." Grace pulled her phone out of her purse, tapped the screen, and began scrolling. "Mom sent me all the information last week, asked if I knew anyone. Here, I'm forwarding you her e-mail now."

I pulled out my phone as my mail beeped and read the e-mail. "India Ferrer? Unusual name."

I also had missed four calls while we'd been having lunch. All of them from Luke, practically one right after the other.

"She's an unusual woman," Grace said. "Oh, damn, damn, damn . . . I've got a meeting in fifteen minutes." She stood up. "Do you mind—?"

"Of course not," I said. "Go ahead and go. I'll see you."

"You'll see me tomorrow at seven. Right?"

I nodded. "Tomorrow at seven."

We exchanged kisses and she ran off to hail a cab as I hit Redial, calling Luke back.

He answered on the first ring, his voice harsh as though he'd been running or was out of breath.

"I think they found Ali."

"Who found her? Where is she?" My heart began slamming slow and hard against my chest.

"The Fourteenth Street Bridge down by the Jefferson Memorial."

I swallowed and said, "What was she doing there?"

"I have no idea. But they just pulled her body out of the Potomac."

TEN

Half a dozen electric blue paddleboats whose occupants were outfitted in orange life vests churned across the wind-riffed Tidal Basin as I turned onto the Outlet Bridge at Maine Avenue twenty minutes later, heading toward the Jefferson Memorial and East Potomac Park. I spotted Luke's Jeep at the curb near the concession stand by the memorial and angled the Vespa so I could park behind him. He was standing at the edge of the Tidal Basin with his back to me, staring across the water. A plane landing at National Airport roared overhead, skimming the Rosslyn skyline. Across from us the two enormous white granite stones of the Martin Luther King Jr. Memorial gleamed like beacons, and behind them the frieze of the Lincoln Memorial was just visible above the tree line.

I touched Luke's elbow. "Are you all right?"

He looked down at me and it nearly broke my heart to see the anguish in his eyes. "I should have driven her home."

"Don't," I said. "You would have had to throw her over your shoulder and carry her off kicking and screaming. You couldn't have stopped her, Luke."

He nodded, but it felt more like a tremor of anger, and laced his fingers through mine.

"We're meeting the detective who called me at the George Mason Memorial across the street," he said as we walked toward the Inlet Bridge still holding hands.

"I never knew there was a memorial to George Mason down here."

"According to the detective who called, a lot of people don't know about it. It's behind that grove of trees and it's pretty secluded."

Beyond the Tidal Basin I could see the shimmer of the gunmetal Potomac River and, above it, the huge green-and-white highway signs spanning the traffic lanes of the 14th

Street Bridge, indicating the turnoff for Alexandria and the airport. A big arrow pointed south to Richmond.

The George Mason Memorial, directly across from the Inlet Bridge, where the river and the Tidal Basin met, was a tribute to one of the lesser-known Founding Fathers. Mason wrote Virginia's Declaration of Rights, a document that profoundly influenced two other Virginians: Thomas Jefferson when he wrote the first part of the Declaration of Independence and James Madison when he drafted the Bill of Rights. But Mason never signed the Constitution and that decision destroyed his friendship with George Washington. Luke and I walked into what looked like a small park and I wondered if its scruffy appearance and dilapidated state was a metaphor for the deterioration of that relationship and his decision.

Patches of weedy grass, concentric gardens of mostly hard-packed dirt planted with tired-looking purple and yellow coneflowers, and a pollen-coated pool with a tiny fountain that was doing a poor job of circulating water—that was it. At the far end, under a bare trellis that looked like climbing roses or wisteria should have been gracefully twining through it, was a larger-than-life bronze statue of George Mason. Seated on a marble bench, one leg thrown casually over the other, head tilted back, a faint smile on his face, and a finger marking his place in a thick tome, Mason looked as though he'd come to while away a pleasant afternoon, instead of watching over the grim-faced metropolitan police officers wearing grape-colored gloves who were now searching the area in front of where he sat.

"Folks, the memorial is closed." A female African-American officer in a light blue shirt and dark trousers stopped us. "Police investigation."

"We're supposed to meet Detective Bolton here," Luke said. "He called me. I'm Luke Santangelo. This is Sophie Medina. I believe we know the, ah . . . person you found."

"Stay here," she said. "I'll get Detective Bolton."

Bolton was compact, ruddy faced, and stubble haired, and had a jutting jaw that reminded me of a bulldog.

"Thanks for coming by, folks," he said. "We got a purse one of our officers found under a bench near that statue. Only

ID was your business card, sir. Could either of you tell us if you recognize the purse or any of the contents?"

Bolton was looking at me, more so than Luke, and I nodded. "Follow me."

Someone had left Ali's black patent leather evening bag on the seat next to Mason's bronze tricorn hat and walking stick. Laid out alongside it in separate plastic bags were her zebra-striped makeup bag, a small hairbrush with a sparkly handle, breath mints, a pretty packet of tissues with butterflies on them, and three keys on a heart-shaped key ring. All on its own: Luke's business card. Ali had colored a smiley face on the *O* in *Focus,* where the camera lens was.

I swallowed hard and said, "It's Ali's purse. That's her makeup bag and key ring. She joked that it was the key to her heart."

"Where's her phone?" Luke asked. "And her wallet?"

"We're still looking," Bolton said. "If they're around here, we'll find them. The K9 guys are on their way. Did you bring that photograph with you, Mr. Santangelo?"

Luke pulled a snapshot out of his shirt pocket and handed it to Bolton, who took it and pressed his lips together. A candid shot of Ali taken only last night in front of the Firebird ice sculpture, her head thrown back, laughing, dark eyes flashing as if she'd just accepted a dare. The deep red spotlights cast a glow like a fire spreading around her, turning her jet-black hair copper colored and making the sequins on her evening dress glitter like hundreds of rubies.

Bolton stared at Ali's picture for a long time. Finally he raised his head and said, "She was lovely. Mind if I keep this?"

"It's for you," Luke said.

Bolton looked hard at me. "You related to her, by any chance? Cousins, maybe?"

"No. No relation," I said. "Do you know what happened to her?"

"We have to wait for the medical examiner to determine the cause of death. Drownings are always tricky, especially figuring out whether the victims were alive or dead before they went in the water." He unclipped a silver pen from the

breast pocket of his shirt and pulled out a small spiral
notebook.

"Are you saying Ali might have been murdered before
someone dumped her body in the Potomac?" Luke looked
stunned. "She was just a sweet kid."

Bolton's eyes softened. "I'm sorry. We don't know. But the
both of you can help by telling us what she did last night, and
that includes accounting for your own whereabouts. Also
whether she seemed depressed, upset, any strange or unusual
behavior."

Luke gave Bolton a detailed chronology right up until Ali
left the National Gallery, including her teasing hint that she
might have met a rich Russian who was taking her out after
the reception. Then we each filled in our own time line, ending
with Luke leaving my place around two in the morning after
we'd finished editing. Bolton wrote it all down.

"So neither one of you actually saw her leave the National
Gallery with anyone?" he said. "She didn't say who the guy
was, didn't give a name?"

"No." Luke shook his head. "Her car was in the shop so I
drove her to the reception last night. She said she didn't need
a ride home so I figured whoever it was, he had wheels."

"Then we're not looking for her car, at least." Bolton chewed
on the end of his pen and glanced over at me. "You got anything
to add, Ms. Medina?"

I did. Something that had been forming into a small knot
in my stomach and was now gnawing at me: the conversation
Ali overheard between Arkady Vasiliev and me. But I wasn't
going to tell Bolton about it right now with Luke standing
there.

"No," I said.

Bolton gave me a look indicating he didn't believe me, but
didn't push it. "One final thing," he said. "Would you mind
taking a look at her so we've got a definite ID? It can be real
quick."

"Of course," Luke said, his voice catching in his throat.

We left the park and the road curved around so it now
paralleled the Potomac. The lane nearest the river had been
blocked off to accommodate the line of police and emergency

vehicles spread out under the two spans of the 14th Street Bridge: red, white, and blue MPD cruisers and a fire truck. An ambulance pulled up, and a fire and rescue boat hovered offshore.

The noise of the overhead traffic reverberated as we walked under the first bridge, echoing inside my head until I felt like it would explode. A freight train traveling south across the railroad bridge farther downstream made a steady *chunka-chunka* sound.

"What in the hell was Ali doing here at night with some guy she didn't know?" Luke asked.

"I could see her coming here," I said. "It's romantic, the kind of edgy danger that she would go for. Maybe he took her to the Jefferson Memorial first and then they headed over to the George Mason Memorial."

"Which is," Bolton said, "a more private place for making out or going all the way if you get your thrills from doing it in a national park. The park police guard Jefferson all night. Mason just gets a drive-by every now and then. It could work except for her purse getting knocked to the ground and her leaving without it. That just doesn't fly."

"How did she end up at the river?" I asked.

"Right now we don't know. What I want to know is who was with her," Bolton said. "Do either of you know if she had a regular boyfriend? The guy she left the party with last night was someone new, right?"

Luke nodded. "No regular boyfriend, but a lot of guys had crushes on her, older men mostly. She sang at the Goodnight Club a couple nights a week. There was always someone buying her drinks between sets."

"Would that include you?" Bolton asked.

"I lost my wife of eighteen years to cancer two years ago, Detective Bolton. Ali was a sweet kid and I went to hear her sing a couple of times after I hired her, but that's as far as it went." Luke's face had turned red and his voice was tight with anger.

"I'm sorry for your loss," Bolton said, pulling out the note-book and writing "Goodnight Club" in it. "But we need to cover all the bases, rule people out."

We had stopped near a small parking lot that looked like overflow parking for the Jefferson and Mason memorials. In front of us was a large marble urn with an outstretched eagle carved on it. A tarnished plaque had an inscription in Spanish and a marker read CUBAN FRIENDSHIP URN. I wondered who had chosen this out-of-the-way spot to commemorate the U.S. friendship, such as it was, with Cuba.

"Okay, let's cross the street," Bolton said.

"She was found here?" I said. "By the bridge?"

Bolton nodded. "A fisherman found her. You don't want to know the details."

Luke and I exchanged glances. He looked like he was about to be sick.

A police officer in high shiny boots and a bright orange safety vest stepped into Ohio Drive and stopped a silver Hyundai so we could cross. Between the road and the river was an area about ten feet wide of broken paving stones interspersed with tall weeds. We had to take a few steps down a slope to get to the dirt path that ran along the river. A low guardrail reinforced by chain-link wire provided minimal safety against falling in—it wouldn't take much to hop over it—and a brown-and-white National Park Service sign said PLEASE WATCH YOUR STEP.

Maybe this had been an accident, a lark that had gone completely wrong. Ali and her date had been sitting on that railing, talking and kissing and clowning around. I could see her doing it: pretty, flirty Ali courting the daredevil thrill that comes with the youthful certainty of immortality. Somehow she'd lost her balance and fallen into the river. Maybe the guy tried to save her, but he couldn't. Then he panicked and fled.

Couldn't it have happened like that?

Luke braced himself as we knelt and Bolton unzipped the body bag, exposing Ali's face, just down to her neckline. The minute I saw her, that tangled tumble of long dark hair, all makeup stripped away so she looked even more vulnerable and childlike, I knew her death had been violent and that she had fought for life.

"It's her," Luke said, rising quickly and walking over to where he could lean over the railing by himself.

I made the sign of the cross and heard Luke retching a few yards away.

"Did she suffer?" I asked. I was sure she did, but I needed Bolton to say she hadn't.

"I don't know." Bolton zipped up the body bag with the tenderness of a parent covering a sleeping child and said, "Was there something you wanted to say earlier?"

I nodded. "Luke doesn't know this."

We stood up and walked away from the bridge to where the branches of a weeping willow screened us like a pale green filigree curtain. I told him about Ali eavesdropping on my conversation with Arkady Vasiliev and the possibility that she'd walked by one or both of the men I'd overheard discussing a plot to assassinate a Russian who was coming to D.C. I left Scott Hathaway out of it, but I ended by telling him about my talk with Napoleon Duval this morning. Bolton furiously wrote all of it down in his notebook. As soon as I mentioned Duval, his head snapped up.

"Jesus, Mary, and Joseph," he said. "This is a hell of a mess. You know how I can reach Special Agent Duval?"

His card was still in my jeans pocket. I pulled it out and Bolton copied down the information he needed.

"Do you know for a fact that she ran into one of the guys you heard talking in that conference room?" he asked.

"No. She was in a rush to leave so she said we'd talk about it in the morning," I said, and at that moment I wanted to join Luke at that railing. "Now we'll never know."

Bolton tapped his pen on his notebook and leaned in close. I smelled cigarette smoke on his breath and the faint vinegary tang of sweat mingled with dust and heat and weariness.

"Well, I guess I'll be talking to Agent Duval. Then maybe you and I'll have a chat again. I have a feeling we're not done." He angled his head in the direction of the bridge. "Here comes your friend."

Luke looked ashen faced as he joined us. "Sorry. That was tough to take."

"You two are free to go." Bolton gave me a bland look. "If I need to talk to you, I'll be in touch. And call me if you think of anything else." He pulled his wallet from his back pocket and gave us each a business card. Mine had a smudged thumb-print on it. "Thanks for your time."

Then he walked over to where Ali lay a few feet away in that body bag like a fallen angel.

She had died in a part of Washington where they put the neglected and forgotten monuments like the Cuban Friendship Urn and the George Mason Memorial. If she had screamed or cried out for help—even with that powerful voice of hers—no one had heard her and come to her rescue as the Potomac swept her away, claiming her in its swift, deadly current.

ELEVEN

Luke and I went back to the studio. Katya Gordon had sent an e-mail asking when she'd be able to review the reception photos, and we still had pictures that needed editing. Not only that, but now Bolton wanted a set as well and told Luke the sooner he could have it, the better.

Neither Luke nor I could get our heads wrapped around work except for one thing: Since the photographs were in chronological order, we were editing the last pictures of the evening. A lot of guests had departed, but Ali's mystery man should have been hanging around.

"I give up," Luke said finally. I'd moved my laptop into his office and was sitting at his desk, across from him. "We don't have a clue who we're looking for—young, old, tall, short, Russian, American. Ali had very catholic taste in men. All they needed was a Y chromosome. I saw her with guys at the Goodnight Club old enough to be her grandfather . . . old enough to be *my* grandfather."

"Well, this guy had to be someone without a date," I said. "Which ought to narrow it down."

"You see any likely candidates in these photos?"

"I don't know. Everyone or no one."

Luke ran his hands through his hair and blew out a weary breath. "It's coming on four o'clock. If you want to take off, go ahead. We're done for the day. I'll post the pictures to our website and give Seth, Moses, and Katya their password so they have access. I probably ought to call Seth anyway, tell him about Ali. He shouldn't find out by seeing it on the news."

"Are you going to say anything to him about Napoleon Duval, tell him about the other meeting last night?" The question slipped out before I realized it and suddenly the air in the room was as thick as smoke.

God, wasn't Nick right? If you don't know, you don't have to lie. I was growing so tired and confused by all the stories

I had to keep straight, the secrets I couldn't divulge. Was Luke going to pick up on my tiny slipup? He knew about only one meeting in the conference room: the conversation I'd overheard between the Russian and the American.

What would he say now if he knew what I'd told Bolton down by the river, about the second meeting, the one between Arkady Vasiliev and me, how Ali had stumbled into the middle of it, and my slowly blooming fear that something had happened last night—maybe she'd said something to the wrong person—that might have cost her life?

Luke held my gaze for a long time while he considered my question, and I wished I could read minds. "I don't think it's a good idea to mention anything," he said at last. "Seth and Roxanne Hathaway are really close. I just . . . don't want to go there. If Duval finds out something, he can handle it."

I closed my laptop and hoped he didn't notice my relief. "That sounds like a good idea. I guess I'll see you in the morning."

"Actually," he said, "why don't we just meet at Hillwood, say around eleven? Katya Gordon's talk doesn't begin until noon, so that ought to give us plenty of time to get squared away."

"Sure," I said. "See you there."

Hillwood was a jewellike museum set on twenty-five acres of land near Rock Creek Park in northwest D.C. The estate, with its acres of manicured gardens, included a Georgian-style mansion, a dacha, a rustic log cabin, a visitor center, a green-house, a café, and a pet cemetery. It had been the home of the Post Cereal heiress Marjorie Merriweather Post, who had been a passionate collector of Russian imperial art. During the 1930s she lived in Moscow with her third husband, who was the U.S. ambassador to the Soviet Union, where she, like Armand Hammer, took advantage of Joseph Stalin's need to raise money for his cash-strapped country by selling paintings, icons, porcelain, and other valuable items that once belonged to the Romanovs. By the time Marjorie Merriweather Post died in 1973, she had acquired the largest collection of Romanov treasures and imperial art outside Russia—including two Fabergé eggs given by Nicholas II to his mother, Maria

Feodorovna. As a Russian art scholar, Katya Gordon had been invited to discuss the lost Romanov treasures on display at the National Gallery and we had been hired to photograph her talk and a VIP reception in the gardens afterward—more photos for the coffee table book on what they were calling "the Vasiliev Collection."

I went back to my desk and packed up my cameras and laptop. As I was leaving, I stopped in Luke's doorway. "Are you going to be all right? What are you going to do after you're done here?"

He looked up. "Have a liquid dinner at the Goodnight Club in honor of Ali."

It sounded like he meant it. "Luke—"

He waved a hand. "Don't worry. I won't do anything stupid, if that's what you're thinking. But if you want to come by, I'll probably be there for a while."

It was a backhanded invitation, not really a date.

"Thanks," I said. "I think I'm just going to go back to the apartment and get some sleep."

"That's probably a good idea. See you tomorrow, Sophie."

It didn't take long to get back to the Roosevelt. I left the Vespa in the parking lot and, because the elevator was waiting when I walked through the back door, I took it rather than the stairs, as I usually did.

I hardly ever ran into anyone on my floor, but as I stepped off the elevator, I saw a repairman—medium height, medium build, white shirt with a logo on the breast pocket, navy trousers, small black satchel, and a baseball cap pulled low so it shielded his face—walking down the hall. It took a split second before I realized he must have come from my apartment or my neighbor's across the hall doing whatever he'd been doing.

I hadn't called anyone to fix anything.

"Excuse me," I said. "What are you doing here?"

He didn't look up, just spun around and ran for the fire exit at the other end of the hall. I was right behind him, but he had a good head start and I was carrying my equipment. By the time I made it down the two flights of stairs, he was gone. I took a guess he'd chosen the rear door since it was the nearest exit, but when I stepped into the parking lot, there was no sign of him.

I ran inside to the lobby. If he'd used the main door, he would have walked by the front desk. The assistant day manager, a motherly soul who projected an air of brisk efficiency and liked you to think of the Roosevelt as your home away from home and its staff as your extended family, looked up from a computer.

"Did a man come through here and go out the front door just now?" I asked.

"I'm sorry, I didn't see anyone, dear," she said. "I had to step into the office for a moment. Is there a problem?"

Dammit, he was definitely gone for good.

"Did you send a repairman to my apartment or my neighbor's apartment this afternoon?"

Her face creased into a worried frown and she put on a pair of red cat-eye glasses that were hanging around her neck on a beaded lanyard. She picked up a ring binder with a handmade *Visitor's Log* label on it. "It's Ms. . . . . Medina, isn't it? 2F?"

"Yes."

She skimmed the first page. "Let's see . . . we had a plumber in earlier to take care of a leak on the seventh floor and someone came by to fix a computer in 3A. They both signed out."

"I see."

"You know, dear, a number of new guests have moved in over the past few days. Maybe you just didn't recognize one of your neighbors."

"Maybe." I felt the itchy urgent need to get upstairs to my apartment. He was no neighbor. "Thanks."

I took the elevator one more time. He was gone, long gone, and there wouldn't be anyone waiting for me, lurking behind a curtain or hiding in the bathroom, like *Psycho* in reverse. Still, my palms were clammy as I fished my key from my pocket. At least he'd locked the door, but only the bottom lock, not the dead bolt. I pushed it open and the memory of walking into our cottage in London the night Nick vanished flooded through me with such fierce intensity I grabbed the doorjamb and clung to it.

Nothing could have been worse than the scene I found that

awful night, the trail of blood and the upended furniture, but this had its own stamp of violation, as unexpected and shocking as a hard slap across the face. As soon as I walked in I could tell he'd gone through the desk in the living room. The top drawer wasn't completely closed and the shade on the desk lamp was askew.

My brain switched to automatic pilot, as it had done that night in London. The first thing I needed to do was check my expensive cameras and my equipment, which could be sold on the street in a heartbeat and I'd never see any of it again. A Leica M7 and Hasselblad H2F, each worth thousands, and the irreplaceable specialty lenses my grandfather had given me were the obvious items to steal. Value: priceless. I kept them in two locked cases in the bedroom closet, along with my other gear.

I slid open the mirrored closet door and felt like I'd been punched in the stomach. The two padlocks were hanging open by their hasps. But when I knelt and opened the cases to check the contents, everything was exactly where it belonged except the Hasselblad, which hadn't been placed correctly in its fitted compartment. I held my breath, removed it and the Leica, and pulled out the false bottom in the case. Nick's grandmother's exquisite Fabergé snuffbox was still there in its pink velvet bag wrapped in tissue paper and protected by a layer of bubble wrap. I left it where it was, put back the false bottom and the cameras, and closed the case.

He'd searched the closet and the dresser, rifled through my clothes and lingerie, and even examined my makeup bag in the bathroom. In fact, the whole apartment had a weird off-kilter feeling to it like I'd suddenly discovered that the floors sloped down at the edges of the room, causing all my things to shift ever so slightly out of place. I shuddered, imagining his hands running over my clothes, and walked back into the bedroom, pulling everything out of the drawers and throwing all of it on the bed. Then I stuffed as much as I could in the washing machine and turned it on.

There was only one reason why he had searched the entire apartment but taken nothing.

Because what he wanted wasn't here.

Nor was he a run-of-the-mill intruder who happened to choose my apartment. He'd been looking for Nick's well logs, and he thought I might have left them under my bras or next to the shampoo bottle in the bathtub.

Had Arkady Vasiliev learned where I lived and sent him here?

I got my phone and found Napoleon Duval's card. Halfway through dialing his number I hit End Call. What was I going to tell him? That I saw someone in the hall whom I suspected had been in my apartment? That I found the dead bolt unlocked and the padlocks to the cases where I kept my camera equipment unlocked, but nothing was missing? And, no, I hadn't forgotten to lock those locks.

Already Duval had doubts about my credibility, maybe even my sanity. Telling him this story would only confirm them.

After Nick disappeared, I had stayed in a hotel in Maida Vale paid for by the CIA until Scotland Yard took down the crime scene tape at the front door to the cottage and cleaners and painters had erased every trace of blood and violence. Friends urged me to find another place, but I'd insisted on going home because I felt closer to Nick, connected to him, if I stayed there.

This time felt different. I didn't want to stay at the Roosevelt anymore. I found Grace's e-mail with India Ferrer's phone number and called her. India had a sweet high-pitched voice and a bridge club date this evening with friends. She told me she was free tomorrow morning at ten o'clock to show me the apartment. I told her I was looking forward to meeting her and would see her then.

After I hung up, I threw my clothes in the dryer and phoned Father Jack O'Hara.

"I was just about to call you," he said. "Grace called and said she had lunch with you today."

"A picnic at Dupont Circle."

"You sound funny. Is everything all right?"

"Not really," I said. "Someone broke into my apartment. Do you think you could put me up for the night?"

Jack didn't seem surprised by the request. "Sure. Both guest rooms are free, so no problem. Did your intruder get anything?"

"No, but I saw him as he was walking down the hall afterward. I called out and he took off down the fire stairs. I lost him outside."

"You went after him?"

"Of course I went after him."

"Good God. What would you have done if you caught up with him and he had a gun?" he asked.

"Well, I didn't and he wasn't waving anything around. So it doesn't matter."

"Did you call the police?" he asked.

"And say what?" I said. "I can't prove anyone was actually in here. Plus nothing was stolen and no one was hurt. The police won't bother with a case like this—they probably wouldn't even file a report. And, Jack, do not tell Grace about this. I mean it. She'll throw a net over my head and take me home to Middleburg and leave me with my mother."

"Okay, okay," he said. "I can keep a secret. When they gave me the funny clothes it was part of the job description. Come on over and I'll make us dinner, too. I've got a new recipe a parishioner gave me, if you don't mind being experimented on. Italian sound okay?"

"Italian sounds great." He always cooked Italian, ever since his days in the seminary in Rome.

"I'm still in my office on campus. How about if I meet you at my place in half an hour?" he asked.

"Sure. I've got to finish some laundry, then I'll be on my way."

"Speaking of laundry, bring your running gear," he said. "We'll need to work off dinner. It's artery clogging but worth every calorie."

When my clothes were dry, I got my big suitcase out of the closet and put everything in it, except for a nightgown, my running clothes, and a blouse and dress slacks for tomorrow at Hillwood. Those I put in an overnight bag to take to Jack's. It wouldn't take long to pack up the rest of the apartment, probably less than an hour.

On my way out, I stopped at the front desk and told the assistant day manager that I would be terminating my lease at the Roosevelt when it ran out in a few days. She seemed surprised at the abruptness of my decision, but she put the red glasses on, pulled out the book of leases, and made a note in my file.

Then she wished me well and told me she hoped I'd be happy wherever I was going next.

TWELVE

Jack lived in Gloria House, which took its name from the Jesuit motto, *Ad majorem Dei gloriam*: For the greater glory of God. A four-story redbrick building overlooking Stanton Park on the edge of Capitol Hill, it had once been someone's grand nineteenth-century mansion, but over the years a hodgepodge of additions with no particular vision transformed it into something that couldn't be characterized by any architectural style. The facade still looked Victorian, but the back of the building, thoroughly modernized with gated parking underneath and rows of nondescript balconies, reminded me of a generic motel off the interstate. The Jesuits bought the old building after they built Georgetown Law School over by Union Station and also because it had been near St. Aloysius Catholic Church, which had been one of their parishes until the church closed. Then they renovated it, added a chapel, and turned it into a house of religious studies for about twenty or so seminarians and a few professors on the law school faculty.

The gate to the parking lot was open so I chained the Vespa to a metal post that supported the balconies and went around to the front entrance. Jack answered the door, a broad smile on his handsome face as he pulled me to him for a kiss and smothered me in a hug.

It had been two years since we'd seen each other, but he hadn't changed. To be honest, he hadn't changed since we were at St. Mike's and he'd won the senior superlatives for "best eyes" and "best hair." He also got "worst car" and "heart of gold." He deserved all of them. Eyes the intense blue of sapphires and dark wavy hair that he still wore a bit long—he looked like a Shakespearean actor—but now going gray at the temples. Worst car—I'd been in it dozens of times when it died, so enough said. And the kindest and most compassionate soul I knew. Grace's other nickname for him behind his back was "Father What-a-Waste."

"He's so damn gorgeous in that delicious dark Irish way," she said to me more than once. "Why'd he have to decide to be a priest? What a waste of a good man. What a loss for womankind."

He picked up my bag after that bear hug and looked me over. "You look great," he said. "I've missed you."

"Thanks. You don't look so bad yourself and I've missed you, too."

I followed him into the foyer, where a grand spiral staircase with a hand-carved railing coiled up four floors. The Jesuit IHS emblem hung on a shield above the stairs and a statue of the Virgin Mary stood on an altar table across the room flanked by flickering devotional candles in ruby hurricane glasses. Through the open doors to the chapel, the stained-glass silhouettes of the four Evangelists in the chancel window were backlit like a vision in the afternoon sunlight.

My breathing slowed as I followed Jack up the steps. Here I would find peace. We reached the second-floor landing and he opened a door on which a plain wooden cross was fastened below a sign that said GUEST.

"Here's your room. Want to change so we can go for a run? I'm across the hall. Come on in when you're ready. Door's unlocked."

My room was functional and spartan: a bed with a white matelassé coverlet, a dresser, a desk, a chair, a crucifix, and a window that overlooked Stanton Park. I had my own bathroom—no sharing—with a tiny stall shower. Jack's suite, which I'd never seen, was also quite simple: living room, bedroom, and bathroom. An antique oak bookcase that I remembered from his parents' home was filled with books on theology, ethics, law, and spirituality. A carved crucifix that looked African and an icon of Our Lady of Vladimir hung on the walls. A well-worn blue recliner I guessed was a favorite chair had a floor lamp next to it and a small table beside it with his leather breviary and St. Ignatius's *Spiritual Exercises*. He also had one of the building's original west-facing arcaded balconies, which reminded me of a Florentine loggia.

"Rank has its privileges, I guess," I said. "That's a great balcony."

"Yeah, I feel like the pope looking down on the crowds in St. Peter's when I go out there." He grinned. "It's pretty cool."

"Nice little garden you've got, too. Who knew you had such a green thumb?"

"I don't. When those plants die, I buy new ones. If God intended geraniums to live forever he would have made them out of cast iron. But I do grow all my own herbs for cooking."

I opened the balcony door and stepped outside. His hanging planter baskets of geraniums looked overgrown, parched, and leggy.

"You might try watering these sometimes. It does help, you know. But you do have cilantro, three kinds of parsley, chives, dill, sage, rosemary, and oregano. And a statue of St. Francis of Assisi."

"My secret weapon," he said. "He's the only reason everything's not dead."

He got two water bottles out of a small refrigerator and tossed one to me.

"I haven't been running much lately," I said. "Except from gunfire in war zones—and that was a while ago. Be kind to me."

"You look good," he said. "You look like you're in great shape."

I turned red. "So do you."

He grinned. "Don't be such a girl, Medina. I'm not cutting you any slack."

"Father," I said, "that's not a very charitable thing to say."

We clomped down the stairs and went outside. The traffic light turned red at Massachusetts Avenue and we jogged across the street.

"Why don't we make a big loop, head up Mass Ave for a few blocks, and then cut over and come down East Capitol so we finish in front of the Capitol by the Library of Congress and the Supreme Court?" he said. "We ought to make it in time to watch the sun go down behind the Capitol."

"'Where you lead, I will follow,'" I said. "Who said that?"

"Ruth. And Carole King. Ruth said it first, but Carole King got paid a bundle for saying it."

I laughed and said as we ran toward 6th Street, "Now I'm going to have that song stuck in my head for the rest of the day."

He seemed to be deliberately keeping a slower pace—Jack ran the Marine Corps marathon every year—to give me the opportunity to start the conversation. For a couple of blocks we ran side by side and I thought about how much I'd missed him, his unvarnished way of distilling a situation to its basic components, his clear-eyed sense of justice and why it was important to do the right thing, to be true to your values, to act with integrity and compassion for others.

"Want to talk?" he said after a while. "Or do you really want me to put on my stole and we can do this back at the house with all the bells and whistles?"

We turned onto East Capitol Street at 8th Street by Morton's Pharmacy. Ahead of us, the Capitol dome filled the rosy evening skyline.

I smiled. "It's not that. There are things I'm not supposed to tell anyone."

"Anything you say stays with me," he said. "I made a deal with the man upstairs when I became a priest."

"It's so complicated I don't even know where to begin."

Jack reached over and threw his arm across my shoulders in a brotherly hug. "Yes, you do, Soph. Just start talking. It'll come out the way it's meant to."

Something in that sweet, comforting gesture undammed all the bottled-up secrets and loosened the constricted vise around my heart. He never would—or could—reveal a single thing I said, even if I'd just committed murder. We slowed to a walk and I told him everything, beginning with Nick's clan-destine work for the CIA, the truth about his disappearance, Colin's death, and Crowne Energy's problems with the increasing menace and threats from the Shaika in Abadistan. By the time I got to the rainy meeting with Baz Allingham in Westminster Abbey, we had reached 1st Street in front of the Capitol. To our left was the Library of Congress; the Supreme Court was on the right.

"There must be something going on at the library this evening," Jack said. "All those people milling around . . . I think it's the last outdoor concert of the season. Why don't we go over to the Supreme Court and find someplace to sit where we can keep talking?"

We turned right and climbed the low steps to the sprawling plaza with its inlaid gray-and-white marble pattern of circles and squares that had been copied from the Pantheon in Rome. I'd read somewhere that the Vermont marble chosen for the plaza and the building's exterior purposely had a high content of mica so the stone would shimmer with a near-blinding brilliance on sunny days. Directly in front of us at the top of the one-story marble staircase was the templelike entrance to the Supreme Court, the words EQUAL JUSTICE UNDER LAW carved into the frieze below the pediment. Two flags on either side of the plaza fluttered in the light breeze, flanking identical fountains whose turquoise water looked tropical.

"How about if we take one of those benches by the fountains?" Jack pointed to two figures seated on enormous plinths on either side of the staircase. "The female statue on the left is the Contemplation of Justice. The male statue on the right is the Authority of Law. Which side do you want to sit on?"

"I'll take justice," I said. "I've had enough dealings with the authority of law today."

We sat on the semicircular bench and watched the jet of water from the fountain cascade gracefully back into the pool and the thin strips of clouds turn orange and red behind the Capitol dome. Across the street, congressional staff and their bosses streamed out of the House and Senate, leaving work at the end of the day. Jack spun his empty water bottle in his hands and waited for me to go on.

"I don't know what to do anymore," I said finally. "Baz told me there are people who believe Nick might have murdered Colin in order to get the well logs and now he's selling them to the high bidder . . . I know that's not true. But I don't understand why I haven't heard from him . . . it's eating at me, Jack. I can't stop thinking about it."

It felt like a weight rolled off me to say it, to finally get it out in the open. Why hadn't Nick contacted me? *Why?*

"Nick's a good man," he said. "I'd trust him with my life, Soph, and you know I'm a good judge of character. There could be a dozen reasons he hasn't called or e-mailed or got word to you through someone he trusts. Maybe he was injured—you said there was a lot of blood at the house and in that car—and he's got amnesia. Maybe he's keeping silent to protect you."

"I wish I knew." I threw up my hands. "Sometimes I feel so alone."

His arm went around my shoulders again. "You poor kid. I pray for you every day, you know that, don't you? You *and* Nick."

I nodded and bit my lip.

"I don't know if this helps," he went on, "but over the past couple of years people have started reaching out to me—from the White House, the Hill, administration policy makers, lobbyists. What they wanted was . . . I guess you'd call it spiritual guidance. How to deal with a professional conflict that troubled their conscience or went against their values and ethics."

I sat up and looked at him. "What do you mean?"

"Well, for example, do you take money from a corrupt government or a company that uses child labor in China that wants to hire your public relations firm to promote their interests in America? Or what if you work for a senator who supports the Second Amendment because of all the hunters in his state and you're in favor of gun control because your niece was killed by an illegal handgun bought on the street?" he said. "That sort of thing. A lot of the people I've counseled have been from the intelligence community."

"You never told me this," I said.

He shrugged. "It's not like I hung out a shingle. Now I guess it's word of mouth because all of a sudden someone calls and wants to talk. But let me tell you this: All of them are tremendously challenged and conflicted about where trust and honesty fit in their lives and marriages. Sometimes they can work it out. Other times, they choose loyalty to country over loyalty to family, believing that's the greater good and the honorable thing to do. Except the spouse can't handle being frozen out, never knowing what's a lie and whether he or she—and maybe their children—are being set up or used as bait."

"What are you saying?"

"I'm saying that it's a hard life and that the choices aren't always easy. You know that better than I do, especially after everything that's happened to you. But you're going to make it through this, Sophie, however it turns out. You're tough as nails, you always have been."

I gave him a twisted smile. "I hope you're right."

"I know I'm right."

"There's something else," I said.

"What?"

"The receptionist who worked for us at Focus was found in the Potomac River this afternoon," I said. "Her name was Alicia Jones, Ali. She was just a kid, twenty-one or twenty-two."

"I'm so sorry." Jack made the sign of the cross. "What happened to her?"

I told him, and about my gnawing worry that I was indirectly responsible. "What if someone made a mistake and thought it was me? Ali said we looked like cousins and even Bolton made a comment about it."

Jack shook his head. "You're not accountable for the actions or the behavior of anyone but yourself. Not for Ali, and certainly not for whoever did this to her if it was a homicide. So don't go there or you'll tear yourself to pieces."

"That's easier said than done, Jack . . ."

"Don't beat yourself up, Soph. I mean it." He stood and held out his hand. "Come on. Let's go back to the house and get showered and changed. We can have cocktails in my room until the kitchen and dining room clear out downstairs. Then I'll wow you with my fabulous gourmet skills."

"I'd like that." I let him pull me up. "I don't know if I ran off enough artery-clogging calories. We did a lot of walking. And sitting."

"We can remedy that," he said as we jogged down the steps. "Last one back to Gloria House does the dishes."

*   *   *

We sat by candlelight on Jack's balcony drinking a bottle of Antinori Chianti Classico, a birthday present from a parishioner at Holy Trinity in Georgetown, where he occasionally helped out saying Mass. Afterward, we brought our glasses and the rest of the wine downstairs to the large communal kitchen, which we had to ourselves. Jack put me to work making pasta dough and showed me how to run it through his pasta machine and turn the thin sheets into fat strips of linguine.

We were standing across from each other at an old marble worktable in the middle of the kitchen and my apron was spattered with flour, as was my side of the table. He'd put newspaper on the floor under my feet and it looked like I was standing in a dusting of snow.

"What's this dish called again?" I asked.

He dumped a can of tuna in oil into a food processor. "Linguine with tonnato sauce and arugula. You're gonna love it."

"Do you have to use the anchovies?"

He opened the tin. "The anchovies make the sauce. Take my word."

"I hate anchovies."

"Suck it up, cupcake. More wine?"

I nodded and he filled our glasses.

"Something else on your mind?" he asked. "You've been kind of quiet."

"I didn't tell you everything when we were at the Supreme Court," I said. "There's something else."

Jack stopped working and stared at me as I told him about the assassination plot and Scott Hathaway's name being mentioned.

"You overheard two guys planning a murder that might involve the Senate majority leader?" he said.

I nodded. "I ended up telling Luke about it, and this morning he ran into a neighbor who works for Homeland Security and casually brought up a what-if hypothetical situation. Then voilà, an hour later Special Agent Napoleon Duval, my CIA contact, who now works for a counterterrorism task force, showed up at the studio for a little chat like someone rubbed the magic lamp."

"What did Agent Duval say when you talked to him?"

"I think he believes I've been listening to the strange voices in my head," I said, "and that Nick's disappearance has made me a little unhinged. He also thinks I deliberately went after the job at Focus so I could meet Arkady Vasiliev."

"That's crazy," Jack said.

"Tell that to Duval."

"What makes you think the person these guys want to assassinate is Taras Attar?" Jack asked.

"The timing fits. He's coming to the States in the next few days on a book tour." I shrugged. "Though Luke says it can't be Attar because he and Hathaway are such good friends—and Hathaway supposedly knows about this plot."

"A friend of mine, another Jesuit who teaches at the university, knew Hathaway and Attar when they were Georgetown undergrads thirty years ago. Hathaway's pretty loyal to his old alma mater."

"That's right. Hathaway and Attar went to Georgetown, didn't they?"

"Go Hoyas."

"I wonder how they got to be friends."

He shrugged. "I could ask Sully, my friend. He seemed to know them pretty well."

I brushed my hair off my face with a floury forearm. "Would you mind?"

"Nope." He pulsed the food processor. "But getting back to Vasiliev—and you—why are those well logs so valuable that Vasiliev called you in to talk to you last night and someone tossed your place today? Crowne Energy must have found something when they drilled for oil."

"Nick couldn't talk about it, but I know he and Colin were really excited about some development right before he disappeared. When Crowne Energy decided to drill that test well in Abadistan, they were the laughingstock of the industry. The geology in that part of the world wasn't considered conducive to finding hydrocarbons—a large quantity of hydrocarbons, that is—meaning you'd also find oil or natural gas. Any drilling is a bit of a guessing game—there is only a ten to thirty percent chance of finding anything anyway. When you throw in the ethnic violence between the Russians and the Abadis, the threats and intimidation Crowne had to deal with from the Shaika, and Abadistan being a major supply route for drugs and arms from Afghanistan and Pakistan, on paper it looked like a terrible decision to go in there. No one could understand why they took such a huge financial—and personal—risk."

"Maybe because the reward on a long shot like that would be worthwhile if it panned out?" he said.

"Nick used to say that for a small company like Crowne Energy it would be like hitting the jackpot."

"If they did find oil—which it sounds like they did—then what?" Jack asked.

"Once you make what they call 'a discovery,' it takes another few years to drill more wells and build the infrastructure to develop them," I said. "It's not like some Looney Tunes cartoon where the oil gushes like a big black geyser and suddenly everyone's rich."

"So maybe Arkady Vasiliev wants to cash in on the risks Colin and Nick took, get in on the ground floor, and take over their operation?"

"I don't think there's much 'maybe' about it after what he said to me last night," I said. "I guess what I'm wondering now is whether he's also behind the plot to get rid of Taras Attar."

"If Attar's gone, it's a huge blow to the Abadi independence movement," Jack said. "Abadistan remains Russian and so does the oil. No one benefits from that more than the guy who owns the biggest oil production company in Russia. I don't know much about this, but I would imagine it wouldn't be hard for Vasiliev to take out a contract on Attar, especially with all his connections to the Shaika."

"But why would Scott Hathaway be involved?" I said. "Luke's right about it not making sense."

"Maybe Sully could shed some light on that." Jack put mayonnaise, capers, and the anchovies into the food processor. "I think the water's ready. Did you finish making the pasta?"

"Yup. Want me to cut the lemons?"

He nodded and poured a steady drizzle of olive oil into the food processor. I handed him the lemons and he added the juice to his sauce.

My phone vibrated in my jeans pocket and I pulled it out. A text message from a phone number I didn't recognize. *Can you meet me tonight to talk?* It was signed Moses Rattigan.

I wrote back. *About what?*

Will explain. At KenCen fund-raiser. Do you know Bar Humbug? Barracks Row, 10:30pm?

"Something wrong?" Jack asked.

"I'm not sure," I said. "The public relations director at the National Gallery wants me to meet him tonight at a place called Bar Humbug after he leaves a fund-raiser at the Kennedy Center. He says he needs to talk about something. Luke was going to send everyone a link to our photos this afternoon. I hope there's not a problem."

"Are you going to meet this guy?" Jack asked. "At least Barracks Row is only on the other side of the Hill, so it's not far away."

"I think I ought to. Maybe this isn't about the pictures. Maybe Moses talked to Duval . . . or Bolton. I guess I'd better find out."

"All right, but you're not going alone," he said.

"Don't be silly. I love you, but I'm a big girl and I can do this. I've been in war zones. I can handle Capitol Hill."

Jack shook his head. "Did you think you'd drive through this neighborhood on your windup scooter at this time of night? No way, sunshine. I can nurse a Perrier in a corner while you talk, so I won't cramp your style."

"Jack—"

"Someone broke into your place today and a car chased you down the Mall last night." He was using his don't-mess-with-God's-earthly-representative voice. "I'm coming with you."

"Okay. You win."

My phone buzzed again. *Are we on?*

I sent a reply. *See you at 10:30.*

THIRTEEN

I n the dozen years I'd been away from Washington, the city had changed, not all of it for the better. Unlike London, which seemed timeless and eternal, D.C. still felt as though it were searching for its identity, trying to prove itself and fill its own oversized boots as the capital of the leading world power. The most striking change, at least to me, was the number of federal buildings that had become walled-off fortresses and the proliferation of ugly barricades that now were the permanent post-9/11 landscape. My stepfather, Harry, called Washington the place people who didn't want to live in America went to live.

But the 8th Street corridor, newly rechristened Barracks Row, was a success story, a neighborhood that had reinvented itself by coming back from near extinction. The city's oldest commercial center, it had been chosen by President Thomas Jefferson as the Marines' first point of defense for the Capitol and the Navy Yard. Over the years, especially after World War II, it grew seedy and run-down, nearly closing for business after the 1968 riots. On the drive over, Jack told me I wouldn't recognize it now: a thriving neighborhood of restaurants, bars, and shops, all the old buildings renovated under a program sponsored by the National Trust for Historic Preservation.

We parked across the street from the Marine barracks and walked one block down 8th Street to Bar Humbug. When Jack opened the front door, heads—mostly male—swiveled to check us out. The place looked comfortable and unpretentious, a long narrow room with a bay window overlooking the street, plenty of dark paneling, high-backed booths, and red pendant lamps that gave off cones of sepia light. The whitehaired bartender waved a greeting. The clientele was a mix of easily recognizable buzz-cut Marines and folks who looked like regulars.

Whoever owned Bar Humbug had a sense of humor because the walls were filled with photos and prints of legendary scam artists and charlatans. Charles Ponzi and Frank Abagnale had places of honor. We sat down at the far end of the bar across from a picture of Victor Lustig posing in front of the Eiffel Tower, which he once tried to sell, and Gregor McGregor. Jack ordered two Perriers and I read him the caption under McGregor's photo. A Scotsman who fought for South American independence in the 1800s, he returned to Britain as the "cazique" of the Central American nation of Poyais, where he recruited investors and colonists to invest their toil and treasure in a patch of water off the coast of Honduras.

The bartender set down our drinks. "Either we're going to need a bigger place or else we have to start hanging pictures on the ceiling. The owner wants to add Madoff, Ebbers, Kozlowski, the Enron guys, and Alan Stanford to the wall of shame." He shook his head. "You'd think people would learn that too good to be true is too good to be true. Haven't seen you guys in here before. Welcome to Bar Humbug."

Jack said thanks, but I could tell he didn't want to get lured into small talk about sports and the neighborhood, which would inevitably lead to having the details mined about who we were and how we'd ended up here. The bartender gave us a curious sideways look before drifting to the other end of the room, where a flat-screen television showed a West Coast game with the Dodgers being annihilated.

Jack clinked his glass against mine. "You all right?"

I nodded. "Fine."

In London my favorite local pub had been a wonderfully atmospheric place called the Holly Bush and, when we were both in town, Nick and I had dined there at least once a week. It was a higgledy-piggledy rabbit warren of rooms, the building dating from the 1600s, a former stable with worn oak floors, the original gas lamps, and—my favorite—a great roaring fire in the fireplace all winter long. Maybe someday I would stop comparing every experience in D.C. with something I'd lost and left behind in London, but this was my first time in a bar since that night in the Cheshire Cheese with Perry and everyone from IPS.

"Your nose just grew longer," Jack said to me now. "You don't look so fine."

"Sorry. I was thinking about London."

"You really miss it, don't you?"

"I do. I miss everything."

He reached over and squeezed my hand. "It's going to work out, Soph. You and Nick are going to be together again. This is all going to be in the rearview mirror someday and you'll be stronger for coming through it."

I blew out a long breath. "How can you be so sure?"

He pointed to the ceiling. "Connections."

I gave him a weak smile. "I hope you're right."

"I know I'm right," he said. "In the meantime, where's your friend? It's ten to eleven."

"Maybe he got hung up getting out of the Kennedy Center parking lot or the fund-raiser went late." I checked my phone. "Wonder why he didn't send another text?"

"Ask him."

After five minutes with no reply, Jack said, "Maybe you should call him."

But when I did, the phone rang and rang until I got an automated message saying that there was no mailbox set up for that number yet. I tried two more times with the same result.

"That's odd," Jack said. "He's the public relations director for the National Gallery of Art. Those people are accessible twenty-four/seven."

"Maybe he got a new phone today. I wonder if Luke has a different number for him, his work number."

Jack shrugged. "Worth a try."

I clicked on my contacts and found Luke's number.

When he answered, loud music and a swirl of voices blasted through the phone. "Sophie?"

I said to Jack, "I'd better take this outside."

More swiveled heads followed as I left the bar without Jack and moved under the light of a streetlamp. I had to raise my voice to be heard above the din still blaring through the phone.

"Luke, are you at the Goodnight Club?"

"I tole you that's where I was goin'." He was slurring his words. "You comin' over here?"

"What? No, I'm sorry, I can't. Are you okay?"

"I'm jes' havin' a li'l whiskey to remember Ali."

He sounded like he was jes' havin' a whole bottle of whiskey. "You didn't drive there, did you?"

He snorted into the phone. "Hell, no. I'm not stupid. I walked."

"Can you get someone to take you home or get a cab for you?"

"Is that why you called?" He sounded irritated. "To check up on me?"

"No," I said. "But promise me you'll be careful. I called because I was wondering if you have Moses Rattigan's phone number?"

"What for?"

"He sent me a text message a few hours ago and asked me to meet him at a bar on the Hill. I figured it was either about the pictures or maybe he talked to Duval and wanted to hear my side of the story. He's almost half an hour late and I can't reach him on the number he texted me on."

Luke snorted again. "You think I been drinking? How much have you had? When I sent the photo link to Seth and Moses tonight, Seth wrote back and said Moses had a family emergency. He left for New York this afternoon. He'll be back Monday."

My throat went dry.

"Hello . . . hello? You still there?" he said.

"Are you sure about that?" My voice cracked.

"Of course I'm sure." Suddenly he sounded alert and sober. "Are you sure it was Moses who sent that text?"

"Not anymore."

"Sophie," he said. "What the hell's going on?"

"I don't know."

"Call me when you get back to the Roosevelt," he said. "And you're the one who should take a cab, not be driving all over town this time of night on that damn Vespa."

"I'm staying with a friend," I said. "We came in his car. Don't worry, I'll be fine. I'll see you in the morning at Hillwood. I'd better go. Good night, Luke."

Jack took one look at my face as I walked into the bar,

slapped a bill on the counter, and told the bartender good night and to keep the change. He met me before I'd taken half a dozen steps, grabbed my arm, and spun me around. "Let's get out of here," he said. "It wasn't your friend, was it?"

"He's in New York." By now we had the attention of almost everyone in the place. I looked around the room and said in a low voice, "What if whoever sent it is here right now?"

"Don't move." Jack disappeared and circled around the rows of booths at the back of the bar. When he emerged, he caught my eye and shook his head.

"Is there a problem, sir?" the bartender asked.

"We thought a friend might be here and we'd crossed signals finding him," Jack said. "False alarm." To me he said under his breath, "A booth full of Marines and two couples who are more interested in each other than anything going on around them. I don't think he's here . . . whoever he is."

"It's someone who wanted me to come here," I said. "I wonder why?"

"He probably expected you to come alone," Jack said, sounding grim. "Now I'm really glad I insisted on being your date. Let's get out of here."

We walked outside, tense and alert, as a man moved out of the shadows and started weaving toward us. Jack put his arm around me.

"Spare some change, buddy?" A drunk who was unsteady on his feet.

"Sorry, not tonight." Jack hustled me past him. "Get over to the McKenna Center at St. Al's. They can help you there." To me he said, "Come on. The sooner we get to the car, the better. Let's run for it."

His car was where he'd left it, sitting in a column of moonlight at the end of the street. I heard the click of his doors unlocking as he hit the button on his key ring.

"Get in," he said.

"Wait. There's something on the windshield." I pulled an envelope out from under a wiper. Nothing written on it.

Jack started the engine and checked the rearview mirror. "Someone could be watching. Don't read it now. Let's get out of here."

He set his phone to speaker and called Gloria House.

"Everything okay there?" he asked when a deep voice answered.

"Everything's fine. Is there a problem?" the voice said.

"I hope not. See you in two minutes."

We sped down 8th Street through the quiet darkness of residential neighborhoods, occasional yellow squares of lighted windows flashing by us, and turned left on Mass Ave. Jack's eyes kept straying to his mirrors; I watched my side mirror for headlights or even a vehicle without lights moving down the shadowy streets trailing us like a ghost.

"We're not being followed," I said finally.

"Maybe not now," he said, "but someone knew you were at Gloria House and followed us to Bar Humbug. How else would he have known this was my car?"

It was hard to argue with his logic. "How could I have missed someone following me to Gloria House? They would have tailed me all the way across town from the Roosevelt."

"Were you paying attention?"

"I think I would have noticed a car, especially after what happened when I left the National Gallery."

"Have you got your phone's GPS turned on? There are programs that can monitor a person's whereabouts by tracking their phone."

I groaned, got out my phone, and turned it off as Jack made a sharp turn into the parking lot at Gloria House. He punched in numbers on a keypad and the wrought-iron gate opened. He waited until it closed behind us and pulled into an empty space near the back entrance.

"Let's make sure everything's okay in the house," Jack said.

"Why would anyone want to break in here?" I asked.

"I don't know," he said. "But until we know who we're dealing with, I think it's a good idea to make sure no one tried."

We ran quietly up the basement stairs into the foyer. Jack reset the security alarm and made a quick tour of the first-floor rooms and the chapel, turning on lights and checking around. I heard him speaking to someone in the chapel, probably the priest he had phoned.

"I'm going upstairs," I said.

"Wait for me," he called, but I'd already disappeared.

My room was just as I'd left it.

"Everything okay?"

I hadn't heard him come up the stairs behind me. "Jesus Lord, you scared me. Yes, everything's fine."

"Good," he said. "Come on, I need a drink. I'll fix us a couple of brandies and we can see what's in that envelope."

While he got the bottle of brandy, I sat on his sofa and slit open the envelope. Inside was a folded sheet of paper. When I pulled it out, a photograph and a news clipping fell onto the glass coffee table. I looked at the picture first. Taken with a telephoto lens, it was a crowd shot of a bustling commercial district along a lake or river, a busy outdoor café next to a small marina, the bistro tables filled with patrons enjoying a meal or an aperitif at sunset. A male figure in the middle of the crowd caught my attention and I squinted at him. Dark blond uncombed hair, a scruffy beard; he wore faded jeans and a rough-looking leather jacket. The way he stood with his hands jammed in his pockets, the slope of his broad shoulders, the way his straight hair fell across his forehead like it always did when he didn't bother with hair gel: The beard was a surprise and so was the hair color, but it was Nick.

I picked up the article. The typescript had the familiar look of something that had appeared in the *Telegraph*; the dateline was last Sunday. Had whoever sent this to me recently been in London?

VIENNA, 10 September. Austrian police are cooperating with Scotland Yard in light of "new information" concerning the suspicious death of Colin Crowne, principal at Crowne Energy LLC, a British oil exploration and development company most recently involved in an exploratory project in the Abadistan region of Russia. The lifeless body of Mr Crowne, 55, of London, was discovered floating in a section of the Danube River that flows through Vienna—where OPEC headquarters are located—on 12 May. Mr Crowne, who was unable to swim, was originally believed to have fallen into the river

*near a commercial district filled with shops and restaur-
ants, possibly after becoming ill whilst on an early
morning walk. A preliminary investigation had revealed
no physical signs of violence on his body. Two weeks
before Mr Crowne's death, his business associate and
close personal friend Nicholas Canning was reportedly
abducted from his home in Hampstead and remains
missing to this day. Recent reports have surfaced about
a dispute between Mr Canning and Mr Crowne over
business matters prior to Mr Canning's disappearance.*

The folded piece of paper was a grainy photocopy of an
article from the *International Herald Tribune* reporting the
discovery of Colin's body in the Danube back in May. There
was a headshot of him taken from his profile on the company's
website and a photo of the place along the river where a
passerby had seen him and called the police.

Jack sat next to me and handed me a brandy snifter. "What's
all this?"

I stared at the *IHT* photo and the photo of Nick. They were
taken on or around the same spot, a nearly identical view of
the Vienna skyline across the Danube. I turned over the photograph. Someone had written 12/5 in black marker on the back.
In Europe they write dates with the day first: this was May
12, not December 5. Nick had been in Vienna the day Colin
died, just as Baz told me that day in the Abbey.

I took a fiery gulp of my drink and said, "Someone's trying
to frame Nick for Colin's death. Baz told me MI6 is looking
into the possibility that Nick might have killed Colin to get
his hands on the well logs. With Colin out of the way, Nick
would be the only person who knew what was in them and
he knew how valuable they were. That newspaper article says
Nick was 'reportedly' abducted and claims he and Colin were
arguing right before Colin died. Someone's leaking information to the press because they found out Nick's still alive and
they're setting him up for murder."

"Who sent this?" Jack asked. "Why?"

"One of Arkady Vasiliev's acolytes, probably. As to why, I
think he's starting to dial up the pressure. Last night at the

National Gallery, Vasiliev was polite, but he was livid when he left the room because I wouldn't admit Nick was still alive. So first he has someone search my room to make sure I don't have the well logs. Then he delivers these." I gestured to the papers on the coffee table. "Supposedly that photo proves Nick was in Vienna the day Colin died. Vasiliev's trying to scare me, let me know he's watching me so carefully he can pretend to be someone I know, like he did tonight."

"Just because someone wrote a date on the back of a photograph doesn't mean it's correct." Jack picked up Nick's picture and studied it. "I wonder where Vasiliev got this."

"Me, too."

"Do you think Nick has the well logs?"

"I don't know," I said. "But what matters is that Vasiliev believes he has them and he also believes I know where Nick is."

"What are you going to do?"

I looked at my watch. "Call Baz when it's morning in London and ask him about this investigation. He knows people at Scotland Yard."

"You ought to call Napoleon Duval before you talk to Baz or anyone else," Jack said. "I know he's not your favorite person, but he is your contact. The break-in at the Roosevelt today and now this. You need to let him know. I hate to bring this up, but what about Ali? What if what happened to her was a case of mistaken identity and someone thought she was you?"

I shuddered. That thought had crossed my mind, too. "God, I hope not."

"So do I. But it's one more reason you need to call Duval."

"Duval is no fan of Nick's and, to be honest, I don't think he told me everything he knew. I'm not sure how much I can trust him."

"Sophie, do the right thing here, okay? First of all, he's not going to tell you everything because it's in his DNA. But you also know Nick didn't kill Colin. If you don't share all this stuff with Duval, he'll think you've got something to hide. Because eventually it's going to come out."

I stared at the photo of my husband. Jack was right. Better to get out in front of this than have Duval come to me later.

"I'll call him first thing tomorrow morning."

"Good." He finished his brandy and walked me to my door, where he gave me a brotherly good-night kiss. Like Luke had done the night before, he waited until he heard me lock the door to my room. A moment later his quiet footsteps padded across the hall followed by the metallic click of his own door closing.

I lay in bed and wondered if I could fall asleep. The next thing I knew Jack was knocking on my door.

"It's quarter to eight, sleepyhead. I'm back from Mass. Breakfast in my room when you're ready."

I bolted out of bed and showered and changed into the slacks and blouse I'd packed for my photo session at Hillwood. Fifteen minutes later I flew into Jack's suite. A morning news show was turned low on the television and the door to his balcony stood open, letting in a cool, sweet breeze, golden sunshine, and the sound of traffic zooming around Stanton Park.

"Coffee's still hot," he yelled from the bathroom. "And I left you the cinnamon raisin bagel."

I fixed my coffee and toasted the bagel in his toaster oven. He joined me on the balcony while I was finishing breakfast, dressed in his clerical garb, short-sleeved black shirt minus the Roman collar and perfectly creased black trousers. His coffee mug had JESUS LOVES YOU BUT I'M HIS FAVORITE written on it in flowery script.

He saw me staring at it and grinned. "Birthday gift from Gracie. She's made it her life's mission to give me tacky religious gifts and cards."

"She would do something like that."

"I read the morning papers," he said. "There are articles about Ali in both of them. And the story made the local news on Channel 7 . . . I'm sorry, Soph."

We went inside, where he turned up the volume on the television and handed me the papers, each folded to the page with the piece about Ali. Both the *Washington Post* and the *Washington Tribune* used the same photo, a sexy siren picture of her in a hot pink one-shoulder cocktail dress. It looked like a candid snapshot that might have been taken at the Goodnight Club and the caption underneath mentioned that she sang there.

"Here it is on Channel 4," Jack said.

An attractive fresh-faced young anchorwoman read the introduction and cut away to a reporter standing near the 14th Street Bridge. When a different photo of Ali in a more revealing evening dress flashed on the screen, along with the account of her possibly leaving the National Gallery reception in the company of an unidentified stranger, it started to sound like a she-had-it-coming cautionary tale of a pretty young girl who sang in bars for lonely guys and ended up where she did because of loose morals and poor judgment.

"She wasn't like that," I said. "She was cute and fun and flirty, not a Mae West 'come up and see me sometime, boys' sexpot."

The reporter ended the story with a clip of an MPD press spokesman asking for the public's help and for anyone who had any information concerning Ali to come forward.

"I hope they find the bastard who killed her," I said, "and he pays for it."

"Calm down, kiddo. They will." Jack turned off the television and slipped on his Roman collar. "What about that call to Agent Duval?"

"It's a little early."

"Soph. Don't mess around with this after what happened last night. Do it now."

I made a face at him as I pulled out my phone. This time Duval answered.

"I had a long talk with someone about you yesterday," he said by way of a greeting.

"I presume you're speaking about Detective Bolton and I also presume you know who this is."

"The very one, and yes, I do, Ms. Medina."

"I need to talk to you," I said.

"Where are you now?"

"Stanton Park."

"Stanton Park?"

"I'm staying at Gloria House with a friend who teaches at Georgetown Law School."

"Really?" He sounded mildly surprised. "All right, then I would imagine you know St. Al's?"

"Of course."

"How about a little prayer session in, say, half an hour?"

"You mean, in the church? It's closed," I said.

"It is, but you'll be able to get in."

"I'll be there," I said.

"So will I," he said and disconnected.

On our way out to the parking lot, Jack said, "Where are you staying tonight? You can always come back here, you know."

"Thanks," I said, "but after I meet Duval I'm going to look at a furnished place owned by a friend of Grace's mother. If it works out, I might be able to move in and stay there."

"Let me know," he said. "I don't think you should be spending any more nights at the Roosevelt."

He kissed me good-bye and got in his car while I started the Vespa. I followed him down Mass Ave, and at North Capitol Street I turned right and he kept going; the church was a couple of blocks up North Capitol on the left.

Last night while we had been killing time at Bar Humbug, Jack had told me that St. Aloysius Gonzaga Church, which had been around since 1859, had closed its doors just a few months ago when the pastor was transferred and the Jesuits could no longer staff the church full-time. The McKenna Center, which provided food and social services for the poor and homeless, was still open for business, and Gonzaga High School, the elite boys' school next door, still used the church for Mass. But as a functioning parish, St. Al's had ceased to exist.

I parked the Vespa in the alley next to the enormous neoclassical redbrick building and wondered how Duval managed to have a key to the place. The Roman numeral clock in the bell tower showed a few minutes before nine. I climbed the two flights of stairs to the main entrance and tried the front doors. The farthest one on the right was unlocked.

Inside, the church—cream-colored walls with accents of blue and gold leaf, bright blue carpet, and dominated by a painting over the altar of a young St. Aloysius making his first communion—seemed eerily silent and the air felt thick and undisturbed. I saw Duval sitting on the far left in the last pew next to the wall. Automatically I blessed myself and genuflected before sliding in next to him.

He didn't waste any time. "Good morning," he said. "What's on your mind?"

We spoke in hushed voices even though we were alone; habit on my part, maybe on his as well. I told him about the break-in at the Roosevelt and handed him the envelope with the clippings and the photo. After he finished reading the articles and studying the picture, he said, "May I keep these?"

I would have liked the picture, but I said, "Go ahead."

"You don't have any idea who sent you those text messages or left this package on your friend's windshield?"

"Someone who works for Arkady Vasiliev. That's my guess."

Duval leaned back and stretched his legs under the pew in front of us, crossing one foot over the other. Today he wore jeans and a black polo shirt and I wondered if he might be off duty.

"Mr. Vasiliev and his band of merrymakers left town yesterday morning on his private jet. Apparently following the National Gallery reception he threw a hell of an after-party in the presidential suite at a Georgetown hotel that may no longer roll out the welcome mat next time he's in town. He didn't leave a forwarding address, but rumor has it he's in the middle of an ocean somewhere on a boat the size of Bermuda," he said. "My boss won't okay the overtime and the Learjet to fly out there, wherever the hell there is, to talk to him in person and ask him a few questions, so I'm at a bit of an impasse right now."

"Look under a rock. He left at least one merrymaker behind, probably more than one," I said.

"Oh, we're looking," he said. "Don't you fret."

"Was Ali Jones at that party?" I asked.

Duval gave me a startled look. "I don't know. Why would she be there?"

"She dropped hints at the National Gallery reception about trying to meet a rich Russian . . . she could have been joking around, or maybe not. I just wondered if it was possible that she did meet someone who brought her there before they ended up at the river. There's also a chance she bumped into one or both of the men I heard talking in the conference room . . . we're not the same age, but even Ali said we could be mistaken for cousins."

Duval was watching me closely and seemed to be making some rapid mental calculations. "I'll check into that. Unfortunately, Mr. Vasiliev didn't have a formal guest list for that little shindig."

"Since we're discussing Mr. Vasiliev and his friends," I said, "you are looking into whether the Russian I overheard planning that assassination works for him, aren't you?"

Duval gave me a reproachful look. "I can't possibly comment on that. You know better."

"But surely you're at least taking it seriously that there'll be an attempt on Taras Attar's life when he's in Washington next week?"

Duval shifted in the pew, leaning his back against the wall so he faced me. "It is a known fact that there have been threats against Dr. Attar's life, particularly from factions of the Russian mafia, and that some of that pond scum has floated across the Atlantic to our fair shores. When Taras Attar is in my town, he'll be extremely well looked after, believe you me. That's all I'm prepared to say."

"What about Scott Hathaway?" I said.

He pursed his lips and shook his head. "Nice try. No comment."

I stood up. "Don't let me take up any more of your time, Agent Duval. Thanks for the chat. I'm glad I got to see St. Al's again one more time."

"Sit down."

I glared at him, but I sat.

"Let's get something straight," he said. "I run this rodeo, understand?"

He waited until I said, "Yes."

"Excellent. Now what I'm dealing with at the moment feels a lot like sand. You ever pick up sand when you're at the beach and try to hold it in your hands? It slides right through your fingers. So here's what I got so far: I got you, I got Arkady

Vasiliev, I got your husband, and I somehow got Taras Attar because of you." He ticked us all off on his fingers and wiggled them. "And I got more questions than answers trying to figure out the way you all intersect, because I believe you do. Here's what I am prepared to tell you. If Arkady Vasiliev had someone search your room, the good news for you is he now knows you don't have the documents he wants. But here's what he does want, and so do you, and so do I: your husband."

"I don't know where Nick is. You know that."

"Well, here's the other piece of news I'll share with you," he said in a conversational tone. "Apparently Nicholas Canning is no longer in Russia. So if you hear from him—I don't care if it's e-mail, airmail, voice mail, or blackmail—I'd better be the next phone call you make. Do I make myself clear?"

I was stunned. "Where is he?"

"No idea," he said. "Like I said yesterday, he can't stay on the run forever. Sooner or later, he needs to find a safe harbor. And you, Ms. Medina, are still top of my list for where he'd go. So let me repeat: If you hear from him, I hear from you."

I'd had enough of him talking to me like a kid who needed to be disciplined.

"And then what?" I said.

"Pardon?"

"What happens next?"

"He's a CIA operative who faked his own kidnapping and has been missing for nearly four months. We want to ask him about the weather in Abadistan this time of year." He glared at me. "What do you think happens next?"

"That's what I'm asking. Nick's people in London told me I couldn't even tell his sister or my own family that he had been seen in Moscow. So how did Arkady Vasiliev find out? And who got Scotland Yard to reopen the investigation into Colin's death? The only people who know Nick is alive work for the CIA and MI6." Duval was staring at me like he was about to spontaneously combust he was so mad, but I kept going. "I don't work for you, Agent Duval. Go ahead and run your rodeo. I don't have to ride in it unless you give me your word that you're going to help Nick, that you're on his side."

Duval shook a warning finger at me. "Ms. Medina, it is not

wise to underestimate me. You do not call the shots here. Believe me, if your husband comes within a ten-mile radius of you, I'm going to know because I'm going to have you watched like a hawk."

I stood up. "Get in line. So is Arkady Vasiliev. You can keep each other company."

FOURTEEN

t took the entire trip across town to India Ferrer's house before I calmed down after that spitting match with Napoleon Duval. If anyone was tailing me as I drove down Florida Avenue to the U Street Corridor, I didn't see him, no car darting in and out of traffic behind me. Even if I was being followed now, so what? I had nothing to hide and everyone knew it. Nor had I been joking about Duval's people and Vasiliev's people tripping over each other—I hoped they did.

I turned off New Hampshire Avenue onto the seventeen hundred block of S Street, Northwest, the pretty tree-lined street of Federal and Victorian row houses where India Ferrer lived. Wrought-iron fences enclosed postage-stamp-size front yards filled with bright splotches of pansies, geraniums, impatiens, and crape myrtle mixed in with the mottled greens of ferns, hostas, and lavender. The trees on either side of the street towered above the houses and grew toward each other in a graceful shade-dappled canopy. India's homes, identical romantic-looking Queen Anne gingerbreads, had stained-glass bay windows, balconies, loads of embellished brickwork, and towers with a witch's hat pointed roof.

My home in London had once been the gardener's cottage of the aptly named Marlborough Gardens, a private gated community of stately mansions lining a circular drive on the edge of Hampstead Heath. The houses surrounded a pretty green of gnarled trees, a gravel path lined with weathered benches, and beds of endless varieties of flowering plants. Something bloomed whatever the season in an exuberant but organized splendor that was quintessentially English; the green itself was never anything but emerald colored and lush as a golf course. I had taken hundreds of photos of that garden over the years, turning my pictures into a coffee table book for the local horticulture society to sell as a fund-raiser. I did not expect to find anything like my beloved English home with its idyllic setting here in Washington, but the peaceful serenity of this street reminded me of London and suddenly I desperately hoped India Ferrer would find me a suitable tenant.

I knocked using a lion's head door knocker and a moment later there were footsteps like a child lightly running. A petite, elfish woman with unnaturally red hair opened the door. India Ferrer wore a flowing amethyst caftan, silver and turquoise jewelry that looked Native American, and the unmistakable scent of Chanel No. 5. She could have been sixty-five or eighty-five. She looked me over with the practiced eye of a livestock judge at the county fair and invited me in.

I had pictured rooms stuffed with furniture; tables and shelves filled with bric-a-brac in keeping with the fussiness and ornamentation of the Queen Anne exterior. But other than the dark, elaborately detailed woodwork, India's book- and art-filled home with its walls painted warm, sunny colors was simply furnished and elegant. She led me into a celadon-and-saffron living room dominated by a painting of a nude hanging above a fireplace. Lighted votive candles sat on a stack of logs on the hearth and Celtic music played through iPod speakers on top of a bookcase.

We sat in her sunny bay window in toile-covered chairs pulled up around a table set for tea for two.

"Would you care for some tea, dear?" she asked.

I nodded. "Yes, thank you. Is that you in the painting?"

India flashed a roguish smile. "Why, yes, it is. It was my birthday present to my husband when we lived in Casablanca many years ago."

India Ferrer seemed like someone I would have liked to be friends with if I'd known her in Morocco. "What a fantastic gift."

"My husband thought so, too." She laughed as she passed me a cup and saucer.

English bone china so delicate I could see through it. I sipped the tea. "Jasmine. It's lovely."

India sat back and touched a finger to her lips. "I think you'll do nicely," she said after a moment. "The apartment's yours if you want it."

"Just like that?" I set down my teacup.

"I've always made decisions based on first impressions and instinct, and usually I never regret them," she said. "I believe Grace told you I was looking for someone who would love the place as much as Max and I do. You seem to be a person who cares about her home; I saw how you noticed my music, my books, the jasmine tea. And the painting, of course." She walked across the room and picked up a book on the coffee table.

"And you did this." She passed it to me. "It's stunning."

The Beauty of Marlborough Gardens by Sophie Medina. I stared at the dust jacket, a favorite photo of blooming wisteria winding through a pergola, and said in amazement, "Where on earth did you get it?"

"A British friend found it in a bookshop near Sloane Square during the Chelsea Flower Show." She took a silver filigree pen out of a small vase stuffed with pens, paintbrushes, and a peacock feather. "Would you sign it?"

"Of course," I said. "And I accept your offer."

"Without even seeing the apartment?"

"I make a lot of decisions based on first impressions and instinct, too."

India smiled. "In that case, how about a tour of your new home?"

She took a set of keys from a red-and-white Chinese ginger jar in the foyer and we went next door. Inside the front door was a small black-and-white-tiled vestibule with two entrances. My door was on the right. We climbed a narrow flight of stairs to the second floor. Maximillian Katzer, the antiques dealer, had the ground floor and the first floor, which included the original living room, dining room, and lower-level kitchen. The enclosed Japanese garden at the back of the house was also his.

My apartment, on the second and third floors, had been remodeled to add a modern galley kitchen with a walk-in pantry and a small laundry area. I also had the library, an enormous sunny space with a reading alcove, carved millwork bookcases, and a working fireplace. Best of all, I had the third floor tower, which I knew would be my bedroom, and a large south-facing balcony that ran along the back of the house.

"It comes furnished, as you know." India opened the sliding door and we stepped onto the balcony. "Grace mentioned that would suit you."

"It does," I said. "I didn't ship much furniture back from England."

"If there's anything you don't want, I can have Max move it to the carriage house." She pointed to a small dull-red doll-house of a building across the alley.

"That's yours?" I said.

She nodded. "Max rents half of it. He keeps furniture that needs repairing there until it's ready to be moved to his Georgetown gallery. The other half belongs to Niles."

"Someone else lives here, too?"

India laughed. "Niles is my car. Or rather, he was my husband's car. Do you drive, Sophie?"

"Yes," I said. "For now, just a Vespa."

"You're welcome to use Niles anytime you like," she said. "If he doesn't get driven regularly, I'm afraid his oil will thicken and his valves won't work properly. Max used to take him out before he started traveling all the time."

"Are you sure you want to loan me your car?"

"You would be doing me a favor," she said. "We'll stop by Max's and get the keys. Surely you weren't planning to use a Vespa to move your things here? You can try him out."

We went downstairs to the little vestibule and India said, "Max leaves an extra key above his front door. I wish he wouldn't, but he insists it's perfectly safe. Could you reach it?"

I found the key where India said it would be and she unlocked the door to Max's apartment. The car key was in a bowl on an altar table next to a set of antique brass wind chimes. A current of air set the chimes off and the sound made me think of mist-covered mountains and Buddhist monks filing silently into a temple.

"Here." India put a silver key chain into my hand. "The key to the carriage house and Niles's key. Keep them. Now, why don't we sign some papers and you'll be all set?"

"All set as in, I can move in?"

"Whenever you like."

"Would today be all right?"

She nodded. "Of course. As I said, use Niles."

"What kind of car is Niles? I mean, I can drive stick, if it . . . if he's not automatic."

Her smile was teasing. "What were you expecting?"

Either Niles was a baby blue convertible ocean liner with fins that belonged in a 1950s drive-in or something Henry Ford would recognize.

I decided to play it safe. "A Cadillac? A Mercedes?"

"A 2003 Jaguar S-type sport sedan with a 4.2-liter V-8 engine. British Racing Green." She laughed as my mouth dropped open. "You two will have such fun."

I left India after signing the lease and promising I'd return for Niles when I finished work for the day. Then I took the Vespa through Rock Creek Park to Hillwood, eventually turning onto a potholey street that led to a gated entrance. A security guard with a Russian accent gave me directions to the Visitor Center parking lot, where fluttering banners proclaimed HILLWOOD, WHERE FABULOUS LIVES. I parked next to Luke's Jeep, got my backpack, and went inside. A woman at the front desk gave me a bright blue "Fabulous" pin to clip to my blouse while I was on the grounds and told me the fastest way to the mansion was the spiral staircase or the elevator to the second floor, which would lead me to an outdoor upper-level terrace. The house was just across the Motor Court.

A collection of black-and-white photographs documenting Hillwood's history lined the wall by the staircase and I stopped to take a look. Sure enough, next to a *Life* magazine photo taken by Alfred Eisenstaedt of one of Marjorie Merriweather Post's many garden parties on the sweeping crescent-shaped front lawn she called the lunar lawn, was a picture taken by my grandfather. Marjorie sat at her opulent dining room table, radiant and laughing, surrounded by tux-edoed men and women in evening gowns, as candlelight and the light from two crystal chandeliers sparkled on her collection of Sèvres china and her gilded lifestyle.

I blew Granddaddy's photo a kiss and ran up the steps to the terrace, where red and white impatiens burst out of hanging baskets and overflowed the border gardens. Across the courtyard was the circular Motor Court, where limousines once pulled up to drop off the rich and famous in front of a large redbrick mansion. A guard in a navy blue uniform opened one of the front doors and told me the lecture would take place in the first-floor pavilion. Entering the two-story entrance hall, I felt as if I'd stepped into old Russia. A massive portrait of Catherine the Great dominated the room above a sweeping staircase and, wherever I looked, portraits of Russia's czars and czarinas covered the walls. Straight ahead was the dining room where my grandfather had not only taken the photo I saw in the Visitor Center but also dined as a guest and friend.

Another guard told me I'd find the pavilion at the end of a corridor off the Russian Porcelain Room, which was easy to find because of the intricate Romanov double-headed eagle inlaid in the floor.

I stopped to study the eagle and Luke's voice said, "Sophie?"

He was in the next room standing in front of a glass case that sat on a malachite table. The sign by the doorway said ICON ROOM. Even in the dim light I could see that he was puffy eyed and hungover. I joined him and he gave me a weak smile.

The case contained Marjorie Merriweather Post's two Fabergé imperial eggs: the midnight blue Twelve Monograms egg and the pink and white Catherine the Great egg, gifts from Nicholas II to his mother.

"Rough night last night?" I said. "How are you doing?"

Luke gave me a weary look. "The inside of my head is an awful place to be right now."

"Poor you. Have you tried drinking lots of water? It'll help."

"Believe me, I've drunk enough to float whatever's left of my liver. Did we have a phone conversation in a bar last night, except we were in different bars?"

"We did."

"Could you refresh my memory of what we talked about?"

Thank God he didn't remember. "Why don't we have that

discussion later? We probably should head down to the pavilion and get set up before Katya Gordon arrives," I said. "She ought to be here any minute."

He picked up his backpack. "I've already checked everything out. There's a second-floor balcony at the back of the pavilion. I'll hang out there for overhead photos; you stay downstairs for close-ups. Anyway, we'll get most of our shots at the luncheon and in the gardens afterward."

The balcony, where he could lay low and nurse his hangover. "Don't fall asleep up there," I said.

"Very funny," he said. "I need to hit the head—again—and then I'm going upstairs. See you in the garden when it's over."

I took a quick look at the Fabergé eggs. The Twelve Monograms egg had been the first Easter egg Maria Feodorovna received from her son, in 1895, after the death of Alexander III. He gave her the Catherine the Great egg in 1914, four years before he was assassinated in Yekaterinburg. As Seth MacDonald had said, each of the imperial eggs had its own story of glory and tragedy.

The blue corridor that led to the pavilion was lined with displays of jade figurines. The pavilion itself had been added on to Hillwood because Marjorie Merriweather Post loved a good party and wanted a dedicated room for after-dinner entertaining. Decorated in shades of eggplant, mauve, and silver, it could be turned into a small movie theater but also transformed into a dance floor for her beloved square dances. Two enormous oil paintings—a boyar wedding and a graceful-looking Russian countess—dominated the two long walls. Photographs of Nicholas and Alexandra and their children sat on a grand piano in front of a bay window that looked out on the garden. Luke's balcony at the far end of the room was where the staff discreetly watched the first-run films Marjorie enjoyed showing. I looked up and saw him moving around. He caught sight of me and waved.

Today the room was set up for Katya Gordon's talk: rows of chairs upholstered in mauve velvet that were beginning to fill up and a podium placed in front of the piano. I found a stout white-haired woman dressed in a bright yellow pantsuit who appeared to be in charge and asked her if the balloon shades could be lowered so Katya Gordon wouldn't be backlit by harsh noonday light.

She said her name was Elizabeth Quick and left to take care of my request. Behind me a cool voice said, "Good morning, Ms. Medina."

Katya Gordon stood there, wearing a sleeveless teal dress with a heavily beaded neckline, her ash-blond hair pulled back in a ponytail. Her lipstick was a slash of bright red and her eye makeup matched her dress. I hadn't heard her come in, nor did I expect her to remember my name.

"Good morning, Dr. Gordon."

"I'd like to have a word with you," she said. "In private." She broke off as Elizabeth Quick joined us.

"Your lighting problem is taken care of, Sophie," Elizabeth said. "And, Katya, I'm glad you're here, dear. I heard your talk in Richmond yesterday was wonderful."

Katya smiled. "Thank you. They had a very good turnout."

Elizabeth noticed my puzzled look. "Dr. Gordon visited the Virginia Museum of Fine Arts yesterday. Many people don't realize it has the largest collection of Fabergé imperial eggs outside Russia."

"I guess I'm one of them," I said. "I didn't know that."

"You must see it sometime. It's a wonderful museum." Elizabeth glanced at her watch. "And now, Katya, we need to do a quick level check of your microphone since we're recording your talk. Would you come with me, please?"

"I'll be right there." Katya leaned close to me. I smelled cigarettes and mints on her breath and the distinct jasmine scent of her perfume. "You and I will talk later."

She left before I could reply. But from her ominous undertone, I knew this wasn't about the photos from the National Gallery reception.

At noon, Elizabeth stepped up to the podium to introduce Katya to the overcrowded room. She repeated much of the biography Seth MacDonald had mentioned the other night, with one interesting footnote.

"Though this is the first time Dr. Gordon has lectured at Hillwood, she is no stranger to this beautiful museum and estate," Elizabeth said. "Many years ago she worked here as a Visitor Center volunteer. Forgive me a bit of indulgence in hoping that experience influenced her decision to continue her studies, becoming one of our foremost scholars on Russian imperial art."

Katya thanked Elizabeth and took her place at the podium to enthusiastic applause. Her talk was more detailed than the one she'd given at the National Gallery and, I had to admit, she was spellbinding as she recounted stories of how Fabergé had racked his brain year after year to come up with ideas for ever more fabulous Easter eggs that would delight first one, then two, empresses.

"I often compare him to Scheherazade, since they both had to use their wits to please and enchant royalty—Scheherazade spinning her nightly stories and Fabergé creating his exquisite concoctions each year. Though I will say that no one ever threatened to behead Carl Fabergé," Katya said, as everyone laughed. "And finally, I'd like to conclude my talk with some news. You all are the first to know that there's been an exciting development concerning the Blue Tsarevich Constellation egg."

Elizabeth Quick clapped her hands and said, "How wonderful. Please, don't keep us in suspense."

Katya gave a rueful smile. "Unfortunately, that's as much as I'm allowed to tell you." She held up a hand, acknowledging the roomful of groans. "I know . . . I apologize. But I promise you, we'll be holding a press conference as soon as a few details have been finalized. In the meantime, if you check the Vasiliev Collection website, we'll give as much notice as possible about the announcement. Thank you all very much and I look forward to speaking with you during lunch in the gardens."

I caught up with Luke outside in a formal knot garden of scrolled boxwood, whimsical statuary, a glass-tiled pool, and ivy-covered walls. Buffet tables had been set up around the corner under the columned portico of the mansion's front entrance, and guests could sit in Marjorie's lawn chairs under blue-and-white umbrellas with views overlooking the lunar lawn and Rock Creek Park beyond. After lunch, everyone was free to explore the acres of gardens for as long as they liked, though the event officially ended at one thirty.

"I'll stay with Katya," Luke said. "You want to do the detail shots again and get candids of some of the guests?"

He looked like he was finally starting to feel human.

"Sure," I said. "I'll take the gardens. A lot of people brought their lunches over to the Rose Garden. It's lovely there."

It was one of Marjorie Merriweather Post's favorite places, still fragrant with the last of the summer roses, a peaceful setting of Zen-like tranquillity. Katya Gordon found me there standing in front of a pink granite monument surrounded by summer begonias and sweet-smelling alyssum where Marjorie's ashes were interred in an urn.

"Let's take a walk," she said.

"Lead the way."

"I know who you are," she said, as we walked under a wisteria-draped pergola. "I know Arkady spoke to you the other night about your husband and some valuable documents in his possession. Arkady will pay any price to have those papers. I hope you understand how important they are to him."

We left the pergola and began to make a slow loop past brilliantly colored rosebushes, each one in a different bed in the circular garden.

"Why is this of any concern to you?" I asked.

Two tiger swallowtail butterflies chased each other, landing on a white Margaret Merrill rosebush. Somewhere in the distance, above the swan song of the summer cicadas, was the gentle beating sound of a helicopter.

Katya gave me an astonished look. "I beg your pardon?"

"Did Mr. Vasiliev ask you to talk to me, Dr. Gordon?" I said. "Because if he did, you can tell him this: I still don't know if my husband's even alive, I still don't know where those documents are, and breaking and entering is a crime in America."

She looked stunned. "What are you saying?"

"Someone searched my apartment yesterday," I said. "I assume he worked for Mr. Vasiliev."

"I know nothing about that." She sounded shocked and I almost believed her.

"Then why are we having this conversation?" I said as we

resumed our stroll. "Why are you getting involved in his business?"

"Because of my daughter," she said. "Why else?"

"Surely she's old enough not to need you to run interference for her."

"Do you have children?" she asked.

"No." Nick and I had tried desperately, but it didn't work out. It was one of the heartbreaks of our marriage, but that was none of Katya's business.

"Then you couldn't possibly understand a mother's wish to help her child," she said, and her words wounded. "Lara is my only daughter. Arkady is ambitious, but he is also generous. He has built schools and hospitals, funded scholarships for young artists and musicians, quietly helped many people who needed it. Together he and Lara can do much good; already they are a powerful and influential couple. It would not surprise me if one day Arkady became president of Russia."

If only he didn't have those pesky ties to the Russian mafia and a reputation for ruthlessness and over-the-top extravagance, he'd probably be eligible for sainthood someday, too. "What does that have to do with Nick?"

"Those papers," she said, "are important to Russian interests."

"They're also important to Mr. Vasiliev's business interests," I said. "Let's not confuse greed with altruism."

It wasn't smart to bait her like that, but Nick was gone, Colin was dead, and the Shaika had destroyed whatever was left of Crowne Energy's operations in Abadistan. She could tell me black was white all she wanted. It didn't make it true.

"How dare you?" Her voice rose in anger. "You have no idea what life is like in my country, how things work there, and how business is done. Arkady wants what is best for Russia. That's all there is to it."

"I can't help you and I can't help Mr. Vasiliev." We had come full circle back to the granite monument. Marjorie Merriweather Post's family coat of arms was engraved in the pink stone, along with an inscription. "Do you read Latin, Dr. Gordon?"

She looked at the words. *"In me mea spes omnis.* All my hopes rest in me."

The motto of a strong, self-sufficient woman who could take care of herself, handle anything that life threw at her.

"Tell Mr. Vasiliev from me that I'm not scared of him," I said. "Tell him that he'd better leave me alone. I think we're done here."

FIFTEEN

I caught sight of Elizabeth Quick's bright yellow pantsuit like a flash of sunshine through the dark green shrubbery, as she climbed the winding stairs from the French knot garden on the lower level to where Katya and I still stood in the middle of the Rose Garden.

"I've been looking for both of you," she said. If she'd picked up on the tension that still hung in the air, she chose to overlook it. "Katya, we have a volunteer standing by to drive you back to your hotel whenever you're ready. And, Sophie, Luke's gone back to the mansion to have another look around. One of the security guards moved your equipment cases to the kitchen for safekeeping and they're locked up. I have the key."

Katya flashed one last warning look in my direction and turned to Elizabeth. "Thank you, Elizabeth, but if you don't mind, I'd rather be driven to the National Gallery. I have a meeting there at two thirty."

"Of course," Elizabeth said. "Your driver will take you wherever you like."

"Luke and I should be leaving, too," I said. "I'll find him and we'll get our gear."

We followed Elizabeth single-file down the narrow stair-case through an ivy-covered archway that led to the knot garden. Over her shoulder Elizabeth said, "Luke told me your grandfather is Charles Lord, Sophie. You do know we have one of his photographs on the wall in the Visitor Center?"

"Yes," I said. "Granddaddy used to tell me stories about Mrs. Post's parties. He loved coming here and he was very fond of her."

"Charles Lord is your grandfather?" Katya stopped walking and swung around so abruptly that we nearly collided. "My late husband gave me one of his photographs of Red Square in the 1950s. It's hanging in my office."

"Your photograph is probably worth a good deal of money," I said. "When Edward Steichen put together his *Family of Man* exhibit at MoMA in 1955, he chose another of my grandfather's Moscow photos for that exhibition—an old woman sweeping leaves with a twig broom in a park by the Moscow River. My grandfather took that picture and the one you have during a trip to the Soviet Union in 1953 just after Joseph Stalin died."

"I grew up near that park," Katya said. "I know it well."

"Granddaddy gave me his original contact sheets of the photos from that trip as a college graduation present," I said. "He took some incredible pictures."

Her voice was soft. "I would love to see them. Those photographs should be turned into a book. Charles Lord really captured the Russian soul, the *dushá*."

The Russian soul. Nick always talked about the *dushá* as though it were something you could see in an X-ray, as real as a beating heart or lungs breathing in and out. Russians believed the soul was inextricably bound up with one's character and that it was the essence of Russianness; it had been written about in their literature by no less than Dostoyevsky, Gogol, and Tolstoy. To know the Russian soul was the key to understanding how a people could endure so much suffering and despair over centuries of history—much of the cruelty self-inflicted—yet nevertheless possess great resilience, compassion, and inner strength. To me the concept was something poetically mystifying—like trying to figure out the geographic location of heaven when I was a kid—but it explained perfectly how Katya Gordon could treat me with icy anger one minute and now be nearly misty-eyed with tenderness and memory.

I said, knowing she would understand the subtext of my words, "Perhaps we can work out a mutually suitable arrangement sometime."

Her chin came up and the chilliness returned. "Yes, perhaps."

A young woman in a white blouse and navy skirt and holding a set of car keys appeared from the house: Katya's driver. Elizabeth and Katya exchanged kisses while I got a brief nod—I was still the hired help, after all—and she left.

"Did I miss something?" Elizabeth asked in a bland voice.

I grinned as she gave me a shrewd look. "You didn't miss a thing. Did you know her when she worked at Hillwood?"

Elizabeth waved a hand. "Oh, goodness, no. I've only been here ten years. She was here long before that. As I understand, Katya was one of the first interns to come to Hillwood from Georgetown's art and museum studies program. Everyone else was clamoring to work at the Smithsonian or Sotheby's . . . she chose us."

"Katya Gordon went to Georgetown?" I said. "When?"

"I couldn't say," she said. "But Hillwood first opened to the public in 1977 and we started our internship program a few years later in the early 1980s."

"So maybe thirty years ago?"

Elizabeth frowned like she was doing mental math. "That sounds about right."

Was that how Katya knew Scott Hathaway? They were old school friends?

"Come," Elizabeth said, "let's find Luke."

He was in the kitchen finishing up a conversation on his mobile.

"That was Roxanne Hathaway," he said to me after he hung up. "She'd like to talk to us about a project she's working on and asked if we could drop by her house."

"Now?" I said.

"Now. The Hathaways live in Georgetown. It's on the way back to the studio."

We said good-bye to Elizabeth Quick and walked back to the Visitor Center.

Halfway across the Motor Court Luke stopped and said, "Can I ask you something?"

"Sure." Behind him, a winged statue of the Greek god Eros pulling an arrow from his quiver was backlit by the afternoon sun.

"Yesterday before you left the studio you made a comment about 'another' conversation at the National Gallery. At first I thought I misheard, but then I started wondering if it had something to do with why you called me at the bar last night and asked for Moses's phone number," he said.

His alcohol-fogged powers of recall had returned and he'd caught my careless slip-up after all. "To answer your question," I said, "no."

"No, what?"

"No, asking for Moses's phone number didn't have anything to do with another conversation at the National Gallery."

"Okay," he said, in a patient voice. "And what other conversation would that be?"

"Arkady Vasiliev asked to meet me in Seth's conference room to talk about something."

Luke folded his arms across his chest. "I have an idea. Why don't you just tell me the whole story and that way I won't have to ask 'and then what?' after every sentence. It'll save a lot of time."

"Okay." I held up my hands. "Okay."

"Good," he said. "I'm waiting."

"Arkady Vasiliev wants to buy some highly confidential documents that belonged to Crowne Energy, my husband's former employer," I said. "They're well logs, data from a test well Nick and Colin Crowne drilled in Abadistan, and now they're missing. I told Vasiliev I have no idea where they are."

"That's it?"

That was it as far as what he needed to know, and according to St. Augustine—as Jack reminded me last night—even though we should always tell the truth no matter what, silence was okay when the outcome would result in more harm than good. It was a loftier version of Nick's conviction that you just stopped talking when you got to the end of what you were allowed to say.

But there was one other matter I couldn't keep from him.

"Not entirely," I said. "Luke, Ali was in the next room, in Seth's office. She overheard our conversation."

"God, Sophie," he said. "Are you serious? Do you think it has anything to do with why she was killed?"

"I don't know. Vasiliev didn't know she was there and I told her not to breathe a word to anyone. But those guys don't fool around. Nick used to talk about the lawlessness and corruption he dealt with every day . . . stuff that would take your breath away. He always said you can't buy an Abadi, but you can rent one."

"What is that supposed to mean?"

"It means that you can get someone to do just about anything you want in that part of the world, however unconscionable, for the right amount of money. But you can never buy his loyalty, or win it, and you never own his trust. Double-crossing is a way of life. They just move on to the next golden opportunity," I said. "I told both Duval and Bolton all of this. They know everything."

"You didn't tell me."

"I told you," I said, "about the 'other' other conversation I overheard, remember? And we agreed that I was going to be the one to report it. Except that's not what happened. Someone jumped the gun."

"That's unfair," he said. "You know it was unintentional, an accident."

"Yes, you told me," I said. "Look, we can't change what happened to Ali. The D.C. police and God knows who else are looking into her death. Maybe it had nothing to do with either of those conversations."

"Coming back to when you called me last night because you thought Moses sent you a text," he said. "If it wasn't Moses, who was it?"

"Someone trying to intimidate me. It didn't work. I can't give Vasiliev something I don't have." I shrugged. "Duval's on top of this. Don't worry."

"Sophie—"

"Come on. You said Roxanne Hathaway was waiting for us. We should go."

He gave me a long, hard look. "All right," he said. "Let's go."

Roxanne and Scott Hathaway lived a few blocks behind Georgetown University on a one-way street of Tudor Revival homes built in the late nineteenth and early twentieth centuries. One side of the street backed up against Glover-Archbold Park, a narrow, sinuous strip of land named for a banking executive and an oil heiress who donated the land to the city, and ran from Tenleytown near American University to the Potomac

River, just past Canal Road in Georgetown. The Hathaways' home sat on a hill overlooking the heavily wooded park, which followed the course of a Potomac tributary called Foundry Branch and was the location of one of Washington's less-well-known nature trails.

The wrought-iron gate to the Hathaways' driveway swung open after Luke buzzed the intercom and said we were expected. A bronze plaque embedded in a brick pillar next to the gate said LINDEN HILL, EST. 1889. We followed the winding drive lined with ancient stately-looking trees that gave the house its name and parked the Jeep and Vespa in a cobblestone courtyard next to a van with the name of an upscale party-planning company stenciled on it. The sprawling Tudor house was surrounded by magnolias, dogwood, and flowering cherry trees and reminded me of the mansions at Marlborough Gardens.

"This place is gorgeous," I said to Luke. "It almost gives Hillwood a run for the money."

"It doesn't have twenty-five acres, but it does have a national park for a backyard and the house is listed on the National Register of Historic Buildings," he said.

"How do you know?" I asked.

"A friend of mine works downtown at their archives. She recommends me for photo shoots when a new building around here gets listed," he said.

Luke seemed to have a tentacle-like network of friends who connected him to plum jobs.

"Have you ever photographed this place?" I asked.

"Nope. But I do know that Lord Somebody or other, who was related to the first British governor of Hong Kong, built it and never moved in. By the time Roxanne Hathaway's mother bought it after she divorced her husband, it was a run-down shell from the slum years when Georgetown went downhill after World War I. She restored it and Roxanne inherited it after her mother died. She's turning it green."

I squinted at the house. "Green?"

"Green as in sustainable living and leaving as small a carbon footprint as possible. Geothermal heat and solar hot water. That green."

"Oh." We climbed the stone steps to the front door and Luke rang the bell.

"Wonder what she wants from us," he said.

"We're about to find out," I said. "Someone's coming to the door."

A Hispanic maid in a dark skirt and white blouse let us into a large art-filled foyer with a long central hallway and a wide staircase on the right-hand wall. A grandfather clock at the top of the stairs chimed on the half hour. From somewhere in the house came the quiet sound of bubbling water, like a small fountain, and the air held the faint smell of lavender.

"The señora is expecting you in her study," the maid said. "It's the second door down the corridor on your left."

"Was that Picasso an original?" Luke asked under his breath as we walked down the hall.

"I think so. Next to the original van Gogh."

Roxanne Hathaway looked up from a Mac laptop on her antique carved desk as Luke and I entered the study. The room was cheerful and feminine: furniture covered in William Morris prints, more original art and antiques, a pair of fiddle-leaf figs in Japanese urns on either side of a blue-and-white-tiled fireplace, and everywhere, silver-framed photos of her husband, three children, and, I guessed, the extended Hathaway and Lane families. A set of French doors stood open, letting in a breeze that smelled of late-summer sunshine and flowers, and the buzzing sound of workers who appeared to be finishing erecting an enormous tent in the backyard.

This was probably why she'd called us: more party pictures.

Roxanne got up and shook our hands. Today she wore her red hair loose, keeping it off her face with a pair of horn-rimmed glasses perched on top of her head. She was casually dressed in ivory silk cropped pants, a tangerine-colored knit top, and tangerine-and-ivory ballet flats. Last night she had seemed cool and standoffish as one of the heiresses of Lane Communications, but here at home she looked relaxed and at ease.

"Thanks for coming by," she said. "Normally I'd suggest we sit on the terrace, but it's rather noisy just now." She gestured to a sofa and two wing chairs pulled around the fireplace. "Won't you have a seat? Can I offer you something to drink? Maria just made herbal sun tea and there's honey from our own bees."

"Sun tea sounds great," Luke said, and I added, "So does the honey."

We took the sofa; Roxanne sat across from us in one of the chairs, kicked off her shoes, and tucked her feet up on the seat.

Maria returned with our tea.

"Looks like you're planning quite a party," Luke said.

Roxanne nodded. "As a matter of fact, it's related to why I asked you to come by. I'm hosting a fund-raiser for the Save the Potomac Foundation tomorrow night." She leaned forward, her hands clasped together. "And before I go on, I'd like to express my condolences about that young girl who worked with you. I saw on the news that her body was found in the river. Seth filled me in on the rest of it. It's dreadful, simply dreadful."

"Thank you, Mrs. Hathaway." Luke balanced his cup and saucer on his knee and it wobbled slightly at the mention of Ali. "That's very kind of you."

"Please call me Roxanne, both of you."

We nodded and she went on. "Let me get right to the reason I invited you here. Two months ago I was asked to take over as chair of the Save the Potomac Foundation, to get things kicked into high gear. I don't know if you are aware that the Potomac has been designated the nation's most endangered river, which I consider a tragedy, if not a national disgrace. Though it stretches nearly four hundred miles from West Virginia to the Chesapeake Bay, I've decided to begin by focusing on the section that flows through Washington, beginning at Great Falls and ending at Mount Vernon. It's a project people can relate to because the river is so inextricably tied to the nation's capital and to the history of our country, as far back as the Founding Fathers."

"You obviously have more in mind than getting folks out with trash bags and gloves to pick up the junk that's accumulated on the riverbanks," Luke said.

Roxanne gave him a sly smile. "Oh, it's much more than that. I'm talking about stopping agricultural and commercial runoff, dealing with polluted rainwater, dead zones for marine life, fish changing sex, larger environmental issues. I'm not under any illusions, Luke. I was asked to take over this project because all I have to do is scroll through the contacts on my phone and make a few calls and big money will start flowing in—at least for a start. I also have an entrée on the Hill to members of the House and Senate who are personal friends, and I can have an impact on getting them to consider tougher environmental laws. The fund-raiser is merely a fun party to make a splash and get us noticed."

"And you'd like us to take photos at the party like we did at the National Gallery?" I asked.

Roxanne shook her head. "Our press coverage is all taken care of," she said. "What I want from you two are photographs of the river. I was impressed by your attention to detail the other night and I did some research on both of you. My staff is already combing archives, working with the Library of Congress to find historical photos and records. I'd like you to take the 'now' pictures to juxtapose with the 'then' photos, but feel free to get a bit creative as you did with the National Gallery photos. We're completely redoing the STP website and we plan to relaunch the public campaign once we get your pictures." She held out her hands palms up. "Interested?"

Luke glanced at me and I nodded.

"Definitely," he said. "Just a suggestion, though: The Potomac has a lot of tributaries that are also polluted. With all due respect—and as you obviously know—Foundry Branch is in your backyard. There's also the C&O Canal just down the street—getting it built was George Washington's project, so it ties in with the Founding Fathers and the history angle you're looking for. What about giving us some flexibility to take pictures of other streams and creeks, as long as they're in the same geographical area?"

Roxanne's mouth tightened. "I think not. The Potomac has more than a hundred and twenty tributaries—and that includes rivers like the Shenandoah and Occoquan to streams and creeks like Goose Creek, Rock Creek, and Foundry Branch. You don't have to tell me how wretched Foundry Branch is—full of street runoff and sewage—and that, too, is a disgrace. At this time of year it's nearly dry. Years ago when we began dating, Scott had a black Lab named Sombra that I used to think he loved more than me. Sombra died after drinking polluted water from Foundry Branch when the two of them were out for a walk one day. Ever since then, Scott's avoided that part of Glover-Archbold Park."

Her voice had grown sharp as though the memory still upset her.

"We'll have no problem getting the pictures you need of the Potomac," I said to placate her. "We'll work with your archivists and historians. I'm sure you'll be pleased with the results."

"I appreciate that." Roxanne sounded calmer. "Obviously I have personal feelings about Foundry Branch, but more important, I think we ought to have one goal and stick to it. It would be too easy to get sidetracked."

"Absolutely," Luke said. "As Sophie said, we'll stick to photographing the Potomac."

Roxanne set her empty cup and saucer on a small table next to her chair. "Then I'll have someone from my staff get in touch and set this up. Thank you for coming. Any questions?"

"We'll wait to hear from your staff person," Luke said, "and see what the 'then' pictures are. I imagine we'll have questions after that."

"Before we go," I said, "would it be possible to use the powder room?"

She nodded. "Of course. Go back to the foyer. It's down the other hallway, first door on the left, across from Scott's office."

The door to Scott Hathaway's office was wide open and I took a quick look inside. The room, as dark and masculine as Roxanne's was cheerfully feminine, was lined with book-shelves filled with leather-bound antique volumes—the senator must be a collector—and dark leather furniture pulled around a carved black marble fireplace. Heavy gold drapes

framed a set of French doors like the ones in Roxanne's office
and overlooked a swimming pool and lush gardens. I heard
the maid's footsteps at the end of the hallway and slipped
into the powder room.

Roxanne and Luke were waiting in the foyer when I joined
them a few minutes later. "My husband just called," Roxanne
said. "We're about to be overrun with cars from the Diplomatic
Protective Division of the Capitol Police. Scott's on his way
home with a houseguest. I don't want you to be blocked in,
so you should try to make a fast getaway. I'll let them know
at the front gate to let you go first."

But the moment Luke and I stepped outside, I knew we
were too late to get ahead of something that was already in
motion. Maybe the front gate person got his instructions
backward or maybe Hathaway's security convoy overruled
him, but as Luke and I walked across the cobblestone drive,
a black Lincoln Town Car and a black Suburban whizzed
around the corner and pulled up in front of the house. A
solid-looking chauffeur in a dark suit got out of the car and
held the door for Scott Hathaway, who waited for his guest
to follow.

Tall, dark skinned, and noble looking, with a distinct mane
of wavy salt-and-pepper hair and a hawklike profile, another
man unfolded himself from the backseat, laughing at something Hathaway just said. The two of them glanced in our
direction before disappearing into the house, followed by their
security guards.

Luke looked at me. "Was that who I think it was?"

I nodded. "The Hathaways' houseguest for the next few
days. Taras Attar."

SIXTEEN

So Taras Attar was staying with the Hathaways, not at a D.C. hotel. Not only that, he'd arrived in town early; his book signing at the Library of Congress, his first public event, wasn't scheduled until Monday. Had Napoleon Duval, who promised Attar would be well looked after during his stay in the United States, known about these arrangements when we talked this morning at St. Al's? If he did, it must have made my story about Scott Hathaway's involvement in a supposed plot to assassinate Attar while he was visiting the States seem even more bizarre and far-fetched considering Attar was now Hathaway's houseguest.

Luke looked like he might have been thinking something along those lines because he gave me a puzzled look and said, "You know, it's been a long couple of days and we've been under a lot of stress ever since the National Gallery gig. Why don't we just bag work for the rest of the day and I'll see you Monday in the studio?"

"Sure," I said, "have a good weekend."

"You got any plans?" he asked.

"Moving out of the Roosevelt to a duplex apartment just above Dupont Circle."

"Nice. Need any help?"

"No, thanks. I'm good. I don't have much to move and my landlady's loaning me her car, so I'm all set. See you Monday."

I followed him down the driveway and eventually down Wisconsin Avenue through Georgetown, where he turned right to head across the river to Virginia and I went left to India's place to pick up Niles the Jaguar and on to the Roosevelt to pack my things and move out for good. Two hours later I was easing Niles back into the carriage house when Grace called to say that Ben would swing by and pick me up for dinner on his way home from the Hill. She didn't mention the break-in at the Roosevelt yesterday or last night's incident at Bar Humbug, hopefully because Jack had kept his word and hadn't told her.

"I can take the Vespa," I said. "Don't worry."

"Nonsense. He drives right past your street. He'll be by around seven. By the way, I saw the story about the girl they found in the Potomac. Did you know her? They said she'd been at that National Gallery reception."

"She was our receptionist. A really sweet kid."

"Oh, God." Grace sounded stricken. "I'm so sorry. What happened?"

"I don't know any more than what they said on the news," I said. "Do you know a detective named Bolton, by any chance? It's his investigation."

"I don't, but maybe someone else here does," she said. "I'll ask around. If I find out anything, I'll let you know. See you in a few hours, okay?"

After she hung up I finally called Baz. It was nearly ten o'clock in London, but he was a night owl and it was easier reaching him at this time of day than trying to catch him at the Foreign Office. His phone went straight to voice mail, so I left a message asking him to call as soon as he got a chance, though I didn't say why.

Then I unpacked my clothes and few possessions, took a shower, and got ready for dinner at Grace's.

When I was growing up, the large, rambling Lowe home was the place everyone congregated. Grace's family was a joyous, raucous, carefree clan who lived, laughed, and loved freely, threw fabulous parties at the drop of a hat, decorated their house to the nines for every holiday, always had enough for dinner so that setting one more place at the table was no problem. As I grew older, some of the untidiness and messiness that I hadn't known about spilled into the open—an alcoholic kid brother, an older sister who got pregnant and dropped out of college, her mom's battle with pain pills and breast cancer—but I loved them all as fiercely as if I were one of their daughters, which is how they'd treated me.

Grace's own home, an elegant Georgian Revival on Mintwood Place in Adams Morgan, was as warm and open as her childhood home had been, with her own urban stamp on it. The house smelled fragrantly of baking bread when Benjamin Glass and I walked through the front door a few minutes after seven. Ben yelled, "Honey, we're here," and she yelled back, "In the kitchen. Be right there."

If blond, ethereal Grace was light, air, and bright colors, then Ben was earth, things that were solid and immutable, dark, sober tones. On the surface they were an unlikely couple—country girl and city boy, Catholic and Jew, extrovert and introvert—but after nearly twenty years together their differences had become their strengths and their marriage as seamless as yin and yang, or as Grace liked to say, she and Ben went together like peanut butter and jelly.

Ben dropped his overstuffed briefcase next to his reading chair in the living room as seventeen-year-old Yale and fifteen-year-old Lily, tall and summer bronzed and perfect looking, clattered down the stairs, flinging their arms around me, hugging and kissing, as they laughed and talked and multi-tasked on their cell phones. Ben held a set of car keys out to Yale, a dark younger portrait of his father, and delivered the be-careful-with-your-mother's-car speech while blond, angelic Lily showed off her clothes to her mother and swore the holes in her jeans weren't too revealing. They were gone as swiftly as they'd come, arguing as they flew down the back stairs to the garage over whether Yale's girlfriend or Lily's boyfriend got picked up first. A door slammed, followed by the whining noise of a car backing out of the driveway and moving down the street.

In the poignant, echoing silence that filled the house, I wished that this could have been Nick and me saying good-bye to our kids as they left for a Friday night high school football game, this sweet tableau of family life that was so down-to-earth and Norman Rockwell American. Nick had not taken the news as hard as I had when we learned we could not have children, but if he were standing here with me now, I wondered if he, too, would feel the acute sense of loss and longing I did at this moment.

Grace, a world-class mind reader, put her arm around my shoulder and said, "Don't be fooled. They put on that show just for you, so you'd think they're wonderful and adorable and well behaved. We love them to pieces, but you can't imagine the things kids get up to these days. It's terrifying."

I smiled and slipped my arm around her waist. "We weren't angels, if you remember."

"Compared to them," she said, "we ought to be canonized. I won't sleep a wink until they get home . . . I never do. Ben, darling, I promised Sophie you'd make us your patented margaritas. God knows, I need one."

We ate outside sitting around their teak-and-glass table on a deck that overlooked Grace's well-tended backyard garden. She lit candles in hurricane lamps and flipped a switch, turning on tiny white lights that outlined the porch and followed the staircase down to where Ben barbecued steaks over a gas grill. More lights sparkled in the trees; the whole scene looked like something from a child's idea of fairyland. By seven thirty, the sun had disappeared as hard and fast as a curtain slamming down, leaving a clear cobalt-blue sky and a sudden cool breeze that hinted at autumn.

After dinner, Grace got sweaters for the two of us and we moved over to a sofa, two high-back rattan chairs, and a creaky glider grouped around a coffee table. Ben went inside to get his pipe and returned with the open bottle of Saint-Emilion as Grace brought the hurricane lamps over to where we were sitting.

"You aren't serving yourself any wine." I plopped in the glider and watched Ben fill my glass and Grace's.

"I'm your designated driver," he said. "I hit my limit a while ago."

"Don't be silly. I'll take a cab home."

"You will not," Grace said, swinging her feet onto the sofa and stuffing a pillow behind her head.

"No, Soph, I'm driving you." Ben pulled one of the chairs closer to the two of us and sat down. "It's settled."

"I told Ben you wanted to talk to him about Hathaway's Hotties, Sophie, so ask away," Grace said, reaching for her glass. "Thanks for the wine, darling."

Ben opened his tobacco pouch and said, "Scott Hathaway works with beautiful, brainy women all day. What's to know?"

Grace pretended to throw a cushion at him and he grinned and pretended to duck.

He tamped down the tobacco in his pipe and added, "You hear rumors all the time and I always figure where there's smoke, there's fire. But Hathaway is discreet, whatever he does. Besides, Roxanne wouldn't stand for any fooling around—at least not in public—and he knows it."

"Roxanne Hathaway hired Luke and me to take photos for the Save the Potomac Foundation," I said. "Apparently she just got asked to take over as the new chairperson. We spent part of the afternoon at her home going over the project."

"Roxanne's a firecracker, all right," Ben said. "She's the reason her husband ran for the Senate. She's the one with the political ambition."

"Seriously?" I said.

"Don't you remember, Soph? Roxanne's one of the famous Lane sisters," Grace said. "Her older sister married a prince from the House of Bourbon and her younger sister married a duke whose family owns one of the largest private banks in Switzerland. She wants Scott to be American royalty, as in running for president one day."

"No one talks about it anymore," Ben said, "but Roxanne and Scott's oldest son was born six months after they were married. He's in his late twenties, I think. Scott Junior. He stayed in New Hampshire after he graduated from Dartmouth and now he's running for Congress next year. Roxanne's been up there campaigning for him."

"Scott and Roxanne must have gotten married not long after he graduated from Georgetown," I said. "Was that where they met?"

"I don't know," Ben said. "She grew up in Europe, as I recall . . . Switzerland. I don't know how they met."

"Sophie was also wondering about David Epps and Eric Nettle," Grace said.

"What do you mean?" Ben looked puzzled as he puffed on his pipe.

"Both of them were at the National Gallery the other night," I said. "According to Gracie, someone from Hathaway's staff tipped off a *Trib* reporter about the scene between Hathaway and Yuri Orlov over the book signing Hathaway's hosting for Taras Attar on Monday. Arkady Vasiliev was adamant about no press and no outside photographs—which boomeranged right back to Luke and me, since we were the event photographers. So I was wondering who might have been upset enough to sabotage their boss."

"Not Nettle," Ben said at once. "He's Hathaway's chief of staff and protects the senator like a bulldog. I don't think it would be Epps, either."

"Grace said David Epps has a reputation as a gambler," I said.

Ben waved a hand. "The Epps family owns a bunch of riverboat casinos in Louisiana. David talks and acts like a good ole Southern boy who just fell off the turnip truck, but play cards with him and he'll take you for everything you've got, except he'll leave your underwear so you've got something to wear home. He really likes the horses these days. Wins a lot at the track, too, or so I hear. A very sharp guy who is not to be underestimated."

A Southerner. So it hadn't been David Epps I'd heard, either. What other man had been at the National Gallery who worked for Scott Hathaway?

"And you know this gambling story how?" Grace sat up, arching an eyebrow.

"One hears things," he said.

"Does one?" she asked. "Or maybe one is the voice of experience?"

Ben flashed a sheepish smile at his wife. "Remember when you took the kids to Disney World about five years ago?"

"You mean, when we came home early and you were sleeping off some epic night out with the guys and you'd spent the grocery money?" She was wide-eyed with indignation. "And to think I let you convince me I balanced the checkbook wrong."

"One learned one's lesson. Never again." He turned to me, avoiding the dagger-filled looks coming at him from the sofa, and said in a bland voice, "How'd that verbal brawl get started between Hathaway and Orlov?"

I held up my wineglass. "Too much of this. Orlov had been

drinking and he started in on Hathaway about his personal friendship with Taras Attar. Told him the book signing is a backhanded way of showing U.S. support for Abadistan."

Ben relit his pipe and said, "We're walking a fine line right now with the Russians when it comes to Abadistan. Hathaway knows that better than anyone."

"Taras Attar is staying with the Hathaways as their house-guest this weekend," I said. "He and the senator pulled up in an official car as Luke and I were leaving this afternoon."

Ben looked surprised. "Well, then, I guess the rumors are true."

"What rumors?" Grace said.

"That Hathaway is taking Attar around town over the weekend for off-the-radar meetings to talk about the unrest in Abadistan and whether the U.S. is going to speak out about Russian human rights violations," he said. "One of their stops is the White House." He glanced over at Grace. "And that, my precious angel, is off the record."

"You still owe me for the gambling fiasco, buddy."

"I bought you diamond earrings a week later. We're even."

She grinned, and I said, "Then what about the book signing at the Library of Congress?"

Ben shrugged. "A smokescreen, mostly. I mean, it's true Attar is on a book tour. But apparently there are concerns about his safety when he's in town so the event has been winched down from a talk and book signing that was open to the public to 'by invitation only.'"

"I didn't know that," Grace said. "Has someone made a definite threat against Attar?"

I didn't know that, either. Maybe Duval had taken me seriously after all.

"It's probably just an overabundance of caution, as they always say," Ben said. "But if there was something, you know as well as I do, darling, they wouldn't be broadcasting it to the press."

"Nick always talked about what a treacherous place Abadistan was to do business," I said. "Over the years, Crowne Energy paid a fortune in protection money to the local mafia—the Shaika—but even that wasn't enough. Eventually they moved in and tried to take over the operation, just because they wanted it. They started threatening workers until they were too scared to show up. Nick and Colin Crowne tried to stand up to them, and look what happened? Colin's dead and Nick is gone."

It was the first time I had mentioned Nick all evening. Grace stared down into her wineglass and Ben busied himself relighting his pipe.

"We miss him, too, Soph," Grace said in a soft voice. "I know this must be so hard for you."

"If there's anything you need or anything we can do," Ben said, "all you have to do is ask. You know that. We love you like family, kiddo."

"Thank you. Both of you." My hands tightened around my wineglass. "I should be going. Ben, you don't have to take me home. I'll get a cab . . . it's nearly midnight."

"Absolutely not," Grace said and Ben shook his head.

"No arguments," he said. "I'll pull the car around front. Meet you there whenever you two are ready."

He went inside and Grace looked at her watch. "Lord, the kids are due home in nine and a half minutes. Someone better send me a text message saying 'We're on our way' any second now."

I smiled. "I'm sure someone will. Thanks for a lovely evening, Gracie. Next time, I'll invite you all for dinner at my place. India left me a well-stocked kitchen. The apartment is gorgeous. I owe you."

She hugged me good-bye at the front door and waited until I got into the car with Ben. "Thanks for doing this," I said.

"My pleasure," he said. "But to tell you the truth, I have an ulterior motive. I wanted to talk to you without Grace around."

My brain flitted to "surprise party for her birthday," but I knew where he was really going. "Oh?"

"My boss serves on the Senate Intelligence Committee, in addition to chairing Foreign Relations," he said. "I'm his designated spook staffer, so I've got clearances that go pretty high. Last spring before our hearings on Abadistan, Langley sent a group over to the Hill to brief us on the deteriorating situation between Russia and the Abadis. Crowne Energy got a big mention."

"I see."

The light turned red at the intersection of 18th Street and Columbia Road, the busy commercial strip that was the main thoroughfare of Adams Morgan. At this hour, the nightlife was in full swing, the streets and sidewalks filled with revelers who had been dancing at Club Heaven & Hell or dining on soul food and listening to the blues at Madam's Organ or smoking hookah at Soussi or frequenting any of the dozens of ethnic bars, restaurants, and clubs.

"It didn't take much to figure out that the CIA was getting some of its information on the ground from someone who knew Crowne Energy inside out," Ben said as the light changed and he swerved to avoid an inebriated couple who preferred walking down the middle of 18th Street. "Colin Crowne was a Brit, so I figured it had to be Nick."

"I see," I said again.

"Look, Sophie," he said, "I know you can't talk about any of this and I'm not asking for confirmation. All I want to say is that I've been keeping tabs on that situation and it sounds like right before it all went to hell, Crowne Energy might have made a significant oil discovery in a place where no one expected to find anything because everyone thought it was dry. If that's true, it completely changes the politics of the region and the Russians are going to be hell-bent to make sure Abadistan doesn't decouple from the mother ship."

He flicked his turn signal and made a right onto my block of S Street. I waited for him to continue, but he was silent until we pulled up in front of my house.

"I haven't said anything to Grace," he said, "but my CIA contacts got really touchy when I fessed up and told them Nick was a friend. I also got the feeling that, as Mark Twain said after learning that his obituary had been published in the newspaper, the rumors of his demise might have been greatly exaggerated."

He leaned over and kissed my forehead. "If I can do anything—and I mean anything—to help, please let me know. This stays just between you and me. If Nick's alive, and I suspect you know this as well, he's in a hell of a lot of trouble. Not just from whoever forced him to disappear—the Russian mafia—but our guys are looking for him, too."

"I know," I said. "Believe me, I know."

"You've got a CIA liaison, I presume?"

"Special Agent Napoleon Duval, though he's not with the CIA at the moment. Do you know him?"

"Duval? No, doesn't ring a bell. I shouldn't be telling you this," he said, "but be careful what you say to him. Sometimes the people you think are on your side have a different agenda from what they tell you. This might be one of those times." He gave me a long look. "What do you think, Soph? You have good instincts. Do you trust the guy?"

I didn't answer him right away. Finally I said, "I don't know."

"That," Ben said, "sounds like a no to me. Watch it, sweetheart."

SEVENTEEN

B en walked me to the front door and waited until I found my house key and let myself in. By the time I got upstairs and looked out the bay window in my new living room, his car was gone and the street was dark and quiet. I went up to the tower room, which I'd claimed as my bedroom, and got undressed. Before I fell into the big four-poster bed, I opened the windows, letting the cool breeze rustle the curtains as a silvery wash of moonlight pooled on the floor. Once or twice a car purred down the street and, for a while, the cicadas sang their fading end-of-summer serenade. Otherwise, all was quiet except for the faint *tick-tick* of the house; comforting little creaks that already seemed familiar as it settled for the night, calming like the regular breathing of sleep.

I closed my eyes, trying to slow my heartbeat to match that rhythm and stop the slideshow racing through my head of people I knew morphing into strangers like a child's mix-and-match book, all crazy with different flipped-around heads and middles and feet until they became unrecognizable. Ben's last remarks rattled me because I'd always assumed I knew who was on Nick's side and who wasn't. He'd asked me outright if I trusted Duval and I finally had to face facts.

I wasn't sure if I did.

Sleep came late. The last time I checked the time it was five fifteen. The next thing I knew, something was ringing in the middle of my dreams. When I finally scrabbled around after knocking my phone on the floor next to the bedside table, the caller had hung up.

Missed call. *Home.*

Either my mother or Harry, calling at precisely nine o'clock. It rang again in my hand.

"Were you in the shower?"

"Harry?" I sat up and ran a hand through my hair, pushing it off my face.

"No, *me.*"

"*Mom?* What happened to your voice?"

"Laryngitis," she said in a raspy whisper. "I'll be quick. You need to be Harry's date tonight at a party in town, stand in for me. You'll wear my dress."

"Wait a minute." I swung my feet onto the floor. "What are you talking about?"

"Too much to explain . . . my voice." She paused for a coughing fit. When it was finished she added, "He'll be there at six with the dress."

"Mom, I'm not staying at the Roosevelt anymore. I moved to a place near Dupont Circle. And I don't need a dress. I have my own clothes." I fell back on the bed, having just capitulated to accompanying Harry to some stuffy event with people I probably didn't know and making only a feeble protest about what to wear. How did she manage to do that to me?

"Not for this you don't. Trust me." Another pause as she sipped something through a straw. "You couldn't tell your own mother you moved?"

"I was going to . . . it only happened yesterday. Look, what party? You didn't even ask if I have plans tonight."

"Sweetheart, I know you," she said. "Doing laundry doesn't count as having plans. It's time you started getting out again. Now, e-mail Harry and me your address so he knows where to be tonight and I know where my daughter lives. Don't forget . . . I've got to go . . . someone's calling on the other line." She hung up in the middle of another coughing fit before I could get a word in.

I threw the phone on the bed, got up, and found my running clothes. Then I went for a long, pounding run during which I tried, for the millionth time, to dissect the convoluted relationship I had with my mother, which I knew was tangled up in an accidental pregnancy and misbegotten marriage when she was a nineteen-year-old student who tumbled into love—and bed—with a soccer player she met in Madrid. The divorce followed two years later, but I would always be the child who reminded her of a mistake and a deeply unhappy time in her life. The person who saved us from each other, and rescued me, was Harry. I honestly never understood what this good man saw in my flighty, self-absorbed mother, but he loved her—and me—unconditionally and we adored him. Eventually we found a neutral place where we could co-exist with Harry as our buffer, and when my half brother and half sister were born, I did my best, for his sake, to make our blended family work.

At the end of my run I stopped by the 17th Street Safeway to pick up groceries and by the time I got back to S Street, it was just after ten. My phone rang as I was climbing the stairs to my apartment. The display said "Private number."

"Ms. Medina?" The male voice sounded familiar.

"Yes. Who's calling?"

"This is Special Agent Duval."

I set the grocery bags on the kitchen counter. "Good morning."

"I hope I'm not interrupting anything important."

He didn't hope anything of the kind. He had an agenda and I was on it.

"What can I do for you, Agent Duval?"

"Perhaps you have time to meet with me? Say, later this morning?"

Again with the imperative tone. He should have just told me where and when.

"May I ask what this is all about?"

"I'd rather not discuss it over the phone. How about Meridian Hill Park at eleven? It's not far from you."

I had spent exactly one night in my new home, but already he knew where I lived. Was Duval or one of his people watching me now? I walked outside onto the balcony and stared at Max Katzer's peaceful Japanese garden. Two squirrels played tag along a stone wall before disappearing up a white oak tree in India's backyard. On the other side of the high fence that enclosed the garden, the alley looked deserted. The sweet jewel-box carriage house was silent and closed up, sitting in a pocket of shade. A stray ray of sunlight glinted off the glass panes of the dormer window, turning them into mirrors. Just for the hell of it, I waved.

"Sure," I said. "Just tell me where."

"I'll be at the bottom of the fountain as you come through the main entrance," he said. "See you then."

He hung up and I went inside, fixed myself coffee and toast, and took it into the living room, where I rearranged a Queen Anne chair and a gateleg table in front of the sunny bay window. I got my laptop and sat down. The morning barrage of e-mail brought nothing from Nick as usual, but Perry had written to say that the IPS bureau in Washington finally brought down the axe yesterday and let five people go, including two senior photographers. There was also a two-line note from Harry.

Hey, kitten, don't forget to send your mom & me your address & thanks for doing this. See you at 6. Love you to pieces, H

I wrote him an affectionate reply, asked what it was I'd agreed to do, and sent the address. Next I looked up directions to Meridian Hill Park: 16th and Florida, close enough to walk, as Duval implied. Last, I did a search for Katya Gordon and Georgetown University, something I'd been meaning to do since yesterday, when Elizabeth Quick had connected those two dots. It took a while before I found a match: a review of a book Katya had contributed to on the Russian avant-garde art movement in which the reviewer mentioned that she had attended Georgetown for one year—he even mentioned which year—before transferring to Columbia. I looked up Scott Hathaway's biography and found what I suspected all along: Scott and Katya were there at the same time, meaning they could have known each other as students.

I opened my photo gallery and studied the pictures I'd taken of them that night at the National Gallery, enlarging them until the faces were so pixilated I could no longer distinguish any features. I still hadn't shown this set of photos to anyone, or told Duval or Luke about the argument I'd witnessed. Now I wondered if it was a lovers' quarrel as I'd assumed that night— or maybe something else.

You have no choice, Scott. You know that.

No choice about *what*?

I closed my laptop, got my camera, and left for my high noon meeting with Special Agent Napoleon Duval.

The moment I walked up the steps past the greenery-filled urns at the 16th Street entrance of Meridian Hill Park and entered the main plaza, I fell in love. Built into the side of a hill on two levels, this could have been the grounds of a romantic Renaissance villa, something you'd expect to come across on a day trip outside Rome. It was a place that belonged to the neighborhood and its residents rather than another tourist shrine, a surprise if you didn't know there could be such beauty and tranquillity in this not-so-upscale part of D.C.

Its centerpiece was a dramatic waterfall of thirteen linked basins that cascaded down a steep slope. Symmetrical staircases of honey-colored stone flanked the waterfall and led to a grand terrace on the upper level. The lower level was dominated by an enormous reflecting pool whose waters caught the swirling greens of the oak trees that anchored each corner and the brilliant blue of the cloudless sky.

I climbed one of the staircases to take photographs, hoping for a panoramic view of the city since the park was directly in line with the White House. Instead, a large apartment building across the street obstructed the view, its solid bulk casting a shadow like an eclipse over the reflecting pool. For a city that had been planned so carefully by Pierre L'Enfant, there were places in Washington that evoked the randomness of a yard sale, with monuments, memorials, and buildings inserted haphazardly into the landscape. This was one of them.

Meridian Hill had its own quirky collection of statues and memorials: an eclectic group including Dante, Joan of Arc, and—my meeting place with Duval—a granite monument dedicated to our fifteenth president, James Buchanan, whose term ended on the eve of the Civil War. It was a good choice for a rendezvous if you wanted privacy: semienclosed and slightly isolated, at the far end of the park beyond the reflecting pool.

Duval showed up at twelve sharp wearing black running

shorts and a faded gray USMC T-shirt, and carrying a small
backpack slung over one shoulder. Wraparound sunglasses,
Nats baseball cap, and a water bottle. Just another D.C. resident
out for a run on a spectacular end-of-summer Saturday.

He sat next to me on a stone bench in the shade of an oak
tree and said, "Thanks for coming. Been waiting long?"

Something told me he hadn't just arrived. Maybe he had
binoculars in that backpack and this was a trick question to
test my honesty.

Maybe I was becoming paranoid.

"I got here early since I didn't know the park or where this
monument was located."

"Seriously? You've never been here? You mean you don't
know about the drum circle?"

"Seriously. What drum circle?"

"It's famous, been going on for years. People show up with
djembes, bongos, timbales—anything that makes noise—every
Sunday, rain or shine, starting at three o'clock. You come to
play, dance, or just listen." He cracked open his water bottle.
"You can look it up on the Internet, see a couple of videos.
There's always a crowd."

"Including you?"

He shrugged. "You'd be surprised how much lower your
stress level is after you spend a couple of hours wailing away
on a drum."

Up until this moment I'd figured Napoleon Duval vanished
into the ether at the end of the day until he reappeared the
next morning wearing his crusader's cape. Now it seemed as
though maybe he lived around here. If he did, then Duval and
I were now neighbors.

"You didn't invite me here to talk about cultural events in
D.C. and broaden my horizons," I said, "did you?"

He set down the water bottle, unzipped the backpack, and
took out a large envelope. "Have a look."

I undid the clasp and slid out an eight-by-ten photograph.
Slightly out of focus, it appeared to have been taken in a hurry.
A hundred or so people—men only, no women—were divided
into two angry groups facing each other. A few of the younger
ones in the front rows had their arms raised, ready to hurl

whatever they were holding. Stones, by the look of it. I didn't
see any weapons.

With all the editing I do in my profession, I'm an expert at
scanning faces even in big crowds, homing in on whether eyes
are open or closed, if the smile is forced or natural, details
like that. Blurry or not, I spotted Nick right away and my
heart lurched against my rib cage. He was standing between
two men on the periphery of that hostile scene, dressed in a
white kurta shirt and a knit kufi cap like his friends. The beard
and dark blond hair were even longer than in the picture I'd
seen of him in Vienna, and his skin was deeply tanned as
though he'd spent a lot of time outdoors. If you didn't know
better, he almost passed as a local.

Where in the world was he? A city street, not a residential
district. Crumbling buildings of brick and concrete block with
corrugated flat metal roofs. A distant minaret and a gold onion
dome, fuzzy through a web of crisscrossing telephone lines.
Weeds poking through cracks in the broken pavement. Cars
that looked old, from a different generation. Gray skies, a pale
blue line of mountains in the background, everyone dressed
in drab colors. These people were poor. I ran through a mental
list of all the places I'd been with IPS that looked like this.
Almost all involved wars or an ongoing conflict; the leaders
were despots, corrupt individuals who swept their country's
resources into their own coffers, living like kings while the
masses endured grinding poverty.

The only clues were the minaret and the gold dome.
Somewhere with mosques and churches, Muslims and Orthodox
Christians. Abadistan fit that description.

I looked up. "Where was this taken and when?"

"See anyone you recognize?" Duval asked.

"Oh, come on."

"Answer the question," he said, "please."

"Of course I do. That's Nick. Right there." I pointed to him.
"But you knew that already, didn't you?"

"We weren't entirely sure," he said. "Thank you for
confirming it. And to answer your question, it was taken in
Iskar fifteen days ago."

I'd been right. Iskar was the provincial capital of Abadistan, a small port city on the Caspian Sea where Crowne Energy had its offices . . . used to have its offices.

"What was Nick doing in Iskar?" I said. "I'm sure you know that, too."

"Actually, we don't know." He held out his hand for the photo and slid it back into the envelope. "But I will tell you this. Fifteen days ago, Nick's CIA handler was found with his throat slit in a warehouse used by Crowne Energy."

I swallowed and said, "Nick didn't do it."

"I understand your loyalty to your husband. I didn't say he did."

"Don't patronize me, Agent Duval."

"I wouldn't dream of it. We don't know who killed our guy, but until this photo surfaced, we had no idea Nicholas Canning was in the region. One of our local informants was taking pictures of this scene just before it turned into a full-blown riot. Imagine our surprise when we started looking to see who was among the boys in the band and he popped up."

I ignored the sarcasm and said, "Why were they rioting?"

"A young Abadi who owned a fruit stall in the local market was shot and killed by a Russian *militsia* the day before. The Russian said the kid was armed and threatened him. When they got to his body, he was holding a banana, not a gun."

"Oh, God."

Across from Duval and me, a young African-American mother chased two little boys playing with a bright blue ball near the reflecting pool. The kids shrieked as one of them threw the ball into the water and it drifted out of reach.

The mother stood there, hands on hips. "Now what did I tell you about throwing that ball near the water?"

"Ms. Medina, if your husband didn't murder his handler, I'll bet you anything he knows who did," Duval said. "Let me repeat what I told you yesterday: He needs to come in and stop running. I can't urge you strongly enough to do what you can to make that happen. Do I make myself clear?"

I nodded, feeling numb. "Yes."

"Good," he said. "Because the longer he stays out, the guiltier he looks. Now he's wanted for questioning in connection with two deaths, not just one. The way we see it, he had means, opportunity . . . and possibly a motive for both of them. If he is in possession of those well logs, they are worth a great deal of money to the right people. In a court of law, you line up means, motive, and opportunity and you've made a good start toward a murder conviction."

"Nick is no murderer."

Duval stood up. "Then get him to show up and prove it. You have a nice day, Ms. Medina."

EIGHTEEN

D uval walked away without turning around because to
do so would have ruined his perfect, devastating exit
line. As soon as he passed the fountain, he veered off
toward one of the staircases and I lost sight of him. For a long
while I sat on the granite bench next to the mottled bronze
statue of James Buchanan and replayed our conversation over
and over in my head until a sharp little wind blew across the
reflecting pool, ruffling the water and skittering dry leaves
across the plaza. Finally, I got up, walked out of the park, and
headed down 16th Street with no destination in mind except
the need to clear my head.

My God, how had it come to this? Nick wanted for questioning in the deaths of his boss and his CIA handler? If
Duval's people found him, they would be merciless. Not
if, *when.*

Sixteenth Street gradually became less residential and more
commercial after I passed the Scottish Rite temple, where the
blocks were lined with embassies, hotels, trade associations,
and think tanks. It felt good to walk, to concentrate on putting
one foot in front of the other and just keep going, counting
off steps in my head, because that way I didn't have to think.

Eventually I ended up at Lafayette Square in front of the
White House. There was a crowd, as there always is, the usual
mix of protesters holding signs or sitting in the park—GET
THE US OUT OF THE UN, NO TO OFFSHORE DRILLING—
and gawking tourists snapping pictures or staring at the lovely,
serene mansion on the other side of the high wrought-iron
fence. Now that Pennsylvania Avenue was closed to traffic
between 15th and 17th Streets for security reasons, a group of
guys played street hockey on the broad, smooth expanse
of granite. If Nick had been here, he would have somehow
sussed out that there would be a pickup game—jungle drums,
texting, whatever—and shown up with a pair of inline skates

and a borrowed hockey stick. He'd have gotten a kick out of playing with a bunch of aging jocks a few hundred yards from where the president of the United States might be watching—maybe with some envy—from a window.

It was one of the many things I loved about my husband—his spontaneity, his delight in something offbeat or quirky, his passion for anything to do with sports. Whenever he traveled, especially on business, he'd take his running shoes and look for a game to join—soccer, basketball, softball, even bocce—or else he'd round up a bunch of people and organize something himself. Even if they didn't speak the same language and nobody understood anyone else, Nick didn't care. He was the Pied Piper; he could talk you into going along with him, doing anything.

I loved that adventurous streak, his zany sense of humor, and his sense of wonder. He was a romantic and a daredevil, a man of great charm and a serious scholar. Right now I missed him so badly the ache hurt like a physical pain in my heart.

I found a bench in Lafayette Square and pulled out my phone, intending to write Nick one more time and plead with him to get in touch with me. Instead a text message from Jack popped up on my screen. He'd sent it ten minutes ago.

At Georgetown main campus having lunch with Sully. He has info. Will fill you in.

Jack's priest friend who had been a classmate of Scott Hathaway and Taras Attar.

I called and he answered right away. "Hey," he said. "I just sent you a text."

"I know. I'm in Lafayette Square. I could take a cab and be at Georgetown in about ten or fifteen minutes. We could talk in person. Would that be okay?"

"Sure." He sounded surprised. "Get the cab to drop you by the stadium. We're at the JesRes around the corner. Good thing there's no home football game today or you'd never get near the place. See you when you get here."

After I hung up, I wrote Nick and this time I didn't bother with any of our coded messages.

Everyone looking for you after incident in Iskar. They have photos. Get in touch. URGENT.

Then I walked over to 15th Street and hailed a cab to Georgetown.

Jack and a man with snow-white hair cut like someone had used a perfect round bowl were sitting on a stone wall in front of the redbrick Jesuit residence hall—the JesRes—when I joined them in the lower-level plaza by the front entrance fifteen minutes later. Neither of them had on their funny clothes, as Jack called them, but there was something in the way they carried themselves—a dignity, or perhaps a certain grace and presence—that marked them as priests, in spite of the jeans and T-shirts.

Jack got up to kiss me and introduce me to Father Patrick Sullivan. Father Pat had eyes the same brilliant blue as the football stadium banner I just saw that said BLEED HOYA BLUE, and his fair skin was covered with so many freckles and sunspots he almost looked tanned. He shook my hand and said with a faint Irish lilt, "Himself's been telling me all about you."

"The good parts are true," I said, and the blue eyes lit up as he laughed.

"Have a seat, Soph." Jack made space for me between the two of them. "I told Sully you were curious about Scott Hathaway and Taras Attar's friendship when they were students."

I nodded. "You knew them, Father?"

"That I did," he said. "We were all on the chess team. I believe that's how Taras and Scott met each other, as well. Both terrifically competitive lads in just about everything. When they played each other, you'd think it was Bobby Fischer and Boris Spassky all over again, the rivalry was so fierce."

"Did you also know someone named Katya?" I asked. "I don't know her maiden name, but her married name is Gordon. I believe she was a friend of Scott Hathaway's."

The blue eyes crinkled in thought and he frowned. The drone of traffic from Canal Road below us, the sound of planes overhead taking off and landing at Reagan Airport, and the hubbub of a busy university campus on a beautiful Saturday afternoon faded to a pleasant background buzz. Two female students passing by on the upper level sidewalk called out to Father Pat.

He acknowledged them with a wave and said, "Katya? No, sorry, doesn't ring a bell. But then, Scott had the ladies hanging all over him. She could have been part of his harem. It was hard to keep track . . . Scott flirted with every pretty girl he met."

So Father Pat didn't know Katya. Not the answer I'd been hoping for, but at least he confirmed that Hathaway had always been a skirt chaser.

"Did Taras have the ladies hanging all over him, too?"

He nodded. "Oh, indeed. Handsome devils, the pair of them, and they knew it. You heard stories about . . . well, competing, as lads do. I'm sure you can imagine. Though Taras was a wee bit more serious than Scott. Had to keep up his grades since he was here on scholarship. Plus, I believe he worked on campus . . . the library, I think it was." He paused and said, "May I ask why you're curious about them after all these years?"

"I was one of the photographers at the National Gallery the other night when Senator Hathaway defended his friendship with Taras Attar to the Russian ambassador. The situation got pretty ugly, but Hathaway wouldn't back down," I said. "I just wondered how the two of them had become friends."

"Ah, yes," he said. "I read about that little dust-up with the ambassador in the paper. No, the friendship's genuine. They were thick as thieves in those days, always had each other's back. The only time I remember any acrimony was when Scott took up with . . . I guess you'd call her an exotic dancer. He met her at a bar off campus. From what I heard she was an absolutely stunning lass. Taras said she was no good and that she'd only bring him grief, but Scott wouldn't listen. He was obsessed . . . missed our end-of-year tournament because they'd been off together somewhere. He caught the devil for it, but he didn't care, which was surprising if you knew Scott."

"Scott Hathaway and Taras Attar argued over a girl?" I asked.

He shook his head. "No, 'twasn't like that. But all of a sudden she was gone and no one knew where she went. The police came round to investigate when the club she worked at finally reported she hadn't shown up for a few days. Scott was brought in for questioning, then his father flew to Washington—he was a well-known criminal prosecutor in Massachusetts—and that was the end of that. But the romance caused quite a rift between Scott and Taras. You had to wonder if Taras didn't fancy her, too, though I'm not sure that was the problem."

"Do you remember the dancer's name?" I asked. "And what year it was?"

"Hard to forget. Jenna. Jenna Paradise. The usual dirty jokes went around about Scott going missing because he was 'in paradise,' that sort of boys' own thing," he said, blushing faintly. "As to when, it was spring of our senior year just before graduation."

Scott and Taras's senior year had been the same year Katya Gordon attended Georgetown.

"How could she just disappear?" Jack asked.

A plane flew directly over us, casting a shadow like an enormous bird. Father Pat glanced up, squinting at it.

"Earlier that year two women were assaulted while they'd been out for a run on the trail in Glover-Archbold Park behind the university," he said. "One in broad daylight, the other at dusk. Jenna was a runner, too, had to keep fit with that dancer's career of hers. So was Scott. The last person to see her, a girlfriend, I believe it was, said she was on her way to the park to meet someone for a run. Scott claimed it wasn't him because she'd dumped him and they'd stopped seeing each other. Jenna never turned up again—it was like she vanished into thin air. There was some speculation that whoever was behind those assaults might have attacked her and that time he went too far."

For the second time in less than twenty-four hours, someone mentioned Glover-Archbold Park along with Scott Hathaway's name.

"How do you get to the park from here?" I asked.

"It's about a three-minute walk down Canal Road," Jack said. "Great place for a run. But if I were a woman, I'd think twice about doing it alone." He gave me a meaningful look.

"I'm serious, Soph. If you want to see it—and I know that look in your eye, so obviously you do—I'll go with you."

Father Pat stood up. "That sounds like my exit cue," he said. "I've got a homily to finish before Mass tomorrow. I'll leave you good people to a pleasant walk in the woods. Perfect day for it."

"You sure you have time to do this?" I asked Jack after Father Pat bussed me on the cheek and gave Jack a man hug before disappearing into the JesRes.

"It's only half a mile each way, at least this part of the trail is. We can walk it and be back here in half an hour, forty minutes tops. Sure, let's go."

"The Hathaways live on the other side of Glover-Archbold Park," I said. "I forgot it also bordered the Georgetown campus."

He nodded. "It follows the western boundary from the sports complex up to the hospital on Reservoir Road."

We walked past tennis courts and down a steep curved drive until we reached Canal Road. Cars whizzed by a few inches away as Jack, always the gentleman, maneuvered me so that I walked on the inside of the narrow sidewalk.

"You all right?" he said. "You seem sort of subdued."

"Napoleon Duval summoned me to a meeting just before I saw you. Someone slit the throat of Nick's CIA handler in Abadistan."

As he had done when I told him about Ali, Jack made the sign of the cross. "What happened? Why was he murdered?"

"They don't know, but they think Nick does. They want me to do everything in my power to get him to come in and talk to them. They have a picture of him in Iskar, the capital, the same day the guy was killed."

"Good Lord. They don't think Nick did it, do they?" Jack looked stunned.

"Duval says if Nick doesn't turn himself in soon, it's going to look like he's got something to hide."

"What's keeping him from doing that? Do you have any idea?"

"I think he's been set up. It might even be someone in the CIA." I shrugged. "Who knows? Duval might even be part of it."

"What are you going to do?" he asked.

"I don't know."

"Well, I'm pulling out all the stops." Jack slipped an arm across my shoulders and hugged me. "I'm praying for you guys."

"By 'all the stops' do you mean Saint Jude?" I couldn't help sounding forlorn.

The patron saint of lost causes, the saint everyone turned to when you despaired of all hope.

"He's on my list," Jack said. "And so is his big boss. Have faith, kiddo. It's going to work out, I promise."

Just before the intersection of Canal Road and Foxhall Road, Jack said, "Turn here."

We walked through a shade-dappled clearing past a National Park Service sign with a list of rules—no collecting natural or historic items, no bicycles or motor vehicles, leash your pets, and no littering—and headed toward a dirt path that led into deep woods. Directly above us, an abandoned trestle bridge surrounded by trees and overgrown vines looked as though it was suspended in midair as it cut across the park.

"What is that?" I reached around for my camera, which was hanging off my shoulder, and lifted it to my eye. "It's fabulous."

"It used to be part of the old D.C. streetcar line that ran from Union Station to Georgetown," Jack said. "Every so often you hear about students who've had too much to drink clowning around up there on the tracks or some bright light deciding to play Superman."

"It looks like it would be fun to climb on," I said. "A massive set of monkey bars."

Jack gave me a stern look and said, "Don't get any ideas. Kids hang out at the top of the hill by that abutment where you can see the graffiti to talk and smoke dope and do whatever, but I'd want to have my tetanus shot up-to-date before I did any climbing on those rusty girders and old tracks. Come on, let's walk the trail."

We passed a brown-and-white park sign that indicated, as Jack said, that it was just over half a mile to the end of this section of the trail, which then continued on for another two and a half miles to Tenleytown. The woods soon closed around us like an enchanted forest where the vines and trees wove together magically and the entrance disappeared unless you knew exactly where to find it again. Though civilization wasn't far away and the sound of airplanes and cars was still comfortingly audible, I could understand why a woman who came alone to this forest would be vulnerable, an easy target for a predator.

"Roxanne Hathaway said the streambed is nearly dry at this time of year," I said as the sweet song of a mockingbird sounded above us in the trees. "I can't even tell where it is."

Jack grabbed my arm as I stumbled over a tree root. "Watch your step. They do a good job of keeping the trail cleaned up, but you can still take a header if you're not careful. As for Foundry Branch, we had a drought over the summer before you moved home and that was the end of the stream. There's one place up ahead where we might still find water."

We had to break away from the trail and clamber over dead limbs and downed trees with Medusa-like root systems to find the spot Jack was talking about. A partially submerged car tire poked up through the mud in a shallow, still pool of water.

I crouched down to take pictures. "It looks stagnant and it stinks of something rotting."

"When the rains come the stream will start running again," Jack said. "From here it flows through the park and into a pipe under Canal Road. Eventually it dumps into the Potomac. Then they turn it into our drinking water."

"Oh, God, they do, don't they." I made a face. "What a revolting thought."

"Well, they do one or two things to clean it up and treat it before it comes out of your tap."

"I feel so much better."

He grinned. "So there you go. Now you've seen Foundry Branch."

"This is it? This puddle?"

"This is it for now. There's a storm grate near the trestle bridge where you can hear it flowing underground." He held out his hand and pulled me up. "Come on. We're almost at the end of the trail."

He was right; a couple of minutes later we stood at the edge a large bowl-shaped field. At the top of the hill we could hear traffic buzzing along Reservoir Road.

"Folks use this field for soccer, baseball, what have you," Jack said. "The French embassy is half a block down the street. Georgetown Hospital's not far away."

"And that's Scott and Roxanne Hathaway's house." I pointed to a series of steeply pitched red-tile roofs visible above the tree line to our left. "Roxanne says the senator won't use this park anymore because his dog died before they got married years ago after getting sick from stream water."

"Really?" he said. "I wonder how long ago that was. Foundry Branch wasn't always as polluted as it is now. There was a time when the water was clean and the stream ran all year."

"Seems hard to imagine."

"Come on," he said. "I think we've depressed ourselves enough for one afternoon. My car is in the garage near the JesRes. I can drop you by your place if you want."

On the drive back to S Street, Jack asked if I had plans for the evening.

"I'm Harry's date for some black tie event. My mother's sick, so I'm taking her place."

"What event?"

"No idea."

"You volunteered for something and you don't know what it is?"

"I didn't volunteer."

He looked disgusted as he pulled up in front of my house. "No comment."

"Don't say it. I need to start standing up to my mother." I sighed. "Thanks for the lift. Can I offer you a drink? Give you a quick tour of my new place?"

"How about a rain check? I'm on duty tonight. I'd better get back to the house."

"Sure," I said. "Another time."

Jack leaned over and gave me a kiss. "Look, I'm not trying to beat you up about Caroline. She's always been the way she is, but one day you need to have the Come to Jesus talk with her."

"I will."

"At least you get to spend an evening with Harry," he said. "Come to think of it, that's probably a good thing. He'll take care of you."

"I'm perfectly capable of taking care of myself," I said. "I've been in war zones, remember?"

"I know you have," he said. "But I was thinking about that conversation you had with Napoleon Duval earlier today. I know they're desperate to find Nick. But you yourself said you think he might be on the run because someone betrayed him from inside the CIA. Duval's playing a dangerous game, Soph. It sounds like he'll do anything to track Nick down. Including using you as his bait."

NINETEEN

When Harry Wyatt, my stepfather, showed up at my front door a few minutes before six, he was dressed in his drinking pinks, the formal evening attire worn to a hunt ball: scarlet tails, white tuxedo shirt, white vest, white bow tie, and black tuxedo trousers. Draped over one arm was an oversized garment bag.

"Hi, kitten," he said, leaning in for a kiss. "I come bearing gifts."

Harry was a master of the Goose Creek Hunt, one of the oldest foxhunting clubs in Virginia whose territory comprised land once surveyed by George Washington. Later it became part of what was called Mosby's Territory, in honor of John Singleton Mosby, the legendary Confederate guerrilla commander known as the Gray Ghost. I'd been to the GCH's formal balls when I lived at home, and the dress code for these events was as tradition steeped as foxhunting itself. Men had two choices: evening hunting attire, which meant their drinking pinks or a tuxedo. Women had one choice: a black evening gown.

"Why didn't Mom tell me this was a hunt ball?" I said. "I have a black dress."

Harry followed me up the stairs to my apartment and said, "It's not a hunt ball. It's a costume party, sort of."

"A costume party? Are you kidding me? It's not even Halloween."

"It's for charity," he said. "Roxanne Hathaway is throwing a shindig to raise money for the Save the Potomac Foundation. She got the idea to tie the evening to the Fabergé exhibit at the National Gallery and she's re-creating the interior of a Paris restaurant that hosted a meal called the Three Emperors Dinner back in 1867. Two of the emperors were Russian and the French food was apparently out of this world. Everyone's supposed to dress in what they wore in those days."

So that explained the ballroom-size tent in the Hathaways' back garden and the upscale caterer. Yesterday I thought Roxanne wanted to hire Luke and me to photograph her party; tonight I would be there as a guest. And so, perhaps, would the Hathaways' houseguest, Taras Attar.

Harry handed me the garment bag and said, "I appreciate you doing this, sweetheart. I know it's not your cup of tea, but you might meet some interesting people. It could be fun."

"I get to spend an evening with you, which is all that counts," I said. "Honestly, Harry, did they really wear drinking pinks in 1867?"

He gave me a roguish grin. "This is as dressed up as this old man gets. I'll just tell everyone I'm a British redcoat."

I smiled and said, "You'll be the handsomest redcoat there. What am I wearing?"

"You know your mother. She said to tell you it's a copy of a dress from the House of Worth . . . she wasn't kidding about the worth part. I just got the bill." He shook his head. "Try it on. You'll look stunning, Sophie."

The dress was fabulous, as Harry said, a blue-green iridescent color that reminded me of tropical water, a Cinderella fairy tale confection of lace, silk, and chiffon that moved gracefully when I spun around, beaded embroidery in the whorled pattern of shells, an off-the-shoulder bodice so low cut I blushed when I looked in the mirror. Happily the shoes were peep-toe satin pumps to match the dress, not the towering stilettos my mother usually wore. I found an antique ivory lace and satin shawl and a silver evening bag that Nick bought me on one of our romantic getaway weekends in Paris and went downstairs to show off to Harry.

He was checking out the eclectic collection of books India had left on the library bookshelves when I walked into the living room, suddenly nervous.

"How do I look?"

He turned around. His eyes widened and he let out an appreciative whistle. "You look amazing, kitten. You'll be the most beautiful woman there tonight. Don't tell your mother, but that dress looks like it was made just for you."

I blushed again and kissed him. "You're great for my ego,

Harry, but I know you said the exact same thing to Mom when she tried it on for you. Didn't you?"

He burst out laughing. "I might have. But I meant it both times."

In the car on the way over to the Hathaways', I told Harry that Roxanne had hired Luke and me to take photographs for the Save the Potomac Foundation. "Does she know Mom's not coming and I'm your date instead?"

"No, but it doesn't matter," he said. "They're expecting over two hundred people, so it's going to be mobbed. Anyway, you know your mother. If I spend ten thousand dollars for a pair of tickets, they're going to get used."

"This is a five-thousand-dollar-a-person dinner?" I asked, stunned. "Are we eating on solid gold plates?"

"Close enough," he said. "Grab that brochure on the back-seat, will you?"

I turned around and picked up an expensive-looking gilt-edged invitation with two tickets tucked inside. On the cover was a painting of an opulent dining room of red velvet walls, gilded mirrors, and glittering crystal chandeliers with *Dîner des Trois Empereurs* and *Save the Potomac Foundation* written underneath in elegant hand-lettered calligraphy.

I opened the invitation and read out loud. "'The Three Emperors Dinner, called the "dinner of the century," was a banquet held at Café Anglais in Paris on June 7, 1867. Legendary chef Adolphe Dugléré prepared the meal at the request of Kaiser Wilhelm I of Prussia, who had come to France to visit the Exposition Universelle, Napoleon III's impressive world's fair showcasing exotic cultures, scientific and technical advancements, and the food and fashion of the Second Empire. While in Paris the kaiser decided to host an extravagant meal to be remembered, with no expense spared for himself and his three guests: Czar Alexander II of Russia; his son, the czarevich, who would later become Czar Alexander III; and Prince Otto von Bismarck. The cellar master was instructed to accompany the sixteen dishes served over eight hours with the greatest wines in the world.'" I paused and said, "We're having sixteen courses and the meal is going to last eight hours?"

Harry shook his head. "Roxanne said if they duplicated that dinner today, it would cost twelve thousand dollars a person, mostly because of the wine. Not to mention the expense of tracking down the ingredients they used in those days. She said her chef was having a hell of a time finding songbirds to put on toast, especially since the species is now endangered."

"Songbirds on toast?" The childhood nursery rhyme of four-and-twenty blackbirds baked into a pie and singing before a king popped into my head. "Just how authentic is this dinner going to be?"

"It's not an eight-hour sit-down dinner, for one thing. And apparently there aren't any photos or paintings of the room in the Café Anglais where the meal took place—Le Grand Seize, it was called, 'The Big Sixteen'—so your mother says the décor is going to be more Moulin Rouge nightclub than Versailles palace."

"It must be killing Mom to miss this."

"I tied her to the bed," he said, "and promised her we'd go to Paris once she's feeling better."

"Harry." I shook my head. "You spoil her. You spoil all of us."

"You only live once, sweetheart. You, Lexie, Tommy, and your mother are my world, you know that."

My throat tightened and I leaned over to kiss his cheek. He patted my hand and cleared his throat.

"So," I said, "tell me how you know the Hathaways. I didn't know you were friends."

"I know Roxanne better than I know the senator," he said. "We met last year when she was looking for a weekend retreat in Middleburg. I showed her a couple of big properties that were on the market. We got to talking and I found out she's quite an equestrian. She grew up in Switzerland and told me her father used to take her on hunting trips. Scotland, Africa—big game, not just shooting rabbits in the backyard. Anyway, I invited her to ride with the hunt anytime she wanted to."

"Did she buy a place?" I asked.

He shook his head and put on his turn signal for the Hathaways' street. We pulled up behind a limousine that had stopped half a block from their house. "No, she didn't find anything that suited her . . . damn. Looks like we're going to be stuck in a traffic jam with everyone arriving at the same time. They're valet-parking cars at the French embassy. Roxanne worked out a deal . . . she's buddy-buddy with the ambassador."

Fifteen minutes later, Harry handed his keys to a man in a charcoal blazer with a logo on the pocket and we joined the queue of guests waiting at the front entrance to the Hathaway mansion.

I leaned over and said to Harry, "I don't see anyone else in formal hunting attire, but not everyone looks like they just stepped out of La Belle Epoque France, either. I hope I'm not the only one dressed like this."

"Kitten," he said in my ear, "be an original, not a copy. You've always danced to the music of a different drummer. Don't go changing on me now, okay?"

I slipped my arm through his and squeezed it. "I won't, I promise. Thanks, Harry."

The house had been transformed, and when we finally walked inside it was like passing through a magic doorway and stepping back in time. The décor was, as Harry said, more French cabaret than royal palace: swags of crystal beads, red, black, and gold fabric draped on every surface; and the flickering light of dozens of gas lamps since we had entered the age before electricity.

Roxanne Hathaway, seductive in a low-cut black velvet gown trimmed in gold, stood alone at the doorway greeting guests. She gave Harry a conspiratorial smile as she took in his contemporary scarlet hunting attire and he bent to kiss the hand she held out.

"Roxanne, my dear, you look gorgeous," he said. "And I believe you already know my daughter, Sophie Medina? Caroline sends regrets, but she's laid up with laryngitis and an awful head cold."

Roxanne's gaze shifted and I caught the tiny flicker of surprise as she recognized me and noticed my couture gown. The look vanished, replaced by the serene expression of a hostess welcoming guests, and she said, "Please wish Caroline better, Harry. We'll miss her, but I'm glad you brought Sophie. I'm sure she's filled you in about the details of how we know each other." To me she added, "I didn't realize you two were related or that you would be coming tonight when we met yesterday." It sounded faintly like a reproach.

"Harry married my mother when I was fourteen, which was one of the best things that ever happened to me," I said. "And my boss asked me to change my name professionally when I first started working because another photographer on staff was also named Wyatt. Once I became established, I never changed it back. Medina is my birth father's name. I'm surprised to be here tonight, too, Roxanne. My mother called this morning to ask if I'd be Harry's date. Luckily we're the same size, because I'm wearing her dress."

Roxanne still seemed taken aback by my presence, but she said, "How very fortunate. The dress suits you perfectly. And now, both of you, please go on through to the garden and make sure you take a glass of champagne. It's Roederer, just as they served at the dinner in Paris. You'll find Scott out there, too."

Harry started to thank her, but the sound of a door closing on the second-floor landing distracted him and all of us looked up. Taras Attar, in a dark suit and a white silk scarf that was very twenty-first century, ran down the wide-plank staircase and crossed the foyer to where the three of us stood.

"Roxanne, my love." He spoke with an aristocratic British accent, and his deep voice was almost a growl. "You look exquisite, darling. I'm already regretting my decision to dine elsewhere this evening."

He kissed her neck as she caught her breath and—there is no other word for it—devoured me with his eyes at the same time. Until this moment, I had thought of Taras Attar only in the abstract, an amalgam of all the disparate things I knew and heard about him: Scott Hathaway's college friend and chess partner, the leader of a people who could trace their heritage and culture back to Alexander the Great, an erudite scholar and a poet, a marked man with a price on his head. What I didn't realize until just now was the full force of his charismatic personality. Nor that he was an even more outrageous flirt than Father Pat had described.

Roxanne removed Taras's arm, which he'd draped over her shoulder, like she was extracting herself from a bothersome seat belt and said in an equable voice, "You can still change your mind, Taras. We've plenty of food and you won't find a better meal anywhere tonight, even if you're dining at the White House. But if you stay, you're sitting next to me so I can keep an eye on you. I can't have you proposing marriage to every pretty woman at this party and breaking her heart when you abandon her for the next one you meet."

Attar roared with laughter, obviously used to the banter, and said, "You can start by introducing me to this gorgeous creature." He lifted my hand to his lips and kissed it.

"Sophie Medina and Harry Wyatt, meet Dr. Taras Attar, brilliant author and scholar, and shameless charmer of women. Taras, Harry's a good friend and fellow foxhunter. Sophie is his daughter and a gifted photographer. In fact, she's doing some work for the Save the Potomac Foundation."

"A photographer? How fascinating. I'd like to see your work sometime," Attar said to me. "Roxy has an unerring knack for finding and working with only the most brilliantly talented people."

The compliment was a throwaway line and nothing to be followed up on, but before I could reply, Roxanne said, "You've already seen her photos, Taras. The pictures from the National Gallery the other night."

"Ah. Those pictures. So I did." Attar's eyes flashed and I wondered if Roxanne had meant to deliberately provoke him by indirectly bringing up Arkady Vasiliev. He turned to Harry and said, "I used to hunt when I lived in England. I miss it."

"Join us sometime," Harry said. "If you're staying this evening we can talk about it."

"I wish I could, but as Roxanne knows, I'm rather bolshie when it comes to anything honoring the Romanovs and Mother Russia, and that includes the exhibit at the National Gallery. I'd be poor company at her nice party, so it seemed a wise move to make other plans." He said to me, "I mean no offense to you, Sophie."

"None taken," I said.

Roxanne flicked a glance across the room as two dark-suited men with wires in their ears who had been standing against the wall came to attention. "Your car is outside, Taras," she said. "Enjoy your evening. We'll see you when you get back."

It was a polite but definite dismissal. I had missed Attar's State Department security detail hovering in the background, they'd been so discreet, and stole a quick look across the room.

Attar made a small, respectful bow to Roxanne, but I caught the sly wink that went with it. "Thank you, darling, I shall. I'm having dinner with an old friend and she and I have a lot to catch up on. I suspect I'll be very late, so don't wait up. I'll see you and Scott for breakfast." He nodded at Harry and me. "Nice to meet you both."

He left with his security team, and Roxanne, who looked like she'd bitten back a parting remark for Taras, turned to us. "I believe I was saying that you two should help yourselves to champagne. There is a well-stocked bar in the tent if you prefer something else, and a particularly good selection of vodkas in honor of the two Russian emperors, Taras's remarks notwithstanding."

Harry thanked Roxanne again and took two champagne flutes from a waiter holding a silver tray. "Interesting fellow," he said, giving me a bland look as he handed me a glass and we walked through the house to the backyard. "Cheers, kitten."

"Cheers," I said. "Isn't he?"

"Roxanne doesn't seem too taken by him."

"I got that vibe, too. But it looked like she already had her shots, so she's immune to his lethal charm."

Harry grinned and said, "Did Nick ever run into him in Abadistan?"

"I don't know. Nick didn't talk a lot about work."

Harry put his arm around my shoulders. "I shouldn't have brought him up. Sorry, sweetheart. I don't want to upset you."

"You're not upsetting me, Harry. It's okay."

We stepped outside onto a sweeping multilevel flagstone terrace. At the bottom of the stairs, a series of formal gardens surrounded a shallow rectangular stone pool with a fountain at the center. The swimming pool was off to the right behind a high fence bordered by evergreens and rosebushes. A pretty white-columned open-air temple stood on a small hilltop to the left. The enormous glass-walled tent I'd seen the workers setting up yesterday was already filled with guests. Lit by crystal chandeliers and dozens of flickering sconces and set against the lacy silhouettes of the blue-black trees of Glover-Archbold Park, it now seemed as enchanted as a fairy tale castle.

I pulled out my phone and turned on the camera. "There's going to be a full moon tonight. Give me a minute to take a picture of that little temple before the light changes, will you?"

Harry gave me a tolerant smile. "Go on, then. I'll meet you inside the tent."

Halfway down the path I stopped to photograph a wrought-iron scrollwork gate set in the high brick privacy wall, a shortcut to the driveway where cars still waited to drop off more guests. Sometimes life really does turn on a dime. Through the keyhole-shaped opening, I watched a limousine and a Lincoln Town Car pull up in the courtyard and jockey for position. Napoleon Duval unfolded himself from the front passenger seat of the limo and came around to hold the door for Taras Attar, who was still waiting on the front steps, just as Katya Gordon, in a head-turning strapless red evening gown, stepped out of the Town Car, helped by one of the valets. Thirty seconds either way and they would have missed seeing each other.

Attar spotted her first. Instead of getting into the limousine, he waved off Duval and went over to Katya. I zoomed in my camera phone and pressed the button.

It wasn't a joyous reunion. Katya looked stunned when she recognized Attar and kept shaking her head angrily. *Go away. Leave me alone.* Attar, no longer the charming flirt he'd been a few minutes ago, took her arm and leaned close to say something only she could hear. Katya yanked her arm free and spoke to him sharply. Instantly Duval and one of the valets surrounded them, Duval hustling Attar to the limo as the valet helped Katya up the steps and into the house. A moment later Attar's car swung past my gate and I caught sight of his face through the open car window.

He was furious.

By the time I walked over to the little temple, the lovely light had turned dull and flat. I took my photographs anyway and wondered what Katya was doing at this party after the falling-out she and Scott Hathaway had at the National Gallery the other night. Perhaps Roxanne had invited her, unaware of the relationship that existed between Katya and her husband. It would be interesting to see what the chemistry was between them this evening and whether the two of them avoided each other. But after our encounter yesterday at Hillwood, I didn't want to run into Katya either.

And what about her unpleasant meeting with Attar just now? Why were they so upset with each other? Was it personal or, more likely, political? I already knew firsthand what Katya would do to further Arkady Vasiliev's political ambitions and her daughter's future. But just how far would she go to make sure that Taras Attar didn't stand in their way?

The other, more remote, possibility was that their feud had its roots in something that happened the year she was at Georgetown with Hathaway and Attar. But more likely, this was a case of Occam's razor, and the simplest and most obvious explanation was the correct one: Katya and Attar sparred just now over politics since they were in opposite camps.

Still, something nagged at me that there was another piece of the puzzle missing. I finally gave up trying to figure out what it was and headed back to the tent. There I found Harry, a bright scarlet beacon in a room of swirling colors, giddy party guests, and free-flowing champagne.

The rest of the evening passed as though we were actually in Paris on the eve of La Belle Epoque—an optimistic era of prosperity, innovation, flourishing arts, and world peace—known in America and Britain as the Gilded Age. An orchestra played Schubert, the Strausses, Lizst, Brahms, Bizet, Tchaikovsky—the nineteenth-century romantic composers—and later in the evening shifted to the dance hall cabaret music of the Folies Bergère and the Moulin Rouge, which had been in their infancy on the night the three emperors had dined in Paris. The meal was, as Harry promised, out of this world and

surprisingly faithful to the original dinner. I tried everything:
a creamy chicken soup and another soup with fresh peas and
sorrel, truffle soufflé, lamb with a puree of broad beans, roast
chicken with adobo paste, lobster cooked in bouillon and
glazed with aspic, quail pâté, stuffed duck, stuffed eggplant,
and, fortunately, no songbirds on toast. A waiter hovered at
my elbow filling my wineglasses with sherry, Madeira, and
so many fabulous vintages I lost count.

Just before dessert—*bombes glacées,* two frozen concoctions of raspberry-rose and blueberry-lavender ice cream
decorated to look like the Firebird and Blue Constellation
imperial eggs—Roxanne and Scott Hathaway got up on stage
as the orchestra took a break. Scott quieted the room, which
had become more raucous thanks to vast quantities of wine
and other alcohol, and introduced his wife, heaping praise on
her for the success of the evening. As he spoke, Katya Gordon
stood up and threaded her way between tables to a doorway
that led to a small side pavilion and the restrooms. Hathaway
spoke for another few minutes before kissing Roxanne and
handing her the microphone in the midst of boisterous applause.

Roxanne's speech about the Save the Potomac Foundation
was passionate as she discussed its work and thanked the
audience for their generosity. I watched Scott Hathaway step
off the stage and, instead of returning to his seat, casually
walk around the perimeter of the room until he was standing
next to the main exit. When he slipped outside, Roxanne
momentarily lost her place in her speech.

"I need some fresh air," I said to Harry. "I'll be back in a
few minutes."

The timing of their departures was too much of a coincidence. Katya Gordon and Scott Hathaway must have already
arranged a private meeting somewhere. I found them by the
swimming pool, standing next to a small waterfall that cascaded
into the lighted turquoise water. Under a bright high full moon
and the flickering reflection of the water, Katya's blond hair
had turned snow white and Hathaway's white bow tie and the
collar of his white dress shirt glowed like they were lumines-
cent. I slipped behind the gate, where I could watch them
screened by a row of ornamental cypresses.

"Did you bring them?" Hathaway's voice carried across the water.

"I said I would, didn't I?" Katya sounded irritated as she pulled an envelope out of her purse and passed it to him. "An eye for an eye."

"Katya, don't."

"Don't act so noble, Scott," she said. "Now we're even."

"Even? Don't talk to me about *even*. This is the last time, you understand? After that I'm done." Hathaway stared at the envelope. "I think you should go."

A thin cloud drifted in front of the moon and in the shifting chiaroscuro lighting, their angry profiles turned as hard and cold as marble.

Finally Katya said, "So be it," and whirled around to leave.

It took a moment to register that in about thirty seconds she would walk right past me. I inched closer to the fence, hoping she would be too preoccupied to realize I was there. But as I stepped back, my heel caught on a sprinkler head. I reached for whatever was nearest so I wouldn't fall. It felt like I'd grabbed a fistful of razor blades: a rosebush, full of long, sharp thorns. I gritted my teeth as Katya swept by and disappeared into the darkness. I stood there, waiting for Hathaway to leave next. Instead, a door quietly opened and closed on the far side of the pool and a light in his office came on, shining onto the terrace through the French doors. After about thirty seconds it went out.

My hand throbbed and my palm was covered in blood from at least two deep puncture wounds and scratches that were bleeding profusely. If I didn't do something soon, I'd have blood all over my mother's beautiful expensive gown.

There was a powder room across the hall from Hathaway's office; I had used it yesterday. His office was still dark and there was a chance he hadn't locked the outside door. I took off my heels and held them in my unbloody hand, slipping through the gate and keeping to the shadows. Just before I went inside the house, I rinsed the blood off under the water- fall—the water was full of chlorine, which made the cuts burn—and then used the last two tissues in my evening bag as a bandage, winding them around my palm.

I knew I was going to look for that envelope when I let myself inside; it was just a question of whether I did it before or after I cleaned up. The tissues had temporarily stopped the bleeding, so I walked over to Scott Hathaway's desk in case this was the only chance I had. He'd been here less than a minute so it seemed the logical place to temporarily stash something of value. He'd left the envelope in his top drawer.

I brought it over to the French doors and took out half a dozen old black-and-white photographs with my good hand. Even in the dazzling moonlight it was difficult to make out much detail of gray on gray, but I didn't dare risk turning on a light. The photos were of a much younger Scott Hathaway, probably in his early twenties. Taken with a telephoto, he appeared to be walking through a field surrounded by woods. Another series of pictures showed him getting on a bicycle with odd-looking handlebars that curved around like a ram's horns and riding away. I turned over the photos. Nothing written on the back and the date was too faded to make out in the dim light.

I had been so absorbed in the photos I hadn't heard the footsteps in the hallway until they stopped outside the office door. For the second time tonight, I moved into the shadows and hid behind one of the heavy gold curtains. If that was Hathaway and he'd returned for the envelope, I was doomed.

The door opened and a woman said, *"No, el senador no está aquí. Creo que ha salido."*

One of the maids. *The senator isn't here. I think he's gone out.*

She shut the door with a soft little click and I flew across the room, slipping the envelope back where I'd found it. My tissues and my hand were blood soaked again and the powder room was just across the hall.

The hall was empty and the powder room door was ajar. I cleaned my hand with soap and warm water, using a monogrammed paper hand towel as a new bandage to stop the blood. A maid was waiting outside when I opened the door, an expression of polite disapproval on her face. Possibly the same maid who had checked Hathaway's office.

"Is everything all right? There are restrooms in the tent, you know."

I gave her my best apologetic smile and slipped my injured hand into the folds of my dress. "I'm sorry. There was a such a long queue."

"A queue?"

The British word confused her. "A line. Excuse me, but I ought to be getting back to my father."

It wasn't until I had nearly reached the tent that I realized I didn't have my purse. Nor could I remember the last time I'd seen it. I'd set it down—where? The waterfall by the swimming pool, when I stopped to rinse my hand? Please, God, no—the senator's office? *On his desk?* Or maybe the powder room?

I ran back to the house, nearly colliding with Hathaway inside the door. The maid who found me sneaking out of the powder room was with him.

"That's her," she said.

My mouth felt dry.

"I believe this is yours?" He held out my purse.

Once again I tucked my bad hand into the folds of my dress. "Thank you. I was just coming back to get it."

"I see. Maria was about to go looking for you." His eyes strayed down and I think he noticed my clenched fist as I took the purse with my other hand. Maybe they would count the silverware after I left.

"I'm glad I didn't have to put her to any trouble." I hoped he'd attribute my obvious relief to recovering my lost property so quickly.

"You look familiar. Have we met?"

"I'm Harry Wyatt's stepdaughter, Sophie Medina. My mother is ill so I came this evening as Harry's date."

"I mean, before tonight," he said. "I've seen you somewhere."

"I was one of the photographers at the National Gallery reception a few days ago."

"Ah," he said. "So you were." He was still studying me.

"I should be getting back to Harry," I said. "He'll wonder where I've been."

I didn't turn around but I knew he was standing there on the terrace watching as I made my way back to the tent. If the purse had been anywhere but the powder room, he would have said something, had questions for me . . . wouldn't he?

On the drive home, Harry said, "You're awfully quiet, kitten. Everything okay?"

"Fine," I said. My hand had finally stopped bleeding and I'd made sure Harry never saw it. "Probably too much fabulous wine and champagne and good food."

He kissed me good night at the front door and made me promise to come out to Middleburg for a weekend as soon as I could.

It took a long time before I fell into a turbulent, muddled sleep. The dreams came right away: Katya Gordon and Scott Hathaway standing together, limned by moonlight, as she said over and over, "An eye for an eye, Scott. Now we're even."

Finally I sat up in bed and said out loud, "Even for what?"

TWENTY

I n spite of all the wine, champagne, and Madeira I drank last night, I woke up surprisingly clearheaded early Sunday morning and went for a quick run while it was still cool. When I got home, I showered, changed, and walked downtown to St. Matthew's Cathedral on the corner of Connecticut and Rhode Island Avenues. Nick had never been much on organized religion—he always joked he was waiting for the Rapture—but since he'd vanished, I'd been faithful about attending Mass every Sunday and it had gotten me through some dark days. In London, I went to a little convent chapel in St. John's Wood, known informally as the American church. Today was the first time I'd set foot in St. Matthew's since I'd been home, and I'd forgotten how beautiful it was, the shimmering mosaics and inlaid stone reminding me of palaces and monuments I'd visited in India.

I'd also forgotten the Latin Mass was at ten o'clock, and when the Gospel reading from Saint Mark mentioned adultery, my mind wandered to Katya Gordon, Scott Hathaway, and Taras Attar. I still didn't understand what was going on among the three of them, but after seeing all of them last night and what I'd learned from Father Pat about the long-ago animosity between Scott and Taras over Scott's exotic dancer girlfriend, I wondered if Katya hadn't also been part of some complicated love triangle. Maybe this was the oldest of scenarios: revenge-fueled jealousy and payback for being spurned. If Katya and Scott had continued to be lovers, perhaps she decided to blackmail him by telling his very wealthy wife about the affair, threatening his marriage and his career. Adultery, as Saint Mark said, could be a powerful motivator.

As for the conversation I overheard in the National Gallery implicating Hathaway in a plot to assassinate Attar, by now it seemed Duval was right and I'd somehow gotten that story completely wrong. On the contrary, Attar was staying with the Hathaways, where it was far easier to protect him from an attempt on his life than if he were in a hotel. And if anyone had murderous thoughts about Taras it was Roxanne, who seemed exasperated at putting up with the ego and Casanova antics of her husband's friend while he was a guest under her roof.

Mass ended at eleven. On my way out, I stopped in one of the chapels, lit a candle for Ali, and knelt to say a prayer for her. Outside, the temperature had climbed to the high eighties and the humidity had returned. Clouds had rolled in and it looked and felt like we'd soon have rain.

I walked to the corner of 17th and Q, where you could get breakfast all day at the Trio Restaurant and ate while reading the Sunday newspapers. There were no new developments in the investigation of Ali's death and the autopsy was still pending. What if they never found out who did it?

How would I live with that?

As soon as I got home I called Grace. An unsolved murder surely weighed on someone's conscience at the MPD: You always hear stories about cops who keep folders and note-books and have sleepless nights about the victims whose killers were never brought to justice. Was there someone like that who still cared about what happened to Jenna Paradise, the girl who caused the rift between Scott Hathaway and Taras Attar?

If I asked Grace to call in one more favor she'd want a full explanation, but maybe she would do it, even if it was farfetched and a long shot. Her phone went to voice mail and I left a message, asking her to call me.

Half an hour later my phone rang. The display said "unknown caller." Not Grace. The only unknown caller I knew was Napoleon Duval. Maybe he wanted to meet yet again and ply me with more questions I couldn't answer about Nick's where-abouts. Reluctantly I answered.

"Sophie, love. It's Baz. Sorry I'm just now getting around to returning your call."

A pang of nostalgia shot through me. I closed my eyes and suddenly I was back in London and Baz was calling to invite me to high tea or sherry at the House of Lords or to make sure Nick and I were coming to some fabulous dinner party he and Lady Isabella were hosting at their lavish home on Eaton Square.

"Baz," I said, "I miss you so much. It's good to hear you."

"Darling, are you all right? It's not . . . Nick, is it? Some news?"

"I'm okay and unfortunately there's no news about Nick. I'm just terribly homesick for London . . . and you."

"That can be easily remedied. I'm in town and I absolutely must see you. I hope you're free for a drink this afternoon? We could meet at my club."

"You're in Washington?" I walked outside to the balcony. "When did you get here? How long are you staying?"

"I arrived a few days ago. I meant to ring you sooner, love, but I've been devilishly tied up," he said. "And I'm scheduled to fly back tomorrow night, if all goes well."

I stood at the railing looking out on Max Katzer's garden and India's carriage house, surprised and a little hurt Baz hadn't found a moment to at least call and say he was in town. But he'd just said he was run-off-his-feet busy, probably in marathon meetings that started early and ended late.

"It's okay." I tried to hide my disappointment. "I'd love to meet you for a drink. Where are you staying?"

"The G. Washington Club on 16th Street near the White House. Do you know it?"

A private club that had been men-only for over a century until they finally broke down and admitted women in the late 1990s. That enlightened decision ended the practice of nude sunbathing on the roof and swimming in your altogether in the lap pool. Harry had been a member for decades and often dined there when he was in town.

"My stepfather belongs to that club. I walked by it yesterday."

"Did you really? What an odd coincidence," he said. "I'm sorry it's only drinks, darling. If I weren't tied up for dinner again tonight, I'd take you out on the town and spoil you rotten. I promise next time."

I smiled. "I'll hold you to it. And at least I get to see you on this trip. What time do you want to meet?"

"Let's say half three in the library," he said. "It's on the first floor. Ask at the reception. The place is rather quiet this weekend, so we might even have it to ourselves."

"Three thirty," I said. "I'll see you then."

The library at the G. Washington Club was more a meeting room for socializing than a place to sit and read or do research. Though the room was lined with bookshelves, the collection that made up the library was an ad hoc assortment of donations over the years that ran the gamut from highbrow literary fiction and serious nonfiction to lowbrow trashy beach reads. A large bookcase near the door had been designated as a showcase for signed editions written by club members.

They'd redecorated since the last time I'd been here with Harry: hunter green walls, matching moiré silk curtains with swagged jabots and heavy gold tassels, glossy white bookshelves that contrasted with the strong dark green. The furniture, arranged in small seated groupings, had been reupholstered in muted shades of sage and raspberry. Large bamboo palms in terra-cotta urns screened several of the seating areas so they had more privacy, and it was behind a large potted plant that I found Baz. He was sitting in a wing chair, impeccably dressed in a three-piece bespoke charcoal gray suit, subtle red-and-gray paisley tie, red silk pocket handkerchief, his glasses slipped down on the bridge of his nose as he frowned at something in the London Sunday *Times* crossword puzzle. A glass of sherry sat on a marble-topped table next to him.

"You're in America," I said as he stood up to give me a kiss on the cheek and a hug. "You could at least be doing the *New York Times* puzzle."

"Lord," he said, "I finished that ages ago. In ink."

"Showoff." I sat in a leather club chair next to him.

"Penology repeater. Ten letters. There's a v and at least two i's."

"Recidivist."

"Excellent." He filled in the word and set down the paper and his gold Montblanc fountain pen as a pretty redhead in a white jacket and black trousers appeared.

"Something for your guest, Lord Allingham?"

"What would you like, Sophie?" Baz asked.

"A glass of sparkling water, please."

"No wine? No sherry?" he said.

"No thanks. I had a late night last night."

"Oh?" He raised an eyebrow.

"I filled in for my mother as my stepfather's date at a fundraiser."

The waitress left and returned a moment later with my water and a bowl of mixed nuts. Baz picked up his sherry.

"To old friends in new places."

"To old friends."

We drank and he said, "You look rather tired, love. More than just one late night. How are you? How's the new job?"

"The new job's okay," I said. "Interesting work . . . it's a change from IPS."

"How are you doing otherwise?"

"Fine. I just moved to a new place two days ago, so I'm slowly getting settled into life back in America."

He drank more sherry and said, "Darling, I was referring to Nick."

Our eyes met. This wasn't just a social get-together. Baz had information to share, but first he wanted to know what I knew about my husband, just like he'd done that day at Westminster Abbey.

I set down my glass. "Everyone is looking for him and those damn well logs. If he even has them."

Baz nodded. "What else?"

I told him about my meeting with Arkady Vasiliev at the National Gallery and what Napoleon Duval said yesterday about Nick being wanted for questioning in connection with the death of Nick's CIA contact in Iskar.

"You know Nick's with the agency," I said. "So there's no point pretending anymore. In fact, I figure you've known for a while."

He nodded again, crossing one leg over the other. "What made you think I knew he was CIA?"

"I guessed that day at the Abbey, though I wasn't sure. And, of course, I couldn't say anything or ask you," I said. "When did you find out?"

"One develops a sixth sense about these things," he said. "Sometimes you're wrong, but most times you can tell when someone's part of the community. I've known for quite a while . . . a couple of years."

"And you also know Nick isn't capable of murder," I said. "He didn't kill Colin and he didn't kill that agent in Abadistan, either."

Baz wagged a finger at me. "I know, love, but there but for the grace of God go any of us. In the heat of the moment, under extreme provocation, anyone—and that includes you and me—is capable of doing something, committing some act, we'd never believe we'd do. Including murder. Neither of us knows what Nick's been through, what he's had to do to survive."

"Do you *know* what happened in Iskar? Do you *know* Nick murdered his handler?" My voice rose.

"Darling, not so loud." He signaled for the waitress. "I'll have another sherry and Ms. Medina would like a glass of Chardonnay." He glanced at me. "Or would you prefer something stronger, Sophie? A whiskey, perhaps?"

"Chardonnay is fine. Thank you."

After the waitress left, Baz said, "You look like you could do with a drink after all. I hate to see you so distressed."

"You didn't answer my question, Baz."

He steepled his fingers as though he were considering his reply. Outside in the corridor, a Westminster clock chimed the full hour and then struck four.

"I'm worried, darling. It looks bad for Nick from the CIA's point of view. He was in Iskar the day that chap was killed and he was in Vienna the day Colin was found in the Danube." He shrugged and his smile seemed tinged with regret. "What did Nick always say about coincidences?"

The waitress set down our drinks.

"In the intelligence world, there's no such thing," I said. "But that doesn't mean he couldn't have been set up . . . that it couldn't have been a conspiracy."

Baz drank his sherry. "Why? For what purpose?"

"Because maybe all the speculation and the rumors are true. Crowne Energy made a significant oil discovery where there was supposed to be nothing and someone leaked that information." I frowned at Baz. "You know everyone in the industry. Can't you find out?"

"If I could, I would. Believe me." He leaned forward and lowered his voice. "Sophie, I know what you told Agent Duval about not knowing where Nick might be, but this is me. *Do you know where he is?*"

I drank my wine and said, "No. Duval said he probably left Russia. He seems to think Nick will come to me."

Baz nodded. "I agree. He'll go someplace he knows. You'd be my first guess, too."

"What about London?"

"A possibility. But he's got to be running out of money," he said. "Look, I can help. I can get Nick enough cash, whatever he needs, until this gets straightened out. Plus I've got friends who owe me favors. If I tell them to back off, they'll back off."

"You would do that for Nick?" I said.

"I would do it for both of you," he said. "Just let me know when you hear from him and how to contact him and get him the funds. I'll take care of the rest."

Money. Baz was dangling a hell of a carrot. "You could get in a lot of trouble, Baz, if anyone finds out."

"I'll take that risk." He stood. "I'm sorry, love, but I need to dash . . . paperwork to finish and then a business dinner. All work and no play. I'm becoming a very dull boy, I'm afraid."

I finished my wine. "You're leaving tomorrow?"

"Tomorrow night."

"Next trip stay a little longer and we'll visit the tourist sites in Washington together."

"I'd like that," he said. "I did manage to get in a quick visit to that Fabergé exhibit after reading your e-mail."

"What did you think?" I asked as he walked me to the front door.

"You were right. It's fabulous. Quite astonishing they actually found the little items that belonged to the Blue Constellation egg as well."

I said, puzzled, "Do you mean the surprises? They turned up somewhere?"

"Why, yes," he said. "Didn't you know? A miniature clock

made of the same blue glass and crystal as the egg, and a solid gold lion to represent Leo, the zodiac sign under which the little boy, Alexis, was born. Someone approached Arkady Vasiliev and told him he owned the items—it came quite out of nowhere. He paid a king's ransom, but of course now he'll be remembered for reuniting the last imperial Fabergé egg with its lost treasures."

This had to be the new development Katya Gordon had hinted at during her talk at Hillwood on Friday.

"I didn't know that information had been made public," I said. "I was told Vasiliev was going to announce it at a press conference."

Baz waved a hand. "Perhaps he is, but it's an open secret at the National Gallery."

Had Seth leaked the news? It didn't sound right, given Vasiliev's insistence on controlling everything that had to do with the exhibit and the imperial eggs, but Duval said Vasiliev was on his supersize yacht in the middle of the ocean so maybe there had been a communication slipup.

Baz's mobile rang in his pocket. He pulled it out and checked the display. "Oh, blast. I'm sorry, darling, but I've got to take this. I'd better go. Be in touch . . . love and kisses."

He blew me a kiss and turned away to answer his phone.

I walked back to S Street and thought about Baz's unexpected offer to help Nick. He'd be taking, as I'd told him, a huge risk. Of course there was the other side of the coin, something I didn't want to contemplate.

The money was bait, to lure Nick in.

And Baz had just extracted a promise from me that I would set the trap.

A note written in purple marker was taped to my front door when I got back to the house half an hour later.

Please drop by. Something arrived for you.

—India

I went next door and knocked on her front door. Today she wore flowing pink-and-purple harem pants, a matching embroidered tunic, silver bracelets that sounded like wind chimes when she moved her hands, and her trademark Chanel No. 5.

India smiled and said, "I believe you have an admirer." I must have looked dumbfounded because she added, "Perhaps it's that tall, good-looking gentleman I saw you with last night?"

"That would be my stepfather."

It was her turn to look surprised. "Wait here." A moment later she returned holding a bouquet of red roses. "You weren't home so the delivery boy brought them here. I put them in water so, mind, the stems are wet. There doesn't seem to be a card. He said you'd know who they're from."

I took the flowers. "When were they delivered?"

"About an hour ago."

"On a Sunday?"

"Apparently those were the instructions." She gave me a sly look and said, "So do you know who they're from?"

I did.

"You were right. They are from my stepfather. He and my mother sent them as a housewarming gift. Thank you so much for taking them in."

"No trouble at all." India looked nonplussed. "Why didn't he bring them last night instead of going to the expense and trouble of having them delivered when the florist is closed?"

"Oh, my parents are like that. They wanted to surprise me."

I walked back to my apartment fairly certain India guessed I was lying. My parents would have sent their daughter pink, yellow, or peach roses, but probably not red, the color of love and passion.

I didn't need a card to know who sent them.

The roses were from Nick.

TWENTY-ONE

Nick was *here*. He was in Washington and he had come, as Duval and Baz predicted, straight to me. It felt as though the world had suddenly tilted on its axis, spinning faster and leaving me so breathless I could scarcely keep up.

For the next hour I paced the apartment and tried to avoid looking out the bay window too often, because somewhere out there people were watching me and waiting for Nick. As risky and dangerous as it was, he was going to find a way to be with me. That's why he sent the roses: He wanted me to know.

Just after six o'clock the skies turned dark and the rains finally came. Along S Street, lights appeared inside homes and the sodium vapor streetlamps flickered on earlier than usual. By now I knew what I was going to do. The only thing left was the interminable wait.

At eleven, I turned off all the lights in my apartment as though I were going to bed and made my way downstairs in the dark to the front vestibule. Earlier I had swiped the doorjamb key to Max Katzer's apartment and left a basket with a bottle of Montgomery Estate Cabernet Sauvignon, some homemade sandwiches, and a couple of chocolate bars inside his front door. I let myself into Max's place, got the basket, and walked out the back door to his garden. India's lights were still on, shining like friendly beacons in the darkness. If she happened to look out her windows at the wrong moment, she would have a clear view of me in Max's garden and she would know I could only have gotten there by breaking into his apartment. I didn't look up, as though some magnetic pull would bring her to the window if I did. The gate creaked when I opened it—I'd been afraid it might—but it was too late to do anything now. I closed it and sprinted across the alley, unlocking the door to Max's carriage house office. Before

I went inside I scattered half a dozen rose petals in front of the door, just like Nick used to do on the staircase in our cottage when a bottle of champagne was chilling, to be drunk in bed by candlelight.

There was one windowless room at the back of the carriage house and it was stacked with furniture in need of repair. I had covered the beam of my flashlight with a red gel filter from my flash equipment, so I turned on the muted light and searched until I found a coffee table, which I dragged in front of a humpbacked velveteen sofa. Then I turned off the light and sat in the darkness as the rain pounded the metal roof like hundreds of ballpeen hammers.

He arrived at midnight.

The front door opened and closed with a faint click and someone began moving stealthily around Max's office, a tiny floorboard creak, little whispering sounds barely audible above the steady drumming of the rain. A moment later, the red beam of a proper night vision flashlight picked out the piled-up furniture surrounding me.

"Sophie?" His voice was a hoarse whisper.

"Nick!"

I flew across the room, nearly knocking him over as we fell into each other's arms. He was soaking wet as if he'd just been swimming, crushing me to him in a fierce embrace, stroking my hair and whispering my name over and over. Then his mouth was on mine and we were like a couple of desperate teenagers, kissing and ripping at each other's clothes as we undressed each other.

Somewhere in my brain a warning bell went off. He had changed. My husband hadn't exactly become a stranger, but something was different, alien. Not just the physical changes—the beard, the longer hair, a different color, and his deeply bronzed skin—but even his clothes seemed foreign and his kiss tasted and smelled of an exotic scent I couldn't define: traces of wind, dust, spices with unpronounceable names, some faint fragrance that belonged to a life I didn't know.

"I'm so sorry," he said into my hair. "I've put you through hell."

"Shh." I pushed back my own fears about what this ordeal

had done to him, how it would change us. "Don't talk about it now . . . how long do we have?"

I heard his sharp intake of breath and he said against my ear, "Two hours at most."

He lifted me up and I wrapped my arms and legs tight around him as he carried me to the sofa and laid me down. I think I was shivering from the cold, but all I remember was pulling him on top of me and closing my eyes, ignoring the rough velveteen fabric abrading my skin as we moved back and forth in the old rhythm. Two hours . . . at most.

We needed to make it last a lifetime.

The sofa was barely the width of a twin bed but we made it work. Afterward, we got dressed because it was chilly and, though neither of us mentioned it, because we might need to move fast, get out of there quickly. Nick had a gun, a small revolver, which he placed on the coffee table.

I tried not to wonder if he'd used it.

I unpacked the picnic basket and took out two votive candles and a book of matches. "There aren't any windows in this room. I think we'll be okay to light these . . . I want to see you, Nick."

His smile was a quick flash of white teeth in the darkness. "Wait a minute." He got up and found a couple of pillows on another sofa in the corner of the room, propping them against the doorjamb. "In case the jamb's not flush with the threshold."

He pulled my rose petals, now bruised and soggy, out of his pocket as the flare of a match lit up his handsome face. In the sharp golden light he looked exhausted, and I already knew when we made love that he'd lost a lot of weight. I wanted to ask about his health, what he ate, was he sleeping, but we were running out of time.

"I found these outside by the door." He set the crushed petals on the coffee table. "Better safe than sorry."

"The roses were beautiful. I left the petals so you'd know where to find me."

"You're my true north," he said. "I always know where to find you."

I blinked back tears as he opened the wine and set the cork faceup on the table, a familiar little quirk of his. For a split second we were back in London and this was one of the indoor picnics we used to have in front of a winter fire in the sitting room, lying on the wedding ring quilt from our bed. But those days were gone and he was on the run, a wanted man. And this was no romantic evening by the fire: It was a dangerous clandestine meeting, our own little council of war.

We touched glasses and he brushed my cheek with the back of his hand. "I love you, Sophie. I've missed you terribly."

"I love you and I've missed you terribly, too," I said. "Nick, there are people in the CIA who think you had something to do with Colin's death and the death of your contact in Abadistan. They have a picture of you at a riot in Iskar on the day your CIA contact was murdered. And someone sent me a photo of you standing in the exact spot where they found Colin's body in the Danube."

His eyes grew dark. At first I thought it was shock, but then I realized he was angry. "It's a setup," he said. "Colin and I met in Vienna right before he was killed—he gave me the well logs—so it's true I was there. But I wasn't at any riot in Iskar the day Dani was murdered. The pictures must have been doctored. What do you call it . . . a multiple exposure?"

"With the right computer software it's not hard to do. Sometimes it's as easy as swapping your head for someone else's."

He stared into his wineglass. "I'm sorry you got dragged into this. The agency must have given you a contact. Is that how you saw the Iskar photo?"

"Yes. His name is Napoleon Duval. He used to be CIA, but now he's with something called the National Counterterrorism Task Force. Do you know him?"

"Doesn't ring a bell," he said. "And you don't ever 'leave' the CIA, darling. What's he like?"

"If you crossed a superhero with Dirty Harry, that's Duval. I think bullets bounce off his chest," I said. "Unless he catches them between his teeth."

He flashed the ghost of a smile. "A hard-ass. Is he giving you grief about me?"

"I don't think he trusts me," I said. "Though I'm not sure I trust him, either. He says the longer you stay out, the guiltier you look. What happened, Nick? How did this start? Why did you have to fake your own kidnapping?"

He rubbed his thumb back and forth across the pulse point on my wrist and I caught my breath. His touch was warm and sure.

"I wish I'd been able to warn you, baby. Colin called me that night you were flying home from Istanbul and told me to get the hell out. He said they were coming for me. I'm pretty sure Dani set me up."

"Your CIA contact?"

He drank some wine. "Yeah, the guy I supposedly murdered in Iskar." He said it casually.

It hung in the air between us, and my eyes went automatically to the gun. We had never, ever talked about whether he'd used it before, but this time was different. I needed to know.

"You didn't kill him, did you?" I asked.

"What do you think?" he asked in a calm voice.

The rain had let up and the sound of it beating on the metal roof had become a muted, steady thrumming, white noise that shut out the rest of the world. Nick kept secrets from me all the time, but I knew if he'd killed a man this would not be one of them. He sat there and waited for my answer.

"I told Duval you didn't murder anybody," I said.

He nodded and relief flooded through me. "What did he say to that?"

"He said if you didn't kill him, you probably know who did."

Nick snorted. "I wonder if Duval's ever been anyplace more dangerous than a desk in Langley. Jesus, Lord. That's what I'm trying to find out before whoever it is finds me."

"You don't know who you're looking for?"

He refilled our glasses. "Not yet. But I do know this: If I hadn't told Dani what we discovered when we drilled that test well, I'm pretty sure Colin would still be alive. Colin was killed because of what he knew. I'm next on the list."

I shuddered. "Whose list? The Shaika?"

"Those guys will shoot you just to see if their gun works. Arkady Vasiliev is a buddy with the *pakhan,* their big boss. I'm guessing it's a joint venture."

"Vasiliev wants your well logs, Nick."

"I'll bet he does. I'm pretty sure he wants what's left of Crowne Energy, too," he said. "And unless I can stop him, he's probably going to get it. With his money and political connections he could steal the iconostases from every one of the Kremlin churches and get away with it."

"How are you going to stop someone like Vasiliev? He's on one of his ocean liners in the middle of nowhere, according to Duval. Didn't I read that there's a submarine on board in case he needs to make a quick getaway and surface-to-air missiles in case of an attack by God knows who?"

"He can't stay in the middle of nowhere forever. First I need to find out who sold out Colin and me."

I frowned. "I thought you said it was Dani. Do you think he was working for both sides? The CIA and the Shaika?"

"I'm sure of it. But there's one more traitor, one more Judas in the bunch. Someone's setting me up to take the rap for Colin and Dani . . . whoever faked those pictures, the one Duval showed you and the one someone sent you."

I passed Nick a sandwich and he devoured it. "I don't understand. The reason Colin and Dani were killed, and now someone's after you, is that you discovered oil in Abadistan?"

He wiped his mouth on a napkin and said, "It's more than that, Soph. We drilled a rank wildcat and guess what we found? Light, sweet crude. It doesn't get any better than that." He grinned at my wide-eyed look of shock. "Yup. The real deal."

Light, sweet crude was the best, most expensive oil in the world, on par with Saudi Arabian oil. And a rank wildcat was the riskiest well you could drill because it meant you were looking for oil far from where anyone expected to find it. The combination of the two was the equivalent of hitting the biggest megamillions lottery jackpot ever, two days in a row.

I had guessed that Crowne Energy discovered oil, but nothing like that. "My God, Nick. Are you serious?"

He took another sandwich. "If there's as much oil as we think there is, that region will go from abject poverty to un-imaginable wealth. You have no idea how much money we're talking about, the fortunes that will be made."

Yes, I did. Enough to kill for.

"Vasiliev knows you found oil, or at least he's got a pretty good idea," I said. "And somehow he knows you're alive. Why is he doing this? Why is he trying to destroy Crowne Energy? He already owns the biggest oil production company in Russia."

I rummaged through the picnic basket for the chocolate bars and handed one to him.

"Because it's the Russian way." He unwrapped the choco-late, broke off a piece and gave it to me, and took another for himself. "In America, if a man has one cow and his neighbor has two cows, the guy with one cow aspires to be like the richer neighbor. In Russia, the guy with one cow kills one of the neighbor's two cows, so now they both have only one cow and they're equal. It's a completely different mentality."

I licked my fingers. "That's crazy."

"Welcome to Russia."

"What about the well logs?" I asked. "Everyone's searching for them like they're the Holy Grail."

"They're in a safe place," he said. "Don't worry."

"Vasiliev told me to tell you he'd pay good money for them."

"Vasiliev can go to hell," Nick said. "One way or the other he's responsible for Colin's death. I don't want his blood money. It's bad enough I have to live with my own guilt for what happened to Colin."

"It's not your fault. You shouldn't blame yourself—" I stopped.

He didn't miss a beat. "What happened, baby? What's wrong?"

I told him about Ali.

He pulled my head down on his shoulder. "You couldn't have known what would happen to her. You're not responsible for someone else's actions."

"Then you're not responsible for Colin's death, either," I said. "Jack O'Hara said the exact same thing. I know it's true, but I don't feel any less guilty. Just like you."

He kissed my hair. "I'm glad you have Jack . . . he's a good friend. I miss seeing him."

I sat up. "You know who else I saw, speaking of good friends? Baz. Just this afternoon. He's in town on business for a few days. Nick, he figures you're broke by now, with no access to money. The CIA knows you're not using your phone, your e-mail accounts, or your credit cards. Baz wants to help. He said if I set up a meeting, he'll get you some cash until this gets straightened out."

"No." Nick was adamant. "No meeting. You can't tell Baz or anyone else you saw me, okay? I don't trust anyone except you. And I'm already putting you at risk just being here."

"Don't say that. We're going to get through this."

"We are. It's going to be over soon."

"What do you mean?"

"Taras Attar, the Abadi political leader, is in Washington this weekend." He offered me the last square of chocolate. I shook my head and he ate it.

"I know. Harry dragged me to a fund-raiser at Scott and Roxanne Hathaway's home last night. Attar is staying with them. I met him."

He stopped chewing. "You met Attar?"

"For about thirty seconds. He has no idea who I am. Why did you bring him up?"

"I'm meeting him during his trip here to brief him privately," he said. "Attar is pro-U.S. Vasiliev, on the other hand, has been getting friendly with the Iranians—we have information that he flew to Tehran for meetings with their energy minister. You know how easy it would be to transport crude across the Caspian Sea from Abadistan to Iran? If Abadistan should secede from Russia, that oil would belong to a friendly ally, not controlled by someone who wants to get in bed with a country we've got sanctions against because they're trying to build a nuclear weapon."

"I thought the United States didn't interfere in the internal politics of another nation," I said, my expression deadpan. "Or at least, that's what Scott Hathaway said the other night to the Russian ambassador."

Nick made a face and drained his wineglass. "You know better. Of course we do. We just try not to get caught."

I didn't want to look at my watch because I knew our two hours were almost up. "Before you go, there's one more thing you should know about Taras Attar," I said and quickly told him about the conversation I'd overheard at the National Gallery.

"Are you sure about Hathaway being involved?" Nick asked.

"You sound like Duval. He doesn't believe me, either."

"It's not that I don't believe you," he said. "But Attar's in D.C. to take a pulse on how much U.S. support he'd get if the Abadi separatist movement heated up. The book tour's a convenient cover. Hathaway's chaperoning him all over town. Sorry, baby, but it doesn't really add up."

I felt like the kid trying to insist the monsters hiding under my bed were honest-to-God real. "I know what I heard."

His eyes searched my face. "Well, it wouldn't surprise me if someone tried to go after Attar while he's in the U.S. Makes a hell of a mess for us if they succeed."

"Probably a hell of a mess for Attar, too," I said and he grinned. "How are you going to meet him when you've got Duval and God knows who else stalking you?"

"I have a friend or two left," he said. "They don't all work for the CIA. And some of them happen to be pretty highly placed."

"What are you saying?"

"I've said enough. More than I should have."

"Then what? What happens after you talk to Attar?"

"I'm going after whoever killed Colin and Dani," he said. "And find out who set me up."

"Nick—"

He stood up and pulled me to him. "It'll be okay. Don't worry, darling."

I tilted my face to his. "When am I going to see you again?"

"I don't know," he said, kissing me. "But I know where you live. And I know a great florist."

TWENTY-TWO

I waited until Nick was long gone, vanished into the rain-slicked night as silently and stealthily as he'd come, before I cleaned up our picnic and moved the furniture back where I'd found it. By the time I walked across the alley to Max's place just before three, the rain had tapered to a light drizzle. I restored the key to its spot above the doorjamb and let myself into my own apartment and went straight to the tower bedroom. When I finally fell asleep, Nick's scent, which had stayed on my skin and embedded itself in the fabric of my clothes, filtered into my dreams. For what remained of the night, we were both on the run from faceless men who chased us and would not give up.

My phone rang at eight o'clock, the noise slicing through my druggy sleep. I sat up in bed and wondered where I was and what day it was.

"Soph? Are you all right?" Grace asked. "Did I wake you? I figured you'd be getting ready for work. Sorry I'm calling so early. We were out of town all day yesterday . . . this is the first chance I've had to call back."

My message yesterday . . . what was it? I climbed out of bed and opened the curtains. Last night's storm had blown away the clouds, leaving behind a clear pale blue sky. Then I remembered: I wanted to ask Grace about Jenna Paradise, Scott Hathaway's girlfriend, who had vanished without a trace.

"I'm fine, Gracie . . . I slept through my alarm. It's a good thing you woke me up."

"What's going on?"

I told her and asked if she knew anyone at the MPD who might be willing to look into a cold case.

"A priest friend of Jack's from Georgetown told me Scott Hathaway was questioned by the police after Jenna Paradise disappeared. His father, who was a big shot lawyer, flew to

D.C. and intervened, so that was the end of the questioning. I wondered what happened to the investigation," I said. "There must have been a report."

"Thirty years is a long time ago," she said. "Look, I'm taking a detective who helps me out from time to time to breakfast this morning. I'll ask him, but don't hold your breath."

"Thanks," I said. "I owe you."

"I doubt it," she said. "I don't think I'll find out anything. But if I do, I'll let you know."

Baz called next, while I was finishing breakfast. Unknown caller. This time, I recognized the phone number.

"I just wanted to hear your voice, love," he said. "And to apologize for rushing you out the door yesterday. Sorry about that call . . . I had to take it. You know how it is."

"You don't need to apologize," I said. "I know you're busy. How was your dinner last night?"

"Long and dull," he said. "Listen, darling, I thought I'd check in and ask if you've had any word from our boy?"

You can't tell Baz or anyone else you saw me. I don't trust anyone except you.

That was the real reason he was calling, to ask about Nick. I said, smooth as silk, "No. Nothing."

"Keep me posted, will you, Sophie? Make sure you let him know I'm there to help."

"Of course," I said. "Have a safe trip home. And give my love to Isabella."

"I shall," he said. "Cheerio."

I hung up and cleared away my breakfast dishes. Was it my imagination, or had Baz been fishing because he knew Nick was in town?

More important, had I been a convincing enough liar?

I got dressed for work, found my IPS press badge, which Perry never asked me to turn in, and called Luke.

"I thought I'd cover Taras Attar's book signing at the Library of Congress," I said. "It starts at noon."

I waited during the long silence on his end, guessing he already knew he couldn't tell me not to do it. Still, he sounded irked.

"First, I think you need to be accredited, and second, we're not a news agency."

"I think I can swing the accreditation and I know we're not. But I'd like to do it."

"I could use you here. I got a voice mail from someone at the Turkish embassy who wants to talk about a project. She asked me to give her a call to set up a meeting at my earliest convenience," he said. "And Roxanne Hathaway's people went into high gear. A huge package of historical photographs arrived first thing this morning. We really don't have time for something no one asked us to do."

"I'll be in as soon as the signing's finished. I promise."

When he hung up I knew he was mad. I nearly called him back, but I'd already decided to do this, and I'd probably only get him more irritated and spun up. I rode the Vespa to the IPS Washington bureau on DeSales Street next door to ABC News and a block from St. Matthew's. The bureau chief was a short brunette named Monica who was a good friend of Perry's.

"I heard you laid off two shooters on Friday," I said, "so I know you're short staffed. You got anyone covering Taras Attar's book signing on Capitol Hill?"

She looked at me like I'd just dropped in from a remote planet. "Are you kidding? We've now got precisely one and a half people covering the entire Hill. You can bet your ass no one's going to be covering a book signing."

I wondered who the half person was and said, "Then let me do it. Can you get me in?"

"What's so special about this one?"

"Senator Hathaway's sponsoring it and the Russian embassy is furious. It might be newsworthy."

"We haven't got any money. You'd have to do it on spec."

"I just want the accreditation."

She shrugged with a look that said, *It's your funeral,* made a call, and found me talking to a reporter I knew from a couple of TDY rotations in London.

"Medina," Monica said. "Get going. You're on the list."

Half an hour later I chained the Vespa to a streetlamp on 2nd Street behind the Supreme Court and walked over to the Library of Congress. It had turned into a spectacular early autumn day, the light breeze a warm caress on my skin and the kind of sharp sunshine that made colors so vivid they hurt your eyes. The Capitol dome looked like a cutout pasted on a perfect cobalt sky.

The bronze doors to the library were closed and signs outside on the plaza informed all visitors they needed to use the old carriage entrance on the lower level. As I walked down the broad granite staircase, a limousine pulled into the narrow drive, stopping under the portico. Scott Hathaway's bulky driver got out and went around to open the rear passenger door. I expected Hathaway to emerge, but instead Taras Attar, in a well-cut double-breasted suit and red tie, was the only one who got out. He took off his sunglasses and checked something on his phone.

I stopped to watch him. Even after thirty years it wasn't hard to imagine Attar and Hathaway cutting a wide swath through the female population of Georgetown as Father Pat had said. But where Scott Hathaway was the all-American golden boy your mother wanted you to marry, Attar was the one you wanted to know: dark and dangerous looking with the hardened features—hawklike nose, firm mouth, penetrating eyes—of a warrior-king.

"I'll expect to find you here when I'm finished," Attar said to the chauffeur as Napoleon Duval, also dressed like a New York banker, got out of a second car that had pulled up behind the limousine.

"Yes, sir." The driver nodded and took a handkerchief out of his pocket as he sneezed and blew his nose. As he hustled Attar into the building, Duval looked up and noticed me hanging over the railing. He gave me a grim nod and followed Attar inside.

By the time I passed through the metal detector and had my equipment bag searched and my credentials checked, Attar and Duval were vanishing into an elevator with an ascetic-looking man in a pale gray suit.

"The book signing has been moved from the Main Reading Room to the Members Room off the Great Hall," the security guard said to me. "Up the stairs and take the corridor to your right."

I nodded. "I know where it is. Thanks."

Much of the federal architecture of Washington pays homage to the ancient Greek and Roman civilizations because the Founding Fathers, who saw temples like the Parthenon in Athens and the Roman Pantheon as symbols of democracy and liberty, wanted their new capital to reflect those same ideals. But by the time plans for the Library of Congress were drawn up in the late 1800s during the Gilded Age, its architects chose the elaborate Paris Opera House as their inspiration, building a lavish, richly decorated Italian Renaissance–style palace of mosaics, paintings, and statuary depicting mythology, legend, and flesh-and-blood icons of poetry and literature.

The Members of Congress Room was a dark, elegant jewel with heavy paneling, coffered frescoed ceilings, Oriental carpets, and two enormous marble fireplaces at opposite ends of the room that could have been plucked from the residence of a Venetian prince. Today rows of red velvet chairs facing a podium had been placed in front of one of the fireplaces. It looked like they were expecting a good crowd; I counted roughly one hundred seats. A table with neat piles of copies of *Growing Up Among the Holy Shadows of the Dead* by Taras Attar stacked on it, a small bar, and a buffet table with platters of sandwiches, cheese, fruit, and cookies were at the other end of the room. A few people had already taken their seats, but most of the invitation-only guests from the library, the Hill, and the State Department were enjoying the free lunch and a glass of wine.

Except for a young woman manning a camera for C-SPAN's Book TV and a gray-haired reporter in a navy blazer, T-shirt, jeans, and red high-tops from the AP, I was the only member of the press. I staked a place between two windows with views of the House of Representatives across the street and made a couple of test shots.

"Where is everybody?" I asked the AP reporter, whose name was Keith. "Nobody else is covering this after the blowup the other night between Senator Hathaway and the Russian ambassador over Hathaway sponsoring this book signing?"

"I think it lost a lot of traction when Hathaway pulled out," he said.

"What are you talking about? He did what?"

He scratched behind his ear and shrugged. "Our Senate correspondent says Hathaway plans to give a floor speech later today that's probably going to throw Attar under a bus. Reaffirm our relationship with Russia, dating back to our days as allies in World War II."

Hathaway had decided to placate Yuri Orlov at the expense of his old friend Taras Attar? "Are you serious?" I said.

Keith nodded.

"I wonder when Attar found out," I said.

"Here he comes now. You can ask him yourself."

Taras Attar looked stone-faced and subdued, so I didn't need to ask when he learned Hathaway decided not to show. The ascetic-looking gray-suited man who had greeted Attar at the door also had walked in with him, followed by Napoleon Duval. Duval surveyed the room, placing himself next to the doorway, hands clasped in front of his waist.

"That's Gregory Feinstein, the library's European Division director," Keith said, indicating the man in the gray suit. "Guess he's introducing Attar."

On cue, Feinstein stepped up to the podium and said into the microphone, "Will everyone please take a seat so we can begin?"

Two more sober-suited men—probably diplomatic security—had taken up posts on either side of the far door down by the bookseller and the food and drinks. I glanced at Duval, but he looked implacable, scanning the audience while people slowly made their way to the chairs at the front of the room.

As Attar moved to the podium, he, too, surveyed the crowd. When his eyes fell on me, I caught the tiny flash of surprise before he smiled and nodded. I smiled back without looking at Duval who, I knew, was probably making a mental list of questions as to how, where, and when I'd met Taras Attar.

Gregory Feinstein gave a short, thoughtful talk that steered clear of politics and focused on Attar's book. As Attar acknowledged the audience's applause, a waiter walked through the doorway with a bottle of water and started to pass it to Attar.

"I'll take that," Duval said.

The waiter looked annoyed, but he gave Duval the bottle and left. A moment later he entered the room through the far door and took his place at the bar. Duval unscrewed the cap and set the water bottle on the podium.

Taras Attar's half-hour talk was sprinkled with references to philosophy, poetry, and history as he spoke about his book, about Abadistan, and, most poignantly, about how Russian influence was gradually erasing the culture of the Abadi people until eventually it would disappear and they would live, as Alexander the Great once said, among the holy shadows of the dead. I only knew Abadistan through the dystopian filter of what Nick had told me, but I had been in enough places like it to understand the Darwinian order of life and the transmogrifying effect so much hardship, poverty, and corruption had on people who were desperate to survive. Beneath Attar's poetic eloquence, I was pretty sure beat the calculating heart of a cold-eyed realist who had made concessions to the Shaika and whoever else he needed to, or he would not be in the position of leadership he now occupied.

Crowne Energy's discovery of oil and the promise of vast fortunes to be made by whoever owned that land would change everything. As Perry told me once during yet another custody battle with an ex-wife, "Blood is thicker than water, but money is thicker than blood." Once it was known just how much oil had been found in a godforsaken corner of nowhere, there would be plenty of blood. Nick knew that better than I did, but there was no turning back the clock now: They couldn't undiscover oil.

There was a burst of applause as Attar finished talking and thanked the audience. Fifteen minutes into the question-and-answer session, Keith, the AP reporter, gave me a sideways look and raised his hand.

"Dr. Attar, I understand Senator Hathaway plans to deliver a speech on the Senate floor later today on U.S.-Russian relations and our strong support for that country. Also he isn't here with you even though he's responsible for arranging this event," Keith said. "Do you perceive this as a slap in the face to Abadistan and what impact will his actions have on your personal relationship?"

Taras gave him a tight smile. "No and none," he said. "Any other questions?"

Gregory Feinstein stepped up to the podium, coming to his rescue. "I'm sorry, Dr. Attar, but that will have to be the last question so we have time for the book signing. A representative from the library's bookstore is selling *Growing Up Among the Holy Shadows of the Dead* at the back of the room. I hope everyone will purchase a copy."

There was more applause as Feinstein led Attar to a heavy wooden table with legs that were carved like enormous eagles.

"Are you sticking around?" Keith asked me.

"For a while. I want to get a few more pictures. Then I'm going to buy his book and ask him to sign it," I said. "What about you?"

"I'm going to see if I can nudge him again about Hathaway," he said.

"Good luck."

The room had started to clear out. Duval left his place by the doorway and now stood directly behind Attar. I walked back to the bookseller's table and purchased my book. Though the buffet table had been thoroughly scavenged, there was still punch in the punch bowl. I helped myself while a couple of waiters removed empty food trays and cleared up the debris of used plates and glasses.

My phone vibrated in my pocket. A text message from Luke.

Going to Katya G press conference at Nat Gall. They want photos. Text me when you're done at LC.

If Katya Gordon was holding a press conference, she was probably going to finally announce that Arkady Vasiliev had purchased the surprises for the Blue Tsarevich Constellation egg. I slipped the phone back into my pocket and walked up to Attar's signing table as Keith waved to me on his way out. The Book TV reporter was gone, too.

Attar was gathering up his notes, preparing to leave. When he saw me holding a book, he stopped and picked up a pen.

"Sophie," he said, smiling. "What a pleasant surprise. You're very kind to buy the book. How shall I sign it?"

"I'm looking forward to reading it. Please sign it to me," I said. "And it's Medina. M-e-d-i-n-a."

He wrote something that I couldn't read upside down and signed his name with a bold scrawl across the title page. As he handed it to me, I said, "What's next for you?"

"I'm going back to Scott and Roxanne's after this," he said. "Then I fly home tonight."

If he was leaving today, I wondered whether he had already spoken to Nick or if their meeting hadn't yet taken place.

"I hope you have a safe trip."

"Thank you. Do you think it would be possible to have copies of the photos you took today? They would be nice souvenirs."

"Give me a way to contact you and I'll send them," I said.

He pulled a leather cardholder out of his inside jacket pocket and wrote something on the back of a business card. "My private e-mail address," he said. "Use that."

"Thank you."

I turned around to leave, distracted by reading what he'd written on the card, and collided with one of the waiters.

"I'm sorry," I said. "I wasn't looking where I was going."

It was the waiter who brought Attar the bottle of water. "Don't worry, it's nothing," he said in a flat, toneless voice. "No problem."

He was Russian.

It's nothing, no problem. In Russian, he would have said *nichevo.*

I stared hard at him and heard Ali saying, *What a klutz I am, I'm so sorry,* when she bumped into this same waiter the other night. And then I remembered that monotone voice telling the American in the conference room to keep his mouth shut and everything would be okay. No problem.

"I've met you before," I said. "You were at the National Gallery the other night."

"You are mistaken." His eyes were so pale they seemed colorless, but they held barely controlled anger. "It must have been someone else."

I looked over at Duval. "This guy," I said. "He's the one I overheard."

The waiter didn't hesitate. He shoved me hard, ramming me into the heavy table Attar had used for the book signing and took off. Attar's book flew out of my hands and landed on the floor.

I saw the flash of Duval's gun as he shouted to the other dark-suited men who had already started to move. "Get him. I'm staying with Warrior."

There was commotion in the hallway outside the Members Room and men shouting. Duval spoke into the parakeet microphone on his shoulder. "Send backup and get the car. Warrior's safe. Move it."

Gregory Feinstein helped me up as Duval said to the three of us, "Stay right here until we get this guy."

"Are you all right, miss?" Feinstein asked me. "He threw you pretty hard against that table."

I felt my ribs, which I knew would be bruised and sore later on. My head throbbed when I nodded. "I'm okay."

"They got him," Duval was saying. "All right, we're going to move."

Two uniformed Capitol Hill police officers and two more men in dark suits showed up so speedily that I figured they must have been waiting outside because Attar's evacuation plans had already been worked out.

Attar took my elbow and leaned close to me. "How do you know that man?" he asked in a soft voice.

He seemed surprisingly calm and composed.

"I overheard two men talking the night of Arkady Vasiliev's reception at the National Gallery," I said. "It sounded like they were talking about you. I told Agent Duval . . . When that waiter spoke just now, I recognized his voice and I remembered him from the reception."

Attar gave a short, mirthless laugh. "Vasiliev? Well, then, I suppose they wanted to kill me?"

"It sounded like one of them did."

"Then I must thank you for your intervention," he said.

"Sophie." Duval gave me a warning look. He'd been following our conversation and I knew what he meant.

Don't mention Hathaway.

"You should thank Agent Duval," I said.

Duval turned to Attar. "Go with these men, please, sir, and do exactly as they say." To me he said, "You stay right here."

Attar murmured something to Duval that sounded like thanks as he left the room flanked by bodyguards.

Gregory Feinstein looked shaken. "What just happened?"

"Nothing," Duval said. "Fortunately. But my people need to talk to the head of that catering company about that waiter. Give me a minute alone with Ms. Medina."

"Of course." Feinstein walked back to talk to the remaining catering staff, who looked like they were in shock.

"You knew about the waiter?" I asked.

"We weren't entirely sure until a few minutes ago," Duval said. "Attar never drank that bottle of water, by the way."

"You switched them?"

He nodded.

"What about the other guy, the American?" I asked. "Where is he? Who is he?"

Duval gave me a rueful smile. "You were right about his employer. The only person from Hathaway's staff who showed up today." He waited for me to figure it out.

"The chauffeur," I said. "He had a cold . . . he was sneezing. I thought the guy I heard had allergies."

"He managed to give us a good enough description of the waiter when we picked him up in the parking lot," he said.

"What about Hathaway?" I said. "The chauffeur said he was involved, too."

"Tell me how that part of the conversation went," Duval said. "Tell me exactly what you heard."

My head ached and so did my ribs. "I think the chauffeur said something like, 'You expect me to believe Hathaway is going to go along with this crackpot idea.'"

"To which the waiter replied?"

Duval waited for me to think it through. "He told the chauffeur he couldn't back out because he'd already been paid and he knew too much."

"But the waiter never said, 'You're right, Hathaway's going to go along with it,' did he?" Duval said. "He let the chauffeur believe what he wanted."

"Are you saying that Senator Hathaway's not involved?"

"Senator Hathaway gave us complete access to his staff's personnel records once we went to him. He cooperated fully."

"He still didn't show up today," I said.

"I can't go into the politics of that decision," Duval said. "Look, you're free to go."

He left before I did.

I packed up my camera, and by the time I left through the carriage entrance, I knew my walking-wounded status was going to slow me down getting back to the Vespa. Grace called while I was waiting at the light at East Capitol and 1st Streets.

"Sometimes you get lucky," she said. "My detective buddy was a brand-new cop walking a beat in Georgetown when Jenna Paradise went missing. He's never forgotten the case. Apparently she was gorgeous. He said they never found her and it's still on the books as open-unsolved. The last concrete information they had was an interview with her roommate, who said Jenna took off on her bike to meet a friend. She and the friend were going for a run on one of the trails down by the canal. After that she disappeared. No body, no bicycle, nada."

"Who was the friend?" I asked.

"The roommate didn't know. Jenna kept her business to herself."

"What about the bicycle?" I said. "Is there a description of it in the report?"

"I don't know. Why?"

"Can you ask your detective friend if Jenna's bike had handlebars that looked like a ram's horns?"

"I will if you tell me why."

"Right now I can't, but I will," I said. "Word of honor. Please, Grace?"

She let out a long breath. "I can't believe I'm saying yes, but okay. Then you tell me everything. Got it?"

"Yes. It's just a hunch," I said. "Once I'm sure, I'll tell you what I know."

I disconnected as the light changed and crossed East Capitol. If I was right, Scott Hathaway had intimate knowledge of what had happened to Jenna Paradise, and Katya

Gordon had the photos to prove it, or at least she'd possessed them for the last thirty years until she gave them to Hathaway the other night.

In return for what? What did she want from Hathaway that was significant enough to make her hand over such incriminating photos? Duval seemed to think Hathaway wasn't involved in the plot to assassinate Taras Attar, but maybe there was more to that story. Katya Gordon knew things about Hathaway that would end his career, maybe even result in criminal charges being brought against him.

Whatever bargain Hathaway and Katya had struck, was it something compelling enough to commit murder for? And if so, perhaps not for the first time.

TWENTY-THREE

L uke was probably still at Katya Gordon's press conference at the National Gallery and I sent him a text message as he'd asked me to do.

He called back while I was unchaining the Vespa from the streetlamp on 2nd Street.

"We just wrapped up here. Arkady Vasiliev acquired two surprises belonging to the Blue Constellation egg last week," he said. "A miniature crystal clock and a gold lion representing Alexis's zodiac sign. Katya announced it this morning. Apparently someone contacted Vasiliev and said the items had been in his family for decades but until they saw a story about the Fabergé egg, no one knew what they were. Vasiliev had them checked out and was told they were the real deal. Over the weekend he had them flown to Washington to be part of the exhibit."

"I heard about that," I said.

"You couldn't have," he said. "Unless you're thinking about the hint Katya dropped at Hillwood."

"A friend who visited the National Gallery already knew about the surprises and told me what they were. He said the word had already gotten out."

"Not from anyone at the National Gallery. I talked to Seth, and Moses is still in New York," he said. "I also had a quick word with Roxanne Hathaway before she and Katya took off for lunch. She's eager for us to get started on the Potomac River project."

He kept talking, but I had stopped listening. Why would Katya and Roxanne be having lunch together? Had Roxanne found out Katya was blackmailing her husband?

"Where were Katya and Roxanne going for lunch?" I tried to keep the urgency out of my voice.

"What?" He sounded annoyed again. "To Roxanne's house. Why?"

"I was just wondering," I said. "Luke, I need to do something. I'll be in later."

"Sophie—"

"I'm sorry, but I've got to go."

My next call was to Duval. His phone went to voice mail and I left him a tense message telling him to call me and that it was urgent. By now Attar was probably back at the Hathaways' house and Roxanne and Katya were on their way as well. For all I knew Nick was either there or he'd be there soon, since Attar was leaving tonight.

It would take at least half an hour for me to get to Georgetown. I pushed the Vespa for all the speed it would give me and raced through downtown Washington.

The person who answered the intercom at the Hathaways' front gate believed me when I said that Roxanne had asked me to meet her and Katya Gordon for lunch. I parked in my usual spot, the only vehicle in the driveway. If Roxanne was already home, maybe her car was in the garage, but where was the car that had driven Taras Attar from the Library of Congress? Where were his security people?

The Hispanic maid and I recognized each other, and she informed me that Roxanne had taken Katya on a garden tour before lunch.

"Dr. Attar told me he'd be here this afternoon, too," I said.

"Yes, he returned about an hour ago."

"I'd like to thank him for the inscription he wrote in the book he signed for me," I said. It had been a quote from Thomas Jefferson.

When the people fear the government, there is tyranny.
When the government fears the people, there is liberty.

"He went to the Greek temple. He often likes to go there to write because it is so peaceful."

It was also where Katya and Roxanne were headed.

My heart started to pound. "What about his security people? Are they with him?"

She waved a hand. "Do not worry. He sent them to get

lunch. He does not need them until he leaves for the airport. There are many cameras and alarms here. No one can get in."

"Sure," I said. "I'd better go find everyone."

Alarms and cameras and security gates with intercoms were fine for keeping out intruders, anyone from the outside. But what if the real threat was someone trusted, a person who was already inside the grounds?

I took off running.

Photographers and journalists are the people who run toward gunfire, a blazing building, a plane crash, or stand at the edge of the ocean as the hurricane is about to make landfall so you can watch or listen or read about it at home or work or somewhere else that's safe. It's hard to explain why we do it, but here are a few reasons: a love of risk taking and the need to always be where the story is, plus the ego-feeding adrenaline rush that lets you believe you won't get hurt. The minute you lose your nerve, you may as well get a desk job.

I wasn't sure what to expect when I came upon Roxanne and Katya at the Greek temple with Taras Attar, but it wasn't the scene that was unfolding in front of me. Instinct warned me to keep off the paths where I might be seen as I made my way around manicured terraced gardens and privacy hedges of evergreens and hollies until I caught flashes of color through the trees—Taras's red tie, Roxanne's sunshine-colored blazer, and Katya in a pale blue dress—and saw the three of them facing each other, their dark, angry profiles silhouetted by slanting afternoon sunshine. I moved behind a bank of rhododendrons and found a place where the tangled branches parted so I could still see without being seen.

"I want you to take this and shoot her, Taras," Roxanne was saying in a calm, reasonable voice. The sun glinted off a flash of metal and I saw the gun in her hand. "When the police arrive, we'll tell them she was part of the plot to assassinate you. Her daughter is Arkady Vasiliev's girlfriend and she'll do anything for him. Her husband left her with massive debts when he died, and Vasiliev, with all his billions, can take care of them for her. So she went after you with the gun. It's not

registered so don't worry. It went off when you were trying
to get it away from her and you accidentally shot her. I brought
her here after her press conference at the National Gallery to
discuss other projects . . . I had no idea she would try something like this."

There was a moment of stunned silence before Katya
said, "That's a lie. Why are you doing this?"

Roxanne's composure gave way to anger. "You *know* why.
You've been blackmailing my husband for thirty years for
something he didn't do. It's over, Katya."

"No. He's guilty. I saw him." Katya took a step toward
Roxanne, who raised her hand and pointed the gun at Katya.

A crack shot, I heard Harry saying. *She grew up hunting
with her father.* And she was standing at point-blank range.

"Roxanne, for God's sake, put that down." Taras held up
his hands like a shield. "What are you two talking about?
What's this about?"

"It's about Jenna Paradise. Remember her, Taras?" Roxanne
gave him a challenging look. "I tracked down her roommate.
She lives in Oregon now. She told me Jenna had just
learned she was pregnant and that she'd had a fight with
the father of her baby the day she disappeared."

"Jenna? Wait a minute." He stepped back like she had
physically struck him. "Why did you go looking for Jenna
Paradise's roommate? Did Scott ask you to do it?"

She shook her head. "He doesn't know."

"Come on, Taras," Katya said, her voice low and vicious.
"Don't you get it? Roxanne found out Jenna was pregnant
with Scott's child and now she's trying to protect her husband
by covering up a murder. Scott killed Jenna."

"No." Roxanne turned to Taras. "Scott didn't kill her. She's
lying. And it wasn't his child. It was yours, Taras, wasn't it?"

There was a painful silence before he said, "How did you
know?"

"That's not true. Taras, tell her . . ." Katya began.

"Yes, tell her." Roxanne sounded triumphant. "Jenna broke
off with Scott and started sleeping with you, Taras. Her roommate described you perfectly. But you never told Scott about
it, did you? When Jenna went to see him on that last day,

Scott said she was hysterical. She tried to convince him the baby was his, but he knew it was impossible since they hadn't slept together in over a month."

"But Scott, who still loved her—who was out of his mind crazy about her—killed her out of jealousy." Katya, too, had stored up her own anger and it now boiled over like the fury of a rejected lover. "I saw him get rid of her body. He stuffed it down the storm drain by the trestle bridge like she was garbage that needed to be thrown out. Then he took her bicycle and got rid of that somewhere, too."

The color had drained from Taras's face. He gave Katya an anguished look. "Is that true?"

"He didn't kill her." Roxanne's voice was harsh and insistent. "She fell and hit her head on one of the trestle bridge pylons. It was an accident. You never asked Scott about her, Taras. Not once. You kept your own secret because after she was gone you didn't have to worry about a pregnant girlfriend. You're just as much involved in this as Scott is." She tilted her head at Katya. "That's why we have to get rid of her. Now take the gun and do it."

She shoved it at him as a hand came over my mouth and a voice against my ear breathed, "Don't say a word."

I nodded, slumping against my husband, weak-kneed with relief. He whispered, "We need to get that gun from Attar before someone starts shooting. Create a distraction somehow. We don't have much time."

"Wait," I said. "Listen."

"I'm not doing it," Taras was saying. "I'm not shooting her like an animal that needs to be put down."

"What are you talking about? You owe it to Scott. He can help you . . . help Abadistan. Don't be a fool, Taras." Roxanne seemed unprepared for Attar to thwart her plans and now she sounded like a petulant child. "She works for Vasiliev and he wants you dead. If she had the gun, she'd kill you. She wouldn't think twice."

"There are other ways to handle this."

I didn't see how or where Roxanne had concealed a second gun, but all of a sudden she was pointing it at Taras. "Oh, for God's sake, kill her before I shoot you both. You don't want to die, too. Think of your people, think of Abadistan. They need you."

Taras started to laugh. "Roxy, don't be so bloody melodramatic. You won't shoot me."

"I'm warning you. I'm counting down from ten."

"No."

"Ten . . ."

Nick swore under his breath. "Christ. That's all we need. A bloodbath."

He picked up a dead tree branch from the ground. It was about four feet long and two inches thick. He passed it to me and said, "I'm going to move behind her. Don't let her get past three. See if you can knock her off balance. If I get her gun, I think we're good. I don't think Attar will use his."

He disappeared.

"Six . . . five . . . four . . . three . . ."

I aimed and threw the branch. It hit Roxanne across her shoulders. She stumbled forward and Katya shoved her hard. Roxanne went down and the gun skidded away. Katya picked it up.

"Whoever you are in those bushes, come out," she said. "Or I'll start shooting."

I stepped out where they could see me.

The three of them stared. Katya swore; Roxanne, who had a cut lip, muttered something; and Taras looked like he'd seen a ghost.

"Sophie," he said. "What are you doing here? Katya, please, leave her alone. She has nothing to do with this."

"Shut up, Taras," Katya said. "You have no idea who she is. You, Sophie, get over there next to Roxanne."

She spoke to Taras in Russian as I obeyed. I didn't understand the words, but her meaning was clear. She turned the gun on Roxanne, who had managed to get up on one knee. Her lip was bloody and she looked like she was in pain.

"Don't shoot me," Roxanne said.

"You invented such a clever story about why Taras should kill me. If you had your way I would be dead. Why should I show you any mercy?"

"Put the gun down, Katya." Taras trained his gun on her. "Or this time I will use it."

I don't know who fired first, but Taras's bullet hit Katya in the arm and hers struck Roxanne in the chest. Roxanne groaned and slumped over, her hands filling with blood as she tried to cover her wound.

The British Special Forces instructors in our hostile environment training course drilled into our heads that even an infinitesimal moment of inattention was the difference between living and dying. Still I could not take my eyes off Roxanne, kneeling in a bloody pool in this serene little temple, like a high priestess who had come to make a sacrificial offering.

When I looked up, Katya had switched the gun to her uninjured hand and her aim wavered between Taras and me. As Taras aimed again at Katya, Nick moved into view.

"No!" I shoved Taras's arm skyward as he fired.

Nick grabbed Katya from behind, wrestling the gun from her hand. It went off and Taras hooked an arm around my shoulders, pulling me with him as we dove for cover, tumbling down a grassy embankment.

"Sophie, Attar, are you okay?" Nick shouted. "I've got her gun and she's not going anywhere."

Taras was on his back, lying a few feet away. "Are you all right?" he asked me. "Who is that guy?"

I felt my ribs. No broken bones, maybe not even anything cracked, but I would ache for the next few weeks. "I'm okay. He's my husband, Nicholas Canning. Thank you for saving me."

His eyes widened. "Your husband?"

"Yes."

He called to Nick. "We're fine." But as he got to his knees he winced.

He helped me up and we climbed the hill to the temple. Katya was sitting on the ground, bloody and disheveled, leaning against a column. Nick had bound her hands and feet with what looked like shoelaces. When she saw us, she moaned and spoke to Taras in Russian.

"You'll live, Katya," he said. "It's just a superficial wound."

Roxanne lay in a widening pool of blood, her breathing rapid and shallow and her eyes closed. Nick was kneeling by her side, both of his hands on her chest in an attempt to stanch the bleeding.

I pulled out my phone and hit Redial. "Is she—?" I asked.

"Barely," Nick said.

This time Duval answered.

"I'm at the Hathaways' house," I said. "Roxanne Hathaway and Katya Gordon have been shot and I'm with Taras and Nick. Send two ambulances. I think you'd better hurry."

TWENTY-FOUR

He came at midnight as I asked him to. The door to India's carriage house opened and the beam of his flashlight played over Max Katzer's office.

"In here," I said. "The back room."

Baz appeared in the doorway, dressed in jeans with pressed creases, a black turtleneck, and a black leather jacket. He was carrying a small backpack. "My darling," he said. "Where is he?"

"He'll be here soon. Have a seat." I pointed to the barrel chair opposite where I sat on the humpbacked sofa.

His eyes darted around, taking in my furniture arrangement in the viscous golden light of two candles guttering on the coffee table.

He sat with the backpack on his lap and crossed one leg over the other. "What's going on, Sophie? I didn't think you were going to be here."

I am a fairly decent actress, but it's tough to con a pro. I knew I didn't have much time until he figured it out.

"Can I ask you something?"

"I don't know. Can you?" His voice was sharp.

"*May* I ask you something?"

"You may ask." He looked tense and on his guard, both hands now gripping the arms of his chair.

"How long have you been working for Arkady Vasiliev?"

A small smile played across his face and when his eyes met mine, they were almost merry. "Whatever are you talking about?"

"Katya Gordon held a press conference today at the National Gallery," I said. "It was the first time the news was made public that Vasiliev had acquired the surprises for the Constellation egg. You knew about it yesterday and you implied you'd known for a few days. The only way that could have happened is if you talked to Vasiliev himself. Katya's terrified of not being in his good graces, so she wouldn't have said anything to you."

He sat back in his chair and steepled his fingers. "That's a lovely story, but I don't work for anyone except Her Majesty's Government."

"Oh, I think you do. Perhaps it was a poor choice of words. Partners? Colleagues? It would explain a lot about why you're so keen to see Nick," I said. "Vasiliev wants the well logs from Crowne Energy. Nick told me someone from the inside has been setting him up for the murder of Colin and his CIA contact in Abadistan. All this time he thought it was someone from the CIA. But it was really you."

Baz stood up. "Nick's not coming, is he? This was just some sophomoric game of yours, some half-cocked story you invented—"

"Good evening, Baz." Nick stood in the doorway.

Baz swung around and the small revolver slipped easily from under his jacket. "As I live and breathe, Nicholas Canning. I think we can dispense with the pleasantries and cut to the chase. Where are the well logs, mate? Tell me or I'll shoot your wife. Sophie, love, get over here. And put your gun on the table, Nick, or I'll kill her right now. I know you brought one. You're getting sloppy, old man."

Baz yanked my arm and I stumbled over to him. The barrel of his gun was hard and cold against my temple.

"Let her go," Nick said, but he put his own gun down. "I'll tell you where they are, but I want your word as a gentleman no one gets hurt."

Baz put Nick's gun in his holster and said in a calm voice, "Fair enough. And just to show you what a gentleman I really am, I brought money as I promised." He picked up the back-pack. "Fifty thousand dollars in unmarked bills. It's yours. Take it."

Nick looked at the backpack and shook his head. Baz's gun was still pointed at me.

"Who killed Colin and Dani, Baz?" Nick said. "Was it you? Or does Vasiliev give the orders? I know you mortgaged the house in Eaton Square and you can't afford your family's estate in Surrey or Isabella's house in Cap d'Antibes anymore. I heard the stories in Iskar about a high-ranking official in the British government who was spending a fortune on prostitutes, young girls kidnapped by the Shaika so they could be sold for sex or as maids in the West. I met one of them in Moscow who managed to escape from her captor. She knows who you are, Baz. That's how Vasiliev got you, isn't it?"

A muscle tightened in his jaw and I could feel him tense. "I have nothing to say. Now tell me where the logs are if you want Sophie to live."

"You wouldn't kill me," I said to Baz, and my voice cracked. "You couldn't."

"I'm sorry, love, but I could."

I looked at my husband. "Tell him what he wants to know, Nick."

"He's going to kill us both, anyway, Sophie," he said. "Before you do, satisfy my curiosity, Baz, and tell me about Dani and Colin. Maybe you weren't the one who killed Dani, but why did you have to go after Colin? You were in Vienna the day he was murdered. Why did you do it?"

Outside, the distant wail of a police siren startled everyone. It receded and I heard Baz let out a long breath.

"Just tell me," Nick said. "The CIA believes I did it. The man was my partner and friend."

"I didn't kill him," he said. "It was an accident."

"What happened?" I asked.

"I suppose there's no harm in you knowing the truth." He shrugged and I tried not to remember the evenings we'd been at one of his dinner parties, how entertaining and charming he could be, all the fascinating people he knew.

"We went for a walk by the river. Colin knew I wanted to talk about what Crowne Energy had discovered in Abadistan. It had been raining . . . we went down to one of the marinas for privacy. It was late and there was no one around. Bloody cold for late May with a wicked wind."

"Go on," Nick said.

"He told me you drilled a rank wildcat and found light, sweet crude. He was laughing like a giddy lunatic," he said. "The next thing I knew he tripped over a cleat, lost his balance, and went headfirst into the water. It was dark . . . he had on dark clothing. I heard him scream that he couldn't swim . . ."

"You didn't try to save him?" I asked. "You couldn't even find a rope to throw him, if you were at a marina?"

"I didn't kill him. He drowned." Baz's grip tightened on my arm. "Don't bloody judge me."

"Don't worry," I said. "It's not up to me."

The carriage house door opened and clicked shut. Baz put his arm around my throat, the gun still at my temple, as Napoleon Duval walked into the room, his gun aimed at Baz.

"You set me up," Baz said in my ear. To Duval he said, "Whoever you are, I've got enough bullets to kill her and myself. I'm not going anywhere. You're not going to subject me to that humiliation."

"Special Agent Napoleon Duval. I'm sorry, Lord Allingham, but you are walking out of this room with me. As for your bullets, do you think we'd let you come here with live ammunition? We paid a visit to your room earlier. Your gun has blanks. So does Nicholas Canning's."

"I have diplomatic immunity. You can't touch me."

"A few of your friends from MI6 are in town. They'd like a word with you as well."

Baz winced at the word "friends" and, in the painful silence that followed, I knew he was considering his dwindling options. He lifted his chin and gave Duval a defiant look.

"This isn't finished." He released me and crossed the room. "All right, let's get it over with."

He stopped in the doorway and turned around. His eyes met mine and his gaze was steady, without a trace of repentance or remorse. "I was always good to you, you know. I was there when you needed me," he said. "When you think of me, love, think of me kindly."

The door closed and a moment later we heard the whine of a car engine quietly leaving the alley. I looked at my husband and saw in his face the strain of the ordeal we'd both been through, how we'd been tested, what it had done to us and our marriage.

"I'm done thinking about him. I'm done thinking about any

of them," I said. "Baz, Katya, Vasiliev, Roxanne. I want our life back, Nick."

He came over and pulled me into his arms. "I know, sweetheart," he said, stroking my hair. "I know. When we walk out of here tonight, we go forward into the light, not back to the darkness."

EPILOGUE

Nick took me to London in November to visit friends who were overjoyed that he was alive, to make a sentimental tour of our old haunts, and to get away from the barrage of news stories for what had turned into the perfect Washington scandal: sex, blackmail, murder, politics, spies, and nobility.

Scott Hathaway resigned almost immediately as majority leader, stepping down from his Senate seat because, as he said, he didn't want the distraction of his complicated personal situation to interfere with the important work of the United States Senate. He also wanted to care for his wife, who was still recovering from a gunshot wound that had left her partially paralyzed.

According to the press and some off-the-record information Grace passed along, Hathaway was cooperating fully with the D.C. police, which had reopened the case into the disappearance of Jenna Paradise. Katya Gordon's photos weren't incriminating enough to charge him with murder and, when questioned, she admitted she hadn't actually witnessed the argument between Scott and Jenna. But she said she had gone to take photos at the top of the trestle bridge for a photography class assignment just as Hathaway was shoving Jenna into the storm drain. In the fading light, those photos hadn't turned out, but she did manage to get pictures of him leaving the park on Jenna's bicycle.

Hathaway exacted his own revenge against Katya, though it turned out to be—in the words of Sir Francis Bacon—a kind of wild justice. He had kept all of her correspondence over the years, turning a file box of incriminating documents over to the FBI. It wasn't long before Katya was facing charges of blackmail and extortion against a U.S. senator for the purpose of benefiting her late husband's Wall Street investment firm. If Hathaway was going to go down, he was taking Katya with him.

In the tangled legal matter of the shootings at the Hathaways', the media was having a field day with the bombshell news that well-known philanthropist and Lane Communications heiress Roxanne Hathaway had been charged with conspiracy to commit murder. Both Taras and Katya had pleaded self-defense, and I suspected any charges against them—especially Taras—would be dropped sooner rather than later. There would be no trial until Roxanne recovered enough to appear in court, though lawyers for both sides had already spoken to Nick and me, letting us know we would be summoned to testify.

The waiter who had been picked up that day at the Library of Congress was charged in the murder of Ali Jones, who had, as I suspected, asked too many questions, after Detective Bolton turned up witnesses who remembered seeing them together that night at Arkady Vasiliev's wild hotel party. Luke went to the arraignment—I couldn't bear it—and watched as the waiter was held without bail and led away in a prison jumpsuit and handcuffs. Predictably there was no evidence to link Arkady Vasiliev to the waiter or the plot to assassinate Taras Attar, but Vasiliev retained a top New York law firm anyway, claiming harassment by U.S. authorities.

Baz's picture turned up almost daily in the British newspapers while we were in London. The story of how he'd been allowed to leave Washington while under investigation in the United States—he was, after all, a minister in the British government and a member of the House of Lords—had been a flurry of diplomatic maneuvering that sorely tested the U.S.-U.K. "special relationship." Eventually it had been determined that Baz's celebrity status made him an unlikely flight risk and he flew back to London, where he continued to insist he was the innocent victim of overzealous American law enforcement agents.

"What are they going to charge him with?" I asked Nick. "He didn't kill Colin. Or so he said. He can probably weather the sex scandal—a lot of politicians have been involved with prostitutes and, after a while, they claim they're rehabilitated and move on. Isabella's sticking by him, so that helps."

"Don't worry, besides the fact Duval overheard him threaten to kill you, there's plenty more to find," Nick said. "Corruption. Selling classified information. It's all going to come out. He'll get what's coming to him."

But not everything had come out in public. Nick had slipped Taras the well logs the day of the shootings at the Hathaways' home and, so far, there had been nothing in the news concerning the discovery of a potentially abundant supply of high-quality oil in Abadistan.

"How much longer is Taras going to be able to keep that quiet?" I asked.

"He isn't," Nick said. "To quote Madame de Staël, 'In Russia, everything is a mystery but nothing is a secret.' Why do you think the fighting between the Russians and the Abadis has escalated? Everyone wants that oil."

"Taras is a good man," I said. "He'd be a good leader if Abadistan ever became independent."

"He would," Nick said. "And you certainly made an impression on him."

The thank-you letter Taras Attar wrote me after I sent him the photos of his talk at the Library of Congress had accompanied a book of his poetry. There was an inscription on the flyleaf.

> *Come to Abadistan with your camera. I promise to show you the beauty of my country so you may know its people and understand its soul.*

But first, it was time to return to Washington. We were leaving London in the morning, the day before Thanksgiving, skipping the annual service for the American community at St. Paul's Cathedral. Though I loved the pageantry—especially the soaring sound of the congregation singing "America the Beautiful" as a Marine Color Guard retreated down the aisle of London's most famous church—it was always the day I felt the most homesick.

This year Harry and my mother were hosting a family celebration for Nick and me at the farm in Middleburg. Nick's sister was flying in from California, and even my brother, Tommy, had managed to get leave to come home from Honduras. My mother had been making plans for weeks.

We decided to spend our last day in London visiting all the iconic places in Westminster—the palace, the Abbey, Parliament, Big Ben—ending in Trafalgar Square, where the Norwegian Christmas tree had just been set up in anticipation of the lighting ceremony the following week. The rain began as Big Ben chimed five and we climbed the steps from the Victoria Embankment in front of the Houses of Parliament. Directly across from us was the House of Lords, where Baz had so often invited me to tea on the terrace. I laced my fingers through Nick's as we turned away and headed down Whitehall.

Nick squeezed my hand as I glanced over my shoulder one last time. "We could move back here if you want, Soph," he said. "Perry would take you back in a heartbeat and I know I could find work. We could look for another place to live, maybe try Chelsea or south of the river."

I looked at my husband. He had shaved his beard and his hair was back to its normal color. A couple of weeks of pub lunches and he had gained back all the weight he lost in Abadistan. During the entire visit we had avoided discussing the subject of returning to London, though it had been the elephant in the room.

"Do you want to live here again?" I asked.

We were walking past the gated entrance to 10 Downing Street and the large Palladian Horse Guards building, where two cavalry officers on horseback stood sentry in the steady drizzle.

"It's up to you," he said. "I've put you through hell these past few months. I'll go wherever you want to."

Where you lead, I will follow.

It hadn't been so long ago that I had said practically the same thing to Jack, joking about the path of our run that had taken us to the Capitol as the sun was setting over Washington.

"I love London," I said. "We were really happy here. But America is home, where we have roots and family. If we stay away much longer, we'll become gypsies. I think we need to go back . . . at least for a while."

"Then that's what we'll do." He leaned over and kissed me. "Tomorrow we go home."

ACKNOWLEDGMENTS

I had considerable help from individuals in the United States, Russia, and Britain who shared their professional expertise while I was researching *Multiple Exposure* and there are many people to thank. My usual rule applies: it's not their fault if it's wrong; that's on me. With this book I knowingly took liberties and bent rules—though that's one of the advantages of writing fiction, since you don't get in trouble for making something up.

I am grateful to June Stanich of June Stanich Photography; Ruthi David of R. David Original Photography; Detective Jim Smith, Crime Scene Section, Fairfax County (VA) Police Department; and Twyla Kitts, teacher program coordinator, Virginia Museum of Fine Arts, Richmond, VA. Jan Neuharth, fellow author and good friend, set me straight on formal attire for a hunt ball. A number of people, including individuals in the intelligence and diplomatic communities and the energy business, spoke with me on the phone, in person, and on Skype and, for understandable reasons, preferred not to be mentioned by name. You all know who you are, so, again, my thanks.

Thanks also to everyone who read and commented on drafts of the manuscript, especially Donna Andrews, John Gilstrap, Alan Orloff, Art Taylor, Martina Norelli, and André de Nesnera. Special thanks and love to Tom Snyder for editing help and friendship.

At Scribner, my deepest thanks to my editor, Whitney Frick, and to Susan Moldow for giving me the extra time and encouragement to go back and do some serious revising to an earlier draft of this book. I'm also very much indebted to Maggie Crawford. Thanks to Gwyneth Stansfield, Tal Goretsky (for the great cover), Katie Rizzo, Cynthia Merman, and Anna deVries, as well as everyone else at Scribner who works so hard behind the scenes.

Last but not least, thanks and much love to my agent, Dominick Abel, who makes it all happen.

To learn more about Karl Fabergé and the Russian imperial eggs, I highly recommend Toby Faber's excellent book *Fabergé's Eggs: The Extraordinary Story of the Masterpieces That Outlived an Empire* (Random House, 2008). The Firebird egg described in *Multiple Exposure* is completely fictional, but the Blue Tsarevich Constellation egg does, in fact, exist, though it was never finished after Nicholas II abdicated. It was the last imperial egg Fabergé ever designed and was discovered in 2001 at the Fersman Mineralogical Museum in Moscow. According to museum records, one of Fabergé's sons had sent it and other items there while making an inventory of imperial treasures for Joseph Stalin.

Also, in an effort to forestall future letters and e-mails from folks who know better and are familiar with the Posse Comitatus Act, I would like to state that a CIA agent such as Napoleon Duval would not be assigned to protect a visiting dignitary: that is the responsibility of the Diplomatic Security Service of the State Department.

Finally, the Russian republic of Abadistan, a potentially oil-rich region with a fascinating culture and history dating back to Alexander the Great, exists only in my imagination.

CPSIA information can be obtained
at www.ICGtesting.com
Printed in the USA
JSHW080849170423
40353JS00001B/1

9 781448 308590